A Man of TWO Centuries
And
YOU JUST NEVER KNOW

Don Littlewood

A Man of Two Centuries and You Just Never Know

By Don Littlewood

This book was first published in Great Britain in paperback during September 2023.

The moral right of Don Littlewood is to be identified as the author of this work and has been asserted by him in accordance with the Copyright, Designs and Patents Act of 1988.

ISBN: 979-8859772094

A Man of TWO Centuries

The large noisy diesel engined lorry towing an equally large caravan of the type much favoured by circus performers, stopped at the crossroads and the driver looked with intense curiosity at the opposite corner. Not that there was a lot to be seen. Just a large rundown looking old house, now surrounded by a recently erected board fence denoting a building site. Dan Stone the driver and new owner of the house, grunted to himself, at least the contractors have done the fence as promised, that's a start.

At that he drove across the road and up the side of the house until he found the gate that allowed him to pull across the back of the house and with great relieve, park, step down from the cab and stretch like a man who had sat too long. Taking a set of keys from his pocket Dan made his way to the front door and let himself in, to be greeted by the smell of dust, damp and neglect. Well, he said, what did you expect Coco Chanel? After a careful look round, he shook his head thinking well my lad this will keep you busy and hopefully out of trouble for a change. Leaving the house and looking over the grounds he remembered there should be a derelict cottage and an old stone barn which came with the house, of no use to me. but a possible source of materials he thought. There they are, not too far away, handy that. Mind you there is something odd about that house, good god the chimney is smoking, now what? Oh well sod it! it will wait until tomorrow I've a caravan to stabilise and a meal to get.

Day dawned and Dan refreshed, fed, showered and dressed, felt ready to face the mysterious smoking chimney. I hope its squatters he thought I'd enjoy a run in with a couple of yobs. His first surprise was the neat and tidy, pretty, garden around the cottage. With a bemused shake of the head he knocked the door and waited. The door opened and surprise number two stopped his breath, as he thought now that's my kind of woman. Tall, straight backed and curvaceous, handsome more than beautiful, with a face full of character.

'Well,' said the vision When you've finished gawping what do you want? Oh! said a somewhat disconcerted Dan, sorry I'm Dan Stone I've just bought the house; I see you wasted no time coming to tell me you want me out she said in an increasingly loud voice, bad luck I'm going nowhere!!! With that she slammed the door in Dan's face. He started to walk away, but thought, sod it, she's picked the wrong man if it's a fight she wants a fight she shall have!!! Turning back, he hammered on the door and shouted, "open up missus or I'll kick the dam door in", getting no immediate response he gave the door a hefty kick to prove the point.

As that the door was snatched open and his very irate advisory stood ready to resume battle. Shut it!! said Dan you had your say now it's my turn. Point one until you opened the door I didn't know you existed and came here expecting to find squatters. Point two the bloody cottage is supposed to be derelict and unoccupied. Point three the ball is now in your court and I will give you a couple of weeks to let me in so I can decide what is best for us both. Or I'll put the whole thing in my solicitor's hands, and we will find out who's going anywhere. Cheerio, you know where to find me, and made good his escape.

Well; Annie, she thought that went well, I don't think. You may have met your match, but he won't have it all his own way.

What a woman, thought Dan. She is going to be a handful, but I can live with that! Might even enjoy it. Then told himself off, that kind of thinking will get you into trouble, again!!

A few days later Dan was stood by the house, enjoying the morning air and found himself thinking back to his old life before he was exiled to the 20th. century some 70years ago. He was born, or at least grown in a laboratory in the 25th. century. An age when average life span was 350 to 400 years and population control was subject to global laws and strictly enforced.

In the 25th. century all work and a lot of design and planning is done by robots, mankind becoming almost obsolete. Even social and sexual needs could be catered for by very high-class Androids. As Dan had been known to remark at least they don't get headaches or tired.

With humans, all but ruling classes and the super-rich are produced in laboratories to perform as entertainers of all types, or sport and games players. The elite of this strata of 25th. century society are the Gladiators who perform in the Ancient Roman style games. In these games fights take place between fully armed gladiators with injuries commonplace and death not unknown. Dan had been "born" to this class and had trained since childhood to be able to compete in the games.

What Dan didn't know, was, by mistake he had been given other attributes normally reserved for scholars and skilled artisans. Not now considered necessary due to the advanced abilities of robots. Which combined with his 6ft.-4ins 16stn. frame had made him a mighty force in the gladiatorial games. Dan had become the greatest of the gladiators. with the title of "No.1 of 100". The 100 being the best of the gladiators.

While Dan daydreamed of the past "or is it the future" Annie was on her way to see him bent on continuing the fight. Seeing Dan she called "you can come on Thursday, I can spare half an hour". Sorry missus shouted Dan I can't make Thurs. I'm busy all day! At this Annie snorted angrily and turned to walk away. Dan, smiling broadly, called hang on Mrs Lloyd, only joking! I would be pleased to call at your convenience, now would that be morning or afternoon?" So you now know my name, at least that's an improvement on "missus", afternoon will be fine". O.K. missus said Dan laughing loudly. At which Annie hiding a secret smile left in an apparent huff.

Dan spent the next couple of days working very hard on the house moving the rubbish on all three floors and attic to selected rooms at the back of the house where it could be conveniently thrown into a skip. His inbred strength and extra large heart enabling him to carry on after 20th. century man would be exhausted.

On Thursday Dan duly presented himself at the cottage, hoping for the best, but fearing the worst. Against his normal inclinations, he had changed from his working dress, wearing what he described as his second best drinking clothes. Annie had been watching for his arrival and met Dan on the garden path, apparently not noticing his sartorial endeavours.

"Morning" said Dan and received a nod of the head in reply. At which he started a thorough inspection of the outside of the cottage. To his surprise it appeared to be sound, needing only attention to the stonework and that only cosmetic. Until he reached the back of the cottage, where he found a poor quality single story extension. Above which the stonework had signs of having been crudely patched where there had been a second story.

Dan called to Mrs. Lloyd to ask what had happened, not sure she said, before my time. I've been told a tree fell on it, there's a large stump near the fence so it might be true.

May I see inside now please Dan asked. Yes said Annie the best way is through the front, and led him inside. The living room was all he could have asked for. With mature oak beams rough finished plastered stone walls and stone window frames. All in good order except the fire place, which to Dan's eye needed rebuilding, don't know how any smoke ever gets to the chimney he thought. Passing through a door into what he hoped was the kitchen, he found himself in the extension, and the poorest kitchen he had ever seen. A sink with a single cold tap an old wooden draining board and two shelves for pots and pans. A door took him to a narrow passage and the stairs. Two good sized bedrooms led off a small landing. the front one a very pleasant room all in good order. The back O.K. except for the patched wall where the extension had been. The attic and roof gave no problems. So Dan went outside and began measuring around the damaged area and all along the back of the cottage.

All finished, he jumped the garden fence to take a look at the dere-lict barn he had been landed with. One end was just a pile of stone blocks end rotting roof timbers. The other enough wall standing to possibly be of interest in the future. Happily the fallen blocks were the same stone as the cottage and would be useful once cleaned up. Not that I have time to spend cleaning old stones thought Dan.

With that he jumped back over the fence, and called to Annie that he would be in touch, and strode off.

Annie watched him go with a quizzical look, just who is this man, she wondered. First he jumps a 4ft.6ins. fence with no effort and then walks off faster than most folk can run, making it all look effortless. I'm going to see what I can find out about him!

Unaware of Annies frame of mind, Dan had settled himself in his small office at one end of the caravan and was busily converting his meas-urements into plans for renovation of the cottage. For most of the years of his exile Dan had worked in all branches of the construction industry and was highly skilled in most trades.as well as being a more than com-petent draughtsman. He soon decided a new two story extension the full width of the cottage. with a new kitchen, scullery and downstairs lavatory.

4

On the second floor a modern bathroom, storeroom and airing cupboard. Rebuild the dodgy fireplace and get back to the big house. No doubt Mrs. Lloyd will have some complaint!!

Dan had decided to use the stone from the old barn for the cottage extension but didn't want to clean the stone himself. Not knowing the availability of labour locally, he had put a large notice on the fence closest to the main road to try his luck.

Builders labourer required.
TOP PAY RATE
For Hard Worker.

He hadn't much hope. but he had to start somewhere.

The next day the skips arrived and he was kept busy throwing out all the rubbish he had sorted. so it was a few days before he had chance to take the plans for Mrs. Lloyds comments.

Meanwhile Annie had been making enquiries to try to learn something about this strange man who had arrived in the area. A friend in the police force assured her he was "not known to them". The company to whom she paid the rent was equally vague about him, except that the transaction had been through his lawyer and was a cash sale. No-one else knew anything, or had even met him.

Knowing nothing of Annies efforts Dan made his way to the cottage to show her the plans for the proposed new extension. To his surprise she thought the plans marvellous, but considered rebuilding the fireplace unnecessary. Although when pressed by Dan agreed it did blow back smoke when the wind was in the "wrong direction". Annie then tentatively asked what the rent was to be when it was all finished. I've never thought about it said Dan, in fact I have never received any of the rent you have paid since I took over. It's going to be a time before I get started let alone finished. So not to worry we will sort something, when the time comes.

I'll get the job done as soon as possible, but I'm trying to find someone to do some of the "donkey" work to save me some time. I saw your notice on the fence and told my nephew Terry and he is coming to see you on Saturday said Annie. He is a very good worker but shy around people because of his stutter. If that means he don't talk much he will suit me fine said Dan I look forward to seeing him, thanks. Right "missus" I'll be in touch said Dan making to leave. I hate that "missus" word my name is Annie please use it. So long as you call me Dan it's a deal, Bye!! With that he left smiling.

ENTER TERRY

Saturday dawned and Annie's nephew Terry arrived late and breathless for his interview "S.S sorry I'm late he stammered and panted the dam bus left early". Not to worry said Dan come into the caravan, sit down and catch your breath, while I make a cup of tea. The tea made and Terry's breathing back to normal Dan made a start. I can see that talking's not too easy so we will try some head nods or shakes O.K.? Terry nodded; have you worked in the building trade? another nod, 1year? Terry held up 2 fingers. So the interview continued much to Dans approval. He had liked the look of Terry from the start and now thought he was bright lad who "caught on" quickly.

Dan explained the first of his jobs would be cleaning stone for use on the cottage, a rotten job, but I'll pay £1 a 100 for all you clean and sort for size. Thats in addition to £15 a week wages. Come and have look at the job and decide if you want it.

Terry seemed completely unfazed by the poor working conditions and nodded an emphatic yes to the job. As he turned to make his way back he trod on an old beam which broke and dumped him in the mud. You don't have much luck do you said Dan helping him up. "YYY you're born, LLL life's a bitch, AAA and then you DDD die". Thats your longest speech so far said Dan, and they both roared with laughter.

Terry soon proved to be ideal for Dan's purpose, whether cleaning stones or helping in the big house. Not inclined to talk much but content to work steadily without constant supervision. His only oddity the way he spent most of his lunch break wandering round the house garden examining the plants which had survived the years of neglect. Assuring Dan that there were some real gems among the rubbish. Dan told him to help himself to anything he wanted, to be rewarded by a double thumbs up and a huge smile.

Seeing Terry's delight at such a simple thing, bought Dan to reflect on how much happier people tended to be in the 20th century than those in the 25th. An early impression of life in the 25th. century would seem that it was roses all the way, and yet when everything comes easily it loses a lot of its value. Not for the first time gave thanks that the council of leaders had exiled him to this time and place. Mind you having fought in two world wars "under different identities", he knew the 20th. century had its problems. Dan's wars had been a strange experience for him, being a born warrior he had frequently been in the thickest fighting, and had often been thought of as fool without fear by his fellow soldiers. From the onset Dan had known that having been alive in the 25th. century he could not be killed in the 20th. Furthermore, he had no marks of any serious injury before his exile and reasoned he wouldn't be badly hurt. As a result, he always considered himself a fraud, how can you be brave when you have nothing to frightened of. He didn't believe he had earned any of his medals and they were in an old box somewhere in the caravan, forgotten.

Of course having concluded he couldn't die in the 20th. century, he realised he would one day return to the 25th. A feat beyond him, which meant he would have to be collected and transported by order of the world council. The question was why would they?

25th. century.

For the first time in many decades the was discord and ill feeling in the world council, with the leading member of the Oriental delegation demanding extra privileges and laying claim to additional land to which he had no right. The member in question was the one responsible for Dans exile. while making a "state" visit to the European regions, a Gladiatorial contest had been arranged in his honour. The top 50 of the 100 leading gladiators were to fight a knock out competition until a winner was found. After several hard fought hours Dan was left to fight the number 2 of 100, a strong and vastly experienced Gladiator, and the closest friend Dan had.

Both were proud men who liked nothing better than to beat the other in a fair fight. The fight this day was to be spoken of for years after, as the greatest battle ever, with both men giving no quarter nor sparing any effort. The fight swung to and fro with neither man able to put the other down. Until Dan in a moment of brilliant invention half turning to avoid a fierce thrust from his opponent instead of turning back to face him continued the turn full circle putting himself on 2's blind side giving him a clear shot at his exposed thigh. Dan needing nothing more struck fast and hard with the pommel of his sword handle paralysing the thigh sending his friend to the ground. Pausing only to kick away his opponent's sword, Dan held his sword point against 2's throat in the signal of victory, he received the corresponding signal of defeat from his opponent. Turning to the members of the Council Dan made the customary bow of homage, while his head was still bowed he was alarmed to hear a large groan coming from the crowd. On straightening Dan was amazed to see the Oriental member giving an outdated signal commanding him to execute his downed opponent. This signal had never before been used in Dan's years as a Gladiator, although it had never been rescinded.

Dan instantly decided that he was not going to kill his friend on the whim of someone who knew nothing about either of them. Holding his sword in two hands he lifted it high above his head before bringing it swiftly down and breaking it over his knee. Looking directly at the oriental council member he threw the pieces away and then turned to help No2 to his feet. The crowd were on their feet alternately cheering the Gladiators and booing the Council Member in an anti-leadership display not seen in years. The sound of the crowd changed again and Dan saw the members of the 50 of 100 running, fully armed into the arena. Quickly forming a guard around Dan two of them helping No.2 they marched them of the field to the Gladiators quarters. Several of the Gladiators began to barricade while others guarded the windows, Dan pleaded with them to stop as he alone was at fault and he was willing to take his punishment." Anyway" he said smiling, the leaders had no need to use force, we have no food so they can starve us out, and with the way you all eat it wouldn't take long. Why don't you all go about your business and I'll wait here and see what happens. O.K. they said no barricade but we all stay with you. Dan, had never realised he was so popular and was deeply moved by their loyalty, and tried to tell them so, but was soon shouted down by a chorus of ribald insults.

Some 24hrs. were to slowly pass before Dan and his fellow Gladiators received a visit from a member of the council of leaders. To the Gladiators great surprise the visitor was no less than the president of the European Council of Leaders, the most important person in the European region. The assembled Gladiators immediately stood to attention out of respect for their visitor. To be told to please gather round as he had much to say and didn't wish to shout. First let me thank you all for your decisive and prompt action in removing your comrades from the arena and for your very civil greeting. What has been decided, at the insistence of the Asia and Oriental council, is that No1 shall be executed, for his defiance, and his body given to you, the 50 of 100, for disposal as you deem fit.

At this a growl of anger and cries of NO!!! ran through the Gladiators. Gentlemen please hear me out called the Leader holding up his hand for silence. I have told you what has been decided, now I will tell you what is going to happen! No.1 will go with me and a technician whose help I shall need and sent to a place of complete safety which only I shall know. A body will be given to you, which you must then burn in sufficient heat to ensure no trace of bone, flesh or skin remains. Rest assured gentlemen that spies of his enemies will make every effort to catch us out. You must of course carry out such ceremony as you see fit in homage to your lost friend and No.1. Needless to say, I would not trust a secret of this importance to so large a group as yourselves, had I not complete faith in your loyalty and discretion.

Come then No.1, time is of the essence we must go. Pausing only to salute his comrades No.1. followed the Leader from the building. The 50 of 100 stood in silence for some minutes taking stock of all that happened and all they had learned. After a short pause No.2. stepped forward and called for order. Today he said we have lost our No.1. though not perhaps in the way we may have expected, we must now plan to give him the greatest send off ever. Numbers 2 to 10 will stand by to receive and guard the body, 11 to 15 will seek out a suitable site for the cremation, I suggest near the sea so that the remains of the fire can be scattered as an extra precaution. Nos.16 to 25 will obtain flammable material for the "pyre". The remainder will hold themselves ready to assist in any way and to be ready to guard the site to keep out any none Gladiators wishing to trespass.

Meanwhile No.1. had been hurried along a series of secret passages by a surprisingly energetic Leader. They finally arrived at a large laboratory containing a two-seater vehicle unlike anything No.1. had seen before. The only human occupant was an elderly looking man wearing a "lab" coat which marked him out as being an old school technician." Is everything prepared" asked the Leader, the harshness of his tone a clear indicator of the stress he was feeling. The warm up procedures going well we should be able to go in ten minutes, the technician confirmed. Have the documents I requested arrived? was the next query. Yes sir; said the technician, indicating a small brief case lying on the bench.

The Leader quickly opened the briefcase and called No.1. over, saying No.1. I have much to explain and less than ten minutes in which to do it. Please give me your full attention and save any questions until I have finished. First the contraption behind you is a time travel machine in which I am sending you to the early part of the 20th. century which at present is the limit of our ability. You will be given all necessary identity papers showing you to be Danial Stone a British Citizen 25years old, you have £500 of the local currency for immediate expenses and banking details showing a deposit of 5,000,000 pounds to ensure your future prosperity. Both the £500 and the £5,000,000 are large sums of money and there are criminal elements in the 20th. century who would kill to get their hands on £500. Even being the man you are I must warn you to be careful until you become accustomed to your new environs. The area you will be left in is rural and isolated, as we cannot risk our machine being discovered. All I can advise is you study your new documents carefully and use your money frugally until you have learned its true value. So good luck and success in all you do. Should you ever feel hard done by then please remember you committed a crime for which the penalty is death, and you are lucky to be alive. Now any questions? No sir was the reply, but if I may a small request, I feel a briefcase may be out of place in the country-side, and would prefer a haversack if possible. The Leader began to shake his head, when the old technician interrupted to offer his own shoulder bag should it be suitable. No.1. was quite happy to accept and thanked him for his kindness.

At that moment there was a loud knocking on the door; who the hell is that!!! snapped, the Leader hurrying to unlock it. The person who had knocked had fled leaving a pile of 20Th. century clothing and a holdall which contained a second set of similar clothing. At the sight of the cloth-ing the Leader cursed loudly and then apologised to No.1. for having for-gotten he needed to change his clothing before his journey. The technician pointed out time was very short as it was time to leave as power was being used to no purpose. which was critical due to the heavy load he was to carry. At this No.1. who had been examining the time machine, said if this seat is easily removed I could sit on the floor with my back to the bulkhead, if that would help. With respect I will not need the second change of clothes, as thanks to your generosity I shall be able to buy all I need. While speaking No.1. had hurriedly changed into the strange and seemingly heavy 20th. century clothes. he was impressed to find the old technician had removed the seat and was climbing into the machine. paus-ing only to salute and thank the Leader No.1. joined his fellow traveller, thinking here we go!!

MEANWHILE BACK IN THE 1970s.

Work on the large house was temporarily held up, the architect Dan had hired had completed the plans, and was now battling to gain planning permission. This left Dan and Terry with time to start on the cottage ex-tension. Dan set about digging the footings, while Terry set up the board for mixing the mortar etc. Annie", who had taken time off work to keep an eye on proceedings" and Terry watched in amused astonishment at Dan digging the footings; his pick and shovel swinging in a none stop rhythm. Terry was prepared to swear he was clearing a yard of trench every minute, and realised he had better finish his preparations or he would be holding the job up.

Annie had wandered to the front garden when the two men were surprised to here her shouting angrily at an unwelcome visitor. "What are you doing here "she cried "get off my property and don't bother to come back". Watch your tongue!! said the visitor you're not too big for a slapping". At this Dan and Terry both looked round the side of the cottage, and saw the visitor, a large florid looking man; muscular but running to fat, approaching Annie in a threatening manner. Dan started towards them when a human thunderbolt in the form of Terry flashed past him, and without breaking his stride cannoned his shoulder into the strangers chest knocking him heavily to the ground. Terry stood over his victim shouting an incoherent babble of swearing and stuttering and waving the hammer he had been holding in a far from friendly manner. Dan, who by this time had realised Terry was threatening to kill the stranger, which he had previously promised he would if he ever came near Annie again. Timing his actions to avoid Terry's wild swings, Dan plucked the hammer from his hand and threw it across the garden, then wrapping a long arm round his shoulders and pulled him away from his victim still stammering and cursing. "Simmer down tiger", said Dan leave some of the fun for me. With that he turned to the battered looking stranger and lifted him bodily to his feet, before giving him a good shake and none to gently batting the dust off him. You will probably have realised by now that you're not welcome here, Dan advised, so let me see you off the premises. Should you have any idea of revenge or any such silly thought you will find Tiger and myself either here or at the big house, where we can play some more. Now don't struggle with the gate allow me, at that he picked the man up and dropped him onto the road.

All that was good fun and all that but am I allowed to ask what it was all about? asked Dan. He is my Ex husband said Annie, the trouble is he thinks he can sponge off me whenever he is broke, which is most of the time. Well! said Dan any future bother and we will come running; I'll kill him said Terry.

Dan and Annie both laughed at this and Dan slapped him on the back saying Terry Tiger you will do for me, you truly will. Now go and find your hammer and we will get some work done.

Some days later Dan was off chasing the architect over the delayed planning for the big house, Annie and Terry were chatting over a cup of tea, how do you get on with Dan in general asked Annie. No problems he said, he works twice as hard as me, pays well and doesn't moan when I make a mistake. Mind you I don't think I would want him as an enemy Terry mused. What do you mean? asked Annie; well you know how strong and fast he is? it's not just that but sometimes there is a kind of intensity to him that can be scary. How do you mean? she asked. Hard to explain he replied, for example, last week we were meeting in the "Spotted Cow" for a game of darts I got there first and just my luck the McCall brothers were already in. Of course they started taking the mickey out of my stutter. They were in full swing when I noticed Dan had walked in and was stood listening, his face was like a stone mask, a different person! He gave me some money and suggested I got the beers while he introduced himself to my friends. With that he wrapped those arms of his round their shoulders and held them very tight. As I walked away I heard him say," now lads why don't you like my mate Terry"; honestly Aunt Annie you had to be there those simple words were in some way full of menace, a threat. I feel that the arms round their shoulders had them imprisoned by sheer pressure, they certainly weren't comfortable. You know the McCall's all mouth and bluster, they were saying nothing. I took my time getting the beers and it was smiles all round when I got back, even if a bit forced on the brothers part. I've just been telling our friends here that you have had too many years of jokes about your stutter to find it funny anymore, and anyway it's the one fault you have you can't help. I think they should do what I do and take the "mickey" when you do something silly, like treading on a loose plank and falling into a puddle.

That got a laugh for them and a red face for me, but at least it lightened the tone. Dan then challenged the McCall's to a game of darts and we all slowly relaxed. Mind you the brothers told me later that Dan had never said a word out of place, but had scared them witless!

Interesting; said Annie but what about girlfriends any women in his life. None I've heard of, replied Terry. It's an education to go into town with him though, watching all the "Merry Widows" preening and thrusting their breasts out as he passes by.

13

The local small market town was called" Willowsville" and was known to the locals as "Widdowsville". This rather unkind title was because there had been a serious disaster in the local coal mine, with many miners losing their lives. As a result, there is an unusual imbalance of young and middle aged widows in the town. Needless to say, in the years since the disaster this circumstance had become the source of much humour, not much of it in good taste.

Annie was about to launch into more questions, but Terry had finished his tea and was anxious to get back to work. Spoilsport said Annie, maybe said Terry but not a nosy parkers spy!!!

Both nosy parker and spy would have been stunned if they had known how Dan had spent his afternoon. Dan was working in his small office in the caravan when he received an unexpected visitor, a not unattractive lady in, he supposed, her early to mid-forties. "Hello" she said I'm Connie, Terry's mother, I was just passing and thought I'd call in and introduce myself. Hello Connie; said Dan I'm so pleased to meet you, come on in! Now said Dan would you like tea or coffee? although I tell you what! I've a bottle of "plonk" somewhere let's try a glass of that. So saying he disappeared into the kitchen, returning moments later with a bottle of wine and two glasses. "Cheers" he said raising a glass and passing Connie the other. Connie sipped her drink thinking if this is what he calls "plonk" I'd like to try his good stuff. To Dan she said I've been wanting to tell you how grateful I am for the way you treat Terry, he's been so much happier since he's worked with you. He's had so much trouble in the past with being treated as an idiot, just because he stutters. Believe me Connie he suits me just fine, Dan assured her, I don't usually have any help as I prefer to work alone Terry has changed all that and I would not like to lose him.

With that they changed the subject and settled into a pleasant conversation, in which Connie explained her husband had been killed in the mine disaster and she had become one of the "merry" widows of Widdowville. Like many of the other widows she had received generous compensation and with care would be independent for life. Good for you agreed Dan. Shortly after this exchange Connie stood up ready to leave, reaching up to kiss Dan's cheek their lips met seemingly by accident and

they were soon kissing warmly, and then keenly followed by passion-
ately. at which point Dan scooped her into his arms and carried her into
the bedroom!!!

A couple of days later Terry remarked, my mum says she dropped
in on you, don't know what you talked about but you have both been in a
good mood since. We talked about you me old mate what other subject
would cheer us both up asked Dan. Anyway enough of the chitchat lets
go and get your Aunties cottage finished. Thats alright then thought Dan.

Work on the cottage was now moving on at a fast pace, with Terry
struggling to keep Dan supplied with mortar etc. so quickly did he lay the
stones for the walls. He seemed to have an instinctive eye for which stone
was best suited to the course he was laying, enabling him to work more
quickly. The stonework finished Dan and Terry were able to tackle the
interior fittings until all that remained was the rebuilding of the stone fireplace and some decorating. Terry and Annie together made short work of
the decor, leaving Dan to restyle the fireplace. This done to his satisfaction and Annie's delight, they were able to declare the job done. Terry
having left to return tools etc. to the big house, Dan had a last look to see
that all was in order. Are you happy? he asked, Oh yes said Annie it is
better than I ever imagined. Do you fancy some sex then asked Dan standing by the door grinning. No I do not was the furious reply. How about a
lie down while I have some?, stepping out and closing the door just as a
potato Annie had been holding hit the door, and Dan walked away still
smiling.

HOLIDAYS!!!!

On Sunday Dan had an unexpected visit from Terry ,wondering if there
was any chance he could have the next two weeks off. He had been offered a chance to join a group of friends for a fortnight in Spain, one of
them having dropped out. Terry my lad you're a bloody marvel, I've just
been wondering what I'm going to do with you for a few days and here
you are with the perfect answer. The bloody planning permission will be
at least 10 more days, and we are at a standstill. With that he went into

his office and came back an envelope of money which he gave to Terry. Thats your wages up to date and a bonus with my thanks, you did some good work on the cottage. Now off you go and come back all sun tanned, and sand in your shoes.

Thats Terry settled now what am I going to do with myself for two weeks "boring". The longest break he had had for years was a couple of days between jobs. In two days he had caught up with all the paper work, cleaned the caravan and all tools and other equipment and was beginning to get restless. Not good for someone who had been bred to fight. Needing some petty cash he took a train to Markfield a medium town about 30miles away to visit his bank. While in town he decided to make a day of it, doing some shopping, having a meal, and seeing the late showing of a film he fancied before heading to the station for the last train home.

He had been walking for a few minutes when he realised he must have taken a wrong turning and was lost. he appeared to be entering a housing estate, probably post war but not well built or to Dans mind well designed. He was about to turn back when he saw an elderly lady stood at the street corner who might be able to put him on the right road. The film had overrun and he was already in danger of missing his train. As he approached the lady he began to wonder if something was wrong as she seemed very agitated and worried. Approaching slowly and calmly in the hope of not distressing her further, he asked if there was anything wrong and could he help? Not unless you think you can chase that lot off she said, pointing round the corner. Dan looked and saw there were four young men loitering at the opening to an underpass intended to allow pedestrians to cross under the main road. I take it they are trouble then Missus asked Dan?. Yes I'm sure they are the ones who beat up my old man and took his watch and wallet she said. Its nearly a mile longer to go the other way and he will be worrying where I am, and I don't want him coming looking for me! I see the problem said Dan I'll stroll down and have a word. The old lady started to tell about the danger he was putting himself in, but cut her short telling her not to worry. What can I do to help? she asked, just keep safely out of sight Dan said, although I like the look of your heavy walking stick perhaps I could borrow it.

She passed it to him and he set off round the corner leaning on the stick and limping heavily as he approached the waiting men." Well now what have we here" said the nearest one, who Dan took to be the leader, somebody come to make a donation to our beer fund and smirked to his pals. Let's start with your wallet and anything else worth having shall we. He was now standing close up to Dan trying to intimidate him with his stare. Oh dear, thought Dan now I really am scared! Look sonny he said why don't you just get out of my way before you get hurt? Seems we've got a tough guy said the leader lets teach him a lesson he won't forget.

At this they formed a group of three across Dan's front with the forth moving to get behind him, thinking him to be in position the leader gave a slight nod of his head as a signal to begin. That was enough for Dan who immediately straightened up changed his grip to the middle of the heavy cane and whipped the handle backwards at great speed striking the man behind on the knee sending him crashing to the ground. Without losing any time Dan swung the stick forward ferrule first into the lead man's stomach, sending him cannoning into the other two knocking them off balance. Discarding the walking stick he jumped over the fallen leader and while still in midair looped an arm around their necks and crashed their heads together before throwing them at the wall. Hearing a shout of warning from the old lady Dan spun round to find the gang leader lurching to his feet holding a large knife. Now that's a shame, said Dan, we've all been getting on so nicely, and now I will have to break your bones. Hearing this defiance the would be mugger lunged at Dan with a roundhouse sweep of the knife. Dan who had been avoiding attacks of this type most of his life easily evaded the knife but caught his assailant's wrist jerking it forcibly backwards and downwards dislocating the shoulder and dropping his attacker to the ground. Well it's not broken said Dan but it will do for now.

Dan now turned his attention to his first victim who's knee he had struck with the walking stick, who was now using that same stick to support his attempt to hobble his escape. Can't let you do that old son, Dan told him, I've got to give the stick back. At that he picked him up and threw to the wall along side his friends.

The fight had only lasted a couple of minutes but Dan felt it was safe enough to call the lady through and send her on her way.

Rather than call her, Dan decided to fetch her in case she was nervous. As they passed the gang he warned her to keep her face covered, in case she should be recognised. Dan noticed that while keeping her face covered she had along hard look at the four men and was not unduly surprised when she stopped and whispered to him that one of them was wearing her husbands watch. "Is he now" said Dan, wait for me at the corner and I'll get it for you and turned back to where the would be muggers were beginning to get up. Now lads he said don't be in too much hurry to leave the party isn't over yet, I've given you something to remember me by but I've nothing from you. Taking hold of the leaders left hand Dan started to remove his watch, the leader swore at him and tried to pull his hand away. Dan merely squeezed harder threatening to break the fingers until he stopped struggling allowing Dan to take the watch. having watched this little tussle the others passed over their watches without comment. Thank you lads said Dan its been nice to have met you but I have to go.

He ran and caught up with the old lady and introduced himself and learned her name was Mary, while agreeing to walk her home. Mary tried to express her admiration for the way Dan had dealt with the gang of muggers, but he was more interested in how to get to the station to catch his train. Mary explained he had been heading in the wrong direction and would struggle get there in time on foot. When we get home I will get my husband George to run you in the car. Fair enough said Dan that's fine by me.

These plans were soon forgotten when George caught sight of Dan; crying good lord its "Peter Roberts"(the name Dan had used in the army during W.W.11) you remember me Cpl. Foster? Don't be silly George said Mary he is much too young to have been with you. I'm sorry Dan he said but you are exactly like him. He's my uncle said Dan but everyone says we are chips off the same block. He is my mother's brother and they are as alike in looks and temperament as a male and female could ever be, mother was always delighted I followed them. Where is Peter living now? asked George. I'm afraid he and my mother were killed in a motor crash, no doubt driving too fast! They were both adrenalin junkies who hated the thought of growing old,

I doubt they would have any regrets.

He was sorry to lie to this very nice couple, but relieved to have his cover story ready. Enough of this chatter said Mary, I promised Dan you would run him to the station for the last train. Oh! sorry said George but I'm so thrilled at meeting Peters nephew I forgot my manners. Do you have to get back tonight? We could put you up for the night, and you can tell me how you and Mary came to meet. Of course I'll run you to the station in the morning. Dan said O.K. and mentally geared himself for an evening of hearing anecdotes about himself and appearing to find it all new.

Mary busied herself in the kitchen soon reappearing with tea and sandwiches, first handing George his watch and then launching into an excited description of all that had happened. Thanks for my watch said George, it was a present from Mary and is very special to me. I can visualise you sorting those yobs out, I remember Peter tackling four big Yanks who had stolen a little Scots lad's hat, and were pushing him about as he tried to get it back. He put three of them down in quick time then the Scots lad held him back saying "Hold on Jimmy this one's mine". Peter stood aside. and the Scots man threw himself at the American, he didn't have it all his own way explained George but beat his man in the end. This started George on an evening of anecdotes and reminiscences, some of which even Dan had forgotten. Dan did however remember Cpl. Foster and knew him to be a typical British N.C.O. doing his duty with good humour and the minimum of fuss.

George and Mary drove Dan to the station the next morning, and saw him on his train insisting he keep in touch. Dan saying yes he would if he ever got another holiday and waved them goodbye.

Back at the caravan he gathered his thoughts, checked on the big house and set off to see Annie. He found her, as usual, working in the garden. This garden is a credit to you said Dan, did you design it yourself? Me! No she replied the layout and planting are all down to Terry, didn't you know he is an horticultural genius. He knows all the Latin names for plants, as well as everything to do with propagation and cultivation. If you have not seen his garden you really should go and have a good look. Yes I will said Dan.

So to what do I owe this pleasure, I see you so seldom, asked Annie. Since you ask he replied its about the rent for the cottage, the amount you have been paying covers the rates and a bit over so I am content to leave it at that. What about the cost of all the alterations she wanted to know. The stone for the walls came free and anything else can be included in with the big house so no worries explained Dan. Sometimes Dan Stone you can be a very nice man said Annie, doubtfully. Does that mean I can have a kiss he asked, opening his arms to her. You deserve one said Annie but I'm not sure I can trust you!! "Be brave" said Dan taking her into his arms kissing her gently if lingeringly before letting her go, smiling. Really Dan, said Annie two pleasant surprises in one day, I see I shall have to watch you. Dan turning to go, looked back saying, I've just remembered I didn't finish off in your bedroom. You didn't do anything in my bedroom interrupted Annie. Thats true, he said, would now be a good time for you? Go away Dan, and damn you for spoiling the moment said a sorrowful looking Annie.

Dan left, looking and feeling more sad than she did, knowing that if he let himself he could fall for her in a very big way. From past experience he knew this could never work, once before he had loved and allowed himself to be loved with a disastrous outcome.

THE BEGINNING

The time machine carrying Dan and the technician rose vertically, with increasing acceleration through the now open roof of the laboratory. At what Dan supposed to be a preordained height the machine stopped rising and began what seemed to be a forward motion. The sky seemed to be rushing past changing from day to night every few seconds, leaving Dan wondering whether it was the sky or the time capsule that actually moved. He remembered the intercom system and asked his companion to explain. There are many theories about that he said, I believe that we are moving, based on the power we are expending all the time. When we reach the period in time we are aiming for the machine will travel normally until we reach our geographical location. You seem to have done this trip before said Dan, is there to be any contact between us in the future? Not unless the council requests it he said, but rest assured they will always know where to find you. "How"? asked Dan. Sorry No.1. I am not allowed to tell you, but there are more things happen in this century and others than you could ever imagine.

About this time the night and day images stopped flashing by and the time machine began a forward movement. Well No.1. or should I call you Dan, our journey is almost over and I must say goodbye. Please be ready to jump out as soon as we touch down my time on land is strictly limited. Thankyou said Dan for all your kindness and help, may I know your name? With pleasure, he said, I am, like you, known by my standing in my profession and for now I am Top Tech.

Their vehicle ceased its forward motion and began to descend, soon revealing a high hedged field boarded one side by a large wood. Head for the wood and try to hide in case we have been seen or heard and someone comes to investigate. The travel machine landed and Dan leaped clear heading straight for wood. Behind him he heard a rush of air as Top Tech wasted no time starting his return journey.

Once well into the wood Dan stood still and silent to try to detect if anyone else was nearby. Hearing nothing, he began to look for somewhere to hide until morning, cursing himself for not asking for a torch. With his eyes slowly becoming accustomed to the gloom he began to search for a shelter for the night. He had not slept for over 24hrs.and with all that had happened to him in that time, he was feeling exhausted. Luckily he quickly found a dence shrubbery he was able to crawl into until daylight and try to snatch some sleep, if his need to remain alert would allow.

As dawn was breaking he became aware of the sound of two men talking and laughing together as they approached his hideout. Now that it was growing light he realised he was not as well hidden as he hoped, and was sure to be seen. As silently as possible he crawled clear of the shrubbery and stood with his back to the trunk of a nearby large tree. He had just tucked his haversack into the bottom of the tree when the two men came into view. They were carrying a number of Rabbits which marked them as poachers. "Hello" they said in unison, you look as if you have had a rough night, what brings you here? asked one. Ignore Sean here said the other, that's none of our business. With that he put out his hand saying I'm Shamus nice to meet you. Dan shook his hand cautiously on guard for any trickery and introduced himself, shaking hands also with Sean.

You look like you could do with breakfast insisted Seamus our campsite is nearby you will be very welcome. Not knowing where his next meal would come from Dan decided to accept while remaining on his guard at all times. His first surprise came when they reached the camp site, not the collection of tents he had imagined, but a neat area of caravans and towing vehicles. All the caravans seemed clean and tidy and the vehicles well maintained. There was a general aura of pride and discipline over the entire area. The second surprise a selection of exercise equipment and a boxing ring, all well used but in good order.

Dan had barely time to take in his surroundings when the door to one of the caravans opened and a large middle aged man stepped out. He approached Dan with his hand outstretched, shaking hands he introduced himself as Michael and welcomed Dan to join them for breakfast. Over a large meal Dan learned his hosts were from Romany stock and now ran a travelling boxing show. Their main passion was the annual Romany boxing competition which Michael had won some years ago and now longed to train a fighter to do the same. His current prodigy, seated opposite Dan, showed great promise, said Michael, but needs to control his temper.

Breakfast being over, Michael explained he was taking the squad on a long training run. May I join you asked Dan I could do with loosening my joints. You're welcome said Michael, but we don't wait for stragglers and you will have to find you own way back if you don't keep up. Fair enough said Dan. Michael instructed Sean to find Dan some kit to wear, giving them three minutes to be ready. Dan found the run very enjoyable, although not as fast paced as the Gladiators would have set. All went well until about a mile to go, when Michael kept them running on the spot while told them the last stretch will be a race with a small prize for the winner. With that he sent the slower runners of in batches according to ability. Keeping Sean, Seamus, Dan and his protege Dillon as the last group.

Sean set of at a pace that Dan thought to be too fast to be sustainable, followed by Dillon only slightly slower. Dan settled into a pace he felt would give him some reserve speed should he need it, for his part Seamus was content to keep Dan company while he could. As the stiffness caused by his time travel journey and night in the woods eased Dan gradually increased his pace, to try to see how Sean and Dillon were progressing. Seamus soon began to feel the pressure, but before dropping behind he begged Dan to try to beat Dillon, explaining he is disliked by everyone and only tolerated for Michael's benefit. Warning Dan to be careful if he tried to pass Dillon as he would be sure to try to stop him, probably violently.

With this warning ringing in his ear he increased his pace again and soon left Seamus behind.

He soon caught up with a heavily panting Sean who urged him along saying Dillon was only fifty or so yards ahead and beginning to struggle. Encouraged by this Dan kept up his pace, feeling he would still have a bit in reserve should he need it. Rounding the next bend he found Dillon some thirty yards in front, Dan was catching his opponent quite quickly. He slowed his pace slightly and approached as quietly as possible and reached Dillon without being heard. Reaching across Dillon from right to left he tapped him on the shoulder, causing him to turn that way in surprise. This gave Dan his chance and he slipped past on the right and was several yards ahead before his opponent knew he was even close. Dan put on his planned final burst and with curses and threats following him, crossed the finishing line. Only to find two of the early starters had pipped him by a few seconds. Dan was amused by this and congratulated the two youngsters on their success.

The light-hearted air soon evaporated when Dillon marched up to Dan and began to curse and threaten him telling him to watch his step as the next time Dan crossed him he would regret it. Dan was about to reply in kind when Michael dragged his protege away with repeated advice to control his temper. Michael returned shortly and began to apologise for any upset caused. Pleased don't worry I've met his type many times and I'm still in one piece. "I wonder if they all are" muttered Sean to Seamus, who nodded agreement. They had earlier formed an opinion that there was more to Dan than met the eye.

Michael Kindly asked Dan if he would eat with them. Thank you said Dan I'm grateful, but I have to find somewhere to sleep, I have only had about 4hrs sleep in the past three days. Can you guide me to the nearest town, I need to get organised. You must stay with us as long as you wish insisted Michael, Colleen has spare room and can easily fit you in. Incidentally she already has your haversack in her care. My god thought Dan my whole future life is in that haversack and I had forgotten all about it, I hope its not been tampered with. Having had Colleen's caravan pointed out to him, he set of to track down his bag. Colleen welcomed him in, explaining she already been told he needed somewhere to sleep. She showed him his comfortable looking bed hidden behind a folding partition at one end of the caravan. Dan pleased to see his haversack lying on the bed apparently undisturbed.

Smiling broadly Colleen assured him that her bed was at the other end of the caravan and he would be quite safe. If only because she was old enough to be his mother. Dan, who had no experience of women or their sense of humour, could only smile and nod his head. Which seemed to amuse her even more.

Still wearing the running gear he had borrowed Dan collapsed onto the bed pulled a blanket over himself and was instantly asleep. He slept unmoving until the sounds of the camp coming alive woke him the next morning. He wondered what the arrangements were for bathing when Coleen knocked on the partition asking if he was " decent" and could she come in?. Dan replied yes to both questions and she opened the door to pass him his shirt, pants and socks neatly washed and ironed and ready to wear. Dan expressed his sincere gratitude for her kindness and asked about the chances of a bath or shower. Colleen showed him a canvass screened area on the edge of the camp and explained the system of pumping the water from the stream into the overhead tank and using this water to shower. She then handed him some soap and a towel, asking with her usual smile would he please go now as he was "tainting" her home. Ushering him out the caravan she warned him to be quick or the "wolves" would eat all the breakfast.

Having made it the breakfast table and eaten his fill, he was wondering what to do next when Michael told him Dillon would be having a sparing session in the ring and invited him to watch. In his years as a Gladiator Dan had done many hours of sparing against several opponents who had natural prowess at boxing and had learned a great deal about the noble art. Unguarded boxing had not been permitted to prevent accidental injuries to Gladiators. He was very interested to see Dillon in action and joined Michael at the ringside. Dillon was to spar with a man of similar size and weight, who Dan had not met. It seemed to Dan that Dillon had many good points, but was too flash and concerned about his image, looking at the crowd for approval every time he landed a good punch. He finally looked away once too often and his opponent caught him with a solid right to the jaw, which he clearly didn't like. He again lost his temper and launched a savage attack on his adversary using every dirty trick in the book. Striking with his elbows and head as well as his fists, finally pushing him so that he fell against a corner post before landing heavily on the canvas. He stood threateningly over his victim until a very angry Michael ordered him to his corner, while Seamus and Sean got in the ring to help the fallen man. As they lifted him to his feet he called to Micheal "that's it I'm finished one of these days that mad bugger will kill somebody and it's not going to be me".

I've warned you about that temper of yours said a still angry Michael, now you have lost your only worthwhile sparing partner at a critical stage in your training. He was never good enough anyway shouted Dillon, can't you get me better than him?. Seeing Dan watching he pointed in his direction, what about your new friend the "big fellow". I fancy taking him down a peg or two, come on big man what do you say?!!! Oh! shut up said Michael before I do something I might regret. Why not see what Dan has to say suggested Sean, you might be surprised, and beckoned Dan to join them.

To Michaels surprise Dan was happy to step into the ring if it would help Michael out. The trainer was not convinced until Dan explained he had done a great deal of sparing in the recent past, although he had never fought in an actual contest. Adding that he had seen nothing in Dillon's ability to worry him. Mark me if he goes for me as he did his sparing partner I will do my best to finish him. Fair enough said Michael, Sean will kit you out while I read that fool the riot act, yet again.

When Dan returned ready for the fray, he was surprised to see most of the camp had gathered at the ring side applauding as he approached. His first reaction was to look at his opponent, noting him scowl angrily at Dan's popularity. Not really helping he thought as he climbed into the ring. Sean had told him they were planning a maximum of six three minute rounds with one minute intervals, but Dan could call a halt anytime he wished. Seamus in Dillons corner and Sean in Dans, Michael observing and time keeping. When everyone was ready a bell was rung and the adversaries met in the middle of the ring.

There was no sporting touch of gloves from Dillon, just a roundhouse right designed to take Dans head off. Dan dodged it with ease and landed a firm jab to the ribs, just hard enough to let Dillon know he was in a fight. At this Dillon began to use his undoubted skill and quick footwork to catch his opponent with his best punch. He grew more frustrated as the round went on as Dan either dodged or took his punches on his arms or gloves. At the same time catching Dillon with several counter punches, not big shots but hard enough for him to begin to feel their effect. This was the pattern for the first three rounds, with Dillon being made to work very hard for little reward.

After ringing the bell for the forth round Michael asked Sean how Dan was coping, I'll tell you boss he said he has hardly broken sweat and his breathing is level and unforced. There is either something odd about him or he is the fittest man I ever met. In the ring Dillon was trying to up his game and was moving quicker than ever, half way through the round he put together a clever combination of punches and finally caught Dan with a hard blow to the ribs. As Dan stepped back to escape the expected flurry of back up punches he was surprised to see Dillon looking at the crowd for their approval. Not one to pass up an opportunity Dan planted a hard right cross to his jaw, sending him stumbling backwards into the ropes.

Bouncing of the ropes Dillon launched himself at Dan in a furious flurry of blows, including elbows, head and any other method he could to bring his opponent down. Dan weathered the storm by increasing his speed around the ring, and his length of reach to keep Dillon at a "safe" distance. At the end of the round he was met at his corner by a very apologetic Michael who wanted to stop the fight to save Dan from further risk. Dan insisted the final round go ahead reminding Michael, of his intention to put his opponent down if he lost his temper again. I've never dodged a challenge yet and won't this time. Ring the bell Michael said Sean and say a little prayer for your champion, I feel he will need it. Michael rang the bell while giving Sean a hard look.

The two fighters met in the middle of the ring and Dillon again ignored the customary touch of gloves to throw a huge right cross at his advisary. Dan swayed back just enough to cause it miss before hammering a right of his own into Dillons ribs, followed by a left to the jaw and a second right to the ribs. This set the pattern for the early part of the round with a rapidly tiring Dillon trying to finish the fight with one punch while Dan dodged his wild swings before countering with combinations of precise punches, wearing his opponent down. Towards the end of the round Dan went into all out attack , launching a barrage of heavy punches culminating in a fierce left hook to the jaw which sent him crashing to the canvas. Not bothering to count him out Michael climbed quickly into the ring to attend to his protege, who soon came round and was led off to his quarters. Sean and Seamus ensured the winner kept warm and took him off to their caravan where they were equipped to attend to any injury.

Sean and Seamus carefully checked Dan for injuries, finding nothing but a couple of insignificant bruises. They then sat down facing him and demanded some answers. Answers to what asked Dan, hoping to gain time to plan his reply. Everything! said Sean starting with the truth added Seamus. Truth about what asked Dan, still stalling. You; who are you really, where are you from and where did you learn to box like that? We are not fools, we have thought there is something different about you since the day we met. The prompt way you hid your haversack, then stood with your back to the tree to protect your rear. You were ready for trouble, but we thought, ready but not afraid. When we brought you to the camp you were on your guard, but still not afraid, you seemed confident you would cope with anything thrown at you! You then go on to run us into the ground, before flattening our "big white hope", without breaking sweat. So Dan the truth please.

Well, thought Dan the truth would be the last thing you would believe. First my name really is Dan Stone, I am what I think is called a foundling never having known my parents. I was shunted from one institution to another, until I was taken in, at about seven years old, by a traveling group. I later found they were involved in many types of fighting shows including a particularly dangerous type illegal in many countries, but popular in the far east and South America. They began my training from age nine and, by nineteen I was a regular in the illegal fighting games. As for boxing, I have sparred for many hours with first class opposition, never a proper fight in case I hurt my hands. After four or five years I tired of the training routine and asked for permission to leave. The couple who had raised me from childhood consented readily, as they were aware of my growing lack of interest. Their fear was I would become careless and suffer an injury as a result.

Sean and Seamus looked about to ask many questions, but Dan told them he had said all he intended to say. Assuring the brothers he was not accustomed to discussing his private life. You must tell us about the illegal fighting they begged. No! said Dan the only thing my guardians asked of me was to keep silent about it and I fear I have already said too much. O.K. they said let's go and eat. You go said Dan, I'll go for a run to ease up, then a shower and I'll join you. With that he jogged off, leaving the brothers shaking their heads. That was all very interesting said Seamus, I think what he didn't say would have been a lot more interesting Sean replied.

After the meal during which many of the camp residents expressed their admiration of his pugilistic skills. A few adding their thanks for him teaching Dillon a much needed lesson. Dan made his apologise and retired to his space in Colleen's caravan, intending to check his papers etc. In preparation for his early departure.

The next morning saw Dan dressed for leaving and rearing to go, he had enjoyed his time with the Romanies but felt this was partly because the life was similar to the one he had left. Now he was eager to move on and begin an entirely new life. However, it was not to be!

At breakfast he learned that Dillon had disappeared in the night,

taking all his belongings with him. Sean and Seamus lost no time in asking Dan to stay and take his place, if only for the boxing competition in
two weeks' time. Michael is too much of a gentleman to ask you but we
are sure he would be grateful if you volunteered. Dan shook his head,
saying "I really don't want this" I need to find myself a new life away
from fighting. As it is I don't know where to go, or what to do when I get
there. I only have a little money and the clothes I'm wearing. We understand that said Seamus, while Sean nodded in agreement, but it will only
take about ten days of your time and we will assist in getting you started
any way we can.

I see this means a lot to you sighed Dan, as you have shown me
nothing but kindness since we met I will agree. Thats wonderful chorused
the brothers, but can we ask one more favour? You're pushing your luck,
but ask away said Dan. Would you go to Michael to volunteer so he does
not know we have been involved they asked. You two really are the limit
said Dan, but yes, I'll give it a try. True to his word he sort out Michael
and offered to replace Dillon.

Michael made it clear that he felt Dan would be the ideal replacement, but wondered if he could really expect such commitment after so
short an acquaintance. Dan assured him he would not be incovenienced
and would be proud to represent the camp. He did however insist on running his own fitness regime, although he would rely on Michael for anything to do with boxing and ringcraft.

So thought Dan after less than a week in the 20th. century I'm back
in the old routine. The extent and severity of his fitness soon became the
talk of the camp. Even Michael had never seen such a routine, nor such
discipline from an athlete. In the ring Michael found he only needed to
fine tune Dan's footwork and general ringcraft. His balance and punching
were already first class.

Only two hectic days had passed when Sean announced the party
going to the tournament would be leaving the next day. He advised Dan
to get as much rest as possible, as the journey could last all day. Colleen
would not be going so he need not be disturbed. After a good night's sleep
he awoke to find two of the smarter looking caravans hitched to enormous
lorries ready to move. Dan said farewell to Colleen who had looked after

him so well. She asked if she would see him again, but he truly didn't know.

As expected the journey lasted all day, with frequent stops to allow the overheated lorries to cool. Dan spent some of the time jogging alongside the convoy, otherwise he was content to study the scenery and was fascinated by the villages and towns they passed through. Their destination proved to be a large racecourse near a large built up area. Where is this place asked Dan, this is Aintree racecourse on the outskirts of a city and port called Liverpool was the reply. You should have time for a look around after the tournament if you wish Sean and I would be glad to join you added Seamus.

Michael explained the competition would start the next day. Starting with a field of sixteen, with the eight winners going through to the next round the following day. The two finalists having a days rest between the final and semi final. After three fights in three days I imagine they will be ready for a rest said Dan thoughtfully. I will follow any instructions you care to give me Michael, but my inclination will be to get through the early rounds as quickly as possible, while taking a minimum amount of punishment. I agree said Michael, but no doubt your opponents will have the same idea. Now attend to your exercise routine, and remember not to eat or drink too much before the fight.

Dan's first bout was set for 11am. his opponent proved to be a heavily built muscular young man, not more than 5ft.11ins. in height giving Dan an advantage of height and reach. Don't get over confident Sean warned, I managed to sneak a look at him on the heavy punchbag and from what I saw he has a right hand that will take your head off if you give him chance.

No butting, gouging, or hitting on the break I want a clean fight. Now shake hands return to your corners and at the bell come out fighting. With these words the referee launched Dan's tournament. At the sound of the bell Dan leapt from his stool and was across the ring almost before his opponent got to his feet. Caught unawares the youngster had no defence to the lightning fast straight left to the jaw which rocked him back into his corner where Dan followed up with right and left hooks to the body. The fight could have ended there and then, but the young man was alert enough to pull Dan into a clinch and hang on, gathering his wits before the ref separated them. Stepping away from the clinch Dan circled clear of the big right-hand Sean had warned him of. For the rest of the round his opponent stayed in the centre of the ring while Dan circled looking for the chance to end the contest. In the break the youngster's seconds worked hard and sent there man out for the second round looking better for their efforts. At the bell he left his seat very quickly, only to find Dan had risen more slowly and was still in his own half of the ring. Disconcerted by this Dan's adversary wavered in his approach allowing Dan to catch him with another straight left followed by a barrage of blows to the ribs and stomach. These were followed by a crushing right to the chin. Which brought the bout to an end with the younger man being counted out. Once his adversary had recovered, Dan went across to check he was O.K. and praise him for his courage. You were just too good he said ruefully. Well said Dan I had been warned about your right hand and had to make sure you didn't get chance to use it. Go on and win the tournament for me was the reply, I'll feel better if I can say I was beaten by the champion. I'll do my best said Dan smiling and allowed Sean to lead him away. You have it all to do again tomorrow said Sean so let's get you checked over, fed and rested.

Dan's second bout was in mid afternoon against a much lighter opponent, who had outpointed his opponent over 6 rounds which showed him to be a clever boxer even if fighting bigger men. You won't find him so easy to hit warned Michael, you will have to use your extra reach. He will want to keep moving and pick you off every chance he gets. So keep well clear, use your reach to keep him unsettled and tire him. At this Dan found himself becoming irritated by Sean and Michael's warnings to be careful of his opponents various skills and supposed power. After all he was No.1 of the 100 and was accustomed to his opponents being wary of him.

It was in this frame of mind and with Sean's renewed warnings ringing in his ear, that he sat on his stool waiting for the bell to start his second fight. From the beginning Dan began to hunt his opponent down using his innate speed and long arms to harry his advisory allowing him no chance to settle into a rhythm. Late on in the round Dan caught his man with a

31

series of heavy punches, hurting him badly and leaving him hanging on until the bell. Carry on like this and you can finish him this round said Sean. I intend to said Dan and stood to wait for the bell. Then that is what will happen thought Sean. Sure enough Dan attacked right from the start of the round and soon had his opponent in serious trouble, and was pleased when the opposing corner threw in a towel to save their fighter from unnecessary harm. Having checked that his opponent was O.K. Dan left the ring tent as quickly as possible before any inquisitive spectator could start asking questions.

Back in the brothers' caravan having the customary post-fight checkover Dan explained his anxiety to avoid any publicity, and in particular photographs. The brothers felt it was difficult for them to guarantee complete privacy, but promised to do whatever they could.

For Dans semifinal fight his opponent was a large powerful man, who had reached the final on a previous occasion. Sean and Shamus were quick to warn Dan that his opponent, "Kirk Adams" had a mighty right hand was able to absorb a lot of punishment and had never been knocked out. Repeatedly advising Dan to watch out for his right, insisting if he landed it the fight would be over. Thanks for that said Dan, I hope you are going to be fair and warn him about mine.

On meeting Kirk in the fight tent, Dan was curious to see the number of bruises he was carrying from his earlier fights, he may be able to take punishment, but he looks like he has to. I'll have to have a close look for holes in his defence.

For the first round he did just that, trying various types of attack to find the most successful strategy. By the end of the round, having dodged several huge right hand punches, Dan felt he had learned all he needed to know. Coming out for the second round he upped his speed and peppered his opponent with fast straight and hooked rights. By the end of the round Kirk was blowing hard and showing the punishment he had received. Keep this up and you could win this enthused Sean, no could about it Dan said he goes down this round. Sean sensed that Dan was serious, and wondered, not for the first time who this man really was. True to his word Dan increased his speed again, and continued to harry his man with a rapid barrage of punches, causing Kirk to attempt a huge swinging

righthand punch while not correctly balanced. Seizing the opportunity offered, Dan parried the attempted punch with a strong left arm and hammered a powerful right cross into the body. Kirk lowered his guard to
protect his body, allowing Dan to land his hardest blow of the competition
so far flush on the jaw, and the fight was over!!

When he crossed to his opponents corner to check he was O.K.,
Kirk insisted on shaking Dan's hand. I've had a great many fights over too
many years, but today you have shown me a different class. I couldn't
stand another punch like that last one, I'm through. Where did Michael
find you he asked, I reckon I could have taken that Dillon one handed. I
was visiting Michael when Dillon did a runner and offered to help out,
said Dan. Things here would not be the same without Michael would
they?. At that Sean and Seamus hurried Dan away to prevent any more
questions.

Dan spent the rest day arranging his few belongings, ready to make
a quick getaway after the fight, he thought the Romanies he had be-
friended were good people but needed he to move on. As usual he wanted
to avoid publicity, and planned to leave as soon as possible after the fight.

His opponent for the final, Kerry White, a tall well-made man was
clearly very fit and well trained. Sean assured Dan he was a skilled boxer
and crisp puncher, although not really a knockout specialist. At last, I
don't have to worry about a big right hand thought Dan. I think this time
I'll let him worry about my right, and the left come to that.

The day and time for the final arrived and Dan and Sean made their
way to ringside, to find a large crowd had gathered eager for the fight to
start. Michael had spoken at length to Dan, about tactics for the bout, but
concluded that he felt it inappropriate to warn him about his opponent as
he was the better man all round. Baring an unforeseen accident Dan
would come out on top.

The bell went and Dan stepped forward to meet Kerry in the centre
of the ring, to his surprise his adversary stayed well away content to keep
as much distance from Dan as possible. Dan was puzzled by these tactics
and decided to pressure Kerry as much as he could, throwing a barrage of
punches not worrying if they got through his opponents guard or not.
Content that any that landed would hurt and any striking his arm muscles

would reduce the power of Kerry's punches. Dan kept the pressure relentlessly driving his man backwards, until late in the second round he trapped his man in a corner and was able to land a combination of punches to the body. Kerry fell into a clinch and was able to hang on until the bell for the end of the round. Back in his corner Dan asked if this was his opponents usual style of boxing, no said Sean opinion is Kirk has told how hard you can punch and he is running scared. A shame if that's true thought Dan this could have been an example of true boxing.

Either way I have a job to due so let's be at it. At the bell he left his stool very quickly, catching his opponent in his own corner and again subjecting him to severe punishment. When Kerry tried to fall into a clinch, Dan was ready and held him off allowing himself room to land a second combination of heavy punches. His opponent was now breathing hard and tried to keep well away from Dan. The ring was too small and Dan too quick for this tactic to work, and he was soon once more trapped in a corner. This time there was no escape and the fight ended in a K.O.

Dan was disappointed in the fight feeling his opponent had not thrown a quality punch throughout. I'm glad I didn't pay to see that he told Sean, you played your part, it takes two to have a fight replied Sean. Lets go and get you cleaned up, and let his corner worry about it.

As soon as he had showered and changed Dan's intention was to find some way to sneak away without any fuss, and before anything else happened to stop him getting on with his life. Unfortunately when he slipped out of the caravan to make his escape, he was immediately surrounded by fans wishing to shake his hand and congratulate him on winning the competition. He was glad to get back to the caravan to regroup and try to find another way of dodging any publicity. His reverie was broken by the return of a breathless Sean full of news.

You have got your wish he announced, there is to be no publicity and no medal presentation. Normally there would be a ceremony giving Gold, Silver and Bronze medals to the top three, but it has had to be cancelled. Kirk Adams refused to fight for the bronze position, and after his poor showing in the final it is felt Kerry White cannot be presented with the Silver. You will get your gold award at a private ceremony later today, and did I mention there was an exit collection after each fight your share is £372, in cash. Frankly we all think you earned it!

The promised ceremony took place early that afternoon with Dan embarrassed by the flattering things said about him. When it came to his turn to speak, he called Michael to the front and handed him the trophy as thanks for his kindness. Explaining to the audience that without Michaels guidance he probably wouldn't have got through the first round. Sean and Seamus led the applause for this action giving Michael no chance to refuse. Once the ceremony was over Dan drew the brothers to one side and gave them the odd £72 to give to Coleen with his thanks for all her kindness. With that he shook hands with Sean and Seamus collected his few belongings, and left, to at last start his new life.

His first reaction on reaching the city centre was dislike for all the noise, everything and many of the people, of whom there seemed to be hundreds seemed to be competing to see how to make the most noise. He had always taken for granted the silence of 25th century traffic, together with the quietness of the robots who formed the majority of the "pedestrian" traffic. Most humans used the continuous, and free, public transport, walking only from the "tram" to the building of their choice. Dan headed away from what he took to be the high street, searching for a small hotel or guest house. He was unsure what a guest house was but he had been told it was his best option. Since he wanted, above all else to remain anonymous, he felt the more low key the better.

After only a few minutes walking he came to a street of large Victorian houses several with signs advertising "rooms to let". He chose the cleanest looking, called "Monarch Guest House" and knocked on the door. He was admitted by a friendly couple of indeterminate age and shown to a clean pleasant room, complete with wash hand basin. Use of the communal bathroom by appointment for a small extra charge. Dan supposed this to be normal for the 20th. century and accepted gratefully. Having received advice on the best shops and directions on how to get there Dan set off to do some much needed shopping. Without Colleen administering his laundry he had attempted his own washing and ironing with less than perfect results.

The next morning after a good breakfast and having arranged for his hosts to take over his laundry, "for a small extra charge" he set off in

search of some way of earning a living. He had come to realise the
£5,000,000 he received from the "leader" was sufficient to keep him in
comfort indefinitely, but was determined that when he was recalled to the
25th. century he would hand all or nearly all of it back.

Fine sentiments but what was he going to live on in the meantime,
he had already spent more of the original £500 and the £300 boxing pay-
out than he hoped.

Dans first call was at a local branch of the bank holding his
£5,000,000 and arrange to have it transferred. Having carefully checked
his identity they agreed to set things in motion without delay. They then
suggested if he needed investment advice they had specialists available,
and were happy to arrange an appointment for the next week, when the
transfer would be complete. Feeling he made a small start, Dan started an
on foot tour of the city looking for something that would offer him a career.

In his room that night he decided to list his preferences in the hope
of getting a pointer to what he was looking for. The list of wants soon
showed he wanted to work with his hands, learning new skills along the
way. The work would need to have a physical element, outdoor if possible. He would want to be his own boss, if not immediately, then as soon
as possible. While determined to hand back the £5,000,000 if and when
released from exile, he was prepared to use it to fund his activities in the
beginning.

From the first he was sure he did not want a clerical career, or anything that would put him into the "limelight". Michael had assured him
he could have gone far as a boxer, even to the top of the professional
ranks. The idea of exposing himself to public and press scrutiny alarmed
him, he was unsure of how well his new identity would stand close inspection.

All very well thought Dan, I now know what I want, but I'm no
closer to finding it. Tomorrow I'll move further away from the city centre
and try again. Having made his way into the suburbs he found many roads
of Victorian houses both terrace and semi-detached. A number of which
were undergoing repair with even more in obvious need of some attention. For a time he watched a workman building a brick wall and was

impressed by the speed and accuracy of his work. perhaps I should find out more about the building industry he decided.

The next day he attended his appointment with the banks investment expert. Who having confirmed that the transfer of Dan's £5,000,000 had gone through successfully, began to offer Dan a variety of investment opportunities he felt would meet his requirements. Before we get too deeply into this, Dan asked, if there was any risk that he could lose money as well as probably gain. Of course there is always a risk that investments can fall in value as well as increase, that of course is why the returns are generally higher, replied the banker. Leaving my capital deposited with you will pay interest in excess of £30,000 per annum in relative safety, enough for my immediate needs I think. My more pressing need is for a suitable occupation, I would welcome your advice on a industry where I can learn as I go. From family experience I suggest the building industry, my brother started with a small capital sum and is now doing very well. He found it hard going for sometime until he gathered the right people around him. Thats the only advice I can offer I hope it helps, said the banker. Thank you said Dan, it's good to have my thoughts confirmed, rest assured any change of mind you will be the first to know.

Feeling better now he had made his decision Dan set about finding out as much as possible about the building trade. A visit to the council planning department showed that all outstanding schemes were already contracted out. Dan enquired about smaller projects he was introduced to a talkative young man responsible for repairs to council housing and public buildings. From him Dan learned that a great deal of Victorian housing was now in need of repair, and in some cases demolition. The council had its own team of builders, but much of the housing was in private hands and this provided for individual tradesmen to obtain work. A starting point for me thought Dan, and thanking his informant for his time, left feeling pleased with his day.

The following day he set out in search of a way to start making his way in the building industry. His main aim was to learn all he could of the various trades without being answerable to a boss. He had previously located an area of Victorion houses, where he had noted many were under repair. On arrival he began to take a closer look at the properties and the type of repair work being done. It soon became clear that while some where being restored to what Dan thought was a good standard, many were being given a poor quality purely cosmetic make over.

Early in the morning he saw the bricklayer he had noticed previously and was again impressed by the quality of his work and the general order and tidiness of his working area. He returned later hoping to talk to him and gain some on the job advice. Unfortunately the builder was engaged in a heated argument with a portly looking man who Dan gathered was the owner of the house under repair. The owner thought the job was taking too long and wanted the builder to cut corners. I told you when you hired me I would do a proper job or none at all and you accepted that, insisted the bricklayer. Thats all well and good, but having these houses stood empty is costing me money, I've a good mind to sell them and cut my losses. With that the florid man left shaking his head angrily.

Excuse me, said Dan approaching the builder I wonder if you could spare me a few minutes of your time, I'd like to pick your brains about the building industry. I could write a book on that subject, was the reply, but I'm behind with this job and can't afford the time until after I finish at five or there abouts. My useless labourer didn't turn up again and I've got the owner on my back. Thats fine by me said Dan, perhaps I can give you a hand while I wait, I've no experience, but I'd like to help if I could. Well, said the builder if you're game, I am. My names Fred and if you do what I say, when I say, how I say, you won't go far wrong. This last remark said with a large smile, to show he wasn't serious. Let's start with what you say then shall we said Dan, having first introduced himself. This place it like a rubbish tip, anyway you can see to clean it up a bit would be a big help. In particular any tools left lying about, cleaned and left locked in the back would be a bonus.

Dan promptly started gathering tools together as Fred had asked, this done he found a brush and shovel and carried on cleaning. Fred finished the section of wall he had been working on a few minutes later and was astonished to find how much Dan had achieved in the time. "Crikey" mate it would take my mate two days to get that much done, and then he would take a day off to recover, said Fred. If he is as useless as that why keep him on? He's employed by the owner and was pushed on to me, If he goes so do I. Anyway that's my worry and I've held you up enough, Fred said ,locking the building and putting on his coat. This being Friday I usually pick up fish and chips on the way home, it gives my daughter a break from cooking. If you like we could get some for you and you can eat with us, then we can have our chat in comfort. That suits me fine Dan replied, thank you, lead me to it!

After a huge plateful of food which Fred had insisted on paying for; "you are a guest in my house" he explained. His daughter, Rose, a young girl in her late teens, left them alone to talk. Dan explained his interest in getting into the building industry, and his confusing wish to be both worker and boss. I want to work with my hands and learn as many skills as possible, but I have never been subservient to anyone and I can't start now. I will happily take instruction from my tutors, and show them the respect they deserve but will want the same respect in return. The only way you will get respect from a skilled tradesman is by earning it, Fred warned, they are a proud bunch who had to make sacrifices to get where they are. I see that you are right said Dan, I'll keep that in mind, thank you.

What you are after is not much different to what any time served tradesman dreams of, a chance to use his hard won skills without unwarranted interference from the money men. We would all like to plan and operate our jobs in our own way, but it don't happen like that. The fellow I'm working for now bought the row of four houses and now wants them patched up to either sell on or rent out. The only way I can see you getting what you are after is if you had the money to buy something similar, and you would still need a patient man to train you.

First things first said Dan, the money is not a problem I have all I need to meet the cost. Before I spoke to you today I had a good look at several sites where buildings were being restored. Some of the workmanship was good and some poor, but none that I saw was better than yours. Having got to know you better, I am hoping to persuade you to become my teacher. I'm not sure we know each other well enough for that kind of commitment, but I'm flattered by your offer and will give it some thought. Bearing in mind that I have expenses to meet that I can't take chances with, my daughter, this house, and my yard next door for instance. If we agreed on everything else I would be happy to secure your finances while we were together. I know I seem to talk big about money, but please believe me the money is there, Dan assured him. At this point Rose came back into the room carrying yet another pot of tea. To Dans surprise Fred began to explain to Rose all that had been discussed. Noting Dan's surprise Fred told him Rose is my best friend as well as my daughter and we have no secrets when it comes to business. Oh dad!, said Rose I hope you will say yes, you're not getting any younger and I would love you to be able to take it a little easier. I'm sure Mr. Stone would be happy to put all he has said in writing if you would be happier.

All very well said Fred but I still have a commitment to Mr. Fraser, the owner, and Dan here still has to find some work for us to do. I'm sure you said Mr. Fraser is always saying he wishes he hadn't bought the houses would he sell them to Mr. Stone, asked Rose. He might, thought Fred, but I have to say I wouldn't buy them, its going to cost a lot of money to put them right and I'm not sure you would get it back. Dan asked them, if I do buy them will you help me with my dream? Aye! I reckon I would said Fred; at which Rose through her arms around his neck and kissed him soundly on the cheek. Having noted Mr. Frasers address, Dan took his leave promising to be in touch with Fred as soon as possible.

Things went well for Dan, he saw Mr. Fraser the following day and quickly concluded a deal to buy the four houses with immediate effect. He thought he may have paid over the odds, but was satisfied having secured Mr. Frasers guarantee he would make no attempt to hang on to Freds services.

He arrived at the site shortly before Fred on the Monday morning and was able to acquaint him with all that had transpired. To his relief Fred seemed genuinely pleased, and shook his hand enthusiastically. They were about to begin a tour of all four houses when Fred's mate turned up, nice of you to turn up said Fred but you've wasted your time your sacked!! You can't sack me he smirked the boss won't let you. Let's ask him said Fred turning to Dan, yes please he said nodding. He's not the boss Mr. Fraser is insisted the young man. You seem to be late about everything Dan remarked, he was the boss, now I am and you are sacked!! What about my money then; since I took over Dan interjected you have done no work in fact you have kept Fred and I from getting on, I reckon you owe me. You will be sorry you treated me like this said the young man nastily, I'll get my own back you see if I don't. At this Dan spun swiftly round and grabbed him by his jacket collar lifted him until their faces were level and shook him. You can come looking for me whenever you like, but if I find you near Fred, his or my property, or any other person associated with us, I will break you. All this said in a low voice full of menace. As soon as he was released he ran off as fast as his legs could carry him.

Dan turned to Fred smiling and asking do you think he got the message? If he didn't he's even thicker than I thought he replied. Shall we make a start then, if it O.K. by you lets get on with the tour and I can see how big a pig in a poke I've bought. The rest of the day was spent in a careful and thorough inspection of all the houses. A useful day in which Dan learned enough about Fred's ability to feel sure he had found the right man for his needs, and for Fred to learn whoever this Dan Stone might be he is nobody's fool. The day ended with both men laughing as Fred tried to knock some of the dirt off Dan's previously clean clothes. Dan's tour had taken him to the dirtiest areas and his clothes had borne the brunt of it.

On arriving back at the "Monarch Guest House" Dan was told politely but firmly that they did not cater for the "blue collar trade" and would he please depart by the end of the week. Having remarked that his money was still as clean as it ever was, he agreed to make other arrangements. Privately he mused on life; from No.1 to one of the unclean in a few short weeks.

Dan told Fred of his reception at the "Guest House" as he would need some time to find alternative accommodation. Jumped up middle class nerds was Freds opinion, they are not so fussy when they need you. If I was stranded on a dessert Island I'd sooner it was with a tradesman than a business man, that's for sure! I've got until the end of the week said Dan so I'll make time in a couple of days to see what I can find. In the meantime if you hear of somewhere suitable please let me know. O.K. said Fred now lets get on, before the new boss gets as fed up as the old one. If I can just show you how to mix mortar, I can get on with the walls while you finish off the clean up you started last week. So began the first day of what became many happy years when the two men would work together. Dan in admiration of the depth of Freds knowledge of all aspects of the building industry. While Fred was astonished by Dan's speed and strength, and his intelligent grasp of all he was taught.

The following day Fred asked Dan if he would like to come to live with him and Rose as they had plenty of room. If you are interested you will have to come and talk to Rose, she wants a chance to earn some money for herself and you would be her lodger. She has my blessing, but the responsibility will be all hers. Dan thanked him and promised to call that evening to talk it over with Rose. As a result of the discussion Dan moved in on the Saturday morning, and was soon comfortably established in homely surroundings. Rose insisting from the start that whatever their relationship elsewhere, in his home Fred was boss. Dan agreed with this and explained to Rose that he had too much respect for Fred to want it any other way.

For the next few years Dan concentrated on learning his new business, to the total exclusion of all all else. His days spent with Fred using his hands, and many evenings spent in libraries and with a private tutor studying theory and improving his mathematics. In time he graduated to studying with an architect and talking to the investment manager of his local bank. The latter in the hope he would one day make a profit independent of the £5,000,000 he had been given.

One night Dan's studies were interrupted by a knock on his, thinking it was Rose checking if he needed anything he called "no thanks Rose" I have all I need. To his surprise the knock was repeated, "come in", he called, and was surprised when Fred walked in. This is a pleasant surprise said Dan sit down make yourself at home. I'm getting worried about you Fred told him, you work hard all day then you are swotting all night, you need a break and to relax a bit. Really Fred, Dan protested, I'm fine!! No you arn't Fred insisted, look how you blew up at the plumber last week. Not like you and quite unecessary. No get your coat and we will have a couple of pints, and I'll introduce you to the noble game of darts. Dan was about to protest, but one look at Fred's face told him he would be wasting his breath. He grabbed his coat and ushered Fred out, asking, this darts, isn't that a game for matronly ladies and old men. Cheeky bugger said Fred smiling, before calling to Rose that they were going for a game of darts. Don't play him for money Dan, was Rose's reply. Is Rose worried You will lose more than you can afford, was Dan's next question. We will see, said Fred with a knowing smile.

Once in the pub, where Fred was greeted very warmly, the banter continued, with Dan asking if he was supposed to drink the beer or creosote the fence with it. Its clear your education regarding the finer thigs in life has been sadly neglected, was the reply, but never fear me and the landlord will soon put you right. So drink and be merry for the next rounds yours. On the dartboard Fred's skill was soon evident, and Dan who hated loosing, soon found he needed all his inherent hand eye co-ordination just to stay in the game. On the way home Dan thanked Fred sincerely not only for a pleasant evening, but for noticing he was in need of a break. Can we please do it again? Certainly said Fred but don't thank me for it Rose has been going at me for weeks about your needing a social life. If you hadn't had a go at the plumber I wouldn't have noticed. O.K. Fred I'll apologise next time I see him.

Work on the four houses had gone well and they were working on the last one when Dan began looking for a new project. I hope Fred you will continue to work with me, and carry on with my tuition. I would like to Fred replied, these past few weeks have been easy for me, the way you have kept the site clean and supplied me with materials, has meant I have been able to get on with skilled work, without having half my mind on other people. The problem is jobs have been coming in from my old customers and I have an obligation to them. I can see that you would like to stay loyal to your own customers, and believe you are right.

I may have the solution Fred but I not sure you will agree, if you would sell me a share of your firm we could carry on as we are now. You would still be the technical head and I could assist with the paper work, material supplies etc. I don't expect you to answer straight away, I'm sure you will want to talk it over Rose. Failing that perhaps you will find someway for me to continue my apprenticeship with you. In any event I would need your expertise if I find another project in the future. Oh!, and I still reckon I can beat you at darts. Freds reply to this last remark was fairly emphatic, but he thanked Dan for the suggestion, and promised to talk to Rose as soon as possible and give Dan his answer without delay.

Rose felt that Dan had already been a great help to her father and thought anything that kept them together was fine by her. Tell him to get someone to value your business with the yard, your tools and stock. Then let him make you an offer I'm sure he will offer more than you would dare ask. Don't forget he needs you more than you need him! You are your mother's daughter, you sound more like her every day. I'll take that as a compliment said Rose smiling, giving Fred a hug, tell him what I said and see what he says.

Dan listened in silence while Fred told him all that Rose had said; then burst into laughter, I'll tell you what Fred that girl of yours is no fool and I will do exactly as she says, and happy to do it. In the meantime can we please carry on as we are.

The firm of Barker and Stone came into being a few weeks later, Dan very pleased to have secured his future tuition. Fred satisfied with the financial settlement and happy to have Dan as a partner. While working with Fred to clear his backlog of work, Dan continued to search for the next big project for them to tackle.

Meanwhile he continued to live with Fred and Rose, content with Rose's thoughtful care and Fred's warm friendship. Their only arguments being over who was the better darts player. Fred was becoming concerned that Rose had begun "seeing" a young friend, and felt she was too young for anything serious. Women young or old were something of a mystery to Dan, so he chose to remain silent.

Life being settled and work at its least stressful Dan found himself with time to look around, and take stock of the world about him. He became aware of the considerable unrest throughout Europe, and the talk of war between Britain and Germany. He began to try to remember the little history he had learned, wishing he had studied more diligently. He was sure the war lasted for four years and cost millions of lives. He knew he would have to become involved in the fighting, having been bred to fight he could not believe he would be able to resist. What if I volunteer and the authorities have no record of me, when I left the 25th. century I didn't have chance to enquire into much detail of how comprehensive the arrangements for my new identity were. I will have to think about this, apart from everything else I don't want people looking for me after the war. Asking questions I can't answer about my life before 1910.

The first problem is how to explain his fears to Fred and Rose without sounding too sure of what he is saying. He took an early opportunity, when they were all sat at dinner a couple nights later. Asking Fred what he thought about all the Sabre rattling in the press. I can quite see the daft buggers won't be happy until they do something silly, said Fred, but whether they will push us into a war or not I can't say. I fear it will be war Dan. I think you are right said Dan, and we ought to start planning how best to get through it. It is fairly certain that I will have to serve in the army, Germany and her allies have a huge well equipped army, and we have a lot of catching up to do. We could have a rough time of it to start with.

Be that as it may; I am more concerned about securing the future of" Barker and Stone" than achieving world domination. In the event of my being absent for a spell I am easily able to leave the company with ample funds for its survival. May I suggest we all have a think about it and talk again in a couple of weeks. Both Dan's partners were happy with this, but Rose wanted to know just how rich Dan was? "Very" said Dan and Rose had to be content with that.

When they met a couple of weeks later Rose opened the discussion saying "I don't want my dad going back to working single handed and making himself ill". Fred was about to protest, but Dan agreed with Rose and suggested employing one or even two experienced labourers. Employ them now and when your war starts they will run away to the army, and we will have wasted our time and money Fred grumbled. What are the chances of you finding a couple of experienced men of about your age who won't be running off to war, but might be glad of some steady employment. That sounds a good idea Dad enthused Rose, surely you must know someone to fit the bill. I'll think about it and check on a couple of chaps I used to know agreed Fred. Good said Dan so I'll leave it to you to sort out, but please remember money is not a problem!

Shortly after the meeting Dan was able to buy two blocks of semi-detached large Villa type houses, of a higher specification and better condition than any of their previous properties. Going upmarket are we asked Fred, there don't seem to be a lot needs doing before they can go back on the market. Thats the thing Fred I want to convert them to multi occupancy, flats or apartments. The days of large families are beginning to die out and these big houses will become obsolete.

Well I hope your right said Fred, because you're now talking a lot of work and a lot of money. Please don't tell me the money don't matter, in my world, sooner or later the money always matters. Have faith Fred, done properly this will make us a lot of money.

Life for those associated with Barnet and Stone settled into a productive phase, the two experienced labourers had been found and were now happily employed. A young forward looking architect had produced plans for the conversion of the two houses. Fred thought they were too elaborate and liable to overprice the work, Dan wanted everything to be as modern as possible and disagreed. Not much point in my only learning about old fashioned ideas, if things are moving on and Fred agreed in principle.

All to soon Dan's prophecy of war came true and brought two major changes to their lives. Dan, having secured himself a second identity, was to join the army once the initial furore had died down. Rose insisting on marrying her fiance, before he to went to war. Her father argued she was too young, Rose was adamant and finally got her way. She duly became Mrs. David Alan Williams, and after a short honeymoon David moved in With Fred and Dan. Time soon came for Dan to enlist, Fred couldn't understand him volunteering, until Dan explained he had been a soldier before they met and felt it was his duty. He knew that having been bred to fight he wouldn't be able to resist.

Remembering a little of the history of the war he took every chance to try to persuade David to avoid going to war if he possibly could. Popular opinion says it will be over by Christmas, my judgement is it will go on for years. Study all that has happened and I think you will agree with me, David promised he would consider all he had said.

Dan's last act before he left was to make extra funds available to Fred, asking him to find a house for Rose and David which would be his wedding present to them. Dan had joined a guards regiment on the insistence of the recruitment officer, mainly on account of his height.

He duly reported for duty, and was amused and intrigued by the efforts of the N.C.Os to enforce their will and instil obedience into the recruits. The Gladiators he had known had all been bred for that life, and were solo fighters. However he grew to see the advantage of a large group of men working as one responding immediately to any given order. Drill came easily to him and his natural athleticism stood him in good stead for any form of fitness training. Weapon training bought no surprises, although Dan proved to be exceptional at grenade throwing achieving longer distance with greater accuracy than any of his contemporaries. Causing the instructor to remark "very good we will give you a shout if we run out of shells".

Like thousands of others Dan was to experience the horror, discomfort and sheer hell of trench warfare. In spite of being involved in many of the worst battles, and being mentioned in despatches for crossing into no-mans land to rescue wounded members of his platoon. He came through the war unscathed, and returned happily to Barnet and Stone.

His homecoming was marred by the news that David had been killed in the last weeks of the war. David had taken Dan's advice to stay out of the war, but had been conscripted in late 1917. Fred had found and renovated a nice house for David and Rose, but Rose had chosen to return home to continue looking after "Fred and Dan". Rose thanked Dan for the house, and asked him what he intended to do with it. Nothing to do with me, he said, its your house please yourself. I can't accept, insisted Rose, I'm not living there and don't need it. I bought it for you as a wedding present, and you got married, therefore it's yours. Talk to your father but I think you should let it out, or sell it and keep the money against a future emergency. Now any chance of a cup of tea?. At which Rose shook her head and hurried off to the kitchen, leaving the single word "MEN", hanging in the air.

The two large houses had been converted to flats and apartments, during Dan's absence, and sold for a large profit. The sale had gone through with a minimum of delay, and trouble free. The property company concerned asked to be given first refusal on any future development by Barnet and Stone. Fred was amazed by the ease at which it had all been settled, confessing to Dan he thought the project had been a mistake. I don't know where you get your ideas from, but from now on I'm a believer.

Dan who got a lot of his ideas and information from the friendly business advisor at his bank, together with his own reading of endless newspapers and trade journals. Often surprising himself by his application. People destined to be "Gladiators" weren't expected to become enthralled by anything else. He now took Fred at his word and suggested they look around for a factory, old school or similar building in line for demolition. Which they could develop from the bottom up. Fred wondered if they could cope with a project of that size, but raised no objection. Rose as usual was worried if her dad would be able to cope, he is not as young as he used to be and I don't want him over doing it!! I'm glad you said that said Dan I would like Fred to hang up his tools and help me with project managing. Except when I need help with learning everything he knows. Well, said Fred I said I would back you and I will, even though a project of this size frightens me to death. If it helps settle your nerves, I assure you I've got money put aside to ensure we won't starve if it all goes wrong.

I read in today's paper my old school, Eastern Rd. Juniors is up for demolition, with the playground included it covers a large area perhaps worth a look. Sounds ideal Fred, can we go tomorrow?. Well the sooner we get on to the council the better, if it's any good that is, agreed Fred. Taking with them the architect they had used previously, they spent several hours the next day taking measurements, and swapping ideas on how best to proceed. A plan of campaign was formulated, and the three men parted in an atmosphere of hopeful optimism. The architect hurrying to start on initial drawings, Fred to look for demolition contractor's and Dan to look into finance and prepare his "pitch" to the local council.

To everyone's astonishment everything fell into place and within three months the site was being cleared, a deposit paid, and outline planning consent granted. The architect was preparing detailed plans with the help of all his colleagues, whether senior to him or not. Dan having insisted the younger man remain the chief, as he wanted his modern outlook and advanced design features. Fred was busy recruiting skilled and semi-skilled tradesmen. A task made easier by Dan's plans for a bonus scheme.

Meanwhile Rose had been coopted on to the board and was to be the director of purchasing. She was already building up a portfolio of potential suppliers. Fred and Dan felt they had made the right choice when they overheard Rose correct a supplier with the words "I am not your Miss anything I am Mrs. Rose Williams Purchasing Director of Barker and Stone Construction, and you would do well to remember it". My god laughed Fred but her mother lives on.

The building soon began to take shape, with all trades pulling together. Dan, Fred and the architect set a monthly expectation of progress and paid all employees a bonus when the targets were met. Which they usually were.

Dan and Rose were enjoying a glass of wine together one evening after a busy work session, when Rose tentatively began to question Dan about his life before they met. We have been friends and business partners for some years now, and in all that time you have never mentioned any family or friends. Are your parents still alive? Have you been married had a girl friend, or anyone at all close to you?. Dan had been dreading this line of questioning, and surprised it had been so long coming, thought the real truth was out of the question and he would need to fall back on some old lies. I never knew my parents, I was found lost and apparently abandoned. he told her. Then told the same story that had seemed to satisfy Sean and Seamus, his former boxing friends. Thats very sad said Rose but what about now, have you never had a girl friend?. Dad says the women at the pubs and clubs where you play darts are always giving you the eye but you never seem to notice. No I have never had a girl friend, to be honest I have never kissed a girl, and apart from shaking hands I've never even touched one. Oh dear she said that's awful, you poor thing. Now don't get feeling sorry for me, I'm quite happy as I am, Dan insisted. Yes but only because you don't know what you're missing was Rose's last word. Last word for now but not for long, thought Dan.

Three nights later Dan was settling to sleep when his door opened and a dark figure slipped quietly into his room. He was about to demand an explanation when Rose told him to keep quiet, "its only me". Yes but what are you doing here?. Rose who by this time had climbed naked into his bed, said giggling I fancied being the first girl you kissed and who knows you might even touch me. Dan had several questions spring to his mind but before he could speak her lips touched his and they ceased to be important. During that night he learned many things, not least the living wonder of a woman's skin and the excitement of her lips.

Dan took the first opportunity to thank Rose for the wonderful night she had spent with him and ask why?. I told you, you didn't know what you were missing, and now you do!! You really should have someone of your own to give your life a meaning other than the accumulation of wealth. In case you are wondering last night was a once only, so look around you at what's out there. Make your mistakes get your heart broken a couple of times, you will be a better man for it. With that Rose kissed him lightly on the cheek and walked away. Your right about one thing he thought, I've got a lot to learn.

The work on the Eastern Rd. project was proceeding seamlessly and Dan and Fred found themselves with little to do to keep things moving. Fred felt he would like a holiday and wondered if Dan could manage without him and Rose, if he could persuade her to go with him. No problem said Dan, let me know if you find anywhere nice, and I might take a break myself. I'll believe that when I see it said Fred. Rose was happy to go with her father and they headed off to Wales for sea, sun and sand. You'll be lucky said Dan. Be good said Rose don't do anything I wouldn't, giving him a cheeky wink.

Worry not, thought Dan I've got the message and may yet surprise you. Sure enough on his next visit to the library, he noticed a rather attractive assistant and waited his chance ro speak to her. Before he could say anything she greeted him: hello Mr. Stone I'm Louise Oakham how may I help you? You can start by telling me how you know my name asked a surprised Dan. Oh! you are well known here, you are one of our best customers she said smiling warmly. You have all been very kind and helped me greatly with my studies he replied. Good of you to say so I will certainly pass that along, we do try. Now what can we do for you today? Dan was about to say you could start by agreeing to come out with me some evening, when they were interrupted by a colleague of Louise, "excuse me sir, Mrs. Oakham you're wanted on the telephone. I'm sorry Mr Stone please excuse me, I'll send someone to you straight away. That was close thought Dan I nearly propositioned a married woman, I must remember to check left hands in future. At that a voice behind him said hello Mr. Stone, Louise has asked me to help, what can I do for you. The speaker a middle aged plump lady beamed at him, and was soon scurrying about finding his requests.

Dan left the library loaded with books his second assistant having proved very knowledgeable and found more information than he expected. Perhaps I came out of it better off after all.

He soon became disenchanted by the "courting" game, finding it difficult to find the paragon of all the virtues he carried in his head. I reckon she doesn't exist he often thought. At one point he decided to try the higher level of local society, but found they were only interested in how much money he may have. To be honest he much preferred the artisan class to any other. In the main they seemed to have there feet on the ground. Rose had taken to asking her father if Dan was acting any differently, he seems to talk to the younger women more than he did, he may even have taken a couple of them out but nothing has come of it he said. Unknown to both of them Dan had decided on two plans of action to help him find a girl friend. First sign up for dancing lessons, and second get a car and learn to drive it. On balance he thought learning to drive would be easier than learning to dance.

He took to dancing with the same ease he found with most forms of physical activity, his natural athleticism, being helped by a surprisingly good ear for music. His tutor a well preserved lady of uncertain age, enjoyed dancing with Dan saying it was a pleasure to partner someone who had such wonderful balance. The car proved fairly simple to chose, once he saw the best available, an Aston Martin tourer, he just had to have it. The car came with free expert driving tuition, and he was soon able to take to the road unaccompanied.

The car soon proved its worth when having given his dancing tutor a lift home, he was invited in and in the course of an enjoyable evening given a long lesson in a much older form of dancing. With this encouragement he was soon a regular at local dances, and quickly built a diary of partners who became friends. He still felt a strong attraction for Louise Oakham whom he continued to meet on his visits to the library, regretting she was married.

The school conversion was completed ahead of schedule and Dan decided to take a couple of weeks break before looking for another project. Packing walking and climbing gear into the boot of his car, he set off for the "Lake District" and the "Scottish Highlands". On his return he was met with good news and bad news. The good news; a provisional offer Fred and Dan had negotiated for the "Eastern School Flats", was confirmed and showed a greater profit than they could have hoped for. Fred in particular was delighted with his share and , announced his intention to retire. Countering all Dans objections with "you have already taught me more than I ever taught you". Nothing Dan could say changed his mind, so Dan shook him by the hand and wished him a long happy retirement. Thank you said Fred, before you say anymore I am signing my share of the business over to you. Naturally I wont accept any payment, were it not for you I would still be working for some money man who never laid a brick in his life. As it is I have enough money to retire in comfort, and no worries.

Dan was now unsure of how to continue with his life. He now had enough working capital to furnish most projects without needing to use his original £5,000,000. Although one more project like Eastern St. school would put his finances on a solid footing. His only complaint was he missed working with his hands.

He was still undecided when he was contacted by the council, asking him to quote for their latest project. A large derelict factory was to be demolished and low cost housing built. Dan's first move was to contact Rose and ask her to resume her role as purchasing director. She was happy to agree, but wondered why he should want her for the position. I believe that your astute buying and no nonsense approach was a major reason we made the large profit we did Dan assured her. He then bought in his usual architect and put him to work asking for a design to give the occupant the best standard of living achievable on the councils budget. The demolition contractors were happy to get involved and agreed to submit their quotation direct to the council, relieving Dan of any responsibility for their work.

After some concern that the design submitted by the architect could not be built to the budget, the council awarded the contract to Barker & Stone. Dan answering their fears by pointing out his company was working to a fixed price and any overspend on the build quality would be covered by them. He had confidence in his architect, but still threatened to " hang draw and quarter him if he cost Dan any of his profit.

Many of the Eastern Rd. tradesman were re-employed Dan offering the same bonus scheme. Once all the contracts were signed and the site cleared work began in earnest, progressing rapidly. At first Dan missed Fred greatly, trying to cover all the ground that had both covered. To ease the strain he promoted two of his senior tradesmen to foremen, they proved very able and solved most of the routine problems. With Rose keeping a firm hand on purchasing and ensuring materials arrived in good time Dan found life easy. Leaving him time and energy to pursue his leisure interests with due diligence!

None of this escaped Rose and all their business meetings ended with her quizzing him on what she called his "love life". Pestering him to find a "proper" girl friend, with a view to settling down. Dan usually countered by asking when she was going to find a potential partner. Finally she gave one of her cheeky grins and told him she was about to become engaged to the head sales executive to one of her suppliers. He found he couldn't beat me, so he's going to join me she added laughing. Dan insisted on giving her a hug, while congratulating her warmly. Am I to be allowed to meet him? Are you having a party? when is the big day?. Stop said Rose, you're worse than my dad, when everything is decided you will be told. I may even send you an invite, now go away I'm busy if you're not.

Dan was very happy for Rose, but began to wonder what he was missing. He had garnered a large group of girls who were friends, and had enjoyed an occasional sexual liaison. Miss Right had not yet appeared. Again Rose was to change all that when after one of her question and answer sessions she casually mentioned she had been talking about him to an old school friend. She says she thought for a time that you were going to ask her out, but you seemed to change your mind and nothing came of it. Am I to be told who this mystery friend is? queried Dan. She works in the library, her names Louise but I can't remember her married name, do you know who I mean? Oakham!, said Dan Louise Oakham: I like her a lot, but felt I shouldn't ask her out once I knew she was married. I don't want to be the cause of a marriage break up. You're a bit late for that, Rose assured him, the Germans did that years ago. I'm not the only war widow around you know. I didn't think of that said Dan thoughtfully, shame, but I expect I've missed my chance now. Maybe, said Rose, but that's not the impression I got. Now go away I've got a man to get ready for.

Dan was more excited by this news than he expected he would be. For the next few days he concentrated on his building project making sure everything was in place, and everyone knew what to do to keep the work progressing. He then felt he had time to concentrate on his social life. His first two visits to the library ended in frustration, Louise was no where to be seen and he didn't want to ask for her and appear over keen. Happily on the third try she was on duty at the reception desk and he was able to talk to her without being overheard. I'm glad I've caught you he said, I'm hoping to persuade you to come out with me one evening. I have tickets for a dinner dance at the golf club if that is your sort of thing?. I have never been to a dinner dance said Louise, but I like to eat and I like to dance so why not! Its Saturday of next week 7-30 for 8-00, look can you meet me at lunch time to cross the Ts and dot the Is. Of course she said I'll see you outside at about 1-10, don't be late.

Both these occasions proved highly successful, and they were soon seeing each other every day. Dan felt he had never been this happy, delighting in the company of a beautiful intelligent woman. When after a few weeks they became lovers, he discovered the difference between making love and having sex, his cup ran over. For the first time in his exile he had no wish to return to the 25th. century. He was so happy he tended to forget who he was and where he came from. He discounted the problems that would arise from his ageing far slower than the people of the 20th. century.

The first sign of problems came on the occasion of Rose and Charles engagement party, when Charles asked Fred how long he and Dan were partners and when told 18years looked at Dan saying you have no right to look that young. Dan covered the moment by joking that Fred wasn't that bad to work with. No more was said but Dan had seen the look that passed between Fred and Rose, and guessed he had not heard the last of it. For the next couple of weeks Dan and Louise continued their happy way, even getting away for a few days touring the Yorkshire Dales. Louise loving the Aston Martin as much as Dan. For a few more weeks they continued their happy way, dancing, eating out and cosy nights in.

Dan, who had entered his relationship with Louise without any thought of the consequences, was beginning to fear there were problems ahead he would have to face. These thoughts were brought to the forefront sooner than he expected, by his dear friends Fred and Rose. They were waiting for him in Rose's office the next time he dropped in to see Rose. Dan instantly knew there was a problem when he saw their worried faces. Fred was the first to speak after the usual greetings, look Dan, he said, you know how fond of you we are, you have always been like the son I never had. There are though things we don't understand, where do you really come from, how did you get here and how come your so rich. Most puzzling of all we have known you for many years, and in all that time you have not aged in any discernible way. Please Dan, begged Rose don't think we are just being nosy, but people are beginning to notice and ask questions. Now that you and Louise are becoming so close, she above all others will need to be told everything.

Dear friends, he replied, I too have begun to realise that I cannot carry on believing no one will ever think I'm in any way different. I have been so happy in my life with Louise, that I haven't thought of the problems that could arise. My problem is that even now I cannot tell you the whole truth. I can tell you I haven't broken any laws and that my money was given to me as recompense for loss of the life I then had. Without my knowledge or permission genetic alterations were made to me that seem to inhibit the ageing process. Until now I have considered this to be an advantage, but now realise the problems it will always cause with my relationships to other people. I cannot tell you more than that, I am bound by vows I made to never reveal where I come from, or who I really am. I am truly grateful for all your kindness to me, I could not face the life that stretches before me without all the things you have taught me and the love you have shown me.

No need to explain yourself to us exclaimed Fred we have gained far more from you than we gave. Not so, said Dan, you have given me a start in my new life and I now know I can survive. Fred was about to argue when Rose interrupted; when you men have done patting each other on the back, what about poor Louise is she to have her heart broken. You can't have a life together with only one of you growing old, sooner or later someone will ask how her son is, or a similarly hurtful remark. You can't put her through that! Of course I know that, he said, and it will break my heart to either lose her or hurt her, but it seems I must do both. Do not leave it too long Rose insisted, Louise will be dreaming and hoping, building her future around you. The longer you delay the greater her pain! We will help all we can, but you are really on your own.

Dan soon came to the conclusion he had no alternative but to move away and make a new start somewhere where he would be unknown. He also realised that he would lose all his friends, and business contacts. Bringing an end to the happiest time of his life. Before he could do anything he had to see the council housing project through his commitment both financial and to his employees left him no choice. Fortunately this meant a delay of only two or three months, which he would need to prepare for his departure.

The three months passed all too quickly, the contract on the housing project was completed and the final cheque safely banked. Less a large bonus for Rose whose buying skills had again increased the profit. He had bought himself the latest model medium sized lorry, which he loaded with all his tools and any equipment likely to be needed.

His final act was to talk to Louise and try to explain why he must go away, and why she could not go with him. He tried to show her how she would suffer as she grew old and he appeared not to. Louise in her turn said she would suffer all that in exchange for the joy of the years before this became a problem. Dan was tempted by this argument, but felt

the longer they were together the more painful their problems would become. He had thought of offering to make a financial settlement on
Louise, Rose was horrified at the idea. Telling him in no uncertain terms;
" It's you she wanted not your dam money you oaf". You have still got a
lot to learn about women!! Dan the, No1. gladiator and world champion,
hoped he would never again experience pain as great as he felt parting
from Louise. Vowing to never again grow so close to anyone.

Having sold or given away anything he couldn't fit in the lorry,
including his beloved Aston Martin, he was ready. He left at 5am. the
next morning, secretly watched by a sorrowful Fred a low key end to what
had been a life changing time for them all.

THE LONELY YEARS.

Dan had only vague thoughts of where to head, thinking to cover at least
a hundred miles before looking to settle. Almost without knowing he
found himself in the Midlands a few miles from Birmingham. Having
parked the lorry and found a small hotel, he walked into the town centre
looking for work. He found himself in a small market town called New-
ton, very pleasant, but tired looking. There were however a number of
people about, so perhaps it was busier than he first thought. He had been
walking for more than an hour, and was beginning to feel his luck had
deserted him. He had paused to get his bearings, when he noticed a poster
announcing "sale by auction of two old semi detached cottages". The auction was in a weeks time, and the poster gave all the information Dan felt
he needed.

The next morning, he made enquiries and was soon on his way to
examine the cottages hoping they would provide him with a project. At
first glance Dan thought the cottages were beyond repair and almost
turned the lorry round to head back to town. Luckily he changed his mind
,and stopped for a closer look. To his surprise the two dwellings were
soundly built in an attractive stone, and would convert to a single dwelling of some character. Their appearance was spoilt by the stone having

been coated in a lime plaster. This coating was cracked and peeling causing the buildings dilapidated appearance. He decided to wait for the auction, and hope to buy them at a reasonable price.

Waiting for the auction he contacted the local bank, and arranged for the transfer of funds, in case he should be successful. He further used his time to check on builders merchants in the area. He hoped some of Rose's skill would have rubbed off on him.

The big day arrived and Dan made his way to the auction house. He had decided on his top bid hoping he had done his homework properly. The cottages were one of the earlier lots, and Dan found himself in competition with one other bidder. His opponent looked to Dan to be a working builder probably hoping to do the same as he was. Fortunately the local man dropped out well before the bidding reached Dan's limit. Having completed the usual paperwork he was surprised to find the local builder waiting for him. I was hoping no one else would see the potential in those cottages, he said, should have known I wouldn't be that lucky!! I'm Bill Scroggs by the way, if I can be of any help anytime you can find me on Wayside Lane, anyone will tell you how to find it. Thank you said Dan I'll bear that in mind, at which, Bill gave a cheery wave and hurried off.

The next day saw Dan hard at work clearing the cottages and grounds of as much debris as possible. he and his lorry making several trips to the council dump. While still light in the evenings he made accurate drawings of the existing layout, and began to plan the new detached house he had decided upon.

Many things were to occupy his time and energy in the ensuing months, but the new building began to take shape to his satisfaction. The upper floor had been refigured into three bedrooms and bathroom, together with a large storage area. The bathroom was fitted to the highest specification he could find, his biggest shock on arriving in 1910 was the poor quality or none existence of bathing facilities. Once the house and gardens were finished, and a paved parking area. Dan had been tempted to build a garage, but decided the time for garages had not yet dawned.

With everything completed, he set off to find Bill Scroggs of Wayside Lane. Dan had a small amount of building materials over, Rose would have been horrified!!, which he hoped the local man could make use of. When he arrived he found Bill loading a horse drawn cart, with tools and materials. He welcomed Dan warmly and was pleased with Dans offer of surplus materials. If you come over tomorrow, Dan explained, we can load the back of the lorry, and I can give you a hand to unload here. Thats great said Bill, perhaps you will let me have a look inside I'd like to see all you have done.

Bill arrived promptly the next morning and as soon as the lorry was loaded Dan took him on the promised tour. Having looked everywhere and exclaimed over the high quality bathroom and kitchen fittings, Bill was glowing in his praise both of the design and workmanship, but wondered why Dan had not kept it at two cottages. He felt this would have been cheaper and less work, and with two properties to sell a better chance of a good profit. Two reasons said Dan, first I needed the experience of this kind of conversion. Secondly with the current economic climate only the better off can afford to buy. The market your two cottages are aimed at is at a low edge I don't think it will recover from for a long time. You may get a farmer to buy for his workers, or a property developer to buy to rent out. Either case is equally doubtful. As for why the high spec. in the kitchen and bathroom it is the wives who chose the houses, please them and your halfway home.

Dan's prophesy proved correct, with the property selling within a month of going on the market. All of the "viewers" saying it was the best designed and finished conversion they had seen. With the wives delighted by the kitchen. During the build Dan had worked long hours seven days a week, stopping only to eat and sleep. In this way he had subdued his thoughts of the dear friends and joyful love he had lost. Now the work was finished, he found his mind again full of sorrow and knew it was time for him to move on. He tried to settle in Birmingham, but felt it was too noisy and dirty for his taste. Work projects were hard to secure as there were several builders chasing every chance. He felt sure he could outbid all of them, this would have meant cutting corners on the finish quality, or making a loss. Neither of which held any appeal.

From then on he concentrated on small market towns, with mixed success. In this way was set the pattern of his life for the next few years.

Until 1939 when Adolf Hitler began his march to world supremacy. Having put his lorry and tools into safe storage, Dan joined the army late in the year. He started as in W.W.1 as a private in the guards. Having escaped from Dunkirk, he was transferred to the Commandos and remained with them throughout the war. He fought in North Africa, Italy and after D. Day. all through France and Germany. Demobbed in 1946 with the rank of Sergeant, he felt he, or his alter ego, Peter Roberts, had done his share. He little thought that his hard won knowledge of guerrilla style would one day come to his aid.

He wandered around many of the counties of "Middle England" picking up work wherever he could. Generally finding that at the end of each year he had made a profit, leaving him able to preserve the original £5,000,000 he had been given. Although he found this life lonely it was not without its passing compensations. Like many others he found the "swinging sixties" an interesting time, but always stopped short of any close commitment.

During this period he bought a large diesel engined lorry and a large circus type caravan. He refitted the caravan to meet his needs, and add to his comfort. As an added bonus he found living in the caravan was cheaper than most hotels. About this time he began to find work difficult to get, it was no longer sufficient to arrive at a new town and hope to find a suitable project. He needed to find a more efficient method to find what he needed.

Talking to an auctioneer, having just missed a likely property, he learned of a national journal listing larger properties for sale in all areas. Dan had not previously considered anything larger than four bed detached family houses. Working on his own he felt this to be his practical limit. Feeling nothing ventured meant nothing gained, he obtained a copy and settled down to study it. He at first thought the properties listed were too large, and likely to tie him down for too long in one place. A second more careful look revealed a house not quite as big as most examples.

Quaintly named the

" Big House", it was situated a few miles from a small market town called Willowsville. At first Dan was inclined to ignore it as a bigger project than he had previously tackled, and perhaps too much for one man working alone. However out of curiosity he sent for additional details, and hopefully detailed measurements. Over the next few days he was busy rebuilding a collapsed wall a small but well paid job, that kept his hand in. It was a couple of weeks before he began to study the "Big House" details. The more he read the more intrigued he became. It became clear to him with careful planning the project could prove very profitable. Making a number of quality apartments, which if he completed each one individually would amount to the same as the work he was accustomed to. Still unsure whether he wanted to tackle this large project, he decided to make an offer well below the asking price to test the market.

To his surprise his offer was accepted, subject to early completion of the sale. He had begun to realise he was tired of always being on the move, and thought a longer stay in one place would make a pleasant change. It was with this thought in mind he concluded the sale without delay. The agent handling the sale was able to give him the name of a local firm, and he was able to arrange for a board fence to be erected around the site.

It took Dan a few days to prepare to leave, with the lorry to service and the caravan to pack for travelling. He had learnt early on that failure to correctly pack the caravan lead to chaos and breakages. The bank arranged to transfer his account to their nearest branch at a market town called Markfield. A couple of days later Dan climbed into his lorry and with a feeling of growing excitement set off for the "Big House".

NOW WHERE WERE WE?

Shortly after his conversation with Annie Dan set off to Terry's house to look over his famous garden. When he arrived it was to find Connie busy with a large hosepipe. Having exchanged "Hellos" Connie explained while Terry was away she was executive director for water distribution. Or to put it another way "general dogsbody". Now to what do I owe this pleasure?. Annie has been telling me about Terry's garden and insisted I take a look, if its convenient perhaps you could show me round. Happily, Connie replied ,but if you have any thoughts of leading me up the garden path; think again!! Dan held up his hands in a gesture of surrender, I have no regrets, quite the opposite, but always saw it as a happening of a particular moment, unlikely to be repeated. Connie nodded agreement, and took him off to see the gardens.

To his surprise Dan thoroughly enjoyed the tour, delighting in the colours and smells, and admiring of the meticulous organisation. Clearly Terry was wasted as a builders labourer. It was not until they were enjoying a cup of coffee, that Connie returned to the subject of their one off liaison. You must know, you picked the wrong sister, she said. What is it with you and Annie?, she says you can be very nice, and then spoil it by saying something rude. What's your favourite saying? " I suppose a shag is out of the question". Court her properly and you never know your luck!! I'm afraid I have nothing to offer Annie or anyone else, any kind of relationship is out of the question. Thats nonsense Connie argued, but Dan shook his head, made his apologise and left. He was very fond of Annie, but had never forgotten the pain of losing Louise. Nor had he ever come to terms with the hurt he knew he had caused her.

With Terry not due back from holiday for a couple of days Dan felt out of sorts with himself, and unable to settle to his normal routine. He had been greatly impressed by the quality of Terry's garden, and wondered if he could start him off in that line of work. On the other hand he had been upset by his conversation with Connie, and wondered if he had perhaps been in one place too long.

The next day he was in the field by the ruined barn, looking for stone suitable for a fireplace he was thinking of building in one of the apartments. For the first time he took a long look at field, and began to walk around accessing its potential. He began to wonder if there was sufficient ground to support a small nursery. He realised he had never seen a farmer or other possible owner in the field and wondered why it was not being cultivated. At the top of the field near where it joined the next field he found a large area of marshy land surrounding a shallow pond, and decided this was probably why the field remained fallow.

Having left the field and made his way back to the caravan he began to wonder why he owned the derelict barn but not the field it stood in. His curiosity aroused he rang the solicitor who had handled the original sale to see if he could throw any light on the problem. While waiting for the solicitors reply he turned his mind to the flooded area of the field, he remembered on one large multi builder project he had worked on some years before, there had been a similar problem in a corner of the site. A team of land drainage specialists were brought in. they found the cause to be a small spring that had its normal exit blocked. on that occasion the drainage team had been able to divert the spring into a nearby brook, pump away the excess water and the area soon dried out.

Dan began to search his many records in the hope of finding the drainage specialists, when the solicitor rang in reply to his enquiry. His findings were rather mixed, the old deeds showed the field belonging to the "Big House", but in later years only the barn was listed, although no record of any sale could be found. Interestingly, prior to the house being put up for sale and left unoccupied the field had been rented to a local farmer, again there was no record of the rental agreement being cancelled. The solicitor gave Dan the address and telephone number of the farmer, and he resolved to go and see him.

Dan and the farmer, Albert Shenton, met up a couple of days later. Dan having been invited to come to lunch, Albert insisting that while he couldn't promise the "Fatted Calf" his wife would rustle up something. Over a large roast beef dinner Albert explained that he had rented the field from the owner of the "House" but was given no warning when the family disappeared overnight. He had heard rumours of debts left everywhere, but that was none of his business and "he kept out of it" he continued to use the field for a couple of years but the flooding got worse and he gave up. He made a couple of phone calls but no one knew who he should pay it to. I suppose as you now own the place I owe you a couple of years rent. If it turns out to be my field, give the money to your wife as payment for the best meal I've had in years. Fair enough said Albert with a broad smile, and they parted like old friends.

He found the details of the drainage company, and wrote to see if they were still in business, and might they be able to examine the field. In addition he instructed the solicitor to try to get the field reinstated on the deeds.

Monday dawned and Terry returned from his holiday. Dan started asking how the holiday gone, but had to call a halt when Terry became so excited with tales of his adventures his stutter took over and he became incomprehensible. Tell me a bit at a time advised Dan, when you've calmed down. In the meantime, the planning permission is through and its time we got stuck into the "Big House". Having got a thumbs up from a still smiling Terry he gathered up the plans and set off for the attic floor. I want to start on the top floor so that we are not carrying materials and tools past parts that are finished.

For the next couple of weeks Dan and Terry worked flat out on the "Penthouse" apartment, until Terry remarked I'll soon be ready for another holiday! If my next plan works out you really will learn about hard work, was Dan's only comment. The solicitor rang the next day and confirmed the field was now reinstated and was confirmed as being Dan's property. He immediately contacted the drainage engineer, who agreed to arrive the next day to begin his checks. Anymore for the Skylark thought Dan, one crazy scheme after another. Just when you should be planning to move on. One thing he was sure of he no longer wanted to convert the Big House single handed, which he would have to do if Terry was to take charge of the planned nursery. Bridges to be crossed as they say.

The next day he explained the basic idea he had for the field to Terry who thought it a great idea, until he learned he was expected to plan, organise and run it. He began a long stuttering monologue, which Dan finally translated as meaning, I'm not qualified, wouldn't know where to begin etc. I have examined your gardens at length said Dan, I liked the flowers and veg of course!, but what really impressed me was the organisation and planning. The smooth way the young seedlings and cuttings are progressed, and then integrated into the displays convinced me you are the man for the job. All you have to do is what you have always done, on a bigger scale, easy!! I shall need you for a couple of hours this afternoon while the drainage engineer is here, but tomorrow you can take a day to think about it, perhaps take some measurements. The drainage shouldn't be a problem we used to play in the field as kids, there is a spring which used to flow into the ditch on the right side of the field. there must be something blocking it, find that and your home and dry. Now he tells me laughed Dan, go and make some tea before I throw a chunk of 4by2 at you.

The drainage engineer arrived as promised and was soon wading up to his waist looking for the spring mentioned by Terry. If you can find a large lump of stone, more to your right, the spring should be in front of it Terry told him. With this help the spring was soon found, declared to be no problem if you can find what is blocking it. The blockage was found to be a pile of building rubble mixed with cement that had set to a solid lump. Probably "fly tipped" by a local builder. The drainage engineer offered to get a couple of his men to clear it, as the water could not be drained too quickly without possible damage down stream. Tery asked if there was anyway a pond smaller but deeper than the flooded area could be made. A source of free water would be a boon to a nursery. In my world nothing is ever free growled Dan, sort out the details with our friend here and he can let me have some costings. All I ask is its deep enough to drown you in!! I'm off to get some work done.

Dan returned to the "Big House", with the help of the architect's plans he began a room to room examination to decide where he could best use outside trades people and where to do the work himself. He soon found his attention wandering to thoughts of having to leave. He would prefer to stay but knew the way his feelings for Annie were growing could only lead to the kind of heartache he had felt when he had lost Louise all those years ago. Dear Connie had told him Annie would respond favourably, if he were to court her properly and not spoil every meeting with some inappropriate remark. In particular the one "I suppose a shags out of the question". Really Dan treat her properly and you never know your luck!! Dan enjoyed his friendship with Terry who he admired for his ever cheerful demeaner, in spite of his speech problems. At least if this "nursery" scheme gets off the ground I'll be able to leave him settled.

Dan decided he would act as site manager, and employ local tradesmen to do the work. This had proved very effective on "The Eastern St. School" project all those years ago. He intended to complete the attic Pent House himself, timing himself. as a guide to introducing his usual bonus scheme. Decision made, Dan proceeded with his usual energy and drive and was soon making rapid progress with the work, while at the same time busily contacting local contractors to complete the other floors.

Terry was being equally busy in the field, measuring, marking, soil testing, and generally shaking his head. The drainage company had submitted their quote, happily much lower than feared! Dan told Terry to contact them and arrange for the work to be done to suit his convenience. He knew Terry hated to use the telephone, and was interested to see how he would get round it. Terry for his part smiled, said O.K., gave his usual thumbs up, and went back to his field. Where to Dan's surprise he was joined by a young looking surveyor, and the pair of them were soon engaged in various areas apparently checking the lie of the land. I said he was in charge, it looks like he's going for it, thought Dan.

Over the course of the next few weeks the tradesmen arrived and work proceeded at pace. Dan had found good suppliers for raw materials and was able to keep them busy. Having persuaded one of the contractors to act as foreman to all the trades, Dan found himself with time to consider where to go for his next move. Although he was unsettled and knew he couldn't stay, his heart wasn't in it, he kept putting off any decision.

Terry brought him back to reality, when he turned up one morning with a well laid out plan of his proposals for the nursery. His plans included outline drawings of a large greenhouse, several growing tunnels and a stone/brick structure where the derelict barn now stood. This was to be the office, staff room, and toilets, being the nearest point to mains drainage. Who is going to run the office, was Dan's first question. No problem there, my mum has promised to set it up and run it unpaid for a year. I will need some qualified help, and will look into that as soon as you give the go ahead. Well done!, said Dan I'll study it all in depth, and give you my verdict.

True to his word he spent all his spare time for the next two days pouring over Terry's plans. Terry had included costings for the greenhouse and tunnels etc., so Dan was able to do some provisional costings as well. All of which seemed to be within his means. He called a worried looking Terry into his caravan office, grab a cup of tea and sit yourself down, and stop looking so worried. The worst that can happen is I say no and you're back where you were hopefully no worse off. I'm not going to say no, I like your plans and hope to get everything set up as soon as possible. Just two points; will your mother stay on after the year assuming you are able to pay her? Why do you need qualified help so soon. Mum has promised me she will not leave until there is a fully trained replacement ready to take over. I shall need the help as I am bringing the cuttings and seedlings from home to give me a start, and will need someone to tend them from day one. Good luck with that then I look forward to meeting him!

Dan offered to get his men to build the office block, A.S.A.P. unless you intend to get your assistant and mother to pee in the pond. Happy now, asked a smiling Dan, receiving a big grin and thumbs up from a relieved Terry. In that case how about a couple of pints in the "Spotted Cow", you can pay if only to knock that grin off your face. Bring your darts I need to win at something today, half seven don't be late.

When Terry told his mother the good news, she was delighted for him, and full of praise for Dan's generosity. Adding she might join them at the pub, giving her chance to thank him personally. When she arrived they were pleased and surprised to see she had brought Annie with her. Connie immediately gave Dan a kiss on the cheek while thanking him for all he was doing for Terry. Oh!, I expect I'll make a profit out of him at some point, said Dan smiling broadly. He saw that Annie had seated herself next to Terry, and decided there would be no kiss from that quarter.

Once drinks had been bought, Terry suggested he and Connie take on Annie and Dan at darts. At first Annie protested she hadn't played for years and wasn't very good then, but agreed after some persuasion to do her best. Terry told her not to worry as Dan was good enough to take on all three of us. Annie nodded and said why am I not surprised!! The games started off quietly but became more and more lively as the evening went on. With Dan and Annie somehow scraping a win most of the time. Until for the last game the ladies challenged the men to a losers buy fish and chip suppers all round. The game was 501, men to start and finish on a double, ladies with a straight start and finish. The scores were fairly level after the men taking several darts to get a double. Once started the men soon went ahead but again seemed unable to hit a double, leaving the ladies to claim victory.

Right! said Dan fish and chips it is, you three make your way to the caravan and I'll dash off and get the food. He was about to hand his keys to Terry when Annie said, I've got a better idea, lets go to the cottage and

I can play mine host for once. For a minute I thought you were volunteering to be the one doing the dashing. In your dreams big man, in your dreams! With that she turned him to face the direction of the "chip shop" and gave him a gentle push, at which he strode off swiftly.

Such was Dan's speed that he arrived at the cottage at the same time of the others. You have been quick said Connie, I was lucky he said there were only a dozen or so in the queue. Fibber! Said Annie, only a little one he replied grinning. The food was soon eaten, and drinks served, and the ladies brought the conversation round to Dan and his past life. Here we go again thought Dan, saying, I'm just a jobbing builder travelling the country trying to make a living. The way you have been laying out money since you arrived, you must be good at it. You can't have made all this money converting old houses. You would be surprised he replied, I've made a profit year on year sometimes a very good one. Yes, the ladies persisted, but how many years, you don't look much over 3oyrs. now. Take away school and apprentice years, and there is not a lot of time for getting rich. I look much younger than I am, and I'm flattered you think I'm only 30ish. Maybe so but you're scarcely old enough to have made all this money renovating old property.

Dan; not happy with the way the conversation was going decided to call a halt. You seem to be implying there is something untoward with my finances, let me assure you I have not, nor have I ever had a penny that was not completely honest and legal. Nor have I ever, knowingly, treated anyone unfairly. Oh Dan!!, said Connie and Annie in unison, we didn't mean to upset you, or to suggest you are dishonest. Please forgive us we are just curious to know more about you. Sorry, said Dan I over reacted, no offence taken, I will tell you my life story one day, but not tonight! Now any more wine in that bottle?

With that normal conversation resumed, with smiles all round. Connie was the first to make a move, rousing Terry from his seat, saying come on we have a business to run and an early start tomorrow. O.K. he said I'm coming and followed her out of the door. Dan finished off the last of the wine, and began to say goodnight. Annie followed him to the door and standing on tiptoe kissed him thanking him for a lovely evening. She then kissed him again thanking him for making her cottage so perfect. At this Dan wrapped his arms around her and kissed her soundly. What's that for asked a slightly breathless Annie. Thats just for being you, said Dan, and calling goodnight over his shoulder quickly left.

Having had an unsettled night Dan was up and about early the next morning. On leaving the caravan he was surprised to find a slim A4 sized package on the step. Going back inside he opened the package, inside was a brief note and a page from a newspaper. The note simply said "There is trouble brewing in paradise, be a good boy scout". The note was signed Top tech (2). Turning to the newspaper he saw the notation, "thought you might have fun with this" along the top of the page. Somewhat puzzled Dan checked the paper carefully, and was amused to find it was the results of a race meeting to be held at Doncaster in a couple of weeks' time. I'll give that some thought as he says it could be fun. For now I'm more concerned about the other message what is meant by "be a good boy scout". Dan was about to give up when he remembered the scouts motto "Be Prepared" it looks like I'm being warned, I'd better get ready I may be going back to the future!

From then on Dan became a changed man, a man in a hurry making unexpected changes everywhere. He promoted the foreman to site manager, told him to appoint a new foreman from the remaining tradesmen. I would like the whole project finished and decorated in a month, take on any extra labour you may need and tell the existing staff I will pay an extra bonus if the job is finished in time. on second thoughts if the men want to work overtime rather than bringing in extra staff, that's fine by me.

He called a meeting with Terry and Connie, and brought himself up to date with progress with the nursery. Terry had been making steady progress and had the site fully marked out for all buildings and cultivation areas. I'm sorry but I'm going to hurry things along a bit, if its at all possible I'd like to have all the buildings, paths, greenhouses and growing tunnels ready in a month. I want the nursery to be ready to concentrate on plants as soon as possible. A stunned and stuttering Terry started to protest aided by Connie, both feeling it was too much too soon. I expect you are right but we have got to give it a try. I will take charge of the building work and paths etc. If you can see to the internal preparation of greenhouses and tunnels. From now on, until I cry stop, expense is not a consideration spend what you need to spend don't bother to check with me. Connie if you could set up the office, buy the furniture and stationery, it would be a great help. I realise you are not on the payroll, but Terry is authorised to recompense you for your time and expenses. I have set up banking facilities in the name of T&C Nurseries and I am having order books printed, you should be in a position to purchase everything by the end of the week.

Connie soon excused herself as Dan and Terry began a long discussion about greenhouses and tunnels. Terry had details of all he required, Dan wanted clarity on the bases he needed to lay down ready for their arrival. A quick check of a couple of measurements, soon satisfied him and he was ready to start. One last thing before go, how are you getting on finding qualified help?.

A huge smile lit up Terry's face, v.v.v. very well he said stammering badly for the first time that day. An old friend of mine; we used to play in the field as kids; has just qualified, and is going to join us. I think you met her father, Albert Shenton, he used to farm the field. I hope you're not mixing business and pleasure said Dan with a mock frown. Shame!, came the reply, I do hope to. Does this goddess have a name? Oh yes, said a still smiling Terry "Penny" Well pay her what's she's worth and not a "Penny" more. Now go and get on with some work, and I'll try to do the same.

The majority of the work on the "Big House" needing bricklayers was coming an end and Dan was able to transfer one of the gangs onto base and path laying in the nursery. He was soon assured that they could be left to carry out the work with a minimum of supervision. He was now able to turn his thoughts to the pressing business of getting himself fit for his return to the 25Th. century. He felt he was as strong as he ever had been, the years of heavy manual labour had seen to that. Strength alone had not got him to No.1. his speed, balance and a supple fit body were equally important. Running and gymnastic style exercises would help with speed and agility, suppleness was another, sadly neglected, matter.

He visited the local library where a charming lady produced books on Yoga and Tia Chi, which promised to be ideal for his purpose. By the end of the week he had worked out an exercise routine using both systems combined. Allowing an hour before breakfast, followed by a seven or eight mile run mid afternoon. Keeping up with his work schedule called for some hectic days. It was after one such day that catching up with paper he found the piece of newspaper left by Top Tech (2).

The Doncaster meet was now only a week away, and as he hadn't been to a race meeting for years he decided to organise a day out. Annie was delighted by the idea and agreed to come without hesitation. Sadly Connie claimed a prior engagement, Terry wanted to come but felt three would be a crowd. Is there any chance your new girlfriend might come asked Dan. Tell her it is all expenses paid, and she gets your company all day, what more could she ask for?. I don't think I could ask her, a stammering, blushing, Terry started to say, but was cut off by Connie, who said he will ask and she will say yes, or I will bang their silly heads together. Fair enough, said Dan I'll make the arrangements.

The day of the races soon arrived, Terry and Penny joined Annie at her cottage, surprised to find Dan had not yet arrived. His highness has rung to say he has been held up and will be a few minutes late, explained Annie. He won't like that said Terry, somebody will have received his stone faced stare. Is he bad tempered then, asked Penny. No, Terry assured her, but he hates to be late, and his stare is usually enough to let you know he isn't happy. Almost before they had finished speaking Dan opened the door and called, "sorry I'm late, lets get going". Leaving the door open he hurried off down the path leaving them to follow. What is up with him this morning he is like a child off to the seaside.

Once outside they could see the cause of all the excitement, Dan stood by a large "Rolls Royce" convertible, grinning widely as he opened the doors, announcing "your carriage awaits". Annie promptly nipped into the front leaving Terry and Penny the back seat, causing Terry to be the one to smile broadly this time. As soon as they were properly underway a smiling Dan was able to tell he had managed to hire a box for the day, so they should be comfortable. They started to applaud this announcement, but Dan interrupted, saying, two more things , in the boot I have a hamper of race going treats, and I have a list of all todays winners, for anyone who likes to take the chance out of gambling. Oh Dan, said Annie, what are you talking about now? Why said Dan don't you believe I've got an hamper in the boot?. Idiot I'm talking about the mystery list of winners! What mystery, here is the list have a look for yourself. Dan this is just a list of horses, no doubt they are all running today, but that doesn't mean they are winners. As Annie finished speaking Terry and Penny Joined in with similar protests of disbelieve. Oh ye of little faith! exclaimed Dan we shall see, we shall see!

Since you dare to doubt my veracity I shall give each of you £10 and the name of the 10 to 1 winner of the first race, which will give you a stake to gamble as you wish. That way your folly will not prove too costly. All said with mock severity, causing his companions to jeer loudly. We shall see children, we shall see, was Dan's final comment. On arrival Dan parked the rolls in the V.I.P. car park, and asked a passing steward for directions to his box. The steward was happy to oblige, and with the help of one of his fellow stewards insisted on carrying the hamper.

They were all delighted with the box which gave privacy at the sides and rear, while allowing a clear view of the course and parade rings to the front. You are free to come and go from the box at will said Dan, the combination number for the lock is 3720 and the box No.48. First here is the ten pounds I promised you, and the horse is "No.7 Fancy That". Please use different bookies to keep the odds high. Be back here in an hour and we will see what the hamper has to offer. Better take copies of my list of winners with you in case you learn to trust me!!

O.K., Boss said Terry we will believe you, as its your money anyway what can we lose. At that he and Penny ran off excitedly. I suppose you are going to make me bet on this "Fancy" of yours, asked Annie?. Well I'm off to back it myself, and truly believe it will win, but I doubt I could make you do anything you don't want to do. So its up to you!! At least come and back something, even if it can't win. Dan, I shall back it, after all I can't lose if it wins I get a purse full of money, if it loses I shall enjoy telling the world what a fool you are. Fair enough Dan replied, all my predictions are going to win, and I shall do some gloating of my own.

They set off to the betting ring Annie hanging on to Dan's hand as he used his height and weight to get through the dense crowd. Seeing his smile, Annie told him not to get too excited she was only holding his hand because she was frightened of getting lost. They made it to the bookmaker just in time to place their bets and make it to the rail to watch the race at close range. Annie was amazed at the noise and speed of the passing horses, but had no idea which horse had won. Listen then said Dan as the "Tanoy" system bleeped and then began to announce the winner; first No.7 Fancy That, that was all they heard as Annie was hugging Dan and squealing with delight. they backed two more of Dan's horses, both winners, then made their way back to the box, as the hour was nearly up.

Penny and Terry arrived a couple of minutes later, both looking flushed with excitement. Terry started to blurt out they had backed all three winners, but his excitement brought the worst of his stammer and Penny had to take over. She ended her account of their success of their efforts, shyly asking "can we really keep all this money". Of course said Dan I'm pleased you have learnt to have faith at last, now lets have a look what this hamper has got to offer! We will miss betting on the forth race, but the winner is the odds on favourite so we won't miss out on much. the hamper was perfect, and was consumed with much laughter and banter. The party only broke up when it was realised that it was time to return to the racing. Dan insisting that any money they didn't intend to spend be left hidden in the hamper locked in their box. There are bound to be pickpockets and worse in the crowd, and you don't want to lose everything.

They made their way to the betting ring all together excitedly discussing how much to bet this time. Don't forget to keep a fairly large bet for the last race, the winner had the longest odds of the day. Keep a sharp look out at all times someone may have noticed how often you have been winning today, and want a share of it. The bets placed, the young ones went off to try to get near the winning post to catch the horses at full gallop. Annie and Dan preferred to go back to the box and watch the race in comfort, enjoying a private cuddle at the same time.

All to soon it was time for them to go back to the betting ring to place bets on the final race. They were accompanied by Terry and Penny, but separated as they neared the bookies each one selecting a different bookie trying to keep the odds at the high level. Dan was becoming concerned by a group of four men who seemed to be hanging around the betting ring but not betting, they were showing too much interested in Dan's group. He said nothing to the others of his concern, but suggested they stay together for the last race, and go back to the bookies together. The ladies were happy with this idea, but he saw Terry give him a look and nod of the head showing he had picked up some of Dan's concern. Good for him thought Dan I always knew he was sharp.

They collected their winnings without any trouble other than a few sour looks from the bookies. Fair enough thought Dan we have probably spoilt their day. Somebody seems bent on spoiling ours though, the four rough looking men were following them while trying to look casual. They stopped following as Dan and friends entered the area of their box, most of the boxes were now full of people packing up and saying their various goodbyes. A bit too public for our new friends thought Dan, probably heading for the car park, this could be interesting.

It was necessary to leave some of their winnings in the hamper otherwise the ladies handbags, and men's pockets would overflow. Dan was worried about the hamper as it meant at least one of the men would be carrying it all the time, when they may need their hands free. As they approached the car park he could see his fears were well founded as the larger two of the four men were hovering near the Rolls, and watching the car park entrance. Dan noted the two men were leaning, in a posed relaxed manner, against the car park wall. The wall was about 5ft. high leaving the men's heads showing over the top. If I can get round the outside I should be able to give our friends a pleasant surprise! Dan quietly alerted Terry to the problem, and what he intended to do. When you see my head appear over the wall make some sort of commotion to attract their attention, and leave the rest to me. Keep an eye on the ladies, I'm worried about the other two men and won't be happy till I know where they are.

Asking the ladies to excuse him a couple of minutes Dan hurried off around the outside of the wall, it proved a longer journey than he had thought. As he neared the area where the two men were standing he heard a loud commotion coming from the general direction of where he had left his friends. His first thought was "Terry is too soon", but he soon realised the two men were beginning to move towards the noise. He immediately ran the remaining few strides and vaulted the wall, as he cleared the wall he kicked one of the men in the face and gabbed the other by the neck dragging him to the floor as he fell. landing on top of his victim he was able to drive his elbow into the mans solo plexus, driving the wind from his lungs. Dan leapt to his feet and turned his attention to the other would be mugger, now climbing groggily to his feet, holding his battered head. Dan became aware of Annie calling for his help and became nervous for his friend's safety. Driven by his anxiety to increased efforts he quickly threw the two men over the wall, muttering to himself " that should keep them quiet!".

Terry and the ladies had been waiting for the all clear from Dan had found themselves faced by the other two men. You've had a good day, taken a lot of money off some friends of ours, we have come for our cut. Just hand it over and no-one need get hurt. As he made his demand Terry had braced himself and charged the nearest man in the chest with his shoulder, knocking him to the ground. As he landed Annie began to belt him about the head with her handbag. Recovering his balance Terry turned to face his other opponent, to his amazement he was just in time to see Penny pivot gracefully on her left foot and kick the man on his jaw and neck with her right. The kick carried such force that the man dropped unconscious to the floor, and did not need the blow Annie gave him, just for good measure.

Terry was about to question Penny about her footwork, when Dan arrived at top speed, ready to come to everyone's aid. Nice of you to join us, even if a little late, said a smiling Annie. Looks like you have been having fun, he replied, but we need to get out of here before "officialdom" comes asking questions. Passing Terry the car keys he told him to get the ladies and hamper to the car, while I get these two out of sight. With that he took the would be muggers by their collars and dragged them out of view behind the wall. Dan arrived at the car by the time his friends had settled in their seats, and lost no time in driving away from the racecourse. Only when he had covered a few miles and was confident they were not being followed did Dan relax and begin to ask what had happened while he was pre-occupied. Better ask the ladies insisted Terry, I stumbled into one of them and when I recovered my balance Penny was kicking one of them in the head, and Annie was beating the other across the head with her handbag.

Hang on Tiger I've seen you "stumble" into someone once before and he ended up on floor in quick time. Well!, said Terry stuttering in his excitement, better let me tell it Tiger while you cool down suggested Annie. You are right Dan he did end up on the floor, and I kept belting him on the head to keep him there. What about the other one? asked Dan. For that I'm handing over to Penny, only she understands what happened next. I happen to be a Black Belt in kick boxing and was able to take him out without much trouble. To be honest I quite enjoyed it, I've never kicked anyone for real before. All of this was said so matter of factly, Terry was left staring at her in open mouthed wonder, while Annie and Dan laughed loudly in their astonishment. I think this calls for a celebration said Dan lets find somewhere to eat and toast our successful day.

A few miles further on they found a suitable restaurant and were able to have the proposed celebration. Annie took the opportunity to ask Dan what happened to the two men who had waited by the car. Odd that!, he replied they saw me coming and jumped over the wall, never to be seen again. Terry tried to quiz Penny about her Black Belt, Terry my love shut up or I will give you a demonstration of how it works. Was all the reply she would give him.

The rest of the journey home passed off without any problems. The young ones in the back became quieter, and Annie sat well down in her seat with her eyes closed. I guess I should have hired a noisier, less comfortable car, thought Dan. At least I can escape difficult question for a while. Having dropped everyone off at their various homes, still smiling at Penny's parting remark, "Do you always have this much fun". While glowing from a warm kiss and cuddle with Annie.

Monday saw Dan back on site at the "Big House", ready to push for the earliest possible completion of the outstanding work. He was delighted to find the builders had been working all weekend and the work was further advanced than he could have hoped. One more day would see the brickwork all finished, leaving the plasterers a clear run. The Penthouse was finished, and the decorators were hard at work supervised by the interior designer Dan had bought in. He also had a local Estate Agent standing by to get the apartments onto the market as quickly as possible. Feeling there was nothing more he could do at the moment, he moved on to the nursery to see how Terry and Connie were getting on.

Again he could only be pleased with the progress that had been made. The paths and bases were all laid, and the office and toilet buildings were under way. Penny was busy with a rotovator turning over the larger growing area. He found Annie in the temporary office she had established in a large shed. Just the man I was hoping to see, she said by way of greeting. I've been chasing the tunnels which are due for delivery today, and I am being given the run around. I was hoping you would throw a bit of weight at them. Many years ago when I was in construction a young friend of mine joined the company as chief buyer said Dan. I once heard her say " I am Miss nothing nor am I your love" I am Mrs. Constance Leyland purchasing director for T&C nurseries, and you will do well to remember it. Once you have got their attention demand to speak to the top man, and be polite but insistent. Give it a try and if you still get nowhere, I will see what I can do.

O.K. said Connie I'll try anything once, And picked up the phone. Dan waited outside rather than cause Connie any embarrassment. A few minutes later she burst out of the office, kissed him on the cheek, saying it worked they are delivering tomorrow and dropping

the delivery charge, because they are a day late. Well done, said Dan, the lady I told you about saved us a lot of money, and every penny was profit.

With that Dan took himself off for his afternoon run, all the time thinking how much he would miss these wonderful people when he returned to the 25Th. century. For the next few weeks life settled into a routine, with Dan spending less time on the "Big House" and nursery and more on training. Until he began to feel he was approaching the fitness level of his days as a Gladiator. All the time wondering what the trouble was in his real time, and why he was being recalled.

He was awoken two nights later by someone knocking at his door.

Sorry to disturb you at this ungodly hour, I'm known as Top Tech 2 and I am sent as a messenger from those who sit on high. Come in said Dan and tell all! You are to be available at 3am a week from today when a high official from the Europe commission will visit you. I regret I have not been given any clue as to why he is coming. Now I have delivered my message, and confess to having a fondness for 20th. century tea if you can provide a cup I have 20 minutes or so to try to answer any questions. Tea coming up said Dan. My question is quite simple, "what the hell is going on!". You will remember the gentleman who had you put to death for refusing to execute your friend, he has for many years been trying to extend his empire. Having had his plans rebuffed at every turn, he has now launched all out war against all who speak against him.

There being no one with any idea how to fight a war all went his way for a time. All his near neighbours capitulated without a fight, only now is the rest of the world resisting. No-one who has not lived in the 25Th. century would ever believe the farcical situation we are in now. Li Pinoe the leader of the Asian council secretly had large numbers of large heavy robots made which were to have been his army. What he and the rest of the world didn't know is, for centuries generations of robots built by robots, have inbuilt systems which will not allow them to enter a situation where they could suffer damage. This is to them a standard precaution ensuring they last there programmed live span. The result means they will not fight, but turn away from any danger.

Li Pinoe had promised his people they would not have to fight, so they now refuse to do so. However our "Asian friend" has persuaded his Gladiators to go to war, opposed in the main by your friends the European Gladiators. I suspect No.1. this is where you come in! How are my lads faring against what must be far greater numbers asked Dan. I'm sorry said Top Tech 2 but those facts and figures are not being released, and you will have to ask your important visitor next week. My time is up and I must go, thanks for the tea. No doubt I shall see you next week. With a last goodbye he stepped out the door, and hurried towards the centre of the drive. So well disguised was the "Time Travel" machine that Dan did not see it until his visitor opened a door and climbed in.

Dan spent a sleepless night his mind in a whirl from all he had learned, he couldn't understand why the urgency to return him to the 25Th. century. He was only one man and couldn't see what difference he could make. By morning he was still perplexed by it all, but had resolved to organize his business affairs to have all in order when he came to leave. He arrived at the "Big House" to find that again the tradesmen had worked all weekend, and as a result all building work had been completed. Leaving the decorators and tilers a clear run. Be sure to put every available man on the Job. I need it to be finished as soon as possible, and let me worry about the cost. In the meantime get the builders on to the nursery site to finish all building work. If Mr. Leyland queries anything tell him I'll explain all later. O.K. Mr. Stone your the boss, was the only reply before they hurried to do his bidding.

Dan went for his training run determined to complete his regular course in the fastest time yet. He found exercising cleared his brain and helped him to plan for return to the future. Back showered and dressed, having clipped 15seconds off his course time, Dan lost no time in contacting his solicitor and bank manager. Arranging appointments for the following day. He had resolved to leave the money he had left over the £5,000,000 original stake to Annie, together with her cottage. Profits from the sale of the "Big House apartments would go to Connie and Terry to help them through the early years in the nursery. In the event of Penny becoming a "permanent fixture" she would be Terry's problem.

For the remainder of the week, when not training, he busied himself in the nursery and supervising the final stages of the Big House. A local Estate Agent had given the contract for sale of the apartments and the penthouse, and were busily preparing the publicity. Dan was pleasantly surprised to learn one of the ground floor flats was sold on day one, and for the full asking price. His surprise was even greater when he learned the buyer was Connie. Next time he saw her he asked why had she not told him of her intention to buy the apartment, you know I would have arranged a better price for you. That is exactly why I didn't tell you, replied Connie, you have already done more than enough for me and Terry. I am selling the house and if I get anywhere near the asking price I shall have money to spare. Dan started to argue but seeing the determined look on her face raised his hands in surrender, blew her a kiss and went on his way.

" Well Connic" he thought you have won the battle, but I hope to win the war. In two days' time I shall learn of my fate, and hopefully I will get the O.K. to dispose of my assets as I have planned. After all, they are getting their £5,000,000 back and the rest I earned.

Come in sir, said Dan showing his important guest into the caravan. Thank you No1. I am called Exec 1. silly but it saves a lot of time explaining my job and position. Can I offer you some refreshments? asked Dan. Thankyou time is of the essence but Tech 2 here has waxed lyrical about 20Th. century tea so I will try that if it is no trouble, perhaps he can take his with him while we have our discussion. Right No.1., I believe Tech 2 has given you a brief outline of the situation in our time. What he couldn't tell you is things are not going too well for us. We have no quarrel with the courage or fighting ability of our Gladiators, but they are heavily out numbered. Our losses are less than half of theirs, but our men are growing tired and many are carrying minor wounds and strains which inhibits their efficiency. I am both proud and sad to hear that, said Dan, but cannot see what difference I, "only one man" can make.

We are fighting this war as if it is some sort of Olympian contest between two teams hoping to win a gold cup. Believe me when I say it is far more serious than that! We are fighting for civilisation as it now is, and all it stands for, you better than most can realise how little Li Pinoe cares for the lives of those he considers his inferiors. Be assured there are none not in that category. What we need is someone to take over and teach our fighting men new methods of warfare. You were No.1., and considered by many to be the greatest ever. In this century you have fought in two world wars and are best qualified to fill this roll. Of course we cannot force you to return, but you will have realised that you must return to the 25Th. century sometime. If you choose to stay and we lose this conflict you will be forgotten, and condemned to work your way to the 25Th. in the way you have for the past few years. Should you decide to accept this position I can assure you of our total support, in all matters, even those we may not understand. I can also tell you we have many fine Gladiators from other districts, such as Canada, Australia and the Americas. These too have happily promised their full support.

Thankyou for the confidence you are showing me, although I fear it may be misplaced. As you know I fought in two world wars, you must also know I only held a low non commissioned rank, and knew nothing of major planning or logistics. I will of course return to the 25Th. century, and do everything I can to help to secure victory. You mentioned civilisation as it is now and all it stands for, I have to tell you I am no lover of your civilisation. If we are successful in our fight, and I survive I will spend the rest of my life fighting to change the system. May I ask why, queried Exec 1. Living in the 20th. century these many years I have come to realise their lives are so much more fulfilled than any in our time.

I find that difficult to understand said Exec 1. surely there is more hardship, poverty and brutal conflict than we have ever known. Certainly said Dan because all those who are not free constantly fight for the right to be free. In our time most freedom has been done away with, and almost no-one is free. In the 25Th. century a successful Gladiator or artisan may get to have sex with a specially designed Android, but never a real woman. You may want to argue that sex is not all important, perhaps not, but men and women are meant to live together, and form family units. The system of growing men in "Petri Dishes", and designing them for individual functions, is immoral and inhuman. Robbing all those created this way of their basic right of choice. I'm sorry sir but I have had many years to think about this, and truly believe our system is wrong.

I can see you are sincere in all you say, and acknowledge you have had a unique opportunity to study your subject. All I can promise is if we are successful in defeating Li Pinoe I will do all in my power to see you

get a chance to state your case to the people who hold the power. For now, may we return to the present, whenever that is, and finalise your return to the 25Th. century. How soon can you be ready?. We hoped for between two and four weeks. I will need to close down my life here, and say goodbye to my friends. On the subject of friends, I have never told anyone the true story of my life as instructed at the time of my exile. I would like your permission to break that vow, to help my friends understand why I must leave. There is also the £5,000,000 stake I was given, I have managed to preserve it in full, having lived on the interest, and my own earnings. By all means tell your friends anything you like, Exec 1 agreed without hesitation, it is unlikely they will believe you anyway! As to the £5,000,000, that is a surprise to me. You have to understand No.1. no record was kept of your abrupt departure, so we know nothing about it. I would say dispose of it how you wish and never mention it again.

After a few minutes more discussion it was agreed Dan should have three weeks to prepare to leave the 20Th. century. Tech 2 would collect him, he would not need any clothing ETC. but insisted in bringing his box of hand tools. Only allowed after Tech 2 had assured Exec 1. he could arrange space and weight capacity for the journey.

The visitors departed, leaving Dan pondering how he could close down sixty plus years in three weeks. Luckily the "Big House" was completed apart from arranging for payment of council taxes and routine maintenance. Terry, Connie and Penny seemed to be progressing well with the nursery. Persuaded by Penny, Terry had taken on two horticulture students for the summer, releasing Penny from ground preparation. She was now transferring plants and seedlings from Terry's gardens. The office and toilet block were now built, and Connie was supervising the office fittings.

Happily content with all outstanding projects Dan felt able to concentrate fully on the disposal of his assets. He spent several hours over a number of days with his lawyer and bank manager. Who, after their initial astonishment at his intention to dispose of everything, gave good advice on how best to proceed. With their firm assurance that all necessary paperwork would be completed in good time, Dan was able to arrange sale of his beloved caravan and lorry. All his clothing, books ETC. were collected.by the local scouts ready for their annual "jumble sale". The scout master called to see Dan a couple of days later carrying a tin box containing Dan's war medals. I'm sure you would prefer to keep these he said, they were mixed in with your kind donation. They have monitory value apart from their sentimental worth. No Dan replied I intended you to have them, if you can sell them privately to gain extra funds all the better. I have no interest in them and had forgotten about them, until your lads knocked on the door. As the scout master left Dan reflected on another chapter of his 20Th. century life closed.

With Annie's help Dan arranged to hold a party at the cottage, a week before his departure. Promising to explain his recent odd behaviour, and finally the story of his life. Connie, Terry and Penny, all promised to attend Dan wishing he did not have to tell them of his imminent departure. The party began as all good parties should, with warm greetings between friends. followed by good food and free flowing drinks. All too soon his friends pressed Dan to tell all. We would like to know why one of the most laid back of men suddenly needed everything done yesterday, asked Connie, with Terry nodding in agreement.

I need to start with a summary of my life so far, I had made a promise to tell no-one the true details, but have been released from this vow, so here goes. I fear you will find what I tell you impossible to be-lieve, I can only say it is all true and I have no intention to fool you. Dan began by explaining that he was from the 25Th. century and how he came to be in the present time. He tried to skim over his "creation" in a labora-tory, and his life devoid of affection and any form of family ties. In spite of his brevity it still bought cries of sympathy, and tears from Annie. He passed over his time with the Romany boxers, feeling it was not relevant to his life from then on.

To speak of his great friends Fred and Rose affected him deeply, causing him to hide behind his wine glass while he recovered his compo-sure. He explained about the large sum of money he had been given, and how it had financed his early projects. I must now tell of my love for Louise, and how I had to let her down, breaking both our hearts in the process. People were beginning to ask how it was that in the eighteen years I had been in the area I had not aged at all. The life Louise and I had planned could not be because Louise would grow old while I would re-main almost the same throughout her lifetime. As Rose pointed out it would be unbearable for Louise to be asked; "where is your son today". I felt then I had no choice but to make a clean break, although it meant losing my friends, my business, and the love of my live.

Since that time I have wandered the country finding work, usually houses needing renovation. Hopefully selling for a profit when com-pleted. During this period I met many very nice people but always took care not to become too attached to anyone. I hope you know I have be-come very fond of all of you, and only wish circumstances were different, and I could spend many more years with you.

I have made certain provisions to prevent the changes I have made in you lives from causing you any undue hardship. To you Annie I leave the cottage, together with £10,000 to cover the cost of rates etc.. I have also arranged an annuity for you which will be available from your 50Th birthday, although you can leave it until later if you wish. To Connie and Terry I give the nursery, lock stock and barrel, together with the profits from the "Big House". I'm sorry that's an unknown amount, but the Estate Agent is confident that everything will sell quickly, at the full price. Penny!!, in the short time I have known you I have grown to like you very much. I am hoping you will accept £5,ooo from me for your own use. Perhaps it will pay for your "trousseau" if and when you should marry. No matter who you marry.

One final thing before I stop talking about money, when I was first exiled I was given £5,000,000 to ensure I didn't starve. I still have it, and have arranged that the interest from it should be available to any of you in need of it. Subject always to the approval of the other three. This system to carry on for five years, after which I hope you will serve as trustees handing the interest yearly to a charity approved by you all. Of course we will said Annie, but why are you talking as if you won't be here.

I had hoped to lead gently into the answer to that question but you are right Annie there is no easy way to say this, in eight days time I am returning to my own time and it is unlikely I shall return. All three of Dan's friends began to express their sorrow at this announcement, with Annie hardly able to speak through her tears. Why now! with so much going on, and we are enjoying our friendship. Please don't leave us now, surely another year or so won't make any difference.

Unfortunately I can only go when my leaders are prepared to take me, and at the moment they believe I am needed, and are anxious for my return. The 25Th. century is fighting its first war for three hundred years and have little idea of how to go about forming and training an army. They feel that as I have fought in two major world wars, and I was bred as a fighting man, I should be able to help. What could they do to you if you refused to go with them? asked a still tearful Annie. Leave me here

to work my way as a jobbing builder for the next 500 years, slowly ageing, until I was finally able to die. Having once lived in the 25Th. century
I cannot die before then, or I would die before I was born.

The sorrowful discussion carried on for a little longer, before peter-
ing out for lack of anything new to say. As was often the case Dan and
Annie were the last two left, and Annie hugged Dan, asking, is all this the
reason you always said something unpleasant whenever we began to get
close? Yes he replied and it was the hardest thing I have ever done. With
that she kissed him warmly, saying now go and don't you dare say a word.
Dan smiling sadly, quietly left.

For the next few days Dan carefully checked that all his plans were
in order and he need not worry about his friends financial future. Sorry
this was all he could do for them. He visited each of his friends individually, including a last evening of darts with Terry. They both drank too
much beer, just as well said Terry as it saved us from getting maudling,
and embarrassing each other. Connie commenting, if only half you have
told us is true, I have to thank you for not leading Annie into false hopes.
I also thank you for not being a pest after our special first meeting. Enjoyable as it was it was always a non starter. With that they kissed
warmly, and parted as loving friends. His parting from Annie was less
happy she was in floods of tears, and soon sent him away to save her from
further upset. On the verge of tears himself Dan could not argue. Perhaps
the most unusual parting was from Penny, when they spent a hectic couple of hours with Penny giving Dan a master class in "Kick Boxing".
Penny was later to tell Terry of how fit Dan was, and how quickly he
learned even complicated moves.

On the seventh night his last full night in the 20Th. century, he was
surprised by a quiet knocking on the caravan door. He was amazed to find
Annie on his doorstep, "come in", this is such a pleasure. I was so saddened by our goodbye. What brings you here now? For her answer Annie
stood close to Dan pulled his head down kissed him then whispered in his
ear; "I suppose a shag is out of the question? Dan laughed and led her into
the bedroom.

Dan was never to forget his last night in the 20th. century.

BACK IN THE 25TH. CENTURY

The return journey to the 25th. century passed without incident, seeming to Dan to be much smoother than his previous experience. He was met by Exec 1. and ushered without delay into an imposing looking building, which he assumed to be the Council Headquarters. No time to look around or ask questions, he was taken directly to the council leader, his saviour of so many years ago. The years had not been kind to the Leader, and he was showing signs of the stress he had no doubt endured these past years. Greeting Dan very cordially he seated him down and asked how he was after his years of exile. Very well thank you sir he replied, thanks to the time I have been given I think I can claim my fitness levels are as they should be. Good very good said the leader, but do you think you will be able to teach us how to fight this war?

It takes many men to run an army most of whom would have nothing to do with actual fighting. An army must be fed clothed, supplied with weapons and not least have trained personnel on hand to deal with casualties. Transport must be available to get fighting men to where they can do the most good. These are just a few of the basics, it will take many top grade men to organise the logistics. So far I have only met Exec 1. and Top Tech 2. but feel these are the kind of men that will be needed.

My first priority is to meet the men who are to do the fighting, and second to learn as much as possible about the enemy. I have been told things are not going too well for us, and I must know all the facts. Please do not at any time try to shield me from bad news, I cannot make right decisions based on wrong information. I think I have said enough for now, and would like get properly settled in, change my cloths ETC.. Then I would like to meet the top ten Gladiators to get their version of events.

Thank you No.1. you have given me a great deal to think about, but I have noted that at no time have you shown any reluctance to take on the role. I am greatly cheered by the first positivity I have seen for some time.

Dan's first meeting with his fellow Gladiators was a sad unsatisfactory occasion, only two of the ten leading men were known to him. All of them seemed to be too young to have had much experience, even the ones he knew had been low ranking in his day. He first enquired about his friend No. 2. to be told he was missing in action. Has any effort been made to find him, asked Dan. To be greeted by a series of seemingly indifferent shrugs. Its every man for himself in this game said a surly looking Gladiator. What is your number Dan demanded? I'm No.8, said the gladiator smugly, and I've killed my share of men in battle. When you had "killed your share" did you look around to see if any of your wounded companions needed help, did you check to see if any had been captured, and if they could be rescued? Or were you too busy counting your kills and patting yourself on the back? I'll tell you this No.8. from now on that sort of attitude will get you a job cleaning latrines.

You can't talk to me like that screamed No.8., leaping to his feet. Your just some has-been from a hundred years ago, I'll bet you never killed anyone in your life. I could take you with one arm tied behind my back. Well my proud friend and indeed all of you I have been appointed by the Euro Council to organise you all into an army capable of defeating our enemies. The changes are going to be vast and numerous, so get used to the idea! Now off you go and spread the word, please parade your men at ten o'clock tomorrow, and I'll speak to all of you then. No.8. please give me a couple of minutes of your time.

No,8. stayed as requested, beginning to speak as soon as they were alone. Dan quickly silenced him saying "You have had plenty to say already" including as I recall something about my being a has-been you could take with one arm behind your back. I'm giving you your chance, go and get your fighting gear and meet me in the courtyard here in half an hour. Now get out of my sight before I really lose my temper.

True to his word Dan entered the courtyard exactly on the half hour, having armed himself with a basic Gladiator's outfit. He found No. 8. already going through an exaggerated warm up. Although fit and strong Dan felt there was something not right with No.8's stance and balance, he could not have learned his basics properly or had become sloppy with time. When they were both ready Dan made the traditional salute to his opponent and raised his guard. We don't bother with all that rubbish now, snarled No.8., we just get to it, and immediately attacked Dan meaning to sweep him to one side by force and aggression. Surprised by the absence of any guile or subtlety in the attack Dan swayed easily out of the way and struck No.8's sword hand with flat of his sword causing him to drop his sword. Kicking the fallen weapon out of reach, Dan held the point of his sword to his adversary's neck. In battle you would now have lost your sword hand and be about to be killed. You got lucky, was the only reply, and you are a slow learner said Dan shaking his head. Get the circulation back in your hand and we will try again.

Soon No.8. was ready and again he attacked with great vigour, instead of avoiding the assault Dan parried it and launched a counter attack of his own. With a series of feints and blows he quickly opened up his opponents defence and began landing a series of blows with the flat of his blade. Before again disarming No.8. and knocking him to the ground. I think I must have "got lucky" a few times then. I hope you realise if any of the hits I scored had been with the edge each would have incapacitated you and no doubt led to your death. The fact that you have so many "kills" to you name must say more about the poor quality of the opposition than your ability. I'm afraid it's back to school for you until further notice. Spare me your bluster, just remember this old has-been could have killed you half a dozen times this afternoon. Even without one arm tied behind your back. Report to my office after parade tomorrow, dismiss.

Dan was not sure he had achieved by tackling No.8., but apart from wondering what story No.8. would tell he was pleased to have given himself a trial at combat. One puzzle was how was someone as inept as No.8. able to achieve the "kills" of which he was so proud. What I need mused Dan is to get to know my enemy.

At the parade he introduced himself to the Gladiators, and explained the role he had been given by the council leaders. Up till now I know you have fought with great courage, and no small skill, holding your own against far greater odds. I believe holding your own will never win the war, and I intend to change the way you have been fighting, and hope to prove to you we can win without the same losses we have so far incurred. On future parades you will be taught to drill act and think as one unit, not the individuals you have always been. I shall never ask how many "kills" have you had, rather how were you able to help your comrades, and how many prisoners were taken. A prisoner can supply valuable information, and perhaps be converted to our cause.

Now any questions? Several hands went up some from a group that included No.8., although his hand was not raised. Dan indicated one of them and asked for his number and question. No.14., why do we have to have all this drill nonsense we have been doing alright as we are. Firstly you will on all future occasions address me as sir, secondly up till now we have lost over 30% of our men killed, injured or missing. The enemy have lost less than 10% of theirs, they may not be able to out fight us, but they can outlast us. Next; No.11. sir, you say you intend to alter the way we fight, could you give a brief idea of how?. Thank you No.11. said Dan, as yet I haven't enough intelligence to have found all the enemy's weaknesses. When I do I hope to be able to take the fight to the enemy, where possible attacking their lines of communication and supply. I can tell you it will be guerrilla tactics, sneak in, do what we came to do, and sneak out again. We will try to avoid contact with their fighting men, until I decide the time is right.

At this point a red faced angry looking No.8. called out, "we are Gladiators not cowards sneaking about trying to avoid fighting". You do not call out on my parades, and when you do speak you will call me Sir, said an equally angry Dan. No.1. take 2 men and escort him to my office and hold him there until I arrive. Now gentlemen please gather round where I can be heard without shouting. Over the next few weeks you will receive intensive training in guerrilla warfare where you will find it generally involves a few lightly armed men, getting close to much superior forces, and causing as much damage and confusion as possible before "sneaking safely away". Any fool can engage superior forces at risk to his own life and those of his fellow men. I intend to win this war, and my hope is to see every one of you survive it, myself included. I have already said I want prisoners not dead men, from prisoners we may learn something to our advantage. In addition we may be able to convert them to our way of thinking. Dead men tell no tales!

Dan went on to explain some of the background work he had initiated to help with his plans. Not least the "admin" boffins searching archives for details of army drill and guerrilla tactics. New combat uniforms, weapons and other equipment are under consideration, and I'm happy to tell you the Leader and members of your council have promised to supply anything found to be needed. You will realise a lot of this will take time, and you will be expected to use this break to recover from wounds or injuries. You will all be given a full medical, and once given the all clear you will be expected to train to the highest level of fitness. You will find me out training in any odd hour I can find, you will be welcome to join me at any time. Thankyou gentlemen; No.2. dismiss the parade, and bring Gladiators 15 and below to my office in an hours time.

Dan hurried to his office to face once again the troublesome No.8.. On entering his office he asked No.1. and his men to remain, and addressed No.8. directly. You will be taken from here to solitary confinement where you will remain until you have cooled down. On release you will be returned to school where you will retrain as a Gladiator and learn there is more to a true warrior than a lust to kill. If you give any trouble to your instructors you will be transferred to a civilian jail for an indefinite period.

You can't do this to me shouted No.8., and launched himself at Dan, who calmly avoided the swinging fist caught the offending arm and twisted it up No.8.'s back. Sensing not all the fight had left his opponent Dan threw him face forward at the wall, and as he bounced back hammered a huge right hand punch into his kidneys. No.8. collapsed unconscious to the floor. Would one of you fetch a stretcher please and take him off to the sick bay. He is to be examined for any permanent injury and taken to solitary confinement as soon as possible. No.1. stay behind please, others are on the way and I would like their and your opinion on a couple of things.

By coincidence the two men carrying No.8. left as No.2. and the other Gladiators were arriving. What happened to him was the obvious question, he attacked the Boss the reply. Then what? the boss hit him once and he has not woken up since! The story quickly spread through the ranks, and " don't mess with the Boss" became the watchword.

Unaware of all this Dan called the assembled Gladiators to order. I am hoping to organise you along similar lines to a 20th. century regiment, I'm sure some of you will feel this is a retrograde step, taking you backwards rather than forwards. I feel that a system that has been proven to work, however long ago, has to be better than no system at all. I need volunteers to teach discipline and guerrilla tactics. Archives are being searched and will very shortly be able to supply drill manuals and details of standard discipline requirements. Digital images of guerrilla fighting will also be supplied. Can I please have Volunteers?, I would also like suggestions for men who although lower ranking are felt to have the right qualities.

No.1. was the first to step forward, I would like to be considered for a role in discipline he said. I feel that discipline has dropped while we have been fighting on an almost daily basis. Thank you No.1. I hoped you would be first to take the lead. An older looking Gladiator was next to volunteer; No.13. I would like to join No.1. on discipline please Sir, I go back to your day and life was easier when we all knew the rules. Yes thank you No.13 I'm sure No. 1. will be glad to have you onboard. In the course of the next hour Dan was able to lay the foundations of training for the new army he had planned. He was particularly pleased to learn of a young Gladiator who was known to be interested in Roman history, including their battle tactics.

Sounds like he might be useful thought Dan, I'm not happy with the every man for himself system when we meet the enemy face to face. I have been looking for an aide-de-camp perhaps he will fill the bill. Dan liked the young Gladiator from the first moment of their meeting, he displayed a extensive knowledge of all aspects of Roman culture. He explained his belief that a variation of the Roman wedge formation would fit in with Dans plans. The "wedge is designed to allow a small group of men to break through a larger force, offering a chance of escape. Dan asked him to consult with Top Tech 2 to find the best way to produce visual images of a "wedge"" in action. One other thing said Dan I'm in need of an aide-de-camp perhaps you would like to give it a try, think about it for a couple of days and let me know. No need for that sir I would be proud and delighted to give it a try, I am a great fan of what you are trying to do and thrilled to be a part of it. Good said Dan, that only leaves what do I call you. As you know sir I am No.147, replied a puzzled A.D.C.. I don't like all these numbers I'm more used to names. I shall call you Terry 2 which will give you a lot to live up to. Thank you, sir, he said and left.

The next few weeks were very busy as the training became more closely directed to the kind of fighting Dan had planned. Terry2 proved to be very efficient and tireless. Dan was able to spend more time on the training ground, improving his own fitness along with his men. Top Tech2 and his team had produced remarkable moving images of a Roman wedge, and it was proving popular with the men. Dan now had Top Tech2 working on personal camouflage similar to that used on the "time Travel" machine. TopTech2 and his team thought this a good idea and promised to give it priority.

Dan's main concern was his lack of information about his enemies movements, he had yet to find a way to learn details of enemy activity in their own territory. He was still anxious for information about his old friend No.2. who took over when he was exiled. He and about twenty or thirty others were missing, no one knowing if they were dead or alive. He asked for a meeting with the Leader and Exec.1. asking for any suggestions for the establishment of a spy network. We have one man planted in the area of their main camp, explained the Leader, we gave him several means of communication. They have all been blocked and we now are unaware of his current status. Meaning you don't know if he is dead or alive asked Dan. Not quite said the Leader, we feel the enemy would have boasted to us had they caught our man. Our signals are being routinely blocked, as we are blocking theirs.

Surely it would be better to intercept and record as much of their signalling as possible, any intelligence gained would be to our advantage. All their messages are in computer based codes not available to us, protested Exec.1. In the 20Th. century a schoolboy using a basic home computer hacked into America's defence systems computers. You will imagine the consternation he caused. Imagine Top Tech. and his team must have a "Hacker" or two up their sleeves, Dan persisted. Things are more complex now than they were, said the Leader, but doubtless you will argue that so is our equipment. We will see what can be done, although this brings us no nearer to communicating with our agent concluded the leader. Thankyou said Dan what we really need is someone who regularly crosses the border but is not connected to the military in anyway. Of course they must be willing to help us, in spite of the risk. As always

No.1. you have given us much to think about, and no less an amount to do, said the Leader closing the meeting.

Having checked and found his training was in full swing and making better progress than he had dared hope. Most of his men had taken to the new style of warfare, and with their inbred fighting instincts were making rapid progress. Dan felt his presence was not as critical as it had been, and he was planning to visit the area where most of the early battles had taken place.

Top Tech 2. agreed to provide transport for Dan and No.1. to visit the battlefield, and was greatly amused when when both men walked past the vehicle without seeing it. When Dan finally saw it he was very excited by the camouflage, and congratulated Top Tech 2. on his achievement. It's all done with camaras was all he would say, I'm afraid your personal camouflage is proving more difficult. I have faith said Dan keep at it. On your way then said the technician, just be sure you remember where you park it I would hate you to lose it.

 Dan and his companion found the "car" very comfortable and completely silent. It was also very quick and they reached their destination well under the estimated time. The Europe Gladiators camp was on a plain near the Asia -Europe border in World Zone A/E2738495D. Dan had no idea what all that meant, but Exec1. thought it could have been Turkey in the old days. Dan was struck, not for the first time, how impersonal everything was in the 25Th. century. Dan's headquarters and training camp was situated 80 miles to the west, in the old East Europe possibly Croatia.

Dan introduced himself to the squad of men stationed at the forward observation post, and found them to be a mixture of experienced fighters and younger lower ranked Gladiators. Their main task was to report any large-scale movement by the enemy and report back to the main camp as quickly as possible. How do you report back? asked Dan, all electronic and wireless communication is being blocked. The leading Gladiator No.28. pointed to a large hill some 15/20 miles away, explaining there is a battery powered telephone wire and we can call HQ. direct. My God!! said Dan I suppose you get there on a bicycle or is it roller skates. You're taking me back to the 14/18 World War. Why wasn't the wire run all the way here? asked Dan. The robots would come no closer to the battlefield for fear of being damaged. Are we gladiators incapable of running a few miles of wire? asked an exasperated Dan. We, all Dan and No.1. would say.

You told me you had 20 men here I can only count 19 where is the missing man, and who is he? He is No. 307. and he is out on patrol. Why is he on his own? no-one should ever patrol on their own, judging by his number his must be inexperienced. He's a bit impulsive and can't keep still, he is always going off on his own. We will talk about that after we find him. said Dan angrily.

What is your best bet for the way he would have gone? Over the brook toward the main battle area, was No.28's best guess! Right!, said Dan, 28 you will come with me in my vehicle, and we will see how good you are at guessing. No.1. you pick out the quickest of this bunch and follow me in their car. Leave the best runner to head to that hill in case it all goes wrong. I've got a bad feeling about this!!

No.28. was astonished when Dan first revealed his camouflaged vehicle, which he did not see until Dan opened the door. Dan set off at high speed, following 28's hurried directions. They soon reach the brook No.28. had mentioned, which was crossed by a narrow but sturdy bridge. Dan parked by a suitable hedge which allowed the vehicle to blend in and virtually disappear. 28 made to get out, until Dan advised him to remain where he was, we can see from here but not seen. I think I saw a movement off to our left wait until it becomes clear.

The movement evolved into a lone figure running toward the bridge. Shortly followed by a group of men in pursuit. Is the runner your man, asked Dan. Yes, was the reply, he is a very good runner, I'd expect him to reach the bridge in the clear. It seemed he was right, until the runner stumbled when within a hundred metres of the bridge. He had clearly hurt himself as he now limped and moved much slower. His pursuers were now closing in on their prey. It is going to be close said Dan if he makes it let him through and be ready to tackle the second of the men following.

The runner No.307. made it over the bridge still a few yards ahead. As soon as he was clear Dan stepped out of hiding to confront the first of the pursuers. Such was the surprise he paused giving Dan time to pivot on his left foot and kick his opponent in the neck, knocking him off the bridge. Thinking thank you Penny!! The next attacker in line had been taken back by Dan's sudden appearance and the unusual way his comrade had been despatched. He was slow to make his own attack, giving Dan time to recover his balance. He took firm hold of the sword arm of his opponent swung him swiftly to where No.28. was ready waiting. Seeing the first two of their comrades dealt with such apparent ease, the next in line hung back from the bridge waiting for the remainder of their force to arrive. Fortunately, No.1. and the remainder of Dans Gladiators arrived, and the opposition fled.

Dan's first thought was to take prisoner the two men who had attempted to cross the bridge. No.28. was holding the second man, who showed no desire to keep fighting. Two men were sent to follow the brook and capture the first man who was trying to escape downstream. He was soon caught and returned to where Dan was waiting. Dan gave instructions for the two men to be made comfortable, and treated well, until they could be taken to headquarters. One of them was suffering severe bruising to the neck and jaw. What happened to him asked No.1? The "Boss" kicked him clean off the bridge, I've never seen anything like it said No.28.

You will all get a closer look at my boot than you want if you don't stop standing about gossiping like a bunch of old washer women. No.1. get together with whoever passes as second in charge around here, and draw up a 24hr. guard and patrol schedule. No's 28 and 307 in the office now!! The rest of you clean this pigsty, it's a disgrace.

Everyone scurried off to escape Dan's wrath, and he joined the two remaining in the office. Dan left the men stood to attention and sat looking at them for several minutes. I had intended to read the riot act to you both for the ill-disciplined and thoughtless way you have behaved. However I have decided that the greater blame lies with me, for the way I have failed you. While I have been in charge I have concentrated my efforts on the main camp, and on retraining my main force. I had forgotten the old adage that an army is only as strong as its weakest link. Now stand easy, in fact pull up a couple of chairs, I imagine 307 that your leg is still troubling you. No 28 I have had a very brief look through your files, but cannot find a copy of your orders. I wasn't given any written orders sir, just told to keep an eye on the enemy and let H.Q. know if they started any large move. Dan looked at 307; I was told do as I was told and keep practising my arms drill, nothing about how to carry out a proper patrol.

My first priority when I get back to H.Q. will to get together a properly trained squad to take your place, and you will be relieved as soon as possible. We can then get your training in my kind of warfare under way. No.307 go and get that leg attended to, you are confined to the camp area until relieved. Now 28 you will follow the schedule being drawn up. Make sure you go no further than the brook and try to find some high point to use for observation. I want you to carry on here until I can get you replaced, you know there is a lot wrong with the way things are here. You must tighten discipline, and stamp your authority on the men. Make sure that anyone not on duty, or resting after duty, is either practising drill or working to improve the camp. I will draw up your future orders and have them sent to you as a matter of priority.

Dan lost no time returning to his H.Q. and immediately sent for Terry2. I found a very poor situation at the front with good men doing wrong things because they know no better, and no orders to guide them. Myself and No.1. are going to sort the problem, but I need you to tell me of any other area needing urgent reorganising. Use my authority and take yourself into every area of the camp and let me know of any problem areas. I do not want to be caught out in the future. Yes sir; the first area of concern is my office. I need more space, and some clerical assistance. Well said Terry2 I should realise I can't throw an extra week's work at you without causing difficulties. Delay that last order until we can get you sorted.

The A.D.C. got his new office within hours, the maintenance robots took away his old building and replaced it with a larger model. "Good" thought Terry2 all I want now is some help. The camp had already exceeded its quota of robots, and he had been turned down by robot allocations.

Having organised replacements for No.28. at wo ladies, whose upper bracket husbands, were detained in and his men, Dan tried to settle down to the constant stream of reports flowing across his desk. I'm a fighter not a writer, was his constant cry. I just wish one piece of this correspondence bought me some intelligence about the enemy. The two prisoners he had taken were willing to tell all they knew, but it added up to very little. His attention was drawn to a hand addressed envelope half buried in his "in tray". The ladies were experienced clerical workers and were hoping they be of some assistance. They realised the jamming of the internet etc was creating more paper files than for many years and felt they could be of use.

Dan called Terry2 into his office and passed him the letter, here you are young man the answer to all your problems, and no doubt a bit of mothering thrown in. Terry2, smiling broadly, said "snap" I've got what might be the end of yours. I found pushed under my door a note, supposedly from a lady, who is offering her services as a spy or go between! She is part of a troupe of entertainers who pass backwards and forwards into Asia. She insists on total confidentiality, and has given me precise instructions how to contact her. Dan was on his feet in his excitement, Terry2 this could be the breakthrough I've waited for. Get your two ladies organised and then give total priority to contacting this person. Don't cause any upset but let her know I want to meet her. If she agrees I'll go anywhere to suit her, it's her call. Now, cancel all my meetings I'm going for a long run to do some thinking.

Dan's run may have helped his general fitness, but not much to clear the confusion in his mind. Every idea he had come down to how much information his new "spy" was able to provide. He knew nothing about her, how intelligent is she, is she capable of working on her own initiative? What freedom of movement does she have? Dan had faith in Terry2 to handle the early meetings with great tact, but couldn't wait to meet her himself. He told himself it was nonsense but couldn't shake off the feeling this was the break he had wanted for so long.

Terry2's ladies soon proved their worth completely reorganising his office and smoothing his way apparently effortlessly. They had an ever polite but slightly imperious manner that tended to get them their own way. That is with all except Dan and Terry2 who were always deferred to. Terry2 was frequently away from his office while meeting his

97

mystery woman, but was able to keep up with his work by leaving his ladies recorded instructions and letting them get on with it.

The day finally came when Terry2 was able to tell Dan his lady had agreed to meet him. Her reluctance had been that Dan was so well known she didn't want them to seen together. After much discussion it was decided a problem should arise over the "troupes" travel arrangements necessitating her making a visit to a Government office, where Dan was waiting. Her name was Dancer1, again more a description of what she did, than a real name. Do I call you Boss?, she asked, Terry2 always does! I much prefer Dan if you don't mind, but call me anything. If you feel you can help me learn more about my enemy, I'll happily put up with most things.

I truly do want to help Dancer1 assured him but I have no idea how. May I ask why you want to help us?, you spend equal amounts of time either side of the border. I'm surprised you want to get involved. Life under the rule of Li Pinoe and his hench men is becoming intolerable, and increasingly dangerous for young women. One of my girls was assaulted and beaten, for no reason except they felt like it. At one time we had a travelling boxing show with us, and they gave the girls some protection. If Li Pinoe is not stopped he will ruin our civilisation, and its not that good to start with. As it happens, said Dan, I agree that our civilisation leaves a lot to be desired, but for now I'm committed to trying to save it.

I'm intrigued by your tale of a boxing booth, that could be useful. For now could you try to discover anything you can about prisoners. I need to know if any of our missing men are still alive, and how they are being treated. Later on when you are more into the role, I hope you can tell me about their Gladiators morale. You have already explained about Li Pinoe's henchmen, I need to know if there is any discord between them and the regular troops. Take no chances, just listen to what's being said, put two and two together, you never know what you may learn. Remember I would rather you returned unharmed knowing nothing, than to know everything and you pay the price.

I understand you are off on your travels in two days, and will be gone about three weeks. While you are gone try to remember all you can about the boxers I will make enquiries at this end and see what we can come up with. Now enough of all this, have you eaten? Tell me what you would like and I will have it bought in. Dan spent the next couple of hours, chatting happily with a bright attractive young woman. For the first time ever in the 25Th. century.

Back at his headquarters Dan began to plan ways to get the most from Dancer1. The first task to do as much as possible to ensure her safety. Calling in the A.D.C. and No.1. he asked that a squad of men accompany her party as far as possible, without going into enemy territory. Don't let them seem to be a guard, more a training squad going the same way. When parting let the troops keep watch until the entertainers are out of sight. In three weeks' time let a different squad meet them and bring them home. Terry2 will you get your ladies going through personnel records to find any Gladiators with boxing experience, or aptitude. I think twenty or so to start with we can thin them out later. No.1. will you get the senior training officer to come to my office A.S.A.P. and will see if he has any suggestions. I do not want this to be the talk of the camp, and any prospective candidates must be sworn to secrecy.

Dan was delighted with the initial response to his search for boxers, several men volunteering and the senior training officer recommending others. As soon as he outlined his idea for a traveling "Boxing Booth", all of the candidates were keen to take part. The twin rolls of "spies" and protectors of the show girls, proving popular. The S.T.O., a grizzled old timer, veteran of many campaigns, revealed himself to have been a boxing trainer and qualified referee, begged to be allowed to take part. Dan was happy to agree, and appointed him manager of the booth and the boxers. With the first task of selecting the squad to become the boxing team. Dan would have liked to have taken the heavy weight position himself, but doubted the governing council would agree.

All the hard work done by Dan and his team was now paying off and the rank and file were highly efficient in all aspects of guerrilla warfare. The A.D.C. and his ladies had the admin. under control. Time seem to hang for Dan, as he waited for Dancer1 and her troupe to return. He worked hard on his own training, finding many of his men easily able to keep up with him when running, but few able to match him in single combat. One of the few being No.1., Who, although no heavyweight, was very fast and clever. Dan had long admired his many other attributes and discipline, fclt he would be perfect for Dan's future plans.

Dancer1 and her troupe arrived back without any problems, better still, she was brimming with excitement over all she had discovered. She and Dan got together as soon as possible, and Dan began to question her urgently. No!! said Dancer1 let me tell you in my own way, then you can ask questions if you like. Sorry, please take all the time you need, I'm all ears.

First said Dancer you were right to ask about relations between the ordinary Gladiators and Li Pinoe's henchmen. I saw several fights between them, and there seemed to be more of them each time. I think there could be big trouble before long. Now my "main" news: they are holding a number of prisoners, my informants vary between dozens and dozens and hundreds and hundreds, so take your pick! They are held in an old schoolhouse on street C12, the building looks more European in design than Asian. I have travelled extensively in both and know the difference. I thought it might be a European architect, and you could have archive records. The strange thing is while I was checking the school building a small squad turned up escorting two middle aged men, who they bundled into the building, locked the doors and marched away. The two men were somewhat dishevelled, but their clothing looked to be of a high quality, and the men had an air about them that I can't explain. I'll bet they are the husbands of Terry2's ladies said Dan. We won't say anything to them as yet, we don't want to give them a false hope.

Now did you get permits for the boxing booth? Are there facilities for them to set up where you are? Do you think there will be any interest, anyone willing to challenge my fighters? Dan, stop, pleaded Dancer, all these questions. One, yes I got the permits, they are happy for anything to entertain the idle troops. Two, plenty of room next to our site, with facilities laid on. Do not want you pinching my audience. Spy or no spy I still have a living to earn and a business to run. Three, as for interest there is so much testosterone flying about, they will be having fights to decide who can have a fight. I hope your men are good, they are going to be busy. You look big enough, will you be coming?

Thank you Dancer for all that I'm sorry I was rushing you. I'm also sorry I have not given enough thought to your business etc. Please rest assured you will be financially secure for the rest of your life. I had hoped to come and fight my corner, but the Governing council have forbidden my going. They feel I am too well known and would be recognised immediately. Quite right said Dancer your picture is all over the place, with lurid details of all the wicked things you have done. If only half what they say is true I'm not sure a nice girl like me is safe with an ogre like you. Should they change their minds my girls and I can do you a makeup job so even Terry2 wouldn't recognise you. I'll bear that in mind said Dan, so long as you guarantee he won't end up fancying me. We are good said Dancer, laughing, but not that good.

Still smiling Dan offered to provide lunch. Thanks, but I had better not, my girls are already asking why I have to spend so much time at the Licence Office. I just tell them there's a war on, but who knows who else is wondering. Thank you for all your good work I am thrilled there are prisoners still alive, I had feared they may have killed them all. Li Pinoe is mad enough for anything. I'll keep in touch until you go in three weeks, any problems you will be the second to know.

A problem arose all too soon, No.46 the boxing squad super heavyweight had a fall during training and dislocated his shoulder. Loss of any of the team would have been serious enough, to lose the top weight a disaster. The booth claimed to take on all comers and there were sure to be contestants too large for the lower weights to tackle. Dan called a conference with all the interested parties, but failed to come up with a suitable replacement. There seemed to be no alternative to cancelling the whole scheme.

Dan asked the Leader and Council to reconsider their refusal to allow him to go. To his regret, but not surprise, they turned him down. Determined the entire scheme should not be cancelled and longing to get a close look at the enemy, Dan set up an urgent meeting with Dancer1. Dan wanted to know how well she could disguise him, and would she be prepared to do the makeover and maintain it for the duration. Dancer was keen to show him what her girls could do, and was confident they could keep him disguised for as long as needed.

Dan duly presented himself at the girls largest caravan to find the girls ready and waiting, excited at the idea of altering his appearance. Having lived for many years in a "circus" style caravan Dan was nevertheless amazed by the lavish comfort and stylish decor of the caravan interior. Tastefully lit, with fine art pictures on all sides, Dan could only guess at the wonderful fabrics used throughout. He was simply speechless at the colour co-ordination and overall design. He had to be contented with staring open mouthed, and the one word "Wow".

The girls while smiling at his reaction were keen to get started; and ushered him into a chair in front of a makeup mirror. He had been asked not to shave and sported a three day stubble, showing dark on his chin and neck. Their first action was to shave his head to a matching length, instantly changing his appearance. The makeover continued for several hours, leaving Dan with scarred eyebrows and chin, and a dragon tattoo on his arm. The tattooist assured a worried Dan that the dragon was not permanent and would start to fade after a month or so as would the scars Etc. A final spray with fake tan to darken his skin and the girls pronounced themselves satisfied.

The next day he presented himself at the Council building, Only to be stopped by a security guard asking what he was doing there. I was told to sit in the visitors gallery until the boss arrives to introduce me, Dan explained. Off you go then said the guard, just remember I shall be watching you! So far so good thought Dan, I hope the Leader and Council are fooled as easily. The disguised Dan waited in the gallery until after the time when he was due to appear before the Committee. Noted for his punctuality, his non arrival soon caused consternation, Dan heard the leader ask if anyone knew his whereabouts. He stood up and raised his arm. Who are you and what do you want?, demanded the Leader. Sir! I was told by the Boss to show myself to you, he wants me to be the new heavyweight to go with the boxers, replied Dan heavily disguising his voice. Well you certainly look the part, said a chorus of voices, including the Leader. All to the good said the Leader but where is our war chief?.

There was a moments silence, before Dan still standing said, " I am here sir, sorry for the subterfuge but I wanted you to be sure the disguise would stand close scrutiny. The leader hardly knew whether to laugh or get mad, No.1. he said, giving Dan his old title, every time we try to protect you from yourself you find some clever, or stupid, way round it. I know how you have longed to learn more of your enemy, and see this will be a good chance for you to do so. I am therefore saying you can go, but get your information! After this I shall expect you to start all out action, followed by a swift victory and an end to this damn war. We have given you everything you have asked for now it's payback time. Message received and understood said Dan. You will have your action and I believe your victory. Get out, shouted the leader you tire me. Dan stood, bowed, and made to leave. As he reached the door the leader called, take care of yourself and waved him away.

Over the next few days before he was due to join the other boxers on their trip across the border, Dan kept out of sight to all except Terry2 and No.1. He gave a long list of things to do to his ever patient A.D.C. who assured him most of them were already in hand. On top of the list to check that Tech2 had ready the supply of camouflaged personnel carriers he had asked for. He then asked No.1. to contact the forward outpost; "The primitive phone line had now been extended all the way", I want details of how many men are stationed at the Asian forward post and a reliable description of the camp layout. The less the enemy are aware of the better.

Once you have the information No.1. I want you to take as many men as you think necessary and attack the enemy forward post, using the methods we have practised so much. I want every man taken prisoner, none are to be harmed unless our own men are in danger. Any who are killed or injured are to be brought back anyway. All documents, computers, radios and other communication devices, to be carefully handled and saved. On return they are to be handed to Tech2. and Exec1 immediately. As little damage as possible, and by that I mean none, to be done, I want the next visitors to be baffled as to what has happened. If they should believe all have deserted, taking everything of value with them, that would be an extra bonus.

As soon as Dan had finished speaking No.1. leaped for joy, crying, thankyou sir; does this mean from now we are on the attack?. If you and your men are successful then yes!, so go get em! No.1. needed no second telling and left at a run, calling for his second in command as he went. He seems happy enough said Dan, yes said Terry2, the only people not happy will be those not chosen to go.

Right then A.D.C. lets see if I can save you from your usual state of boredom and find you something to do. First continue to chase Tech2 for the camouflaged vehicles, and for any advance with camouflaged battle dress. No.1's men will need the best available. We should be hearing about street maps, and hopefully architects drawings of the school on street C12. Chase them up, show them to your ladies they may have been into Asia several times and might know the area. You have probably guessed I am hoping to recover our lost men. No one must know until we are ready to move. I fully understand boss said Terry2, I only request that on all your future adventures you A.D.C. is alongside you where he belongs.

For the next few days until Dan left on his travels, he was aware of a new level of excitement in the camp. he soon realised this was due to No.1. selecting men for his attack on the Asian forward post. As Terry2 had prophesied all the Gladiators wanted to go. Terry2 was hard pressed keeping Dan safe from all the Gladiators who wanted him to persuade No.1. to let them go. Dan had no desire to be seen in his new guise, so poor Terry2 was left to placate the disappointed.

The time for the entertainers and boxers to leave came all to quickly, and in a flurry of last minute orders and reports Dan joined the caravan as it began its journey. At first there was great surprise among the boxers that "Sir" was their new heavyweight, shock at the change to his appearance. Welcome aboard Sir said the S.T.O., you look the part well enough, but are you up to taking on all comers. A good question S.T.O., I am not without experience and will be looking to you to assess my worth. If you will excuse the pun "pull no punches" with my training, and I won't pull any when the time comes. A thought that occurs to me is we cannot continue to call each other "Sir" and S.T.O. ETC. My name from now on will be Dan, sort out names for yourselves and let me have a list in the morning. I shall expect the new names to be the norm by the time we arrive in Asia. Serious training starts tomorrow, get some sleep you will need it; goodnight.

The morning training session was to set the routine for their journey. The S.T.O., or Arch Or Boss as he was now to be called, had his
fighters running alongside the vehicles for several miles. After a rub down
they began stretching exercises, and finally bag and speedball training.
Dan was excused the latter as Arch was anxious to check his all round
boxing ability. He matched Dan against two of his fast punching light-
weights, allowing Dan to defend only, not attack. He soon found he had
his work cut out to keep himself out of trouble. With both his opponents
moving very quickly and throwing a seemingly continuous barrage of fast
accurate punches, he was forced to keep increasing his own speed to its
maximum. By the end of each round he was more breathless than he remembered being in any previous sporting conflict. "Not too bad" was
Arch's verdict, I'll have another look at your footwork when you're not
moving so fast.

In this way they reached the Asian City LI/4156 without incident,
Dan had been surprised at the casual disinterest shown by the border
guards. The Caravan being waved through with no checks of any kind.

The camp show tent, boxing booth and side shows were soon set
up, and the living quarters connected to main services. Dan wondered if
the boxing team was more interested in helping the Dancers set up than
erecting the boxing booth, but felt there was nothing he wanted to do
about it, even if he could. These men would have something to fight for,
and he was sorry for anyone who got in their way.

The first couple of nights passed quietly for the boxers, with only
the lighter weights being called on. To no-ones surprise they proved far
too skilled for their challengers. At the weekend there were far more people about, mainly in uniform as if attached to the military, although Dan
wouldn't describe them as real fighting men. As a first sight of the enemy
he was pleased to have the men of his own army, and not this rabble. It
was not until the Saturday night that he got his first real challenge. A large
tough looking man in a well kept uniform watched Dan dispose of a couple of no hopers, before making his own move. Stripped for action he was
almost as tall as Dan, and probably a stone heavier. From the start it was
clear this was not his first time in a boxing ring, he certainly knew how
to throw a punch. By keeping moving and adroit use of his straight left

Dan was able to keep out of trouble, and look for possible openings.

He felt that although his punching was dangerous his opponents footwork was not the best. Dan was happy to have his opinion confirmed when Arch whispered to him to speed up and harass your man he will lose his balance. For the next round Dan did as he was instructed, moving at close to his fastest speed and rapidly changing his angle of attack. As the round progressed his opponent began to slow and Dan was able to land some heavy blows to the body slowing him further. In the third and final round Dan's opponent slowed even further, allowing Dan to keep out of trouble while looking aggressive. At the bell he went across to his advisory's corner to check he was O.K. "I'm fine was the reply" I didn't expect to win, and you were better than I thought, too good for booth fighting.

Dan thought no more about him until two days later when he was out for a walk, checking the City layout, and met his former opponent coming the other way. "Hello" said the stranger I'm glad I bumped into you, I had hoped we could have a chat sometime. There is a Cafe just round the corner can I get you a drink?. Thankyou said Dan I wouldn't mind a coffee, more from curiosity than thirst. As soon as they were settled in their seats with the coffees the man said I am L54 of Li Pinoe first army. You I believe are, or were No.1. of one hundred, probably the greatest gladiator of all time. Startled!! Dan started to rise, don't be alarmed the man said your secret is safe with me. I was present when you and No.2. had your epic battle, I thought Li Pinoe was wrong then and think he has been wrong most of the time since. I suppose you know we are keeping a number of your men prisoner in an old school, under pretty appalling conditions. Yes I know said Dan, but right now I'm more interested in how you recognised me?

Easy!!, was the reply, I studied you for many years watching all your contests and exhibitions until I knew your every move. Thats why I got in the ring with you, I was sure who you were but wanted to get a closer look. From your appearance I would never have known you, but you have carried many of your moves into the boxing ring confirming what I already knew.

I am too much of a fan of yours to ever do you any harm. Although if we ever come face to face on the battle field I will do my best to defeat you whatever it takes. I think your aims are far better than Li Pinoe's, but I have sworn to fight for him and I am a man of my word. I wonder if you know that we have a serious food shortage and most of Li Pinoe's men spend their pay buying food to supplement their rations. There are two food distribution centres in the city, one for the army and one for the "henchmen" Any disruption of supply would be disastrous. Where are these centres? Dan began to ask. I have said all I intend to say, all I have told you is common knowledge, not a state secret.

With that he stood, shook Dan's hand and made to leave, after two paces he turned back and with a huge smile said, could be I just laid a big trap for you! Bye. Dan sat for a couple of minutes digesting all he had learned and wondering if he should trust his enemy come fan. He decided to take a chance and check all he had been told.

A few minutes later found him hurrying into the camp calling for all his men to meet him in the communal caravan. Catching Dan's excitement the men hurried to join him, asking each other, "now what's floating the bosses boat?" Dan lost no time in explaining about the Asian army being on short rations, and about the two distribution centres. Your priority from now on is to learn where these centres are and how they are restocked. I don't have to tell you we are only here for a few more days. and this information will make the trip worthwhile.

Later that night he was able to have a quiet conversation with Dancer1. Once he had explained the situation she readily agreed to try to learn all she could. Now I think about it there is a military looking building in the northeast end of town, say a mile from the centre. I used to see it when I went that way on one of my runs, I'm sure its got loading bays. I stopped going on runs because the "henchmen" started to be a nuisance. Thankyou said Dan that sounds worth a look. If you fancy a run I can supply you with a dozen or so fit men, who will be only too pleased to fight your corner if necessary. Your on! said Dancer, after lunch tomorrow, I think I can find the way.

Happy with this decision Dan turned to the city map supplied by Exec1., suspecting the Asian army would keep the two supply depots well apart he concentrated on the south side. He soon found a suitably sized building, worth a second look. Built on the same M3 rd. as the other build-ing, it was too square in design to be a school or office complex. Trusting his hunch, but anxious to check it out he walked, trying to look like a tourist, to the south side of town. As he approached the general area of his target he began to wonder if he would gain any real evidence of the buildings true purpose. As he reached the beginning of the building he was accosted by three men in dishevelled uniforms of Li Pinoe's army. They were clearly some of Li Pinoe's conscripts, with none of the attrib-utes he would have associated with true Gladiators. Dan was anxious to avoid any trouble and was instantly on his guard.

It was soon evident he had nothing to fear, the men complained they were starving and asked if he could spare a few credits (money) to help them buy food. I carry very little said Dan, but you are welcome to what I have. As he fumbled in his pocket he casually asked, why are you out here?, wouldn't you do better in the city centre?. This building is the food distribution depot, the men explained, sometimes the guards will give you some food, but no luck today. "Jackpot" thought Dan, so much for military secrets. He handed the men most of his credits, waving away their thanks and thinking he would have paid ten times the amount for the information. Come to the boxing booth at closing time tonight ask for me "Dan" and I will see you get a decent meal. Bye for now, see you later.

When Dancer and her party returned they were able to confirm the building they had visited was the second food distribution centre. A bunch of "henchmen" were there, they didn't seem keen on tackling my escort at close quarters. So they settled for pelting us with eggs, a clue to what the building held! Joining in with their laughter, he took the first oppor-tunity to tell them of his own discovery. Adding that the three soldiers would probably turn up later asking for him, I promised them a meal. I think we might learn more detail from them if we go slowly, and don't let them realise they are being interrogated.

As expected, the three soldiers turned up, and seemed quite happy to talk about the distribution depot with only the minimum prompting. Happily revealing the days and usual times for deliveries of replacement supplies, together with their estimate of the number of guards. All very convenient thought Dan, we will have to check what they have told us very carefully. With only a week before their permits expired there was not much time for Dan to be as thorough as he would like. He decided to take no action to verify the three soldier's comments, concentrating on gaining as much detail of the two depots as possible. For the five days before the need to dismantle the camp and boxing booth ETC. he had the depots watched as often as possible. Runners and walkers wearing pedometers passed and repassed the buildings, and through the nearest streets until he was sure he had covered everything he could.

One item hinted at by the soldiers pleased Dan, there had been some sort of trouble at the Asian forward outpost. An embargo had been placed on all information and no detail was available. Dan was content that No.1. had been successful in his attack, had he not been, the enemy would be shouting from the roof tops not suppressing information. At last the battle has begun!!

The journey back to camp was uneventful, Dan spending most of his time analysing all the information they had gathered. Checking the pedometer readings until he had distances between the two depots and the old school accurate enough for his purposes. On the penultimate night the girls threw a party in their largest caravans. Music and dancing were the order of the day, and Dan found himself truly relaxing for the first time in a long time. He mentioned to Dancer his fondness for ballroom dancing she produced suitable music, and showed him why she was called Dancer1. Dan thanked Dancer explaining how much he had enjoyed himself, having not expected to dance in the 25Th. century.

Dan was greeted by a new aura of excitement and anticipation, and everyone wanting to tell him of the success of the attack on the Asian forward post. All very well said Dan, after receiving No1's report, but you faced no opposition so we cannot call it a baptism of fire. How will the men fare against an opposition fighting back?. The enemy was there Boss protested No.1. we took them by complete surprise, those who showed resistance were overcome before they could arm themselves. You asked for no damage and the men's speed and efficiency ensured that's what you got. Quite right No.1. said Dan I have preached "no casualties", and should be glad when that's what I get. Please pass on my congratulations to the men, tell them they are off to a good start!

Now gentlemen I want comprehensive plans for a three phase attack on the old schoolhouse, and the two food depots. All plans must include a "flying" reserve as cover against any kind of trap. There is just a chance we may be expected. I would like to lead the attack on the schoolhouse, there may be some of our men recognise me and obey my orders, if necessary. I am under instruction from the Leader and Council to carry the war to the enemy, and end this war as quickly as possible. Of course it is taken for granted we will win.

Set the S.T.O. to work I need every man on top flight in training and fitness. Once we get started this next time there will be no time for further training, It will be all out attack. With that in mind I will be glad to hear of any target that will harm the enemy if destroyed. You can tell your men the peace is over we are going to war. Dan knew that the word had been spread when the S.T.O. ordered him to be on the square at 6am. the next morning for weapon training. I have heard you are good with your feet and I know you are good with your hands, he told Dan, but I want a look at the whole package. Fair enough said Dan, smiling, now get out of here.

Things began to move at a pace, Dan passed the S.T.O.'s inspection, and the plans for the three pronged attack arrived on his desk far sooner than he expected. Until he remembered he had told Terry2 of his intention to try to release the prisoners as soon as possible, and guessed he had started work on the plans immediately. Terry and No1. clearly knew their business, the plans met with Dan's approval with only slight changes. Dan was particularly pleased with a secondary plan for the Asian forward outpost to be retaken and held by the men of his own forward post. It would then act as a gathering point for anyone separated from their platoon. Or as a regrouping point in the event of the attacking force failing to meet its objectives. Each group was to carry coloured rocket flares, to signal completion of their task, or to call for assistance from the reserves.

Having expressed his pleasure with the plans, Dan immediately asked how soon they would be ready to move. One week, replied No.1. and Terry2 in unison. Good said Dan, you have got five days. At that No.1. left, and Terry reached for a telephone and began frantically dialling. Dan left to seek audience with the Leader, hoping to make his day.

If you win it will be fine, if you fail I'll send you the bill, was the leaders comment.

For the next four days Dan saw little of his main men who seemed to on the run from dawn to dusk. Dan was also busy trying to check on all sections and platoons, checking moral, and generally making a nuisance of himself. That is what Generals are for, his only excuse. The fifth day was given as a relax and catch your breath day, Dan, No.1. and Terry visiting everyone taking part, Dan promising a real party in a weeks time.

Dawn on the fifth day saw the three units leave at timed intervals, programmed that all groups arrive at their different locations simultaneously. Putting the enemy under the greatest pleasure, on all fronts.

Dan's team, complete with empty personnel carriers, arrived at the old school and immediately charged the building. The door was beaten open in seconds and the leading Gladiators burst in! The Asian guards promptly dropped their arms and surrendered. Slowly realising what was happening the prisoners began to cheer. Silence!!, roared Dan listen to me, who is in charge here, who is the senior among you?. I'd know that voice and stance anywhere, I'm your old No.2., No.1. and glad to see you. Wonderful to know you are still alive old friend, but no time for pleasantries now, we must get moving. We have transport outside, and I want stretcher cases, walking wounded and any non military personnel first followed by the more able bodied. Anyone hoping to join in any fighting forget it, my men all have set roles, and you would only get in the way. Fear not your time will come!

At this the old No.2. called, do as he says men he knows what he is doing. Dan's men were already taking out the worst cases and accessing the others. In this way the wounded were loaded within minutes, and the fitter elements lined up for loading. Dan was delighted to see the two businessmen among them, and hoped they were the husbands of Terry2's helpers. The trucks were ready to move off and a signal flare let off to let the other teams know they were about to set off on their return journey. The group attacking the main food distribution centre signalled they were also about to leave. No.1's group attacking the "Henchmen's" store sent up a distress flare indicating they were under pressure from a large defending force. Without waiting for orders the "reserves" returned to their

111

vehicles and set off to assist, Dan joining them at the last moment. On arrival they found No.1's. force surrounded by a much larger defence than had been anticipated.

No.1's Gladiators had formed a "Roman" fighting square, and were fighting a tremendous battle against a much larger force. True No.1.'s force were by far the more efficient and better trained outfit, dealing severe punishment to their opponents. There was still the danger they may be overwhelmed by force of numbers. Gauging the situation the leader of the reserves ordered his men to form a fighting wedge and promptly attacked where the enemy were most numerous. Totally unused to this style of combat the Asian defence soon started to crumble. Those who did not run away threw down their arms in surrender.

Dan, who had remained clear of the action, was about to join No.1. when a voice behind him said " So No.1. of 100 I thought I might find you here". Dan recognised the voice as belonging to L54 the Li Pinoe Gladiator who had told Dan about the food depots. He stood perfectly still as L54 said I told you if I met you on a battlefield I would kill you, and here you are. No! said Dan you said you would TRY! to kill me. As he spoke the last word Dan spun on his heel and kicked his assailant on his knee knocking him to the ground. Kicking his opponents sword out of reach, Dan turned him over and fastened his wrists behind his back. Two of Dan's men picked L54 up and put him with the other prisoners in a personnel carrier.

I can see we will all have to learn this kick fighting, said a smiling No.1. when he joined Dan a few moments later. You could do worse said Dan, the little I know was taught to me by a sweet 20 year old girl. She only weighed 10/11 stone yet I saw her lay out a 13 stone thug with one kick. I was happy to learn as much as I could, and regret I didn't have time to learn more. Enough reminiscing, are you ready to move? What are the holdups? Many of the guards have run away that we have spare capacity in the trucks. I have the men loading a much food as possible before we destroy the building. Quite right said Dan all the prisoners we have taken will need feeding. Well done No.1.

The extra loading was soon completed and they lost no time in setting out on the journey back to base. On the boarder of the town they met up with one of the reserve who had waited to be sure all was well. Dan was happy to have the extra men available, some of No.1's. squad were injured and the remainder tired from the battle.

On the route back to camp they passed within a mile or so of the Asian forward post, now by Dan's squad from his own forward base. As arranged in Terry2's plan No.1. sent up a flare to let Dan's men know they could return to their forward base. To their dismay the response was a flare asking for assistance. "Now what" Dan wondered, while losing no time in ordering the reserve squad to hurry to the forward point to assess the situation. Lose no time, but make your final approach with caution. If our men have been overrun I don't want to lose you as well!! No.1. and I will follow with the most able bodied of his squad, as soon as we can.

It took slightly longer than Dan had hoped before he and No.1. were able to follow the reserve squad as promised. Dan spent the time in a turmoil of anxiety, wondering what the problem could be. Hoping most of all that he was not about to lose his first man. When he arrived an astonishing sight met his sight, hundreds of Li Pinoe's were sat in orderly rows in front of the outpost building. The seated men were guarded by the men from Dans forward out post, now assisted by the reserve squad. The commander of the outpost saluted Dan and No.1. and apologised for the distress signal. We are not in any immediate danger, but I don't know what to do with them all.

Quite right, said Dan, giving No.1. a questioning look and receiving a shake of the head. Dan thought for a few moments and then began issuing orders. No.1. send your fastest vehicle to catch the last convoy. they are take the trucks loaded with food to our forward base. While at the base I want them to use that damn phone line. Use my authority and get a large mobile kitchen delivered to the base tonight. In addition all available personnel carriers are to be sent to the base A.S.A.P. each with a driver and guard. Tell H.Q. I will want to speak to my A.D.C. early tomorrow morning, and the camp to be on full alert. Have you got all that No.1.? yes sir, my No.2 is with the convoy, and I will send him. Once you're done join me, I will be talking to our prisoners.

No.1. returned in time to hear Dan tell the prisoners, "you all came here to escape the war, having no doubt realised that for you it is a lost cause and the worst thing that could happen to the world is Li Pinoe winning." Fair enough; my men and I will do our best for you. All we ask is your full cooperation while we organise the best future for you we can. To start with we are taking you on a ten mile march for the first part of your journey. A chorus of groans met this, causing Dan to tell them," There will be food available on arrival, but any of you may stay here if you wish, good luck when Li Pinoe's henchmen find you".

There was no further dissention, so Dan ordered No.1. to get them up and moving. Keep to small groups with as many guards as possible to each group. Any sign of violent protest to be jumped on from a great height. They reached the forward post without incident, the prisoners being astonished to see the two truck loads of food waiting for them. The timely arrival of the large field kitchen together with engineers and cooks, convinced the prisoners they had made the right decision. The engineers began assembling the kitchen while the cooks checked the food supplies. The head cook, known to Dan's amusement as Chef 4., assured Dan " kitchen in 15 minutes, food in 45minutes". Thankyou Chef said Dan, please feed half my men first and keep some hot food ready for the other half after the prisoners have eaten.

Dan now found time to phone Terry2 at H.Q.. Having thanked him for the kitchen and its staff, he asked for an update on the personnel carriers. They will be with you shortly after dawn tomorrow, I have asked them not to use their camouflage, the less the enemy learn about our equipment the better. Well done Terry said Dan I hadn't thought of that! Now!! we have got between three and four hundred prisoners here and they will need housing. Get wooden huts erected for them and arrange for them to be fed. Have my old No.2. come and see me no more than an hour after I get back. Anything else you think I should know? Only good news said Terry, the two civilian gentlemen you rescued are my two ladies' husbands. All four are now members of your fan club, and sing your praises to all who will listen. Good!! said Dan, introduce them to the Leader, he is getting a little disillusioned with me. The memos he has left for you tell a different story Terry assured him. Good said Dan, see you tomorrow, and hung up.

Arriving back at camp the next day Dan took short time to shower and grab a bite to eat, before rushing to his office calling out for Terry as he walked through his door. "Hello", thought Terry, are we off for another turn on the merry go round. Terry! There you are, have you arranged for my old No.2. to see me? Yes, Boss he's waiting in my office now, I rather think he wants to see you as much as you want to see him. O.K. said Dan wheel him in and we will see. No.2 hurried in, and the two men embraced with mutual good to see you's, and are you well's. Great said Dan, now what do want to see me about. When I was captured it was partly because I was watching the behaviour of one of our younger Gladiators, No.2 explained, he was skulking round the battlefield killing wounded enemy fighters and robbing the bodies.

I don't know his number, only that he was stockily built and a surly expression. To make matters worse when I was attacked I called to him for assistance and he ran away. The two of us stood a chance against my attackers, and I want to find him. Dan and Terry looked at each other and said in unison, No.8.. Dan went on to explain his dealings with No.8., and asked No.2 to postpone any planned revenge until he had heard Dan's plans for him. Fear not old friend he's not going anywhere in the near future.

I want you for a job I'm not sure you will like but I believe you will be good at. In a few days I hope to attack the main enemy base in LI/4156, which will take all the top line troops I've got. Which leaves me with the problem of all the prisoners we have taken, thats where, I hope, you come in. I would like you to select the best fifty or so of the men who were incarcerated with you and form them into camp guards. I know you will say you are a fighting man and belong on the front line, I more than most know how true that is. Unfortunately after months of life in prison you are not fit or well enough to join my front line. As chief prison guard you will have plenty to keep you occupied, while allowing you time to work on your fitness. I will leave the S.T.O. with you and he will coach you in our new methods. Please tell me you will take it on. With your promise that I will be given my chance to fight as soon as I'm fully fit and trained. While it remains in my power to decide, you have my promise. With that the two old friends shook hands, and the deal was done.

Terry2 here will give you your orders and some idea of how I like things done, said Dan. Basically I want all prisoners to be treated as well as possible, any we can convert to our cause will be a bonus. Any bad behaviour or sign of violence to be jumped on. You will be the Boss, and they will need to know it. Good Luck.

Dan called in No.1. who had been waiting outside, and told him of his plan to attack the LI/ 4156 camp as soon as possible. We have them on the run lets keep it that way!! I think a dozen good men disguised as road menders or something, can take and open the main gate a few seconds before our main force comes down the road at high speed. We can be in the middle of the camp before they know it. I am expecting very little resistance, they are hungry and demoralised, ours, for the taking.

Get together with Terry and finalise the plans, as usual, as soon as possible. In the interim get your team to take the fastest transport available, and see if they can capture a couple of food delivery trucks, before they reach LI's men. I don't want any risk taken, but it would be nice to keep them hungry.

Left on his own, Dan was about to go for a run, feeling he was neglecting his fitness, when he was surprised by a light knocking on his door. He was delighted to find Dancer1 at the door, and more so when she greeted him with a kiss. Hello Dan, she said, I was hoping you would buy me lunch. Happy to, his prompt reply. Pausing only to tell Terry he was off to H.Q. Dan took Dancer's arm, And hurried off smiling. Terry watched them go, thinking H.Q. may be where they are going, but I'll bet its the Exec's restaurant they end up in. One of those jobs he does not get me to do!!

The A.D.C. was quite right Dan and Dancer were heading for the Exec. restaurant, where they were to spend a leisurely meal in animated conversation. Dan felt their friendship had become closer, and was delighted when Dancer invited him to her caravan for a meal. Home cooked by my own fair hand, she promised, and if you're good dancing to follow. I think I can fit you into my busy schedule, said Dan, and received a playful slap for his cheek.

Dan returned to be greeted with more good news, the squad sent to look for food convoys on route to the Asian camp had returned with four fully laden trucks, and 30 prisoners. The squad leader was laughingly explaining how the prisoners had offered no resistance, surrendering their arms without being asked. Their only question "what are you going to do with the food". When told "feed our prisoners" they said good for we are your prisoners. No.1. expressed his opinion, send plenty of food when you attack their camp and they will surrender on mass. O.K. said Dan go and see if your new prisoners know when the next convoy is due, and send a large force to collect it. The Leader will not be happy feeding this lot for long. Oh! and while your at it try to find out where these convoys start out, we might be able to do some wholesale pinching.

Now No.1., Terry, how are the plans for the attack on their barracks going? Quite well, said Terry the basic premise of drive in and take over remains favourite. With the help of one of your boxing team we have managed to find your three friends from Ll/4156. They are proving very helpful with details of the camp layout. Good said Dan, I hope their information can be relied on. Have no fear, No.1. assured him your old friend No.2.has the prisoners in the palm of his hand. I think it is called the iron fist in a velvet glove. Great, laughed Dan I knew he could do it.

As soon as your food hunters get back and rested, take off with every man you have got, and knock them dead. I'm sure I don't need to tell you that each of your teams will need a specific target. One other thought if you find any food double guard it, we don't want any looting. I'm off to see the prison superintendent, I hadn't thought of prisoner interrogation as a source of intelligence and want to hear his views.

Dan's old friend was pleased to see him, and enthusiastic about all aspects of his new role. We have started records of all prisoners, all the time asking for more details than we would want our troops to divulge. I have a team of men going through the extra information looking for anything that might be useful. We already have the location of the nearest enemy camps, beyond LI4156. Dan expressed his delight in this development, and pressed his friend to keep him updated on all he learnt.

Pleased that everything was going so well, Dan was finally able to set off on his exercise run. As always he used the run to clear his mind, and try to plan for the future. The news from the prison camp that he could at last hope for a steady supply of intelligence about the enemy infrastructure, was a great relieve. Would it, he wondered, be feasible to send squads out to capture prisoners from the next two Asian camps. If so, he could hand them over to his old No.2. and see what could be learned. He found, as he tired, it harder to concentrate and his thoughts drifted to Dancer's invitation, and what was behind it, if anything. One thing for sure he didn't want to miss it.

When he arrived back at the office, he found Dancer had left him a note asking him if he could make it for the meal that night. Sorry for the short notice but my other plans have changed. Rather cryptic thought Dan I wonder what these other plans are!! A second note arrived at that point, asking Dan to see The Leader As soon as convenient. The note suggested Dan use the carrier bringing the note as transport, saving time. I guess that means now is convenient thought Dan. Pausing only to ask Terry to contact Dancer and tell her "Yes". Just "yes" asked Terry. "Yes" said Dan, and left in a hurry.

Dan was ushered straight into The Leader's office, and invited to sit. Thank you for coming so promptly said The Leader. Now No.1. or should I say "Boss"? Dan nodded and smiled but didn't speak. You know the council and I have been very pleased with the way things have been going, the capturing of food supplies has been a master stroke. Almost bought a smile to the money men's faces. I know to you it was a military expedient, but we all fight this war on different fronts. Now we are hearing that LI. Pinoe is in financial difficulty and we need to keep the pressure on him. How are your plans for the attack on LI4156 camp? Progressing very well, said Dan, I have my food gathering team out on one last sortie, as soon as they return and are rested we will be on our way. We have been greatly helped by the prison guards, led you may remember by my old No.2., who have been interrogating Prisoners and have provided us with comprehensive plans of the layout.

Excellent; on behalf of the council and myself thankyou, and good luck. Friendly councils throughout the world are becoming very interested in all your doing, and planning ways in which to put more pressure on LI. Pinoe. Your "Roman" fighting methods seem to be of particular interest, but more of that later. You have become something of a figurehead in this war, something like your Winston Churchill I expect. Extra pressure for you I'm afraid, be sure no harm comes to you. I know you like to lead your men, but do it from the rear, if you see what I mean. I will not plan to take any part in actual fighting, should it arise that any of my men are in trouble and I can help then I shall not hesitate. Once a Gladiator, always a Gladiator. At that Dan took his leave and hurried back to camp.

Showered, shaved and spruced, he duly presented himself at Dancer's home, to be greeted by two of Dancer's girls who explained they were hostesses while Dancer was tied up in the kitchen. They proved to have a funny line of banter and kept Dan amused until Dancer called them into the kitchen. Dancer joined Dan and they sat at a beautifully laid table. The girls, now waitresses, came with the first course of what was to prove one of the finest meals Dan had ever eaten. The girls while proving to be efficient waitresses, continued to entertain pretending to be confused between Dan sir, and Dancer. Once the meal was finished and the table cleared the girls said their goodbyes and Dan and Dancer were alone.

Dancer produced suitable music and came into Dan's arms to dance, the music was continuous, and included many tunes from the 20th. century. They danced with great enjoyment for a long time, with hardly a word spoken. Dancer seemed very pensive and Dan began to wonder if something was troubling her. When the music stopped Dan led her to a seat and asked if anything was wrong. Wrong no!, badly timed maybe, I have long wanted to give up my nomadic life, and take up dance teaching. I have been offered a chance of teacher training in Italy, if successful leading to a place at a school in Paris. It sounds wonderful said Dan, although I will miss you, probably more than one would think. There is my problem said Dancer, I am being offered the life I have always wanted, but it means saying goodbye to you just as we are getting to know each other. You must take this chance, said Dan, or you will spend you life wondering, and possibly grow bitter over what could have been.

Anyway never say goodbye, I don't know where this war is going to take me, but I do know I won't be in this area much longer. We are about to be separated anyway, lets use it to our advantage, you go for your dream life with my love and blessing, and I will try to end this war as soon as possible. Believe me I have become more than fond of you in the short time I have known you and I will be looking to find you as soon as

I am free. Thank you Dan, for being so understanding I was hoping you would find an answer, and much as I would like to take you everywhere with me I think you are right.

Content they had made the best decision they could, they spent the rest of the evening in warm companionship. Dancer persuading Dan to talk about his time in the 20th. century. Amazed at all he had achieved, and sympathetic over his parting from Louise. She felt it all pointed to him being more than just a Gladiator. I have often thought about that said Dan and why that should be. Even now among my men are some very special people, No.1. and Terry my A.D.C. are far more than just fighters. Even my old No.2 has taken to his new role as prison superintendent, and expanded it to include intelligence gathering. When this war is over the council could find themselves with problems. I think I understand said Dancer, I am a case in point, I am about to break a tradition of centuries in my family, I just want more than to be a song and dance girl for the next fifty to a hundred years. They talked and planned in this vein, until the night was gone and dawn sent them on their separate ways.

Dan returned to find the food hunting team fully rested and everyone ready to move on camp LI4156. Right said Dan time our departure to arrive an hour after daylight to give the gate openers time to be in position. Your No.2 has provided tatty enemy uniforms for the squad to wear, and a slightly better one for himself. He has learned that a working party would have a wounded "veteran" in charge and has volunteered himself for the part. Cheeky bugger said Dan, but I can't think of anyone better for the job. Tomorrow we go.

Having had an early night Dan was about in the early hours to see No.2. and his small band on their way. The rest of the troops began to form up, a count of all sections showing no absentees. Having allowed time for the gates to have been opened, they set off on the first major campaign of Dan's war. Thanks to the prison

superintendent supplying Dan's men with details of the camp lay out each squad had a specified target, and would head there without delay. With this in mind each truck left in a predetermined order, those pressing deepest into LI4156 going first.

Ahead of the main force No.2. and his "roadmenders" had arrived at the main gate and were unloading their tools. Picks, sledgehammers and crowbars seemed the more popular choice. Unknown to the guards on the gate the heads of the picks and sledgehammers were all loose and easily detached. No.2. sauntered over to the gate and began to question the guards about life on LI4156. No food was the main complaint, I'd sell my soul for a full belly. We have plenty, said No.2., bring your lads over to our van and we will sort you out. They all came eagerly and were soon tucking in. While they ate the workmen formed a ring around them preventing them from returning to the gate.

No.2. was wondering about his timing when he heard a klaxon sound twice, the signal that the troop convoy was imminent. His men dropped the heads from their tools and using the handles as weapons persuaded the guards to get in the back of the truck. This done they threw open the gates just as the first of the convoy sped down the road and rushed through. The last truck stopped at the gate and with No.2's squad set up a blockade to prevent anyone escaping.

Dan his A.D.C. and No.1. were in a separate vehicle parked in the centre of the camp, allowing a few minutes for their men to take control before heading to the headquarters building to try to rescue any documents of interest. They were speeding to the H.Q. when an alarm flare went up from that area. As they arrived a small squad of reserves arrived from the opposite direction. The platoon allocated the task of capturing the enemy H.Q. were seen to be in severe difficulties, being faced with a force three times their number. The platoon square had done sterling work until one man stumbled and fell causing the square to loose its shape and allowing the enemy to gain advantage. Dan immediately called Terry and No.1. to him, saying, Terry pick all the spare men you can, form a wedge and attack from the back of the crush. Join the square as quickly as possible, make plenty of noise to attract everyone's attention. No.1. and I will form another wedge with some of the reserves and attack where the enemy are thickest. Terry left instantly, calling to all spare men to join him. Right!!, No.1. said Dan, lets you and me lead this wedge and show this rabble what two No.1s. of 100 can do.

With the well-trained reserves forming a tight wedge behind them the two top Gladiators drove into the densest part of crowd and began to drive forward. Dan soon found his old form and began to enjoy himself. With his length of reach, dominating presence, and the sheer weight of his blows, the opposition began to crumble with men trying to get away blocking the attempts of the more willing. At his side No.1. with his great speed, perfect balance and accurate striking was being equally devastating. The Gladiators forming the rest of the wedge were maintaining a tight formation, and clearing up many of the enemy fighters fleeing the two No.1s.

Terry and his reserves had now reached the main square, and with the gaps filled the square was again a force to be reckoned with. The opposition began to melt away. Dan was now able to order Terry and his team into the H.Q. building to try to find the records office and secure it. The wedge led by Dan and No.1. Continued to mop up any resistance, while those trying to flee were being hemmed in by Dan's Gladiators arriving from other areas they had secured.

The headquarters area proved to be the last to show resistance and Dan was able to receive his lieutenant's reports giving the overall situation. The last two to arrive both seemed particularly excited, keenly striving to catch Dan's attention. Dan called one of them over asking him what had he discovered. My squad were given the area used by the "Henchmen", which includes a large storage building, heavily guarded until we arrived. On inspection we found it was full of good quality food, presumedly reserved for the "Henchmen" as the rest of the camp are complaining of hunger. We have mounted a guard of our own, and would like some catering personnel to do a proper assessment. Good work said Dan, make sure the hungry element don't get too close, and I will get Caterer 1. to you as soon as possible.

Calling the second man Dan asked him if he too had good news. If I am right sir! very good, I think we have found the apparatus jamming all our communications, it is huge and has its own power source. How sure are you? Dan started to ask but stopped himself, saying of course your are sure or you wouldn't be here. You have probably made the find that makes this whole campaign worth while. Go back and double your guard, nobody to have access without my written authority. Great work thank you.

Dan summoned his A.D.C. and called for one of the small but very fast troop carriers together with driver. Terry sent his driver and one of your best men without delay to the forward outpost. Tell your man to ring H.Q. I want Top Chef 1. as soon as possible. More importantly message to Top Tech 2. I need his top communication experts without delay, Top priority. While he is at it he can mention that camp LI4156 is in our hands. Dan could only imagine the importance of finding the communication blocking equipment, the propaganda opportunities were enough to put his mind in a whirl.

Fortunately, the immediate demands on his time and energy left him no freedom to ponder the many chances to take advantage of the find. First to report to him was his superintendent of prisoners, making Dan smile with his opening words, "Boss there's hundreds of them". For the time being I've got them under guard in their billets, but its not very secure and I could use a lot more men to strengthen the guard. Well done No.2., Find No.1. and tell him you have spoken to me and ask him for all the men you need. We can't have hundreds of them running amok can we. I hope to start a tour of the camp shortly and will be looking for ways to improve security.

Dan started his tour and was pleased to find all his men under close discipline, and all he spoke to completely understanding their orders. Two 20th. century world wars had taught him the best soldier is only as good as his orders. He soon arrived at billets, where the prisoners were kept. Approaching one hut he could hear a voice raised in apparent anger, and found the guards on the door to be paying full attention to the fracas inside. What's the trouble here?, he asked one of the guards. Nothing much sir, he replied just the supervisor laying down the law, and letting them know who is boss.

Dan was about to enter and join in with the fun when his A.D.C. hurried towards him with his assistant newly returned from the forward outpost. Did you manage to make contact, Dan asked, yes sir, the Top Chef 1. should already be on the way, and Top Tech 2.s team anticipate leaving within the hour. They are all excited by the news. Terry 2. interrupted to tell Dan that the Leader required his presence at H.Q. without delay. What now said Dan, cursing softly to himself, with a bit of luck perhaps he is going to sack me. If he does he had better sack us all, came the unanimous reply.

Before setting out for H.Q. Dan took time out to brief No.1. and the A.D.C. with his ideas of how it might be best for them to proceed, Terry2 please continue to go through their H.Q. records I have a feeling that LI Pinoe may be short of money, and this may be the time to keep the pressure on him, see what you can find. No.1. get the prisoner interrogation going again, check on the chains of supply and hit them hard. If you send a large platoon to their docks and take them over we may be able to cripple them. I don't think their "front line" troops seem too keen as it is! Anything you can do to harass them can only be good. I hope to rejoin you very soon but I have a bad feeling about this summons, its not like the Leader to recall me this soon. One last thing, up to now we have suffered no fatalities, lets keep it that way.

DAN STONE AMBASSADOR

As Dan had feared the leader's plans were to end his involvement in the front line of the war. An unhappy man he pleaded to be able to stay with his troops, stating his belief that a strong push now an early victory could be won. The Leader and Council were sympathetic but adamant in their resolve. To Dan's horror they wanted him to tour the friendly nations to explain his methods, and help train troops intending to join him. The more his mission was explained to him the more he thought he wouldn't be doing much troop training. His first duty was to visit the U.K. now known as area EU 1250., where he was to address The Houses of Parliament, "the stubborn British still sticking to their traditional title", for the council of representatives.

That should be fun thought Dan, a Gladiator come builder, making speeches in the "Houses of Parliament", and none of Terry 2's ladies to correct my grammar. I'm afraid, I am who I am, and they must take me as they find me, bad grammar or not.

He received a very warm welcome on his arrival in the U.K. and was surprised by the extensive coverage he was given in the press. His biggest surprise seeing himself on television, he had no idea there was so much archive film about him, most of which he didn't know had been taken. At first Dan was dismayed by his apparent notoriety, but realised it was often an advantage that everyone knew who he was. He was cheered by the thought that when he came to speak in parliament there would be no-one wondering who he was.

On arrival at Parliament he was shown into the upper chamber, which was packed with representatives of all political parties. Following a warm and flattering introduction, it was time for Dan to speak.

Having been warned that unlike the 20Th. century the were no Lords, he began "ladies and gentlemen", thank you for giving me the opportunity to speak to you today, and for giving your time to come and hear me. Let me be the one who says it " I am no speaker". A former No.1. of 100 Gladiator, and a fairly successful builder, but no speaker. I am here to explain my method of warfare, its easy, get yourself an A,D.C. who is a student of Roman warfare, and modify and copy some of their tried and tested methods. Then get a No.1. who is keen on discipline and training, add some experienced Gladiators who are far better at everything military than you have a right to expect. All you then need is reliable intelligence about your enemy, and away you go.

None of our achievements would have been possible without the uncomplaining support of the Leader and the War Council. Even Ll Pinoe has not dared to ignore the long standing international ban on firearms and explosives. which meant the "War" has been fought by Gladiators on our part and Gladiators, Mercenaries and conscripted "volunteers" on their part. Ladies and Gentlemen, we were losing!! Not because of any lack of endeavour or skill on the part of our men, but through sheer weight of numbers. For every one of their number killed, wounded or captured two or three would be pushed forward to take their place. When one of our men was taken out of the battle there were no reserves to replace him. In spite of inflicting far greater losses on them than they caused us, we were being swamped by weight of numbers.

In the two World wars I fought in in the 20Th. century, men fought as part of a unit and not as individuals. My task was to change the mind set of men who had been trained from an early age to fight only for and by themselves, to think, work and fight as a team. I started by introducing standard army drill, where all must work as part of a squad, platoon or regiment. In this I was greatly helped in this by the current No.1. who was keen to reintroduce discipline within the Gladiators. The ideas for Roman style fighting squares and later attacking "wedges" came from a low ranked Gladiator, a student of all things Roman. I was happy to promote him to be my A.D.C., a position he has filled quite brilliantly to the present day. All the success we have so far achieved is largely due to these two men and the teams they have gathered around them.

I have already mentioned the great help afforded me by the Leader and War Council, creating an army from scratch does not come cheap but at no time have I been refused any request for equipment or outside help. Believe me my demands (requests) have been many and extensive. My believe is LI Pinoe will soon be defeated, and one reason will be because he is running out of money. The majority of prisoners we have taken have been close to starvation, and not only because our "guerrilla teams" have captured a lot of their provisions in transit. The average soldier in the Asian army is poorly dressed, hungry, badly trained and disillusioned. From what we have learned from many of our prisoners the civilian population is also unhappy with shortages of necessity's and ever rising prices.

You, I am sure understand the ramifications of these matters far better than I do, I only ask that you give them you earnest consideration. May I close Ladies and Gentlemen with a plea that you keep the faith, and continue to contribute to the "War Fund". You are getting good value for your money. Thank you!!

To Dan's relieve his address was warmly received, and many of the members present promised to pressure the ruling council to keep on with the contributions.

His address to the U.K. Parliament was to form the basis of his address to many councils, saving him the torture of trying to write a new speech for each occasion.

His first stop after London was Paris here he spoke only to the French Leader and his Inner Council. Made possible by electronic instant translation. Dan's speech was received in complete silence, but with many nodding heads, giving him hope it was well received. The question and answer session that followed was more intense than in London, but at least everyone seemed satisfied with his answers. His plea for continued support for the War Council drew a positive response from all present, and a promise of continued financial support.

There was no suggestion that Dan should assist with troop training, and he determined to take a couple of days leave to try and track down Dancer. Asking for help to get started on his quest he was handed a trade journal listing all the dance studios in Paris. His gratitude soon turned to dismay when he realised there were hundreds of them spread all over the city. His first thought was to try all the studios claiming "International" status, a nonstarter as over 50 were listed. There were a few listed as French Italian origin, and he decided to start with these.

He was wondering how best to proceed, when a council member offered him the use of his car and chauffeur for the day. Waving away Dan's thanks, he called up his car which arrived within a few minutes. The driver was a highly sophisticated Android, which when learning of Dan's mission asked to see the list of venues. Having taken a few seconds only explained he had memorised them and rearranged the order making it unnecessary to "back track" between venues. Our route will take us close to many of the sights of special interest should you wish to see them, explained the chauffeur. Thank you said Dan only if it is not more than 5 minutes out of our way.

Dan did not meet Dancer, and found he was more disappointed than he expected to be, not having realised how he longed to be with her. He had discovered the studio "in fact a college" at which she taught, only to find Dancer was back in Italy for an examination, with a view to promotion. Everyone spoke very highly of her as a dancer and a person. I'm thrilled for her thought Dan, but it probably puts an end to my dreams of our being together.

No consolation now, but at least I saw some of the great sights of Paris he thought. The Louvre had impressed with its air of gravitas and constancy. The Elysee Palace by its sheer beauty and grandeur. Both buildings looking as they had looked for hundreds of years, though hardly any of the original buildings remained. The greatest spectacle of all was the mighty full sized "Hologram" of the Eiffel Tower. The tower had been pulled down many, many, years before as unsafe. To Dans mind the "Hologram" was a far greater spectacle.

Dan travelled on through several European countries, finding his by this time well-rehearsed speech, was well received. He was especially gratified that all he spoke to promised to increase or maintain their contribution to the "War Fund". He found himself becoming increasingly curious about the electrical equipment found at camp LI 4156, which he and his men had believed to be connected with Li Pinoe's blocking world wide communications. Surely if they had been right something should have happened to reopen at least some lines of communication. Not too much time to ponder the question however, as Dan was booked on the afternoon rocket to Australia. A flight he had taken many times in his life as an international Gladiator, Europe to Australia in under three hours, to Dan a miracle. The rocket fired aircraft blasted into near space, (wherever that might be), levelled out, boosted to Mach 5. The engines cut, Delta Wings run out from the fuselage, allowing the aircraft to glide to its destination without further use of power. A standard aircraft engine being used for re-entry, taxiing, ETC..

Dan was settled easily in his seat, enjoying a short time of idleness when the captain of the aircraft, asked for the passengers attention as he had received some exciting news.

Following the recent capture of camp LI4156 by the European Council Army, technical staff have been able to break the Asian blockage of world wide communication. Upon your return to land you will find all your personal communication fully restored. I'm sure you will all give a moment to offer thanks to the brave men who achieved the victory at camp LI4156 that made this possible. Thank you!

As soon as the Captain had finished speaking loud cheering broke out, and general rejoicing at this wonderful news. To Dan's horror the chief steward approached him to ask for permission to announce his presence on board. Please do not say a word to anyone begged Dan, believe me I only gave the order for better men than me to do the fighting. I am no hero. To his relieve the steward gave a knowing smile, said, as you wish sir, and left him in peace.

On reporting to immigration Dan was met by an Embassy official who rushed him to meet the Ambassador. The Ambassador, a French man, who looked to Dan's eyes exactly as he should for that role, greeted him warmly and put him at ease. I have some messages to pass to you from the "War Council Leader" which I will acquaint you with shortly. First I must indulge myself by telling you how pleased i am to meet you. I have been a lifelong fan of all things appertaining to Gladiators and their battles. It was therefore inevitable I should be your greatest fan during the halcyon days when you were No.1. of 100. In the opinion of many including myself you were, and probably are still the greatest of them all. May I shake your hand; of course I am also aware of your achievements as the "General" of the European Army, and again congratulate you. Be assured myself and my team will be happy to assist you in any way we are able. Now!, I have taken enough of your time, if you would care to follow my P.A. he will hand over to you the correspondence we have received on your behalf.

Thanking the Ambassador, Dan followed the P.A., and was soon studying a number of messages from the War Leader and his staff. It seemed events were moving apace, and it was difficult for any-one to predict imminent events. Since the discovery at camp LI4156 and the un-blocking of international communications, Europe had been bombarding Asia with the truth about the conflict between them. The European trade embargos, raging inflation, and unfair rationing had reduced their stand-ard of living to an all time low. LI Pinoe's propaganda had assured them that huge sums were being poured into the army, and that victory would soon be theirs. Now they were learning for the first time of the poor equip-ment, clothing and food being supplied to the troops. Lack of payment to the troops and their families, also caused hardship.

Many Asian troops were reported to have laid down their arms and refused to take any further part in the fighting. On hearing this No.1. had immediately set out for the next two camps to discuss surrender terms. Although not met with "open arms" he had not been totally rebuffed, and talks were ongoing. With the rapidly changing situation the War Council were unsure where best to deploy Dan in the immediate future and suggested he fulfil his commitments in Australia, while awaiting further instructions.

Dan was unable to use his much practised speech before the Australian Council as they preferred a less formal question and answer session. He was relieved to find he was able to to answer all their questions, and managed to get in a plug about financial aid for the "War Council". The questions took on a more personal tone later, when he was first reminded the he had said in a radio interview that he had done very little fighting, preferring to leave it to his troops. What fighting did you actually do?, the question coming from a smiling young man wearing a smart uniform showing he was a member of the newly formed Australian army.

You have rather put me on the spot, as the only real fighting I did was contrary to the "War Council Leaders" wishes. He was anxious I did not get injured as I was booked to come on this tour. Things don't always go to plan however, and I found myself getting involved when one of my fighting squares got into difficulties. The square had come under attack from a large number of LI Pinoe's henchmen, when one of the square stumbled end fell breaking the squares shape and lowering its efficiency. Luckly they were able to fire off a distress flare, and we were soon on the scene. We were very quickly able to form an attacking wedge, with myself and the European No.1. at the sharp end. We were able to quickly clear a way to the troubled square and reinforce it. My advice would be to always have your No.1. next to you if you're on the sharp end of a wedge. Assuming of course that your No.1. is as good as mine!! This last remark bringing hoots of derision from his partisan audience, and the meeting to a close.

In the next few days was able to watch his Australian counterparts in training, being very impressed with their high standard. On his last day with them he was coerced into fronting a wedge, during a mock battle. The local No.1. insisting on fighting alongside him "saying he realised Dan needed all the help he could get". Too true Cobber said Dan, smiling broadly, as he took his place. It soon became clear who was the main target in the battle, and Dan found himself under maximum pressure. As usual he soon loosened up and was able to increase his speed, which with his height and reach made him a formidable opponent. The defending

Gladiators had their vulnerable areas marked in red and were instructed to withdraw once struck in any of these areas. Most were happy to comply with this rule as the blows could be very painful.

Dan's fighting stick was soon coated in red die as his years at the top of the list of Gladiators showed him to be a different class to his opponents. With the wedge still a few feet from its target the local No.1. was hit on a marked area and had to fallout. Dan was pleased to note the change over was carried out very smoothly, and the attackers were given no chance to take advantage. He began to feel even he was beginning to tire a little and decided to drive harder to the finish. Calling to the wedge to close up and stay with him he began to drive for the finish line. Having struck an opponent on the wrist he grabbed his fighting stick. With the extra weapon he was able to launch a two handed attack, at the same time, gambling all his reserves, he increased his speed, and charged for the line.

For a short time it seemed he had gambled too much and would fail, luckily a gap opened in front of him. His latest victim was slow leaving the fight, delaying his replacement. Seeing his chance Dan burst through the gap and drove across the line. As he attempted to recover his breath he was surprised when the Australian Gladiators surrounded and applauded him. He silenced them and thanked them for their courtesy, although he didn't know what he had done to deserve it. The S.T.O. explained, at first count you took out 28 of your opponents, doubling our previous best score. I have been a Senior Training Officer for many years and never thought to see a performance of that speed and accuracy of strike. I have been a Gladiator for many years, said Dan, and never thought to be as near to collapse at the end of an exercise. I hope no-one was hurt, in particular your No.1. who carried me most of the way.

Having been assured there were no serious injuries, Dan made his excuses and headed for a long hot soak, promising to join them for a "couple of beers" later. His main preoccupation was to try to contact Dancer, unfortunately there such a huge backlog of calls on all lines of communication, he was unsuccessful. He hoped Dancer was trying to contact him, and would know of the difficulties.

The evening with the "Aussie" Gladiators passed uproariously with Dan trying not to drink all the beers bought for him. The next day he phoned the Ambassador, thinking he had better not let the embassy staff see him "worse for wear". Luckily although there was a communication from the War Council, the Ambassador was unavailable and asked Dan to make an appointment for the following day. The instructions he received were to return to H.Q. as events had progressed faster than they had dared to hope and an important bulletin would be broadcast very shortly. Dan was puzzled why his presence should be required, but hastened to obey and was on the next available flight.

On arrival at his H.Q. he was immediately summoned to a meeting of the War Council. The council had received an approach from LI Pinoe, suggesting a suspension of hostilities and possible unification of the two armies. The communication was couched in very arrogant terms stating the unification of armies was in Europe's best interest. Li Pinoe protested at the treatment of the prisoners held by Europe, demanding they should be rearmed and reclothed before being repatriated to join his army immediately. The impromptu comments from around the chamber left Dan in no doubt of the Councils opinion of these demands.

When asked for his thoughts Dan was in no doubt it was the bluster of a beaten man. May I ask what success No.1. has had with his localised negotiations. The ordinary Gladiator/Soldier is for the war to end and has no interest in further fighting. The camp commander and his staff are all LI Pinoe henchmen and veto all suggestions. Since the men cannot get home without assistance from their Government their hands are tied. That is much as I feared said Dan, but leads in to some of my ideas.

From what we have learned it is fairly certain we can bypass these camps without too much fear of exposing our rear. May I suggest therefore that we send a number of guerrilla bands to LI Pinoe's nearest city stronghold. They should then put a stranglehold on the city's roads stopping all supplies entering or leaving the city. From what the Superintendent of prisoners has learned in the course of his routine interrogations, the people in these cities are already short of everything. I believe we may ignite civil unrest if not anarchy. I suggest you get No.1. and my A.D.C. back to do the planning they are far better at it than me, and I hope, with your permission to take the rest of our army to take the city if necessary. I know of no reason why we couldn't take over the city without any real resistance. If in the mean time you were to flood the area with leaflets giving the true state of LI Pinoe's army, and his empires near bankrupt economy. I feel sure we could bring him down quickly. If you were to also give details of the major fortune he has salted away, his people would possibly do the job for us.

Thank you, said the leader as usual you have given us far more to think of than we bargained for. We will let you know our decision without delay. Dan left with the applause of the council members ringing in his ears. Left to his own devices Dan returned to his efforts to contact Dancer, at first he had no success until after a number of tries he finally got through to the collage of dancing where he believed Dancer taught. After a couple of minutes an answering robot cut in telling him to leave a message. Dan continued to try over the next two days, always with the same frustrating result.

All too soon Dan found himself before the war council to learn their decision. In essence they approved his ideas for the next phase of the war, but were anxious to ensure no civilians were to be hurt, or endangered. They hinted that secret talks were ongoing with senior officials who were against Li Pinoe and his policies. Nothing was to be done to antagonise the local population, latest opinion suggesting they were more in our favour than earlier believed. The Leaders final word, "your fellow conspirators have been recalled" lets get this war finished before I'm driven to fight against you. Good Luck!!

Dan returned to the camp without delay and called the senior men in charge to gather every available man together on the square at 2pm. Thats every man that can march and fight, I want a really big show. With that he took himself off for a long run to help him think and plan. Prompt at 2pm. refreshed by his run and shower he presented himself at the square. The senior man (a veteran Gladiator rated No.10.) bought the parade to attention and greeted Dan smartly. All present sir 1525 in total. Well done No.10. I shall require 9 platoons of 150, the remainder to be selected for their suitability as medical orderlies. Special training to be given where required.

The platoons are to be drilled every day, if all goes to plan they will be marching into an Asian town to take it over. I know you can all fight, this is to be a show of maximum impact. The civilian population must fall in love with you and any cncmy soldiers should be frightened to death. we are going to take this town without a single blow being struck. I have thought about having a band or at least drums with each platoon, but perhaps that's going too far. Right No.10. if you can count the men off into their platoons, parade at the same time tomorrow in platoon formation. Make it no weapons and lightweight clothing, we will be making them sweat.

For the next couple of days Dan spent hours on the square drilling the men in basic marching. Including rapid transition from platoon formation to fighting squares and wedges. His years as a sergeant during the second world war proving useful, at last.

No.1. and Terry arrived having been given V.I.P. treatment, and were delighted to learn the latest plans. Dan hardly needed to explain the need to start the blockade of City LI31198 A.S.A.P., they knew from their discussions at camp LI4156 that it would take very little to bring Li Pinoe's empire crashing down. To Dan's surprised delight Terry2 produced a large scale road map of LI31198 clearly showing main and minor roads into the city. From this they learned there were eight major roads, and the same number of secondary roads.

Dan quickly explained that this tied in very well with his platoon numbers. Do you have enough men to blockade the main roads, and run checks on the minor roads?. I can possibly let you have a hundred or so if you need them. I believe we will manage insisted No.1., I will recall the men holding Li's harbour (there has been no traffic through there for a month or so) and I think it is not the priority it once was. This will give me all the men I should need. I need you to stop any food or other military supplies reaching enemy forces. The catch is I would also like you to allow food clothing ETC. to reach the civilian population. I don't see why it couldn't be handed over free of charge, that should make us popular if nothing else does. You will have a couple of Doctors, several medical orderlies and plenty of medicines. Please treat anyone you can, civilian or soldier, all soldiers will become prisoners after treatment.

Dan offered No.1. and the A.D.C. a couple of nights at H.Q. to catch up on sleep, both declined being anxious to get started on blockading LI31198. Happily Dan could now keep in daily contact with them, and promised to join them, in force, as soon as they gave the word. Never the less he was sorry to see them go, still unable to contact Dancer he was feeling lonely,

Dan continued to spend long hours on the square, bringing his men up to the standard of a 20th. century Guards Regiment. When it became time to parade the platoons as a single unit Dan was proud to lead them. Indeed he was proud of all the Gladiators had learned, and mastered, since he had joined them.

In less than a week he received good news from No.1. his troops had been well received by the population of LI31198, and he felt Dan to move in to take over without delay. No.1. and Terry had found all the supplies arriving were for the army, the civilian population surviving on local grown produce. When the blockading troops began to distribute the army's supplies among the civilians, while taking prisoner any soldiers they could. They soon became very popular.

In three days Dan and his complete army were assembled at LI31198. The original plan had been to march a platoon down each of the roads into the city, in view of the warm reception received it was decided to march on mass to the city square to create the maximum impact. At noon the following day Dan proudly gave the order and over 1300 men began the march into an enemy stronghold. The sun glinting on highly polished weapons, and the feet in perfect time, Dan felt if this doesn't impress the civilians and terrify the soldiers nothing will. He had no need to worry from the first few yards to the city centre, his men were cheered every step of the way. With the few soldiers who dared to show their faces quickly swept up by No.1's guerillas, no problems were encountered.

Once the parade was over Dan was inundated by requests from various civil dignitaries wanting an audience with him. Needing to contact the War Council urgently, Dan passed the task of sorting the relative importance of the petitioners to his long suffering A.D.C.. Thanks to the restoration of communications Dan was able to speak directly to the Leader and the Council members.

All the Council were delighted that LI31198 had been taken without a blow being struck, or a word of protest. The Leader telling Dan that Top Tech2 was already broadcasting the news to all the cities and towns under LI's control. Please convey our thanks to all your men, I had the honour to see your army on parade, and found it a moving and awesome sight. I too would have been on the street cheering had it been my city they invaded.

Dan lost no time is passing the Leaders words on to his men, before relieving Terry of some of his burden. Terry had the Mayor and Council dignitaries gathered in one room, and suggested Dan start with them. As Dan walked into the room They all hurried to their feet and all began speaking at once. Dan waited a few minutes before banging on a nearby table and roaring "SILENCE" in his best parade ground voice. Order restored he explained there were many demands on his time, and he had none to waste on polite protocol.

I would like to hear from the Mayor first, and must warn you that anyone speaking without my permission will be removed. Mr. Mayor if you please!! Given the floor the Mayor was clear as to his requests, to get the City back to normal as quickly as possible. We need to get the markets operating, the schools open, and all branches of industry back to work. The roads must be open and outside traders encouraged back. Local farmers and market gardeners, must have open access to our shops and markets, Thankyou Mr. Mayor for being so clear, but I confess I don't know why you are telling me all this. My blockading teams stopped only supplies intended for the army, and even these were then passed on to the civilian population; free of charge.

My Leaders are anxious that your life returns to normal A.S.A.P. Roads will still be guarded with occasional checks to ensure nothing illegal goes in or out. Our main concern will be to prevent enemy soldiers escaping. No-one else had any questions, except one wine and spirits trader who was worried about his trading licence. Where do you normally get it asked Dan, from the Mayor came the reply. Well he is standing there I suggest you ask him said Dan. and left.

Like the good A.D.C. he was Terry was waiting in the ante room.

Please tell them either you or I will meet the Mayor once a week, otherwise they are to be self governing until further notice. Now let's go back to being soldiers.

Dan found No.1. and his Lieutenants had organised squads to guard the roads in and out of the city. They were to carry out random checks, to try to prevent any illegal activity. Where possible a police officer would accompany each squad. Over the next few weeks life settled into an easy routine, and Dan again found time to try to track down Dancer. He had given up on the Paris phone number, having left a dozen or more messages none of which were answered. Next Dan searched his private files until he found the details of the Dance Academy Dancer had attended in Italy. To his delight Dan was able to talk to a member of staff. His hopes were soon dashed when not only did they not know where Dancer was, but regretted she had left their organisation, and they had no further connection with her. A despondent Dan wondered if he should stick to fighting, it was less painful than loving!!

Certainly his men were to bear the brunt of his mood as he concentrated his energies on keeping them busy. He sent off Guerrilla Squads to blockade any nearby town or city likely to be worthwhile. With orders to return any captured military supplies to H.Q. for shipment to the Superintendent of prisoners at LI4156. As far as possible with some 1,500 or so troops adding to the population he tried to return the life and commerce of the city to as near normal as possible. Dan reinstated the local police, giving his own troops clear warning that all laws were to be obeyed at all times. In this way Dan was able to pass his days busily, while tormented by Dancer's disappearance. He contacted his good friends Exec.1. and Top Tech.2. asking them to use their respective skills and experience to try to track her down. They promised to try but were unsure of what they could do. In the course of Li Pinoe's communication shutdown many people had gone missing, a large industry was growing claiming to find lost persons for a fee. Exec.1. was dubious as to their reliability.

It came as almost a relieve to Dan when he was called back to H.Q. for meetings with the leader and Council, in spite of an initial reaction of "now what"!! To Dan's surprise the Leader told him he was being withdrawn from active duty to prepare for negotiations with Asian leaders in the event of Li Pinoe being overthrown. The Leader and Council felt No.1.'s Guerrillas were bringing much of Li Pinoe's army to the brink of starvation. The local people were also suffering as they tried to feed the soldiers from their own meagre rations. The army are already laying down their arms and demanding a negotiated peace before it became too late. Discussions with the mayor and council of LI31198 suggested the civilian population was ready to join any major uprising.

When Dan suggested he was a soldier not a diplomat the Leader silenced him, saying, " enough of your humble soldier routine", it no longer fools anyone. In the event of our hopes coming to fruition, your role will be the iron fist in the velvet glove. Whenever there is a suggestion they will carry on fighting you will persuade them they can only face heavy defeat. Dan could not refuse the Council's order, but suspected he would find it boring. He would have liked to ask to have Terry accompany him, but realised this would be unfair to No.1.. So Dan was launched into yet another phase of his career "hardman diplomat", perhaps after this I can go back to being a humble builder.

Dan began his studies into the background of the diplomatic negotiations already taking place. It seemed to him LI Pinoe's team were operating delaying tactics, but he couldn't work out what they hoped to gain. Obviously their army had been weakened and had very low morale, Dan could not believe they were foolish enough to planning a counter offensive. Thinking when you don't know ask, he arranged a meeting with the Leader.

"Come in No.1. Boss! or whatever it is you are called" said the Leader when Dan presented himself at his office. Thank you, sir, said Dan you have led me straight into one of the points I hoped to raise. I think it is time we rationalised the Gladiators into proper army rankings, I can only think in terms of 20Th. century ranks with officers, non-commissioned officers, Gladiator would suffice for private soldier. When I achieved my No.1. rating there could only be one No.1., and that only counted until he was beaten. In the army we have now there is a need for several leaders able to command, and they need a recognisable status, be it general or corporal. I know of several deserving of high rank, and I am sure No.1. and the A.D.C. could tell you of many more. I'm sure Exec.1.

would love to get his teeth into that one.

My main reason for wanting to see you sir, I feel that LI Pinoe's team are deliberately delaying progress in your talks but I don't understand why. Their army gets weaker, civil unrest is rife, why are they dragging their feet?. Well done, you have hit upon the thing that has been puzzling us all, agreed the Leader. We are trying to find a way to give them some kind of a prod. Any ideas? Nodding his head Dan pointed to the large scale map of LI Pinoe's territory hanging on the Leader's wall. About 25 kilometres north of LI31198 there are two medium sized towns LI2271 and LI2275, which just happen to straddle two main supply routes. No.1. has these areas under surveillance and tells me they are only lightly guarded, with no increased military activity since we took LI31198. He and I both feel we should move into these towns, in force, and blockade their supply routes.

What do you see will happen if we agree to your plan?, asked the leader, apart from more prisoners to feed. We need to prove to them that we are prepared to press onward until we are in complete control of all the territory previously held by LI Pinoe. Were I our chief negotiator I would make it plain we are aware of their delaying tactics and intend to use the time they are allowing us to capture enough territory to give us overall control. We may as well bleed Asia dry to recover some of the cost of waging war, as let LI Pinoe do it to fill his own coffers.

you may be right! said The Leader. O.K. said Dan lets ask the people of Asia what they think. Ask them where is Pinoe, why are they short of food and other essentials. Why is their army which he told them was invincible being beaten on all fronts. Where is the wealth of which he boasted?. Flood all the media outlets with these questions as your army starts another major advance, and I will lay odds the people will rise up demanding LI Pinoe personally gives them answers. My God!! exclaimed The Leader don't go into politics, or the world be in turmoil before a year was out. Not me, said Dan, I'm just a humble builder, turned humble soldier. Get Out!! shouted The Leader, before I have you thrown out, a large smile on his face softening his words.

Within a few days Dan learned all his suggestions had been acted on. No.1. had his men taking control of the designated towns, and squads of guerrillas blockading the roads. Top Tech2 and his staff were flooding the media with the type of question Dan had proposed.

LI Pinoe's negotiators were unhappy with these events and demanded the media broadcasts cease immediately, and all troops return to their previous positions. Insisting that no further talks could take place, until these demands were met. With a military smart Dan at his side The Leader was happy to tell them he was no longer interested in the talks and he and his team would take no further part. Frankly gentlemen we have tired of your filibustering and time wasting and intend to pursue this war until we have totally defeated your forces, or received your unconditional surrender. You have 24Hrs to leave any delay and you will be arrested as spies and imprisoned accordingly. With a final Good day gentlemen he left, pausing only to instruct Dan to "get rid of them No.1."

Only too happy to comply Dan called in his guards and accompanied the Asian team to their hotel. Gentlemen there will be a guard outside your doors all night, with instructions to notify me when you are ready to leave and we will be happy to send you on your way.

Dan was almost sorry when the Asian team gave no problems, and left on the first available flight.

With no other problems to fill his time, Dan's thoughts turned inevitably to Dancer and to where and what had gone wrong. His attempts to track her down were interrupted by an unexpected priority call from No.1.. Sir; he explained I have just received some delayed private mail addressed to No.1. at the main barracks. None of this mail relates to me, having been put in my mail box by an unthinking robot doing what it had been programmed to do. Our friend Terry2 assures me the mail is intended for you and you will be anxious to receive it. The fastest courier we have is on his way and should reach you within 12Hrs.. I can't thank you enough said Dan if this is the news I hope for there will be the greatest party ever next time we get together. I'm off now to kick a robot in its the mail box. Again many thanks.

The mail when it arrived, was, as Dan had hoped from Dancer. Reading them all, and noting Dancer's growing despair at not hearing from him, brought Dan to near despair himself. It was the very last letter that caused him the greatest pain. Dancer had built for herself a reputation as one of the finest dance teachers in Europe. Her exclusive academy was highly successful but she had run into trouble when a standard business loan had been taken over by a notorious "loan shark". He started by increasing the interest rate, then claimed payments hadn't been made, and imposing penalties causing the debt to grow faster than Dancer could hope to pay. Dancer was in danger of losing everything just as her pupils were about to give an important recital. The pupils had trained hard for months, and she was heartbroken at the thought it would have to be cancelled.

Dan sought an immediate meeting with The Leader, and offered his resignation in order that he could travel to Paris, to give Dancer assistance. The Leader would not accept Dan's resignation, but having heard the full story and been reminded that Dancer had risked her life as a spy for Europe, offered Dan open ended leave. You have never drawn any pay while in our service No.1., I have arranged for you to be given a Government credit rating allowing you spend any amount you wish. In addition you will have a letter signed by me and endorsed by the Council, ensuring you full cooperation at all times. My secretary has your airline ticket, so on your way, there is just a chance we may need to call you back, but knowing how fast you tend to act, I'm sure it won't be a problem. When Dan tried to thank him The Leader waived him away, "saying we have all been in love you know".

Dan caught the next rocket to Paris, having been given priority treatment all the way, a good friend to have, the Leader!! On arrival in Paris he was hurrying across the concourse when a large policeman stopped him; sorry to delay you Sir but I just had to shake your hand. You won't remember I fought you in a competition many years ago, I think I've still got the scar. Dan shook the mans hand and was about to hurry on when an idea occurred to him. I think you may be able to help me, he said to the surprised policeman, will you please read this letter. Dan passed the council's letter and waited while he read it through, right Sir, or may I call you No.1., how can I help? Could you rustle up two or three more ex Gladiator policemen like yourself, and take me to this address as quickly as possible. The policeman took one glance at the address, and assured Dan he knew it well. Without delay he spoke, in rapid French, on his radio. Right No.1. I have the perfect three men for you, men I would trust with my life. They are to meet us at the address you have shown me, if you are agreeable, we will take a taxi and meet them there.

Once in the taxi the policeman, "call me 49", explained I have heard that the dance academy is having problems, and think I may know the gang responsible. We have been after them for years, but they keep such impeccable records their lawyers get us thrown out of court every time. No witnesses ever make it to court! You mean the records are false but you can't prove it, I tell you 49 if any harm has been done to Dancer I'll kill him.

As the taxi began to slow down near the academy 49 told him to drop Dan off then drive on, before dropping him off. There are two suspicious looking men lurking near the entrance, he explained, if they see me they may warn whoever is inside before we can stop them. If you will engage their attention, we can apprehend them as soon as I arrive. Nodding his head Dan made a show of paying the driver, before hurrying to the building where the men stood. The men blocked Dan's access to the door, refusing to let him in. Speaking only English and pretending to not understand their French, Dan held their attention until 49 arrived. As 49 told the men they were under arrest one of them tried to escape through the door, hoping no doubt to warn the people inside. Dan grabbed him and pulled him onto the pavement forcing him to his knees at the same time. I must tell you 49 said to the crooks, my friend here would like to kill you, and I don't have the authority to stop him, be wise don't struggle. The crook did as he was told and Dan released him and fled upstairs. As expected the was another man on guard outside what Dan took to be Dancer's office. At Dan's approach the man turned to meet him ,and started to wave him away, ignoring him Dan looked intently over his shoulder and gave a slight nod. Fearing what might be behind him the door watcher spun round to meet the new threat. Dan immediately jumped on him, and covering his mouth to prevent him calling out rendered him unconscious with a blow to the neck. As Dan lowered him quietly to the floor he heard the sound of Dancers voice, angrily demanding to be left alone. Followed by a man's voice threatening to teach her a lesson, saying its time you learned who is boss.

At this Dan slipped silently into the room unseen by either of the two combatants. Dan tapped the man on the shoulder and spun him around. Who the hell are you snarled the man. Funny you should ask that said Dan, just now you were offering to show us who was boss. I have to tell you the 3,000 men under my command like to call me" The Boss". Your underlings are all in police custody, and I have vowed to kill you; so please give some trouble and I will keep my promise. You're mad, said the man, maybe said Dan but you are nicked. Come in 49 and take him away, before I remember he was threatening Dancer.

As soon as he had gone, Dancer threw herself into Dan's arms, crying, "how did you know I was in trouble"?, where did you spring from?, am I really safe now?. Pulling herself free of his embrace, and standing away from, please Dan why have I heard nothing from you. I have written so often, and Oh how I have missed you!! Dan pulled her back into his arms, darling there has been a terrible mix up in with the mail and I received all your letters only three days ago. I can't tell you the efforts I have been making to try to find you. Never mind we have found each other now, The happy pair started to kiss when a cry of "Oo la la" came through the window from the dance hall. They turned to find most of the pupils looking through the window thoroughly enjoying the scene. Dan do you think we will ever be alone? asked Dancer plaintively, Yes my love I do, but not now. I have promised the police that I will use the authority the "war Council" has given me to authorise a search of his office. We need to find the real records of you dealings with him, and the police will do the rest. Its not quite the use it was intended for, but by the time the council finds out it will be too late to help our friend.

Before Dan and Dancer could make any plans 49 returned with two of his colleagues, sorry No.1. but we have to get moving or the lawyers may get involved. Promising to ring as soon as he could Dan said goodbye to Dancer, and left with the policemen. Feeling like she had been caught in a whirlwind Dancer took a few deep breaths, and began the task of reorganising her students. Refusing to answer their many questions about who Dan was, and where did he come from, she managed to survive the remaining time until the class ended.

The police hurried Dan across town to the building which housed the gangsters office. The office manager and clerks didn't seem surprised when the police arrived waving a scarch warrant. On or two were heard to remark, "it had to happen one day". Nor were they surprised to learn the police were keen to find the real company records. I've been here 5years, the manager told them but I haven't seen any other records. The search was proving futile until the office junior, a young girl no more than 16years old, said I've always been puzzled why the filing cabinet draws don't reach the back of the cabinet. Good girl, said Dan, lets have a look, taking a draw from the cabinet he laid it on the top. Sure enough the draw was 15cms. short. An examination of the back revealed flaps the same depth as the draws, once open the missing records were soon found. In the mist of the general rejoicing Dan hugged the young girl and told her he would buy her whatever she desired.

Oh Sir! she said I am torn, my head says I must have new clothes, but in my heart I would like to continue with my dance studies. My family can no longer afford them since the death of my father. Perfect said Dan, next week when the dust has settled, contact the principle of this academy and all will be arranged. Dan gave the girl dancer's address, and made her promise she would ring. Meanwhile 49 and his team had quickly checked over their find, and confirmed they had all the evidence they would need. Does that mean I can get on with my life, and leave you to it asked Dan. For now yes said 49, smiling broadly, but always remember the law is an ass.

Dan rang Dancer as promised, and it was arranged that they should meet at a favourite restaurant, giving them both time to shower and change. Dan was the first to arrive at the restaurant, and settled down to study the menu. His attention was taken when there was a slight stir amongst the diners with many of them looking towards the entrance. Dan also looked and found the commotion was due to Dancer having walked in. Dan had always known she was beautiful, on this night she was a vision, to Dan's mind the best of Paris fashion worn and carried to perfection. Dan was so transfixed it wasn't until someone said I wonder who the lucky man is, that he remembered to stand up as Dancer approached. They kissed cheeks in the French fashion, and Dancer whispered, loud enough for the nearby tables to hear, again Danial we meet but are not alone!!

Once seated she smiled at Dan saying "that was fun", it worked wonders for my ego said Dan.

Now, Dan she begged please tell all that has happened, am I free of that dreadful man at last?. Yes you are!, he has been charged and remanded in custody pending trial. You may be called upon to give evidence, but every thing possible will be done to keep you out of it. I will need your help with one small matter, we only found the evidence we needed thanks to the office junior, a delightful girl aged about 16Yrs. Her name is Simone, and when I asked what reward she would like she told me her head needed new clothes, but her heart wanted to renew her dancing classes which her family could no longer afford. The lessons I would like leave to you, I have lodged a War Council bond in your name, with the Central Euro Bank, please use it to take Simone shopping for clothes as well. Of course if you see an outfit as good as the one you are wearing, please buy it for yourself. Dancer barely had time to say thank you before the food and wine arrived, neither had eaten earlier and they concentrated on the excellent fare before them. With their early hunger sated they were able at last to talk and plan their future.

Dan believed the war could not last more than another year, and hoped at that time to find a quiet backwater to retire from any kind of public life. Dancer also believed that within the next year she would have fulfilled all her dancing ambitions. Dan feared she could not just walk away from that life. Believe me Dan I have been a Nomad all my life and I long to have a home of my own, In a community where you do not make friends today and wave them goodbye tomorrow. They both agreed that wherever we end up we will be together.

At this point they were disturbed by a minor commotion in the restaurant, looking up they were dismayed to see 49 marching towards their table. He arrived with a crash of boots, and a beautifully executed Gladiator's salute. Begging your pardon sir and your beautiful lady, I regret I am instructed by the war council to deliver this signal to you without delay. Thankyou 49, will you join us for a glass of wine?, you are most kind sir but I must decline. Firstly, I am on duty and secondly were I dining with such a lovely lady, and some man tried to join us I would probably kill him! Well said 49 Dan replied, there is no reply. Unfortunately this means I will be unable to visit your H.Q. as promised. Please give all your friends my apologies. I will sir, said 49, we will all be sorry you have had to cancel. Myself and my car will be outside when you are ready, you shall also have a discreet guard where ever you wish to go.

Once they were alone again Dancer asked Dan what the new orders were, are we to be parted again so soon?. I'm afraid so my love, The leader is sending his private rocket for me and I am to return to the War Zone without delay. The rocket will arrive here within the hour and leave an hour later. I cannot believe the tide of the war has turned against us, so perhaps we are about to enter the final phase. I hate this war for the way it keeps us apart, surely one more year will see it end and then nothing will keep me from your side. I too need another year to see my pupils through their exams, and competitions, if you are free by then I will join you without delay. I now have the personal communicator you gave me and I will contact you whenever and wherever you may be. With a last hug and kiss they sealed their vow and hurried out to find 49. They drove to the airport in silence, and were in time to see the Leaders gleaming rocket arrive.

49 tactfully claimed another duty and left them alone in the police car, they were happy to be alone but sad they were to be parted so soon. All too soon 49 was seen returning and their time together coming to an end. With renewed vows to keep in touch Dan begged Dancer to stay in the car and hurried to meet 49. Dan felt if Dancer came to the lift off area with him he wouldn't be able to leave her.

The rocket was soon airborne, and Dan was able to try to switch his mind to why he was being recalled so dramatically. His thought and hope was that the Asian people currently under LI Pinoe's Rule would have turned against him, and his Henchmen. His problem, if that was the case, what could he do to help their cause. These thoughts occupied his mind for the duration of the flight but brought no firm solution. As the rocket began its final descent, he gave up with the decision that whatever he did would include some kind of bold action.

It was in this frame of mind that he met The leader and War Council a few hours later. He soon learned the uprising he hoped for was well under way. LI Pinoe had been caught attempting to flee the country in an aircraft packed with an assortment of treasure pilfered from many of the countries he had recently controlled. It appeared the pilot and crew of the aircraft had delayed the take off until the angry citizens arrived to take LI Pinoe prisoner.

Most of the towns and cities ruled by Li Pinoe promptly dispensed with military rule, and reinstated their previous Mayor and Councils. Many taking their lead from the towns and cities held by soldiers of the Europe army. The exception being the capital or largest city where LI Pinoe had his H.Q. Known as LI.1. the city was filled with members of LI P's Henchmen, and there was constant fighting and arguments between them and the local people. The Leader and Council feared the Henchmen would create an enclave and become an obstacle in the progress of peace.

Gentlemen said Dan all I have learned cheers me greatly, but like you I do not like having any remnant of LI Pinoe's rule to go unchecked. I have an idea of how we may approach this problem, but need to check with No.1. and his officers to check its feasibility. What's this?, asked the Leader half smiling, "Do you no longer just give orders". No sir I just carry out yours as always, said Dan also hiding a smile. Get out of here Field Marshall, said The Leader, report back in three days, hopefully with a comprehensive plan of action. Be careful how you address your staff they all have fancy army ranks now. Realising he had been out manoeuvred Dan snapped to attention, barked out Sir!, and marched out.

Loosing no time he contacted No.1., now Major General 1., and outlined the situation to him. Please get together with Terry2 and any of your officers you wish, I would like to take a couple of regiments direct to LI Pinoe's capital without delay. Once there we could quell any civil unrest and establish law and order to all aspects of civilian life. We are not going to conquer, but to rescue, of course any trouble makers will be shown the "Iron Fist". I will send you a voice mail giving detail of my ideas, use or reject as you feel fit, but let me have your complete plan A.S.A.P.

With every thing under way Dan was happy to take the chance to contact Dancer. All was going well for her, with her finances back on an even footing she was able to concentrate on her pupils progress. There had even been talk of compensation. Dan briefly outlined his plan for a bold move into LI Pinoe's home ground, if it works it could shorten the war. What if it doesn't work Dancer interrupted anxiously. Then I give my men orders to fight their way out, while I run away to you. Yes Dan run away from a fight just as you always have!!!, I don't think, said Dancer. You be careful Dan Stone I want you back in one piece. Bless you my love , said Dan, I will try. For now I must get back to work, a queue is beginning to form in the outer office.

First in the queue was Brigadier2, or to Dan's mind his old friend No.2. As Dan called "next" he marched smartly to Dan's desk saluted, while saying, good morning Field Marshall. The effect spoiled by the big grin on his face. You big ape laughed Dan I should have killed you while I had the chance. Sit down and tell me what's on your mind. The General has been onto me about your plan to invade LI0001. I have a number of prisoners, real Gladiators most of them, who like the way we took over LI4156 and the other towns. They expected we would ransack and pillage ETC., and are pleased with way we restored order, before handing back control to the civil authority. They would like to offer their services as peace keepers following any future invasion. Excellent, how many are we talking about?. I could muster 50 with ease, probably 75 at a push, all reliable honest men, the Brigadier assured him. O.K. said Dan, you're on, organise a new uniform for them possibly featuring both our insignia. Smarten them up and they could go in with our men. Sort that out with the General.

After a short conversation based on their long friendship, the Brigadier hurried away to get started on his preparations. Dan gathered his thoughts before talking to General1 and the A.D.C.. They were exited by the prospect of invading the Asian stronghold, believing it could shorten the war. Only half joking when they said they liked their new found status and may keep it going for as long as possible. No way, laughed Dan, some of us have lives to begin.

Dan duly made his report to the War Council and gained approval of his plans. At first the council was not keen on the use of men from the Asian army to help with peace keeping, but agreed after Dan explained they would only be deployed in areas already under our control. Dan was about to leave when a new young member of the Council stood to ask a question. "Field Marshall" he began, slightly drawing out the words as if to mock. We realise your bold move may shorten the war, but how many of our bold men must die to gain you more glory. Has there not been enough death and bloodshed already?, without your throwing caution to the wind, in the vain hope of shortening the war. Dan was on his feet as soon as the Counciler had finished speaking. Excuse me Field Marshall, said the Leader, if you will forgive me I will answer that myself. I suspect Sir he said, addressing the new member, that you have not inspected the casualty figures for the time the Field Marshall has been in charge. No!, then let me enlighten you; Dead none, Life changing injuries 8,Injuries requiring hospitalisation 24, Other injuries 237. I know that from the very beginning No.1., as I prefer to call him, promised his troops his first priority would be their welfare. I suggest you take an opportunity to apologise, but perhaps not today he may want to hit you. On that note the meeting broke up, and Dan hurried away to contact the General. Taking a small pleasure in hearing the Leader tell an usher to ask the new member for section 23 to drop by my office, before he goes.

Dan was soon in touch with his leading officers, finalising the plans for taking over LI0001. Even Dan was surprised to learn they would be ready to move at dawn in 2 days time. Not for the first time he counted himself lucky to have found his leading men. Having the rank and file Gladiators accept the new style of fighting was also a bonus. They have certainly made my life easier.

The plan on arrival at LI0001 was to enter the city simultaneously from as many directions as possible. Each platoon would lead with armed Gladiators at the front, the remainder would keep their weapons sheathed unless called upon. The hope was that civilians would not feel too threatened, and perhaps cooperate with the invaders. Once an area had been peacefully occupied the Brigadier's friendly prisoners would move in to reassure the locals of the troops good intentions.

In the early afternoon on the third day Dan's army marched quietly and without fuss onto the busy streets of LI0001. In the main they were greeted warmly by members of the civilian population. It continued this way, until the leading men reached the central area of the city. Having secured one of the main approach roads, a small squad of armed men, together with some unarmed Gladiator volunteers recruited by the Brigadier, were left to maintain order. A large number of fully armed LI Pinoe's henchmen rushed from a nearby building attacking the small squad of armed men. Dan's small squad immediately adopted their defensive square and began the fight of their life. The corporal in charge activated his under attack alarm, and hoped help would not be long in coming. The defence square soon proved its worth holding its discipline and showing the worth of all their training. Men fighting under this pressure are bound to tire, and the henchmen began to increase the pressure. To the corporals surprise there was a sudden thinning of their attackers many of them seeming distracted by a commotion behind them.

The Asian Gladiator volunteers who were accompanying their European counterparts had seized weapons from the Henchmen attacking the Square and launched an attack against the Henchmen's rear. The battle soon began to swing against the Henchmen, who had neither the fitness or fighting skill of their opponents. Many of them broke away from the fighting and tried to run away, running straight into the arms of the relief squad answering the corporals call for assistance. The General arrived shortly after, and having thanked the ex prisoners for their timely assistance told them to keep their weapons.

The fight against the Henchmen was the last serious incident, the main problem thereafter being rescuing LI Pinoe supporters from the anger of the civilian population. LI Pinoe and his closest associates were shipped to Germany to stand trial after interrogation to find the missing billions of credits missing from the finances of the countries he had captured. There was a world wide demand for the death penalty, for him and all those associated with him. Two who did not agree were Dan and his old No.2. Both had been sentenced to death, and thought that to kill in combat was one thing, but put a sentence of death on someone's head before killing them in cold blood was inhuman.

To Dan's disgust it was many months of tedious meetings and seemingly endless discussion before he was able to finally retire from army life. In addition to a generous pension from the War Council he received several large payments from countries rescued from oppression. Dan insisted on transferring a large percentage into a pension fund for soldiers and Gladiators. He would still be, to use a 20th. century expression "comfortably off".

It was decided after much consultation to keep the army, as a peace keeping force active worldwide. The Gladiators would still be available to put on the type of display of man to man fighting that was their tradition. It was soon found that these tournaments were still as popular as they had always been.

After a long discussion with Dancer Dan decided to return to England where he had spent his years in exile. He had a long standing dislike of the design and structure of 25Th. century housing and hoped to find either a building plot, or a very old building he could renovate and remodel. A favourite area from his exile days was the Cotswolds even then a designated area of "Natural Beauty". It now had some regional number and map reference, but was still thought of as The Cotswolds by the majority of people. Dan felt that this could be a good area for him to search, not only was it still beautiful but contained a higher proportion of older buildings. He spent many days searching the area without success. He found some houses that looked ideal from the outside only to discover the inside had been modernised at the cost of all its charm.

He had almost given up and was about to try a new area when he heard of a building which may suit his purpose. The building, a large old house had been earmarked by the local council for demolition. Parts of the building were known to be 200 hundred years old, and the foundations even older. The house had stood empty for many years, no record of ownership being found. Many local conservation groups were protesting against the demolition of the house, believing it should be made safe, and preserved for posterity. The council were adamant that the cost was prohibitive even if someone with the necessary skills could be found. A council with no money for good works in the 25Th. century, nothing changes, thought Dan.

Shamelessly using his rank and recent fame Dan persuaded the council to let him look around the building inside and out. He was delighted with what he found, although the damage due to neglect was everywhere, at ground level the foundations were remarkably sound. Built by craftsmen of carved stone blocks. 300 years old and good for another

300 was Dans verdict. Because of the foundations there was no rising damp, all the problems with damp being due to the collapsed roof. Dan saw nothing which he felt was beyond his ability, and decided to form a plan and make a bid for the property.

Before anything else he took many photographs of the inside and outside of the house, the garden showing the wonderful all round views. These he sent to Dancer together with details of the house's potential. Hoping she wouldn't mind roughing it for a year or two while he sorted it out. Dancers reply left Dan with no doubt of her feelings! "Do not talk to me of roughing it, I spent the first few years of my life living in worn out tents while crossing various deserts to get to the next backwater. There I would be expected to dance my child's legs off, usually in a too large costume that hadn't been washed for a year. All on a diet of Goat's stew and Asses milk". Believe me my darling I will make your idea of roughing it paradise! I thought all of the photographs beautiful, Field Marshall Stone get me that house, even if you have to call up your tame army and invade England to do it.

Dan revisited the house and made drawings of the existing floor plan, and areas where he felt changes could be made. All with careful measurements. He then contacted a west midlands company, advertising themselves as "Specialists in vintage and modern building materials". Again Dan was greeted by the C.E.O. with supressed excitement "No1. you have long been a hero of mine. I can't tell you what a pleasure it was to learn you hadn't been executed". Talk of old fights he had seen Dan in and how great the Gladiatorial battles had been, went on for several minutes. Forgive me No.1. said the C.E.O., let me shake your hand and then anything I can do for you will be my pleasure.

Dan produced his drawing and measurements and explained his need for estimated costings for materials. You may have heard while I was exiled I earned my living as a builder, but I will need help with modern materials. No.1. said the top man (I like to be called chief) you have come to the right place. I can see from your drawings that you are an experienced builder, and assure you we have everything you are likely to need. The good news, we have a range of modern products that work like natural, wood, brick, slate ETC., without any of the inherent problems.

Can you leave your plans with me and I will get my team onto it. We can give you a price for the best combination of old and new and let you have it within the week. Chief, thank you said Dan, you have made a worried man a lot happier.

Dan lost no time in visiting Cotswold estate agents to try to price the plot of land the house occupied. He also located an old established firm of architects, including an architect nearing retirement, who knew more than most of the type of house Dan was hoping to buy. Dan hoped he would not only produce the final drawings, but assist him with the mysteries of planning permission. The estate agents were quickly able to give Dan their estimation of the market value of the plot and derelict building. As usual more than he had hoped but less than he feared. He lost no time in making an offer to the council, with little hope of it being accepted.

It took the council four tedious weeks to reject Dan's offer; leaving a frustrated man wondering why councils always took four weeks to make a four minute decision. The refusal boiled down to the councils believe that Dan's offer was too low. It being their intention to clear the site and sell it with outline planning permission, which would show a more profitable reward. It is about 400 years since my last dealings with council planners and nothing has changed, moaned Dan.

He continued this complaint when talking to Dancer that evening, I've told you Dan, she interrupted, I want that house If you have to call out the army to get it. I almost would if I could said Dan, but its not in my power. I have an idea it nearly is Dancer answered, I think If you dress in your full Field Marshalls uniform, wearing your No.1. Gladiator medal, and trot off to the council offices you might get a different reception. Announce your self as Field Marshall, No.1. Stone, and firmly but politely insist on seeing the Chief Planning Officer, and you may get a pleasant surprise.

I can't believe all that show would make any difference moaned Dan, all that carry on wouldn't impress anyone. Oh! Dan listen to yourself, Said Dancer, you really have no idea of how famous you are, or how loved you are. Those who remember you as World No.1. Gladiator boast unendingly of having seen you fight. Any who cannot remember No.1. hold you in reverence as the saviour who led the army to victory. The other thing to remember council employees all have fancy titles, never heard of the; ATTSSCCR. No said Dan and please don't tell me what all that stands for, I doubt if I could stand it. Anyway you win, I will put on the full regalia If only so i can tell you it didn't work.

True to his word Dan turned up at the council office, feeling like a character in a comic opera. To his amazement he was shown into the chief planners office without delay. Field Marshall, said the C.O.P., we had heard a rumour that you were in the area but hadn't realised you had made a offer for a plot in one of our villages, If you can give me a moment to study the file I'm sure we can find a mutually acceptable compromise. In a very short time a compromise had been reached and a happy Dan was the owner of a plot of land, complete with a derelict house. More importantly the C.O.P. promised to look favourably on any future planning application. Provided it does not clash with our regulations Field Marshall, he added, smiling broadly.

Dan spent the rest of the day chasing the architect, who promised the first draught within the next few days. The materials supplier was as good as his earlier word and promised 24Hr. delivery as soon as Dan was ready.

Dancer was "over the moon" with Dan's news, and gloated at the success of her scheme. Gloat all you want my love but is the last time I wear that damn uniform, unless for a military occasion. Cheer up Dan it was worth it; have you started work on clearing the site yet?. No, but I have rented out a small furnished cottage in the village, so all I need is you!! Dan I promise you I will tell you tomorrow when I shall be able to join you. Good news said Dan it can't be soon enough for me.

A contented Dan started the next day to clear the site, only slightly dismayed by the rubble ETC. created by half a house. It's time you got down to some real work far too long since you did. As a mark of good faith the council had loaned him one of the lorries they were to have used to clear the site. The lorry, (or clearance facility vehicle) came with robot driver/crane operative, enabling Dan to concentrate on clearing while the robot loaded the lorry. Of course the robot would only do what it was programmed to do, no use asking it to help with anything heavy or awkward. Still better than nothing he thought, not for the first time missing Terry 1.

He was interrupted mid afternoon by an unfamiliar "personal transport vehicle" parking at the front of the plot. To his astonished delight Dancer jumped out and came running up the path to throw herself in his arms. This is wonderful, why didn't you tell me you were coming, please tell me you are here to stay. Oh Dan!, yes I've come home and I'm here for as long as you will have me. Dan had much he wanted to say but Dancer pleaded with him to show her round the site, don't forget this is my first real home.

For the next two or more hours Dan spent some of the best time of his life. Sharing Dancers delight at the gardens potential, and joy at the beautiful views all round. Her mind instantly full of plans, whose number was only surpassed by the number of perceptive questions about the house. Steady on, Dan pleaded, I should have the full plans in a couple of days and will be happy to get your input then. For now my love go and plan your garden, I have this Robot for another hour and it has stood idle long enough. Slave driver, said Dancer, leaving Dan to his site clearing. Dan felt he was perhaps treating her a little off hand on their first day back together, but could see her happily pacing out areas of the garden, while making notes in a little book. The lorry finally had its last load for the day, and the robot drove off, I'm sure if that Robot had feelings it would be miserable mused Dan, it seems to give off that aura, Give me a person every time.

There now began a truly happy time in Dan's life when all seemed to go his way. Dancer soon proved to be a perfect partner for him, her outgoing personality bringing him out of his shell and more relaxed with new people. For his part Dan had thought he would never love again as he had Louise and Annie, and now found his love for Dancer had no bounds. believing they would grow old together gave him an added joy, knowing he need never leave her against his will.

The architect produced the completed drawings on schedule, Dancer loved them asking only for a larger window in the kitchen, with both Dan and the architect happy to oblige. Dancer accompanied Dan to the planning department and so charmed the C.O.P. he approved the application in only two weeks.

Now began the greatest time of Dan's life, the rebuilding of the house was the most exciting project of he had known, never before has he built so much from ground level. Spurred by Dancer's Joy and excitement, every brick laid seemed a triumph. He was helped when two injured ex Gladiators turned up looking for work and possibly tuition. Both admitted to Army pensions they could live on, but wanted something to do with their lives. Fair enough thought Dan, Ive been there, bought the tee shirt. One decided to work with Dancer on landscaping and gardening, the other with Dan on the building.

Dancer had produced beautiful paintings of her designs for the gardens, and she and her helper, soon named Muddy, could be seen heads together over them before starting the days work. Dan and his mate "Bob" also studied the architect's drawings being mocked by Dancer for spending time staring at a few lines and meaningless numbers. Offering to do them a nice painting for them to look at. Go away, laughed Dan, before I brick you into a wall and paint you. Give it a few months and I'll be looking for someone who can paint!

Those few months passed as quickly as busy time will, and soon the house was nearing completion. The roof, exterior walls, doors, and windows fitted, leaving just the interior fitting out. Dancer was having a problem finding some particular plants needed for her grand design. I used to know where there was a nursery said Dan, but that was 400yrs. ago, it won't be there now. Oh, Dan, said Dancer, could you find where it was, can we go and look? I told you its 400yrs ago, there is no chance.

Dancer didn't let the idea drop, and a couple of weeks later when robotic plumbers and kitchen fitters were coming, Dan agreed to leave Bob in charge and go and look. Checking a map, he found that Willowsville had been incorporated into the conurbation of Markfield, and now seemed little more than a large area of housing. There did appear to be a small green area on the map which aroused Dan's curiosity.

They arrived in the area where Willowsville should have been but Dan was saddened by being unable to recognise anything. After driving around for what Dan thought was too long, Dancer persuaded him to one more try. Taking a turning they had formally missed they found the road was WV479 (formally Big House Lane). Dancer whooped in excitement, shouting come on Dan now we are getting somewhere. A little further along the road they came to a small park, which Dan thought must be the green area he had seen on the map. Look Dan exclaimed Dancer it says "The Old Nursery Park", that must be the nursery you told me about, lets go and look at it. Dan had already stopped the car, and sat staring at the sign, it can't be he said it's been 400yrs.

Come on slowcoach called Dancer I want to explore. Coming he said and hurried to catch up to her. Walking along the pathways they soon realised much of the planting was of a great age, with gnarled and twisted branches everywhere. There used to be a pond in the back right corner said Dan, let's go and look. Sure enough the pond was there now surrounded by a concrete wall, topped by a metal grill for child safety. Dan stood with his head bowed, repeating, 400yrs. Dancer, imagine 400yrs.. They took a long time walking over every inch of the park, being stuck by how well it was laid out and how lovely it still was. When they finally got back to the entrance and were about to leave, Dan noticed a short path between two flower beds that only led to an ivy covered wall.

Tentatively pulling aside some of the ivy he discovered an old plaque, very dirty but still legible. What does it say pleaded Dancer, come and look was all Dan could manage.

THE PLAQUE
THIS PARK WAS BUILT BY THE LEYLAND FAMILY AND BEQUEATHED TO THE PEOPLE OF WILLOWSVILLE IN
PERPERTUITY. IN LOVING MEMORY OF OUR FRIEND AND BENEFACTOR DAN STONE WHOSE GENEROSITY MADE ALL THINGS POSSIBLE.

Dan and Dancer hugged each other both with tears streaming down their cheeks.
I have told you my darling you are much loved said Dancer, now as you were then. YOU REALLY ARE A MAN OF TWO CENTURIES.

THE END

EPILOGUE

Dan and Dancer were married shortly after completion of the house and garden, remaining together for the rest of their natural lives. Dancer continued to teach dance of all types and to all ages. Dan became the man to go to for restoration of old buildings, Employing and training retired and injured Gladiators.

Search of old records show Terry and his descendants ran the Nursery for almost 200 years before creating the park found by Dan and Dancer.

The Big House and the cottage were lost without trace, buried in modern housing ETC. somewhere in the past.

Dan was often asked which century he preferred but would never answer.

YOU JUST NEVER KNOW

Jim was not happy! but then Jim had not been happy for a long time. It's not that he was miserable, more he was fed up, this growing old lark was not much fun. In fact, it was. "And here Jim had a selection of words and phrases" depending on who he was talking to, for now let's just say its bloody. awful. He was finding life a bit of a struggle, he was not all that old, but knew he soon would be if he carried on ageing at the same rate.

He was healthy enough, no dreaded disease, that he knew of, just plain worn out. Fifty years of work, most of it hard and heavy, had left him with a body of creaking joints and torn muscles. He could still do most things, except bend low or reach high, but everything hurt. Arthritis, which Jim almost never ever mentioned without an added expletive. Only today, he read in the morning paper doctors had been advised to no longer prescribe steroid injections or the usual tablets, as they were costing the N.H.S. millions of pounds and were not thought to be effective. I'll bet who ever dreamed that one up was an arthritis free accountant, thought Jim. Treatment from now to be exercise.

Exercise!!, Jim simply couldn't think of any group of people less likely to take up exercise, than those suffering with arthritis. In theory Jim thought, it might to be a good idea, but not for the sick and disabled. Not that he liked to think of himself as disabled, just someone who struggled a bit. He often took the 15 minute walk to the shops, but had to admit he caught the bus back. In addition to all the other things he could no longer do. Pick things up from the floor, or for that matter reach lower than his shins. He dropped a 50 pence piece the other day, and had to ask a passing child to pick it up for him. Only to have the little bugger run off with it. Bad enough, but he then had to buy a couple of pints to get over the shock.

He had thought a lot of late about the way his life was changing and shrinking. His old group of friends now numbered less than half, and half that half were no longer functioning as of old. Sickness, frailty, and old age keeping them house bound, and generally boring. Of course he had to admit he wasn't the party animal of old. He no longer played golf, for some reason his old playing partners had made no effort to persuade him to carry on, odd that. Darts was another non-starter his old friend arthritis put a stop to that, and he couldn't drink the number of pints needed to play an evening's darts. Jim had been thrown out of the bowls club for throwing the bowl instead of rolling it. He didn't really throw the bowl, well not all the way he just couldn't bend low enough to start the dam thing rolling near his feet. Sorry said the secretary but you are denting the green. I bet I don't dent the green with my bowl as you do with your bloody size 15 feet, said Jim and stormed off.

Well what am I left with?, was the next question, and the more he thought about it the less he liked the answer. The pub of course! But Jim disliked drinking alone, and his mates had all cut down on their drinking and the time spent in the pub. Time was, when he could have dropped in at any time and found a couple of them, now he could be in all opening time and not see any of them. He gave up when one of the wives told him off for keeping her husband out past his bedtime. Jim wouldn't have minded but that was the night he had stayed a bit longer chatting to the landlord, and was still home by half past nine.

I need something to change! But what? The only change I can think of is to drop down dead. It would have to be somewhere inconvenient, like the main aisle in the local shopping centre. Otherwise nobody would notice, and he might lie somewhere cold and wet for days. Not that it would matter if he was already dead, all the same no thanks! All I want is some excitement, mind you what did mother always say, be careful what you ask for, you may be sorry if you get it. Mind you as I recall mother wasn't much of a risk taker, she would wear rubber gloves to switch a light on.

Jim's life got no better!, on the way home he dropped a piece of paper knowing there was no way he could bend to pick it up, so he carried on walking. Who should come round the corner, Jim's most hated neighbour better known as P.C. Plod the local Gestapo. I hope you're going to pick that up he sneered, beginning to enjoy himself. I would if I could but I can't said Jim, I'm disabled "Arthritis". Well said Plod I believe the new treatment for Arthritis is exercise, so you can at least try, who knows it might even do you good. Of course if you can't manage it I can arrange for you to have a hundred or two hours unpaid street cleaning! I've told you its not that I won't, I can't!

Well then I shall just have to book you, said a happy looking Plod, ceremoniously taking his notepad from his pocket. At that moment a huge Artic and Trailer swept past nearside wheels in the gutter only inches from where P.C. Plod was standing. The side draft from the truck almost blew him over, but succeeded in snatching his notepad from his hand while at the same time sending his hat bowling along the road. The P.C. set off in pursuit, leaving Jim to make good his escape, exhibit "A", the piece of paper having also disappeared.

Once home Jim collapsed in his armchair, wiping the sweat from his brow and catching his breath. If that is the kind of excitement you're looking for you can stuff it! Mind you I did enjoy Plod chasing his hat. Oh! And sorry Mum should have known you would be right. My Mum my Wife and my Sister, Between them knew everything, and anything one of them didn't know the other two would soon tell her. I know that's true because they told me.

Right two hours Tele. a cup of cocoa and bed, I've earned a good nights sleep. A couple of hours later he was woken by some kind of disturbance in his garden. He looked out just in time to see a small cloud of steam or smoke disappear in an instant, one second it was there the next it was gone. That was odd enough but what was left behind was even more strange. A strange ovoid metallic looking object perhaps a foot diameter and slightly longer was lying on his lawn. Jim was prepared to swear it was pulsating slightly with red and green light, Jim could also swear it was nothing like any machine part he had ever seen, I'd better get down for a closer look.

When Jim got to the mystery object it had stopped pulsating and although warm was not too hot to handle. Heavier than he expected, but not unmanageable, Jim carefully turned it round and end to end looking for a possible way to open it. No sign of any opening or even a seam, its beautifully made he thought, probably Japanese. I will take it indoors and get an hammer and saw to it, Japanese or not, not a lot stands up to a few hefty clouts with a hammer. Once back inside he put the object on the kitchen worktop, and told himself to get off back to bed.

You had better hide me in case the authorities come looking for me. Jim had these words run through his brain, but was sure he hadn't actually heard them. Where did that come said Jim, why am I "hearing" things that nobody said, and what is this about hide "ME"? He looked again at the overgrown egg and was shocked to see it was pulsating again, Oh! Blood and sand he thought now what is up with it. Do not be afraid Jim, you are quite safe so long as I remain hidden. How the hell do I know what you say if I don't hear you say it, and how do you know my names Jim.

You won't like this my friend, but I have entered your brain in order to learn more about you, and to establish a communication channel between us. Bloody hell mate shouted Jim are you saying you have taken over my brain and are controlling my thoughts. Not at all Jim came the reply I am not controlling your thoughts if I were I wouldn't have let you shout at me. While on that subject you don't need to speak at all, I am getting all your thoughts anyway, and can answer much quicker. Well I'll tell you now if you really are listening to my thoughts you will be hearing some things you won't like! I don't think so Jim I've checked enough of your brain to know you are not at all a bad chap. Why do I have the feeling that bit of flattery is going to cost me? Cost you Jim?!!, how on earth can it cost you? Worry not.

Of course, said Jim through gritted teeth, why would I worry, I'm having my thoughts read and my brain delved into by an overgrown metal egg with its own light show!! Not to mention it demanding I hide it! Jim! Jim! I'm sorry; let me start again and try to clear your confusion, NO don't interrupt! Fat chance I have of interrupting while you're putting words straight into my brain. Well, you just managed it! If you do it again, I will turn off your power of speech until I've finished.

Fasten your safety belt I'm about to blow your mind. Stay cool it won't do you any harm. The "overgrown egg" as you call it is my space capsule, inside is my brain, my body, as you would call it, is in a larger one waiting for me to call it down. I got into difficulties due to the density of your atmosphere. It is twice as thick at ground level than very slightly higher up, causing me to make an un planned landing. Your earlier idea of "belting" it with a hammer would avail you nothing, except a possible injury when the hammer bounced back at three times the speed you swung it. Even your Japanese friends have nothing like it.

162

Now, hiding my capsule, it has carried out a minor repair, and is now recharging the propulsion fuel. The recharging, (which has never been necessary in mid-flight before) will take until mid-morning tomorrow and the capsule needs to be hidden until then. My fellow travellers are monitoring your local communications and are concerned that a search is to be held to try to discover the source of some strange Radar images. I should perhaps point out the official chosen to search this location is none other than P.C. Earnshaw better known to you, we believe, as P.C. Plod. He is due, or so my team inform me, to start a house to house along your street early tomorrow. Will you please hide myself and my capsule until the search is completed.

Well I have to say the idea of getting one over on Plod appeals, I used to hide the kids Easter eggs in the washing machine covered in washing to make it more real I suppose your gadget can stand getting wet, I could pack wet clothes round to deter Plod or whoever from looking too close. Jim if I didn't know better, I would think you are beginning to enjoy yourself. I wouldn't go that far said Jim, but if I can have a run in with Plod on my playing field that I may enjoy.

Jim before you hide me away can I just say, I am, and all my people will be very grateful that you are helping me. Well I'm sure that is very nice to know, if there is anything I ever wanted it's the gratitude of an overgrown brain stealing metallic egg. If we don't get away with this Mr. Egg I'm all too aware that I will be in bother, If we do I'll be looking for more than gratitude. Without giving Mr. Egg (he rather liked that title) time to answer Jim pulled the wet washing out of the machine, thrust the egg inside, covered it with the wet washing, and slammed the door shut. Before he could even begin to relax, the voice in his head said, now Jim temper, temper.

Dawn was beginning to show in the window so he decided not to bother going back to bed, and settled himself in his armchair. As he sat he was too wound up to relax, but was instantly asleep. Too asleep to hear Mr. Egg "say that's better Jim I need you alert for tomorrow.

Jim was woken later that morning by a loud pounding on his door and an officious voice shouting Police open up. All right shouted Jim keep your hair on I'm coming, and opened his door. As he half expected he

163

found none other than P.C. Plod on his doorstep. We are carrying out house to house searches let me in. Of course I'll let you in said Jim, without moving out of Plods way, I'd better just have a look at it though hadn't I? Look at what snapped the P.C. You know said Jim the bit of paper. Wait a minute I remember you now you're the litter bug! That's a bit harsh P.C. Earnshaw, as I remember you're the one who threw his hat and notepad down the road and then ran off. Still, show me the bit of paper and we will say no more about it. I have had enough of your messing me about get out of my way, shouted Plod. Not until you show me the paper, shouted Jim. What blasted paper screeched P.C. Earnshaw. The one required by paragraph 6.131968 (1) said Jim calmly "the important numbers having been fed to him by Mr. Egg". Jim closed his door in his adversary's face and leaned back on it smiling. He had seen over Plods shoulder a police sergeant striding towards them, no doubt attracted by the sound of shouting.

Through the door could hear the sound of a heated discussion between the two Police officers and wished he could hear what was being said. Perhaps Mr. Egg can tune me in, HINT, HINT. No sooner the thought than the deed and Jim could "hear" the police clearly. P.C. Earnshaw was receiving a verbal dressing down, the sergeant asking what he thought he was doing shouting at a resident, in particular, at a time when we need their full cooperation. As for your claim that the resident is being awkward, I think I should tell as a beat bobby this was my area and I always found this resident, Jim Fields, polite and friendly. Now take yourself three doors down, and start again, this time politely and quietly.

Jim waited a few seconds after hearing the sergeant's knock, before opening the door, not to appear too keen. He kept a frown on his face, only letting it drop, when he knew the sergeant could see his face. Sergeant Ransome what a pleasant surprise, how are you, long time no see! Mr. Fields, nice to see you too, it's been too long.

So far so good thought Jim, what can I do for you? Well sir you may have heard a bit of a commotion last night, the powers that be thought they saw something on their RADAR screens, and have asked us to do a house to house search, to see if anyone saw or found anything. May I come in? Of course you may sergeant, said a smiling Jim, stepping to one side. My P.C. was saying you wouldn't let him in!! True but then he demanded to be let in, and to be fair I cannot stand him. Actually I never forbade him entry, just asked to see his search warrant, and he started shouting. Fair enough words have been said and more will follow.

Can I just have a quick look round then sir, and I will get out off your hair, as you have got your coat on, perhaps you could look round your garden to see if there is anything strange and I can catch up some of the time we have lost. A pleasure said Jim and took himself off on a showy look around. Within a very short time the sergeant popped his head round the back door; Anything? Jim shook his head. O.K. said the P.S. I'll let myself out the front, and was gone.

Jim let himself back in the house, paused to draw a breath, and began to empty the washing machine. Are you sure it's all clear, said the voice in his head. Don't give me all that flannel snapped Jim. If I thought there was a problem, you would read it in my brain, probably before I did. He finished unloading the machine and put the "egg" back on the kitchen worktop. As Mr. Egg's reply began to form in his brain Jim interrupted, and said, be quiet I'm talking. Up to now you have called all the shots, now it's my turn.

Sometime in this long wearisome night you were telling me how grateful you and your team were. I am not sure that I want anything more than you get out of my life, and stay out. Too many things about all this I don't understand. With that thought in mind let's hear what's in all this for me, and how soon can I have my life back. Oh, and my brain while you're at it.

I am sorry for all the stress I and my team have caused you. Please believe me had my capsule been found it would cause a world wide disaster. Attempts would made to open it and if successful cause my instant death. Worse would be the military attachment of my team would mount a recovery mission.

The history of your world suggests this attempt would be met with extreme violence. I have to tell you your world has no weaponry capable of causing my military any inconvenience, and no defence against them. I could go on about the world wide political upheaval caused by all the leading nations of the world demanding the right to examine the capsule.

I imagine you have had enough of the idiocy of your political leaders to not want to hear all that.

Well you got that bit right, so lets get to the future, how do I pass you on to your "team", and then what? Quite simple Jim said the voice humans from my team will come and get me tomorrow by the time they do a package of offers will have been prepared for your consideration, Very good said Jim how do I know your visitors from any others. Good point, in the beginning they will communicate direct to your brain, but change to verbal should you wish.

Now! Jim if that's all for now; anything good on tele! You have got nerve Mr. E. I'll give you that, I suppose after Tele you will be wanting my bloody bed. Not at all mate the washing machine will do thanks.

After no more than an hours Tele, Mr. Egg asked Jim to put him away for the night. What's up, are you tired?, asked Jim. Not as such replied Mr. Egg just cannot stand anymore of that Tele. No wonder you humans are known through the Galaxies as a war like species, the stupid violence and apparent disregard for your lives, must have some influence on your every day lives. Not really, said Jim we just let it wash over us, a kind of escapism. Your average working man needs something to relieve the humdrum monotony of his life. Theres more than Tele anyway, music, football and the pub. I wish I had time to visit one of your famous pubs, unfortunately I am behind schedule as it is. Just as well because if you think I am carrying an overgrown metallic egg into my local, you can bloody think again.

Jim again had a very good night's sleep, which surprised him, although it didn't surprise his outer space visitor.

Promptly at ten the next morning, things started to happen. First two council workers in a council van, one came to his front door carrying a piece of paper, as expected his voice came into Jim's head, people are supposed to think the paper is for you to sign, but all I want is the space capsule. He hurried into the kitchen and wasted no time retrieving the Egg. In the meantime the second member of the Egg's team had swapped Jim's bin for the new one. They then put the Egg in the old bin, loaded it into the van, the whole thing over in minutes.

Well, thought Jim gone, gone "and never called me mother". I heard that said a familiar voice in his head, don't worry Jim you haven't heard the last of me. My team members will be with you in 10 minutes.

Sure enough in precisely 10 minutes he opened his door and two people arrived on his threshold. Hello said Jim, Mr Egg said I would find you on my doorstep, and here you are. I'm assuming you are part of his team. Yes, they said in unison, which sounded like an echo to Jim. Come on in he said make yourself comfortable; and tell me all. If you can in normal speech please this voice in my head lark is getting on my wick!

The two team members, one male and one female, agreed to normal speech while apologising for his discomfort. Mr. Egg (he quite likes that name), has ordered a plan for your future, which he hopes you will accept. The team have done a complete scan of your brain and body and have identified several areas we can improve if not remedy. Hold a minute said Jim I don't want end up like Quasimodo, or Mr. Universe for that matter!! Oh! No Mr. Fields answered the female, We are thinking more of curing your arthritis and repairing the damage it has caused in your joints etc. As to your brain, said the male, We are thinking of improving your memory, for instance, but only with your express permission. You can do all that then can you asked Jim. Yes, said the team, Given the full treatment Mr. Egg proposes, you would be as you were in your thirties and forties. Of course if you should require any particular skill, such as Golf or Darts, we could no doubt help. When and where does all this happen, asked Jim. We are completely flexible as to when we start or finish, your decision entirely. Of course if you are to lose the weight (3 stones) we recommend, it wouldn't do to seem to lose it overnight.

Not for the first time since I met Mr. Egg, I'm getting confused, moaned Jim. If it is going to take a reasonable amount of time to fix me up how can you bring me back whenever I choose? Not wishing to confuse you further, we will just say as a culture we are accustomed to "warp time" to fit Our needs. If you agree to our proposals you will be in suspended time, not knowing how long you are with us until we return you to your home, in as many months you choose. So far so good said Jim, but are you able to give me more detailed information about your proposals. Certainly Mr. Fields, Our time with you is totally unrestricted, nothing will be decided until you are satisfied.

Perhaps Mr. Field, you would like us to show you a basic list of our intentions.

BODY
Reduce weight as previously suggested.
Cure arthritis and all damage caused by this decease.
Restore torn ligaments and muscles, throughout.
Restore damaged or worn cartilage, i.e. Knees and lower back.
Clean up skin, i.e. moles warts, rashes etc.

BRAIN
Improve worsening memory.
Improve General knowledge. Plus English vocabulary, and Grammar.
Speed response time.
Perfect your vision and eye health
Finally improve general fitness. (Body And Brain).

We hope you will realise this is a very basic list, be assured while our scientists are working through the list every area covered will be given a complete overhaul. Now sir any questions?

What are the chances of anything going wrong? I notice there has been no mention of my teeth or what is left of them. The team duo began a frantic searching through their notes, to find the missing mention of teeth, believing there was no chance their leader could have missed anything, The missing teeth notice was found on the back of an otherwise full piece of paper. Much to the visitors relieve.

As to if anything can go wrong, all we can say nothing has in the past three hundred of your years.

Your teeth will be returned to as near perfection as your jaw will allow.

When are you expecting all this to begin? I have one or two people to warn I will be away for a time. My milk and newspapers will have to be cancelled, and told some sort of story, not the truth of course. Also you have still to mention how much all this is going to cost me!

To answer your questions in order, Jim, we will begin at a time to suit you but suggest five or six weeks to give you time to explain your absence to any you feel need to know. We suggest you say you have volunteered to attend an experimental course of treatment for Arthritis etc. As to cost, the question is rather insulting, You seem to be unaware that by your courage and kindness you saved one of the most important beings in several galaxies from a dreadful fate. Or even a space war. We would not have given up your Mr. Egg without a fight. Discussion is ongoing to decide what financial compensation you are to be offered.

To be honest, said Jim, I didn't really expect you would charge me, but felt I ought to offer. compensation is another matter altogether, I'll have to think about that. Think all you want Mr. Field but remember Mr. Egg still has charge of your brain and may influence your decision. May my colleague and I assure you from our personal experience, your life is unlikely to ever be the same again. However if you go with all that then your life, like ours, can be wonderful.

You wouldn't like to elaborate on that, would you? There was a brief pause: while the visitors attention seemed to be elsewhere. Are you O.K.?, asked Jim. Yes thank you, was the reply, sorry about that we were just receiving some instructions from the "Master". Briefly, we had a chance to help a much junior member of the team than the "Master". As a reward we too received many health benefits and were given a thriving business, which we have to this day, we are not members of the "team" only called upon for occasions like this.

Are there lots of these occasions Jim wanted to know. Sorry sir but we have told you all we can anything further will have to come from a higher authority.

So what happens next? First we have to ask if you have decided whether to take the treatment or decline. You can of course ask for more time if you wish. I reckon no matter how long I wait it will get no easier. So what the hell Yes!! Congratulations, said the team duo together, we believe you will never regret it.

In a short time you will have a meeting with the scientists, Who will carry out a more thorough examination of your condition and formulate their plan of treatment. This will cause you no discomfort, and will probably take place while you sleep. Later you will be told when they will be ready, and you can decide when to join them. At this Jim's new friends again congratulated him and left.

Jim spent the rest of the day wandering from room to room, unable to settle, his mind in a whirl hoping he had made the right decision. Unable to decide if he was wrong or right, he finally took himself off to bed to try to sleep. In fact he was asleep as soon as his head hit his pillow, unknowingly helped by two scientists, in a far away space capsule. The scientists, watched by Mr. Egg, spent many hours examining Jim in minute detail, not one atom being overlooked. Finding nothing they couldn't cure or improve, they concluded that if only Earths scientists would spend the same time and effort on improving the human body and brain. Instead of finding more and more sophisticated ways of killing and maiming. They could become a mighty race. The "Master" telling them not to be too critical, without studying the early epochs of their history.

Jim awoke the next morning feeling fresh and relaxed. I think I'll take myself off shopping and call in for couple of pints, to see if there is anyone about. It will give me a chance to spread the word about my imminent departure. If I am wanted by any of the "team", I'm sure they will have no problem contacting me. His day was made when he spotted his old friend P.C. Plod on traffic duty watched by a bad tempered looking Sergeant. Oh! Dear, Oh! Dear, said Jim, getting some funny looks as he walked on laughing.

His life carried on in much the same old routine, "boring, boring", at least it convinced him he had made the right decision, anything has to be better than this! For five tedious weeks he did his best to tell people he was to be a Guinea Pig in a medical experiment. Giving up when most people nodded and said that's nice. Without the slightest interest, or idea of what it might entail.

At last; as Jim lay in bed one night wondering if it had all been a dream. An all too familiar voice came into his brain, worry not my old mate, said the Egg get off to sleep and we will come and fetch you tonight. Jim just had time to think some hope of sleep with this lot hanging over me, before he was sound asleep. Oh you of little faith whispered the "Master" Unheard.

When Jim awoke, he found himself in a gleaming white room lying on a seemingly rubber mattress. On a metallic bed, with rails to prevent him from falling off, or for that matter climbing off. Around him a number of sophisticated looking machines, all with lenses for eyes, and vices for hands. Members of the team or robots wondered Jim. Not that it mattered he was committed, and anyway, he didn't think there where many doctors in England could take out their brain so they could space travel in a smaller capsule.

He did not have long to wait before he started to hear voices in his head, now no longer the surprise it used to be. Good morning Mr. Field, said a very pleasant voice, I am one of the scientific team and have the honour of being in charge of all your treatment. It is an honour Mr. Field. since many of my colleagues wanted to treat the human who saved our master from a perilous fate. It seems we all wanted to be the one to take you apart and put you back together. This last sentence accompanied with a very human sounding throaty chuckle. It sounds as if you have a sense of humour, Jim replied, in which case you will do for me. More chuckling!!

We are starting today with curing your Arthritis, repairing any damage it may have caused, and strengthening torn and strained muscles and tendons. This is quite a large task as many parts of your body are showing signs of wear and tear, which even if not troublesome now will cause serious problems in the future. You will feel no pain or discomfort during this and all your future treatments, unless of course you do something we have advised you should not do. I was due for a knee replacement in the near future, will you still be doing that? No, it will not be necessary as our treatment is more effective and far less intrusive.

At this point many of the robotic looking machines came to life, with two of then getting closer to Jims bed. The voice telling him if you have any further questions we will be happy to answer them later, bet for now time is pressing and we must get on. No reply from Jim as he was again fast asleep.

When Jim next awoke he found himself sat in an armchair, fully dressed. The clothing was not his own or anything like it. Not so different in design, there is little one can do with a body, two arms and two legs. Trouser legs and arm sleeves pretty much cover it, Jim thought. It was the material that struck him, Almost weightless yet completely opaque, and he felt weather proof. I wonder if I can stand up he thought, pushing himself up on the chairs arms. To his surprise he completed the manoeuvre smoothly and painlessly, experiencing none of the usual spasms of pain or the momentary loss of balance. He took a painless walk round the room, and emboldened, tried one of the two doors which swung open at his lightest touch. Revealing a bathroom complete with all he could possibly need. So far so good! lets try the other door, again the door swung easily leaving him staring down a long empty doorless corridor.

Now what "Jim Lad", Dare you go any further?, Well I'm very hungry so here I go! He was halfway down the corridor when he was passed by a robot going the way he had just come. The robot was wheeling what looked to Jim like a school hot meals trolley. All there is down there is the room I was in, I think I will follow. Sure enough the robot entered Jim's room, and when he entered was laying out an Earth style meal on the table. What have we here then? Jim asked, to his surprise the robot replied In perfect English, "Food for Mr. James Fields Patient No. 4156." . Without another sound the robot left, closing the door behind it. Jim ate the food with great enjoyment, he thought I'm damned if I can remember when I last ate. I don't think I have eaten since they brought me here yesterday. In Earth time he had actually been there for nearly five months, in space time, or as Jim came to think of it "EGG" time, it didn't matter the team had mastered time, only counting what had been achieved and not how long it took. They could always adjust time to suit their requirements. For now patient 4156 was to be kept in his time lock, to save him from worrying about how long he had been away from home.

After his meal just as he was beginning to wonder what he should be doing, the pleasant voice of his chief scientist came into his mind, asking him to retire as soon as possible as he had a busy day planned for tomorrow. Jim immediately hurried to obey, before thinking they got me brainwashed. Not yet 4156 said the voice, but it can be arranged if you wish: ending with one of her throaty chuckles.

It was only when Jim had undressed and was standing in the shower that he realised his paunch had gone and he was nearly back to his fighting weight. No wonder I felt lighter earlier "I was". Curious to know what else had been done, he began to examine the areas that used to hurt looking for signs of surgery etc. His main problem had been his left knee, with limited movement and lots of pain. Testing he found a full range of pain free movement, and he could also kneel without discomfort. Despite a very close scrutiny he could find nothing to show the work done. Well if they stop now and send me home it will have been worth coming.

The next morning he was taken back to the operating theatre, without being woken. Work on his skin in the morning and his eyes in the afternoon. These operations and treatments were completed in good time and subject to the "Masters" approval it was considered his body's treatments were complete.

Jim was now ordered to take a couple of days rest, to give his eyes chance to recover from some intensive treatment. An enjoyable time as he was given a free run of the space capsule. The sheer size of it took his breath away, the lack of any life forms moving about baffled him, he seemed to have the place to himself. He found many rooms full of the most fantastic machinery, but soon gave up looking as he understood nothing.

After his brief rest, he was taken to a smaller theatre full of highly coloured imagery and brightly lit computer screens. Here he was told work was to begin on his brain, at first he would be sedated, later he would be awake and alert to enable his scientists to test his brains responses. Jim expressed himself as being very nervous but was assured he would feel no pain nor would his brain be damaged. Jims last word "that's easy for you to say" wait till you find how weak it is already.

As usual Jim was instantly asleep, even as he began to wonder how the sedation was to be administered, there being only him in the room and none of the robotic machines close enough to touch him. To Jim he was awoken within minutes of being sedated, no matter how it was done. In fact the minister and his team worked on him for many Earth hours. Only stopping when satisfied that his brain had been given a complete overhaul and improved where possible.

Without further delay Jim was moved into yet another surgery, this time equipped for dental treatment. Previous investigation had revealed all his teeth were either missing or faulty in some way. (another of the joys of old age). Unknown to patient 4156 a replacement set had already been made and were now to be inserted individually into his gums and jaw. The real miracle being that the teeth were permanent and pain free within minutes.

The next day a sleeping Jim was given a complete examination, and with a couple of minor adjustments, declared cured and improved. Having been woken and returned to his room and fed. He was told to remain in his room in the morning, at which time the "Master" and members of his team, will discuss what would happen next. What now wondered Jim, am I to see my saviours at last, or just sit here with half a dozen voices rattling round in my brain.

Morning!, and Jim felt cheated, or did when he stopped laughing. One of the solid looking walls in his room slid aside revealing a number of computer style screen. On each screen was an image intended to show Jim the "team". Screen one, showing the "Master with full beard and the serene look of one of the old masters. Screen two an extremely attractive, rather sultry looking blonde straight from 40s cinema. The other screens filled with Adonis like men, and one statuesque women. The exception being one normal looking man in "Golf" clothing. Following Jim they all laughed none more than the "master"

Order restored the "Master" began speaking, to Jim's relieve in normal speech not just In his head. Explaining that Jims treatments were now complete except his physical fitness needed a lot of work. From your brain we learned you would like to play golf again hopefully to a higher standard. It also showed your desire to return to swimming, although not necessarily to a higher standard. Both these wishes will be catered for by the team members shown in the final two screens, but not until your fitness reaches the required level. Fitness training will be given by the remaining gentlemen. We have given you four instructors for their protection against the time when you want to kill one or more of them. This time it was the team and "Master" that started laughing. Jim smiling ruefully and shaking his head. Even after fifty years he still remembered the sadistic Physical Training N.C.O.s of his square bashing days, in the army.

Fitness training began early the next morning, Jim soon understanding the "Masters" remark about him wanting to kill the instructors. Later in the day Jim asked if there was to be any weapon training! Oh! No sir we have lost too many instructors that way! Even Jim joined in the general laughter. Being awake for the training sessions gave Jim a better idea of the passage of the days. Of course he had no real idea of how long the days were. As there were no weekend breaks he soon lost count of the days anyway.

Towards the end of the training he was spending alternate days in the Gym on and the running track. After the hardest session with the weights so far, the trainers announced he was to have company on the track the next day. A lady of similar age "although younger" who had been training on a different capsule, had been sent to receive her final running training with 4156. Incidentally you will be sorry to learn you have finished your training with weights, from now we will be running your legs off. All said with large smiles, but vigorous head nodding. Oh! Lucky Jim!

The Lady was ready and waiting when he arrived at the track, Jim's first thought, if I had known she was this lovely I would have got here sooner. Hello he said, I'm 4156 Jim, but you can call me anything you like. Jim will do! I'm Sarah, I am looking forward to beating you on the track. If you look as good from the back as you do from the front the pleasure is mine. Cheeky!! Said Sarah and turning her back on him shimmying her way to the start line.

I'm not sure you two need warming up, but we will do some running on the spot and some stretching etc. insisted the trainer. Soon it was time for the first time trial, you are not racing each other but against the stopwatch. They were off. Jim had no idea but decided to stick close to Sarah and see how he felt. Staying a yard or two behind her left shoulder, he watched her long smooth seemingly effortless stride with envy, and began to think he was in for a tough time trying to compete. They were to do two laps of the track, after about one and a half laps Jim was not feeling too bad and decided to push on a bit to see what happened. He quickly drew level with his opponent and drew ahead a few feet. A short lived triumph as Sarah reappeared at his side, smiled broadly, and drew ahead at speed. I should have known Jim thought, increased his own specd. He found Sarah mentioned her lead but drew no further ahead and crossed the line smiling at him over her shoulder.

I told you both not to race, it was to be a time trial only, I wasn't racing, were you Jim? said Sarah. I can't have been or you wouldn't have won so easily, he replied, and they both grinned while the instructor sighed and shook his head. Ordering Sarah to do some stretching, and to cool down slowly/ He turned to patient 4156, again shaking his head this time looking perplexed. 4156 are you convinced your left knee is fully cured of all its problems. Yes said Jim, why? When you run especially when you put on that spurt, you are trying not to put extra strain on it, and losing some of your power potential.

Well I did limp on it for years, perhaps that's why. Just a moment I will check said the instructor, turning his back on Jim and went into the glazed look Jim had learned meant he was receiving instructions. The "Master" says you always were a stubborn bugger, and yes, you did have treatment for that particular problem. There is probably some residual muscle memory, and I am to get you over to the triple jump pit to get you hopping on it. You will get me hopping mad if you are not careful said Jim.

Pausing to say a reluctant farewell to his opponent, saying if I come back on crutches be gentle with me!! No chance the reply I'm here to beat you. Lets have you, snapped the instructor time is a wasting, I thought there was no hurry. Perhaps not for you but I have a lot to do! I always thought these physical training blokes were a sullen bunch, thought Jim, hoping his thoughts hadn't been read.

Close to, the triple jump pit was more impressive than he expected, if you survive this Jim lad you will survive anything. Right then what do I have to do? I need to see you hop. So we will do a couple of "hop steps" to give you the idea. With that he strode a long way up the runway, set himself and came racing back at a speed. Jim didn't believe possible. His "hop and step" so smooth and quick Jim could hardly follow it. If you had done the Jump as well you would have cleared the pit, I hope you have not hurt yourself. Please do the next one a bit slower I could not follow what you did the first time.

Nodding his head the instructor took a much shorter run, giving Jim chance to follow what happened. Can I use the short run this time?, begged Jim. Yes but only this once I want you at full stretch, as soon as possible, Off you go! Jim did as he was told, set himself, and sprinted down the runway, a good "

"Hop and step" and collapsed into the pit. Very good, said the instructor, yes very good! Now could we please try it hopping on the left foot?! Sorry Sir! I forgot, too busy trying to get the run up right. O.K. full run this time and really bang that left foot in. If the "Master" says it will stand it, it will. Back Jim went, and with full run careered into the pit like a dying Swan. Again 4156 please, put your back into it. That set the tone for the next ten or so tries, before the instructor declared enough was enough and called it a day. Well not quite a day as he sent Jim and Sarah on one more two lap time trial, to see how the knee was behaving now As Usual Sarah set off like a Gazelle, with Jim fighting to keep up. After Twenty yards or so his knee seemed to ease and he began to catch up. He drew alongside Sarah who gave him her smile and matched him stride for stride. They stayed like this until there was half a lap to go and she increased her speed until she was yards in front. Where she stayed till the finish line. Class dismiss said the instructor, walking away shaking his head.

Back in his room showered and changed, Jim sat to wait for dinner. To his surprise the robot had a larger trolley loaded with two meals. Before he could ask any questions Sarah walked in with her usual smile. This is wonderful said Jim, how on earth did you find me? On earth I couldn't have!, but here on space "Disneyland" it was easy. I just asked the food robot to bring my meal here, and then followed it. Actually its no distance, next corridor, brown door. Its got some of their symbols on it but I have no Idea what they mean.

Sit, eat, Jim insisted, then we can find more comfortable seating and have a chat. Good idea she agreed, I'm starving! The meal was soon finished, and armchairs relaxed in. With you disappearing to play in the sand pit we didn't get chance to talk, so I thought I would try to find you. You have made my day Jim assured her, I never knew a sand pit could be so painful. I cannot show you the sand grazes, they cleared up after half an hour, some more of the "Masters" tinkering no doubt! I thought you were going to say they were on your bum said Sarah, and they both laughed. Jim saying I wish they hadn't gone now, I would have shown you for your cheek!! This exchange set the tone for the evening, while they both told stories of their normal life, with as much humour as possible. Ending with Jim telling an embellished version of his trials with P.C. Plod, Sarah laughed so much she begged him to stop her ribs were aching.

They parted as friends sharing what Jim thought was a very satisfactory hug, and Sarah saying you can come and find me tomorrow.

The next morning he arose looking forward to the day, not so much the running track, but hopefully seeing Sarah. They did see each other but only briefly as Sarah's instructor told her she was to run a half marathon. Against with two trainee instructors. Sarah to set her own pace which they would try to match. Try to match my eye thought Jim they look about half her age, and have probably been training since infancy. He noticed his instructor giving him a sharp look, serves you right for mind reading, thought Jim.

Jim and Sarah met less often on the track from then on, Sarah was either away running some long distance, or resting after it. Then she would have a week or so light training, before going off on another marathon effort. They managed two or three more evening meals together, until Sarah was put on a strict personal schedule of early nights and constant supervision. They didn't think this was just to keep them apart, Sarah had explained to Jim she was training to run in an international marathon in America, which she was only able to do thanks to the work done to her body after an accident. You are not the only one with a lot to thank the "team" for.

Jim carried on with his track work, and stretching exercises. He now did his time trials with the instructor as his pacemaker. He was told his times were getting quicker but he always lost. No surprise Jim thought the instructor could beat him hopping backwards. The happy day came when the instructor bid him a fond farewell and told him his swimming classes started the next day. Jim and Sarah had swapped Earth addresses promising to get together in the future, but were not to meet again in

Space Disneyland.

To his delight Jim found the swimming instruction was to be for only three Earth weeks and then only every other day. He was to receive golf lessons on the alternate days. The swimming was a pure delight, when he first arrived the statuesque swimming tutor was ploughing up and the pool with what Jim believed was the smoothest yet most powerful front crawl action he had ever seen. She saw Jim at the pool side, and swung herself out of the pool in one beautiful movement. Hello 4156 I gather you're here to do some swimming, but nothing too hectic. Well if its all he same to you I'll just stand here and watch you, especially the bit where you leave the pool, I think I'm in love! From what I hear about you and Sarah, it seems to be a habit with you.

In love with Sarah, where did you get that from? From the "Master" and he is never wrong about anything. Now if you would like to get in the pool and swim a couple of lengths using your favourite stroke, I can see what I am up against. Jim had loved swimming in his fitter days and was pleased to do as asked. Using the crawl stroke he had once been proud of, and completed the two lengths in what he thought was a good time. Oh! There you are 4156 I was beginning to wonder where you had got to, all said through a broad smile. Seriously not a bad effort, all we have to do is completely rebuild your strokes and you should be able to swim properly. Thanks!!, was all Jim could think to say.

Now if you will kindly lie on your stomach on this bench, we can make a start, just demonstrate your arm action for me, without the water, I'll see what can be done. Feeling a bit like a beached Whale he did his best to do it properly. Well 4156 I'm delighted to tell you there is hope. This time a longer reach forward, and your arms angled slightly further out. Now watch me as I lie on the bench and see if you can tell what I mean. At first Jim found it hard to look at her arms, until a very sharp voice said I'm watching you 4156 arms, and only arms. Change places and let's see if you have learnt anything! Trying to redeem himself Jim concentrated very hard really trying to get it right. Very good said "Shark" (as Jim had decided to call her.) See what you can do when you concentrate.

Now 4156 back in the pool and we will try again. Off went Jim amazed at what a difference the small changes made. The longer stretch forward naturally gave him a longer pull back, moving more water. The wider hand spacing created less turbulence around his head, meaning less resistance. Jim really thought he was moving much quicker, until at the turn he discovered "Shark" had been swimming alongside him using a head up breast stroke which allowed her to check his progress.

Back on the bench, he was again asked to demonstrate the arm movement, everyone satisfied. He was sat up and a weird headset strapped on. Shark then called up a scientist, (none other than throaty laugh) and said they were ready to proceed. Just a couple of practice strokes 4156 while we check the monitor, please, and then continual until we ask you to stop. Only a slight adjustment to your muscle memory to enable you to reproduce that stroke every time. You have done very well, for the time left go and have a splash around and enjoy yourself. Do not let the Golfer tire you too much it will be all legwork next time.

Jim was not too keen heading to the golf centre, he always thought he was not a very good golfer to start with and got worse as he grew older. Today, I would like to have a close study of your swing, which possibly means you're hitting the practice ball until you're sick of the sight of it. The practise ball rested on what looked like real grass, but could not be, as when Jim carved out a divot. It immediately "grew" over leaving no trace of being there. Facing the Tee box was a very large computer screen which showed the theoretical flight of the ball. The practise ball moved only a few inches returning to its position as soon as the club passed by.

Passing him a 7 iron the Pro instructed Jim to take a back stroke no more than waist high and swing easily at the ball, making sure you follow through to at least waist high. The computer showed the ball to fly 75 yards, at an angle of 30 degrees to the right. Try again please, this time make sure your club is square to the line of flight at the address. Better! Better! well done, take your time and give me another dozen like that. The instructor seemed quite pleased declaring your swing is better than I expected. Not as good as I hoped, but better than I expected.

Asking Jim to address the ball and stand still. Jim stood as asked, saying "hello" ball how nice to meet you". Are the old ones are the best said the Pro. now concentrate! Please take another dozen swings starting with the short backswing, increasing by degrees until you reach your maximum. The computer showed the ball flew further with the increasing backswing, until the last two strokes showed the ball to swing off line travelling a shorter distance. Those last two swings were too long and threw you off balance. Try again at the slightly shorter backswing. Right Jim very good, have a rest while we fit this band round your head. Muscle training again is it, asked Jim. More or less!, you just did the training, we are just putting your best swing into your muscle memory.

Over the next few days, the golf Pro took Jim through the full range of Golf irons, each time putting the best swing into his muscle memory. The Woods and Hybrid clubs were treated in the same manner, the computer showing Jim hitting the ball further than ever before and with greater accuracy. Putting was to be saved until on the final day he was to be taken to a Golf Course, complete with Putting Green.

The "Shark" in her turn spent over two days getting his leg movements to her satisfaction, only then allowing his efforts to be put into his muscle memory. A quick check on his breathing technique, and the "Shark" declared herself satisfied, provided 4156 agreed. I only wanted you to get me back into leisure swimming, and you have certainly done that and much more. Thank you very much. It has been our pleasure and privilege, and may we remind you when you came to the pool you were already fitter than ever before.

His Journey to the Golf Course was made while he slept, waking in a luxury hotel room, and finding a complete outfit of perfectly fitting Golf clothing. On the putting green he was given a selection of putters to try, but no instruction on putting technique. Every Golfer has their own way of putting and you must find yours. All I will say is try to keep your head still, it may help. Completely happy, Jim spent half an hour on the putting green, finally selecting a nondescript putter on the grounds it felt comfortable. On to the "Pro Shop" where he was fitted with a top of the range set of clubs, adjusted to suit his height and stance.

Onto the Golf Course and Jim was thrilled and excited with the quality of his new swing and game in general. Having completed the Par 72 course in less than 90 strokes, a first for him on any course. The two assistant Pros who had partnered him, full of praise and certain he would soon improve when playing regularly. The Golf game signalled the end of Patient 4156 treatments and exercises, making him wonder how the "new" Jim would fit into his life back on Earth. Worry not said a familiar voice in his head we are not quite finished with you yet. Please stay in your room tomorrow morning, myself and some members of the team would like a chat. The "Masters voice closed down before Jim could answer. Guess I'll be staying in my room, no chance to ask why. "For your own good of course" said another more throaty voice, again closing down before he could reply.

Jim intended to be up and about early the next morning, but soon realised he had overslept by a couple of hours. That will be the team playing with my head again, I guess they are not planning an early start. All very well but I do wonder if I will ever regain complete control.

The Robot waiter arrived with his breakfast and interrupted his ungrateful train of thought. As the robot cleared away the remains, the panelling slid to one side revealing the battery of computer screens. On this occasion the "Master" was in the guise of a benevolent bank manager, complete with desk and papers. "Throaty Laugh" now dark haired, in Doctor/Surgeon whites, the three other men in business suits and earnest expressions.

The "Master" began by offering Jim an apology, we heard, with some dismay, you question whether you will ever regain complete control of your thoughts. Please believe me when I tell you on behalf of the whole team, we have no wish to take over your life. However we wish to be a part of your life while you live. By this we mean that all the decisions you make will be yours and sacrosanct. With your consent we would like to help you to achieve your goals, what those goals may be will be your decision alone.

Jim declared himself happy with that and the "Master" was able to start the meeting. Your treatment and your time with us are almost at an end, but not, we all hope, finally. Your kindness towards me in my hour of need saved a situation which without your help could have been calamitous for all concerned. We feel a great debt is owed you, greater than you could ever realise. With this in mind, we are offering the sum of £25,000,000 to cover your immediate expenses, on your return to Earth.

We realise you have little experience in handling such large sums. For this reason we would like to offer our help in this regard. May we repeat not to take over, but to smooth your path when needed. The team we are offering will include, Accountants, Lawyers, Bank Managers and experts in Real Estate. Other professions are available as required. In the unlikely event of illness, we would wish to bring you back here to us. You know we can do more for you here than is available on your N.H.S.

I hear you are well aware of how much I don't know. At least I don't have to tell you, there is a lot a secondary modern education does not equip one for. I don't feel I can accept the £25, 000,000 it is far to much money for me to handle. I thought perhaps a £100, 000 or so to enable me to buy a decent flat, if I have to move. Jim my old mate said the "Master" we thought the £25, million just a deposit. We will happily multiply that a hundred fold if needed. You have the potential to be a very special person. Buried in your mind we found ideas and dreams which if you follow through will improve many people's lives.

What were these ideas and dreams? Jim wanted to know. That I will not say countered the "Master", they are yours and only you can pursue them. With our combined help the team chorused the "Team Members" as one. Try to accept your life will never be as it was. The old Jim Fields has gone, the first time you run for a bus neighbours will wonder who you really are. You can't play more than one game of Golf with your old friends, they will want to know how the "Rabbit" of old, became the "Lion" of today. Do you have any idea of what you would really like to do with your life?

You are putting me on the spot, said Jim before you came into it I thought the life I had was the best I could hope for. You know!!, not much but my own. I always thought I would have liked to help people who were struggling through no fault of their own. In what way struggling? queried one of "The Team" There was a case in our local paper of a family man, who was knocked down by a drunken driver and is now in a wheelchair and on benefits. I don't know any details so I cannot say if he now needs help, but I would bet on it.

I see what you mean Jim, please let us know if you make progress with it. So you're leaving me to get on with it then, asked Jim. You can't have it both ways, either you are making decisions or being led like some no hoper. Now Jim any questions?

Just two said Jim; first how do I contact you, or your team? Second, and you don't have to answer this if it is secret. Going back to when we first met, why were you on Planet Earth. First question to make contact, simply concentrate very hard, and think to yourself "Jim" to "Master". It may not be me that responds at first, but I will always be in contact at some point. Question Two, Earth has for thousands of years been the most beautiful planet in all known Galaxies. In addition it is a source of many very scarce minerals, and gasses. As you should be aware your industries ETC. are rapidly destroying your planet, and the Council of the United Galaxies are trying to find a peaceful way to help you back from the brink. I should tell you there are other less peaceful Planets who advocate exterminating all Humans without exception, and are totally serious. I am leading a team of the Councils greatest minds in our endeavours to save mankind from itself, and hopefully Planet Earth.

Thank you, "Master", for explaining that to me, we are of course aware of pollution and "Climate Change". Most of the average people of Britain are aware and tend to do what they feel they can, of course their efforts are puny compared to the pollution of the industrial nations. I now know why your team hold you in such reverence, and I know now that I made the right decision on that fateful first day.

I think you ought to throw me out "Team" before the "Master" and I start a romance, I am already wondering whether I want to go or not. I have one word to say to all that, Jim my old mate and that is SARAH, I still say you two are in love and I am never wrong!! True never wrong chorused the "Team".

In unison. Jim grabbed the last word, saying I hope you are right, she is lovely.

All the team said goodbye and applauded loudly and enthusiastically. In the following silence only the voice of "throaty laugh" remained. Saying her own goodbye, and telling him he would be shipped home while he slept while reminding him they would always be there for him. By the way there will be a new car on your drive, taxed and insured, With all your Golf gear etc in the boot.

Jim woke early the next morning, and hurried to the window to see what make of car they had left him. Wow!, Only a Lexus Hybrid Compact, I might just sit in the window all day to catch the neighbours reaction. More sensibly he checked the calendar to see how long he had been away, they certainly packed a lot into the time. I wonder how many Earth years I've really been gone, but decided what he didn't know wouldn't hurt him. Checking for food he found all he had was tea bags and milk, the "Team even knew I don't have sugar in tea. O.K. a cup of tea and off to the bank for some money, and then shopping.

A quick cup of tea, then hurried out to examine his new car. A beautiful blue he had always fancied, and a matching interior, they really do know me very well thought Jim. Checking the boot he found the Golf equipment was the set he had played with earlier. Included was all the golf gear he could imagine wanting, shirts, sweaters, two pairs of shoes and cold weather and warm weather rainproofs. Also in the boot a locked document case, but no keys.

This must be important for them to hide the keys, I had better take it in and look for the keys. Once back inside he had a good look round. Trying to imagine where the "Team" would have hidden them, the lounge or as Jim thought of it "the front room" yielded nothing so he moved into the kitchen. Fridge no, freezer no, Cupboard no and drawers also no. In desperation searching the cooker and the washing machine, still nothing. Come on "Mr. Egg" where are they?, silence! Of course, Jim thought, on the kitchen worktop stood a pottery hen for storing eggs, I bet the keys are in there, A lift of the lid and there they were. That will teach me to think first and panic after.

The case held a surprising number of papers each folder separately labelled. Did I never tell the "Team" I hate paperwork, his first choice of documents covered the car, detailing dealership, date of purchase, insurance, road tax (Free). Next something he had almost forgotten about £25,000,000, (Jim how could you forget). The money was held in a commercial bank he had never heard of, on behalf of EGG Investments sole signatory Mr James Fields. Included in the file where several documents proving he was the said James Fields. WOW!! was all he could find to say.

Buried at the bottom of the case a small envelope, holding a brief note saying, don't forget you promised to contact me, signed SARAH XXX. Another WOW! 3 kisses I wonder if Mr. Egg. Is right. He hurried into the hall and began to sort through the pile of mail and "bumph" that had accumulated in his absence. To his relieve and joy there was a nice letter from Sarah, giving him details of her new address and phone number. She had come first amateur in her age group in the New York marathon, and was now working as coach in a large running club. Fitness and distance running her speciality.

That is some homecoming A £25, 000,000 fortune, a brand new quality car, and a letter from a lovely lady. Life is sure going to be different from now on, I hope I can keep up.

Knowing there was no food in his kitchen, Jim had a quick read in the "Driving Your Car" chapter in the cars manual, and set off to the chip shop for his lunch. After lunch, several phone calls to Sarah's number, only able to leave a message, Sarah probably at work. Jim was surprised how disappointed he felt. Told himself to grow up and ring later. Replacing all the documents in the folder, he took himself off to do some boring but necessary shopping.

The shopping passed uneventfully, except that the check out girls called him sir, and fed him through without any of the usual banter. I reckon they don't recognise the new clean shaven, slim line me. I'm in a hurry today but I will put them right next time. Hurry or not he took a detour on the way home to try to find his new bank. Finding the correct street was simple enough, he had always known were it is. The actual bank was a different matter. He had walked up and down three or four times before he noticed a small brass plaque next to an inconspicuous door. On the door an intercom system allowing the staff to identify visitors before allowing them in. "By gum" you're going up in the world, Jim Lad!

Back home he got through to Sarah first try, I saw all your calls and was going to ring you as soon as I get my coat off. Now that's better, how are you, Jim? I have so been looking forward to speaking to you. Really I am fine, I've only been home two days, my mind is in a whirl. We really need to get together I have so much to tell you the Phone will not do. Just give the brief details please Jim, asked Sarah. Simply then, I have a new Hybrid car, £25,000,000 in a posh bank, a complete set of new Golf clubs with all the best accessories. Have been shopping, and no one recognised me, with luck I'll have a lot of fun with this.

Sarah; when can we get together please, I want to know all about your time in America, you seem to have done very well. America was O.K. too loud for me. I now have a super job coaching and training the Cambridge University track team with special responsibility for the distance runners. I would love to see you, unfortunately, there is a meeting in two weeks time against Durham. I shall be working for the entire time, preparing the teams, and supervising the races. It transpires the coaching I received in Disneyland Space, included some new ideas, which I am getting the credit for.

If you would like to, you can come to the meet, although even then I cannot promise to spend time with you. Get the details from the internet, stay an extra night, and we can spend some time together. I was going to offer to try to find you some cheap "digs", but you multi millionaires can have your pick of the best hotels. Jim, explained he hadn't got his millions yet, but then remembered he had six months pension, that had accumulated while he was in "Disneyland "so money was no problem and he would see you at the meet. Please ring me anytime you can.

Wasting no time he checked on the Internet, got all the details of the meet, including the distance races. As Sarah had suggested the hotel booking was no problem, although a few months ago the cost would have taken his breath away. Time I got to the bank I reckon!

Rechecking the paperwork he found a phone number for the bank and decided to give them a ring. Not too surprisingly he was nervous waiting for someone to answer. Not knowing how his working class dialect would be received. Although he was dammed if he was going to change it. The voice answering was quite ordinary, neither posh nor common. Good afternoon!, Coults bank, Senior Cashier, how may I help you? Hello! Said Jim my name is Jim Fields Of "Egg Investments", I would like to make an appointment with whoever is looking after my account. One moment sir I believe, Mr. Coults our manager, has been hoping you would contact us, I will see if he is free. Mr. Coults is indeed anxious to meet you, but regrets he is in a meeting he cannot break. If convenient for you he can be free at 10-30am.for the next two days. Tomorrow suits me said Jim, I'll be there. If you would care to leave your car in the loading bay outside the door, our porter will park it for you and of course return it as required.

Prompt at 10-29 the next day he parked in the loading bay, and was suitably impressed when the porter opened the door of the bank and introduced him to the chief cashier. Within moments he was being introduced to the manager, and a Mr. Sheerbourne head of investments.

Coffee and biscuits, served by a very attractive young lady who was not introduced. To lowly in the hierarchy to bother with I suppose thought Jim. Now down to business, it is not often we get a new client with £25,000,000 initial investment, free from any ties, or other investments. We are very keen to hear your future plans. That's simple said Jim there are no plans, as yet. It is my hope to establish some form of organisation, to help people and families who have had their lives shattered due to some outside circumstance over which they had no control. It sounds very worthwhile Mr. Fields, can you give us any more detail. No not really, The only clue I can offer is; a case in a recent newspaper where a hard working successful family man was run down by a drunken driver, ending in a wheel chair with two shattered legs, unable to work. He may have been a suitable candidate for the kind of organisation I have in mind. In fact the press had greatly exaggerated the extent of his injuries, and the effect on his life was minimal.

The bankers understood Jim's ambition, but felt it was likely to be long term before he would need the bulk of his capital. They would be happy to offer him an investment portfolio, which would keep the interest rolling in until he needed his capital elsewhere. I believe said Jim the type of investment you are talking about carries an element of risk. Capital can be lost as well as gained, therefore I am not prepared to take any risk at this time. If in six months my plans are not progressing then I may reconsider, but not before.

The bankers where not happy with this believing he was missing an excellent opportunity. Jim remained unmoved by their arguments, and got his own way, as I should thought Mr. Fields!!! Did he get faint applause sounding in his head, he wasn't sure. After all they promised, they surely wouldn't dare. Look out Jim you are getting bolshie and big headed, his next thought.

With a couple of days to kill before he could join Sarah, he contacted a local Golf Club, enquiring about membership. A few short months ago the fees would have left him breathless, but to a man of his new found wealth quite acceptable. A further condition he must have three lessons with the senior Pro. before his membership could be finalised. After some persuasion the Pro. agreed to see him the next day, for his first lesson. Jim was excited at the thought of an expert checking his new swing.

After the lesson the Pro. declared himself impressed by Jim's swing, saying you have obviously had some excellent coaching, I feel your swing is as good as it possibly be could given your age. If you would like to be here at ten in the morning, I am playing a round with two prospective Junior Assistants. If you would like to join us, it would count as your final two lessons and I can tell the committee you are suitable for membership. Always assuming you keep within the rules, and don't wreck the course. Thank you said Jim I'll be here.

Here I go thought Jim later I'm going to call the "Master" wish me luck. Concentrating hard He thought "Jim to "Master" a voice instantly entered his mind "Hello Jim what can we do for you?". Not a lot really he replied, I just wondered if you could implant in my brain the full list of Golf rules. Trivial I know but I have this important game tomorrow and expect to be tested on the rules. Consider it done said the voice, the "Master" sends his best wishes, Knock Em Dead. With that his head went quiet, that was easy enough thought Jim but I'd better not pester them too much.

The next day Jim had one of the best days of his life so far. The two Juniors were very pleasant although in obvious awe of the senior Pro.. Not surprising so was Jim! After two or three holes the senior man seemed to relax, probably believing his three companions where not likely to do anything silly. Once relaxed he proved to be full of fun, relating many funny golfing anecdotes. Making Jim's day saying I think you will be a good asset to the club, and will lose no time telling the committee so. His acceptance arrived a couple of days later and he was free to play immediately.

Satisfied he was on he way, he contacted Sarah and finalised the details of his visit. The meet was to be held over two days, they would try to have some time together, but knew it wouldn't be much. Jim was to stay for an extra day, when they should have more time together. Although missing Sarah He enjoyed the meet very much. He had never realised how fast the sprinters ran, as well as the pace sustained by the distance runners. Delighting in seeing Sarah giving them last minute instructions and encouragement before the races started. He made a special effort to be near the finishing line. Amazed at the final sprint many runners put in. They would pass me with ease if I tried a sprint down their last 100 metres.

At the end of the first day Sarah was able to pinch an hour and they had a meal together, not a complete success from Jim's point of view. Sarah coming down from an adrenalin charged day, was very quiet with her mind full of her day and the work she still had to do. Apologetic, sorry to spoil her own and Jims evening, she left early. Needing to check on competitors carrying injuries who were expected to run in the final heats.

Jim was not too upset as he was tired from the excitement of the day, and happy with the hug and kiss they enjoyed on parting. Day two was finals day, the competitors seeming, to Jim, to be faster than before, if that were possible. Jim watched the beginning and end of all the distance events, feeling sure Sarah's athletes did very well. Happy to see her full of smiles as she greeted her runners as they crossed the finish line. There was a medal presentation at the end, with Cambridge the overall winners. The best bit for Jim, Sarah was given a special mention as her distance runners had taken first and second places in all their races. Jim cheered so loudly, the people near him backed away.

Another evening nearly apart as Sarah was to be on the top table for the celebration dinner. There was to be a dance afterwards, which Jim was invited to attend. For the length of the dance was able to bask in Sarah's glory, as dancing or sitting out she was constantly besieged by people offering their congratulations. It was impossible for them to leave early, due to her popularity, luckily the top table dignitaries did leave early and a riotous night was had by one and all.

Sarah arrived at Jim's hotel just as he was finishing his breakfast, quickly begging a cup of black coffee, explaining she was not used to nights like last night. Your very welcome, just as long as you speak quietly, Sarah hadn't eaten any breakfast, Jim ordering lightly buttered toast, to help settle her stomach. Saying I could get used to this posh hotel lark, one word and they come running, I like it.

They decided to spend a couple of hours in Jims room to give themselves time to get over their hangovers. They stretched out on the two sofas, chatting about events since they last met. Jim thought he had been busy, until he heard all of her experiences. Starting with America on to Australia, for a veterans meet, she hadn't done too well down under reckoning some of their "veterans" were young enough to be her daughter. They both dosed for an hour or so waking refreshed and ready to go.

Sarah produced another surprise, asking if Jim would mind going to a wheelchair basketball match featuring army veterans. I've seen some of that on "Tele" those blokes are crazy, lead me to it. She had booked two seats near the front, feeling sure it would be Jims kind of thing. The match was held in the gymnasium of one of the colleges. All the seating was sold out proceeds to a forces charity.

Jims first surprise was the number of families gathered together at one end, until he realised there were no fathers and guessed their fathers would be playing. Right from the start both teams gave their all and the pace unbelievable. Jim and Sarah were soon engrossed, shocked by the noise of clashing (crashing) wheelchairs team members shouts and the roars of the crowd. Jim found himself watching the children a lot of the time, their enthusiasm, and pride in their fathers clear to see even as their mothers turned away as wheelchairs collided.

At the interval Ice-cream vendors came round, and he saw two young boys look hopefully at their mother who with obvious reluctance shook her head, the boys accepting this with the air of being used to disappointment. Sarah wanted to stretch her legs so he asked her to bring back a couple of ice creams. Getting her O.K. He waited a short time and bought two from a passing vendor, settling back in his seat just as she arrived back with two more. Did you forget you asked me to buy these? Not really he said, you see the two boys in matching school uniforms, please take them the ice creams explain the idiot you are with forgot you were bringing them and would they please eat them for you. The boys checked with mother before excepting, delighting Jim by offering her the first lick. Before waving him their thanks.

What was that all about Jim? asked Sarah, I have a feeling you are up to something. Not really he replied I just wanted those two smashing kids to have a treat which I am convinced their mother couldn't afford. If you can think of some way to invite the family for a meal let me know. I would like their thoughts on a vague idea I've had. Make it simple Jim tell him what you have told me and see what he says. You know I think I will! Let's watch this next half then see if we can catch him. Waiting for the father to appear passed quickly as Sarah was recognised, and soon surrounded by admirers.

The father arrived before too long, to be greeted with flying hugs from the boys, and a smiling hug from their mother. They were busy gathering together coats, bags and what appeared to be Father's spare foot. Jim approached carefully, not wishing to seem overeager, Sarah escaped her fan club and followed closely. Excuse me he said after catching the man's eye, I wonder if you could spare me a few minutes of your time. You will have to be quick he replied smiling, these two rascals have been promised beef burghers, and are hungry. Is it just beef burghers or all the trimmings as well? Jim asked also smiling. All the trimmings we can afford, which won't be everything! Give us a minute, and we will see what our hotel can rustle up.

Dialling as he spoke, Jim was soon through to the Chef, what can you supply for a couple of young men wanting beef burgers and all the trimmings, plus four hungry adults. Listening with an increasingly wide smile Jim hung up. The chef says if you boys can think of an extra he can't supply he will eat his hat. Adults will have to make do with the main menu. Of course it will all be charged to my account, as recompense for my taking up your time, I am sure after that battle you have just taken part in you must be feeling tired.

A short taxi ride, and they arrived at the hotel, to be greeted by the head waiter, and shown to an elegantly laid table in a private booth. The chef appeared as soon as they were seated wearing his tallest hat and sporting an obviously false twirled moustache. Addressing the boys in mock Italian he demanded to know who wanted trimmings, with an added beef burgher. The boys put their hands up and he marched them off to his kitchen, saying I can see you need feeding up, come I will show you the food of your dreams. Getting fathers permission, the lads skipped off bursting with excitement.

The head waiter had waited patiently, handed the adults menus, promising to return when they had chance to study them. Please order you favourite dishes, or whatever else you may want, the cost is on expenses Jim assured them. I am having the most expensive item on the menu, Sarah insisted I happen to know he is a multi millionaire, and does not know what to spend it on. I can't keep calling you Mum and Dad, I'm Jim, and this is Sarah. Harry and Carol, I'll let you decide which is which! Starting with the tricky ones are you?, asked Jim, getting a playful slap from Sarah for his cheek.

If you don't mind talking while you are eating, I would like to tell you what's on my mind. It is true, as Sarah said, I am a very rich man and I'm anxious to put my wealth to some good use. My first thought was to find people whose life had been ruined by circumstances beyond their control. Lack of the ability to retain their current income, or to live life as fully as previously. To simply give them money is not at all satisfactory, and anyway how much money is enough? I'm sure you know the old adage, give a man a fish and you feed him for a day. Teach him to fish and he can feed himself forever.

I don't have any idea of the extent of your injuries, or the effect it has had on you and perhaps more importantly on your family. With families such as yours very much in mind, I have the outline of an idea and would love your opinion. You are right about needing a new chance to keep my family properly, said Harry. We will have no charity added Carol, my children are worth more than that. At which Harry reached over and kissed her.

All I have at the moment is a vague dream of some sort of commune, where families could have their own accommodation, while fathers would receive tuition in whatever occupation they chose. A new thought I have just had, wives and older children could also receive guidance and tuition as required. To earn their keep while being trained all families would be responsible for the care and maintenance of the commune infrastructure etc. I hope you will understand these ideas only came to me as I watched you play basketball. For perhaps the first time I realised your injuries are not who you are, you are more alive than ninety percent of the so called fit and well. I've had my say, let's eat our food and you can think about everything, and tell me the snags.

The food was as near to perfection as it could be and for the next half an hour all that could be heard was the chink of cutlery and murmurs of appreciation. Harry insisted on going to check on his sons, but came back smiling. They had eaten their fill, left the kitchen and were now being taught to play "Pool" by one of the porters. I don't know what you will get out of all this but you are giving our kids a night to remember.

Carol has given the O.K. for me to talk first but will undoubtedly have questions of her own. The principle of being in a kind of "married quarters" while being trained is O.K. by me its what a soldier always does, Carol will give her side of that I have no doubt. The problem is these places tend to be very "clicky" with people of higher rank expecting to run things and give orders to wives and children. The kind of commune you speak of would have to be high quality, and fair to all. With residents able to do their own thing when not working. Are you expecting a quick turnover of families? I imagine not everyone will want to give up what has been their home for a length of time. I understand this is all new to you as well as Carol and me, whatever you decide please keep me posted.

Carol thanked Jim and Sarah for the lovely evening, before adding thoughts of her own. All that Harry has said I agree with but feel with the limited detail you have provided there is little to adhere to. He made no reference to the children, deliberately leaving it to me. I would hate to bring the boys up in a kind of creche under a number of tutors. They are Harry and My children they have our love and a healthy home life in spite of our present problems. If this is to be harmed in any way we will never consider your proposals.

Thank you both so very much for all you have said. I consider myself fortunate to meet you both. At that time I had a very slight idea, you have shown me that I have a big problem to solve, but given me hope it can be done. Do not think I am no more than a dreamer, I have a team of experts in all I shall come up against, who will push me on. Oh and a number of wealthy backers if they like the scheme.

Jim you are a persuasive fellow we have missed the team bus, and have a long train journey ahead of us. Since I became very rich, very recently, I find money solves most problems. Harry if you would like to round up the boys. The ladies and I will see if the hotel has room for you all and you can stay the night. I will drive you home tomorrow, as Sarsh has to go back to work. You don't know where we live and how far you would have to drive. True but I can tell from your dialect that you're from somewhere up north and that's good enough for me. The hotel were pleased to offer the family first class accommodation provided it could go on Mr. Fields account. Jim hoping his guests never find out he had requested the last ruling to prevent any argument.

Harry and Carol agreed to join Jim and Sarah for a nightcap, as soon as their sons were asleep. Jim and Sarah waited in the lounge, were pleasantly surprised by how soon there guests joined them. With all the excitement and a later bed time the boys had fallen asleep the minute their heads touched the pillow. The nightcap proved a good idea with everyone relaxing after the unusual day. Jim at last learning his guests were Mr. And Mrs. Edwards and lived only Thirty miles from Jim. The obvious question soon came "how did you become so rich so suddenly". I've promised never to mention his name, but I managed to save his life in strange circumstances when his "team" were unable to help him. Please no more questions, I expect I have said too much already. Shortly afterwards the party broke up, with affectionate goodbyes to Sarah who had an early start the next morning.

The two boys "Mark" and "Wayne" proved to be keen on cars and impressed with Jims "Lexus", can we please have a look at the engine and electric motor. Yes if you can find out how to open the bonnet, I haven't a clue, confessed Jim. With help from Harry the bonnet was soon open, the boys and their father all enthusing over the compact, tidy mechanics. The journey to the "Edwards" home passed pleasantly, with

Jim admiring the way Harry and Carol patiently answered the stream of questions fired at them by their sons. When he told the parents how impressed he was, Harry replied his ambition was to one day know the right answer to one of their questions.

Jim stayed with all the "Edwards" long enough to enjoy tea and sandwiches, and to get their promise to stay in touch and consider any new plan he might come up with. Jim arrived home very pleased with the weekend feeling he may have found a project for his future. The next task was to get his ideas on paper for his own benefit, and for when he approached the "Team" for help. I'm going to keep control of all this and not let the "Master" take over.

He very soon came to realise the task he had set himself was enormous, wondering if his vow to have control was over ambitious. To even begin he would need a very large area, with established buildings for housing, catering, and conversion to workshops etc.. All this needing to be near some established village or town for schools, shopping, and leisure (Pub), and public transport. Very good Jim Lad now where on Gods Earth are you going to find that lot. Easy!!, a semi derelict farm, a few miles from the coast, with transport links for tourists.

You have cracked it my old mate, farmers are always complaining about their lot, they will be queuing up to take your money. We shall see we shall see! Sighed Jim. All very jolly and glib but what are you going to do really?, thought Jim. Seriously now, how are you going to find somewhere to start you commune? How about at the bottom, go and talk to local house agents, and see if they can help. Try the big one in town they may have branches near the areas you have dreamed about. You are thinking well Jim perhaps the "Team" really have improved your brain. Remember!, being rich is supposed to be more fun, save a bit of time to enjoy yourself.

Arguing with himself was giving Jim a headache, so he took himself off to the pub. At least if there are none of the crowd in I can see if the landlord recognizes me and play him along for a time if he doesn't. As he feared there were none of his old crowd in the pub. The landlords greeting of " good evening sir what can I get you" told Jim he had not been recognised. Good evening landlord, a pint of you best light bitter please. The beer served he asked the landlord if "Jim Fields" had been in recently. Do you know sir I've not seen Jim for months, I heard he went into some special hospital or other, I have heard nothing of how he went on since, he could be dead! Come to think there are a couple of his old Golfing pals in the snug they might know something. Just through that door sir, pointing to his left.

Thank you said Jim, trying not to laugh, while thinking this is getting better I cannot wait to see what this lots got to say. Walking through the door and seeing his former partners he carried on with the same act. Excuse me gentlemen the landlord tells me I may find some friends of Jim Fields, might that be you? Yes he used to play Golf with us some time ago, but gave it up because of his Arthritis, to tell you the truth he wasn't very good said one of them. Jim thinking you should know, I remember you were the expert in playing rubbish.

That is a shame said Jim I had heard he was playing Golf again and was hoping we could have a round while I'm in the area. Jim finished his beer and asked them if they would like another. Yes please they said in unison, nearly choking in their haste to empty their glasses. Jim thinking no change here then they always were a miserly crew. I bet they offer me a round with them and they will want to play for money, thinking anyone who would want to play with me must be rubbish. As expected the trio were playing the next day and would be happy to have him join them. Introducing himself as Eddy Gray, he thanked them and asked where and when. Time and place verified, he promised to be there made his excuses and left. He dodged seeing the landlord in fear of giving himself away.

He arrived at the Golf Course early the next morning, spending some time on the driving range and putting green. Arriving on the first tee in time to greet his partners, calm and relaxed. One of them enthused over his splendid new clubs etc. Jim pretending not to hear the other two whisper the posher

the equipment the worse the player. We usually play a pound a hole and a fiver for the overall winner, is that O.K. for you Eddy? I don't have a handicap will that matter?, asked Eddy. We prefer handicaps, but we can manage without this once, answered their spokesman. Does that mean none of us gets shots on any hole said Eddy. "Yes!", the reply. Thank you said Eddy trying to sound naïve. What a bunch of creeps they really are, thought Jim, we are not supposed to know scrapping the handicaps helps the lower handicap players the most. I think that will suit me fine.

On the first tee Eddy asked if he could go last to give him a chance to see the best line to take. His opponents agreed, but insisted they used the normal system of highest score teeing last and winner of the hole first. Very well said Eddy sounding worried.

In fact his opponents drives were no help to him, one being straight and two left and right. No matter really as Jim had played the course many times and new the best line anyway. Having asked politely that his opponents stayed out of his eyeline, thinking they are pulling out all the tricks today, much good may it do them. Taking his stance concentrating hard he played a fine drive, on the line he needed and thirty yards or so past his playing partners. Oh! I hope I can do that again said Eddy smiling happily.

His opponents seemed less pleased and walked after their balls with out comment. Nor were they pleased when Eddy was the only one to put his second shot on the green parring the hole with ease. The next best a scrambled five. Putting Eddy on pole position on the next tee. Eddy/Jim went on to win every hole scoring "Birdies" on the two par fives and one of the par threes. With four "bogies" a score of one over par for the round, his best score ever. As a final gesture he made a show of putting his £60 winnings in the charity box. His day made perfect when one of the trio said, apart from your swing you remind me of our old partner Jim Fields. You mean the bloke you said was not very good? Well done that's who I am, cured of my "Arthritis" and a better Golfer than you ever will be.

You tricked us said the three in unison, you ought to give us our money back. It is in the charity box help yourselves, but don't let the club secretary see you or you will be bared from every club in a fifty mile radius. You told us you have no handicap, you lied. No! said Jim I've put cards in at the Grange Golf Club. As yet I haven't been rated, these posher clubs tend to take more time, you know. We are supposed to be friends you could have been honest with us. The same as you were honest with Eddy, trying to take him for more money than you have ever bet before.

My Friends!!, I bid you a fond farewell, if I remember the next round in the "Red Lion" is yours.

Well that was fun thought Jim, even though it wasted a day I could have been looking for a site for

my grand scheme. I should have time to catch the large "Estate Agent", If I hurry. Jim arrived at "Country and City Estate Agents" in ample time and was soon seated before an enthusiastic Agent hoping to be of service. I wonder if you have other agencies in different locations, I'm not sure what I want can be found locally explained Jim. Certainly sir, but our branch covers a large area so don't write us of too soon. O.K. agreed Jim, I'm hoping to find a large area with domestic and other outbuildings to set up a commune or similar. I hope to be able to provide a living for disabled servicemen while training them to be independent which is all they really want.

That is a big ask, can you give any further information to work with? My thoughts focus on a run down or semi derelict farm, possibly with Farmhouse, Outbuildings, barns and plenty of land, but I am open to any suggestion. Adding it needs to be near a village or town, providing schools, shopping and Leisure Facilities and a Pub, I thought perhaps near the seaside with tourist local transport, don't offer me too many at once you will confuse me said a smiling Jim. We will try not to confuse you Sir, I'm wondering if a disused airfield may meet your requirements. An Airfield covers a very large area and has ready concreted areas for outbuildings. Some of which have Nissan huts suitable for storage if not accommodation.

May I suggest you give me a couple of days to arrange visits to the Airfields on our books, and check with our Agencies in more rural areas. Suits me fine said Jim, leaving his phone number. Feeling he had rescued a lost day and gained an extension to his ideas. He decided he must take the first opportunity to check on Airfields. With that thought in mind, he rang Harry's number to see if he had any thoughts about it. It was Carol that answered, and after the usual pleasantries explained that Harry was out "basketball training". You can probably help me as well as Harry, to carry on with my dream scheme I have been talking about semi derelict farms. Hopefully with a lot of land and some serviceable buildings. A suggestion has now been made that a disused Airfield may fit the bill. What do you think?

Wow! She said that's a bit of a curve ball, give my a minute while I gather my thoughts. If you want more time I can ring you again tomorrow, Jim offered. No need, Carol assured him, stay on the line. Shortly after she came back. Jim you have really asked two questions, we had no idea you were considering a farm. It seems to me a good idea space for all manner of activities, the children will have to be entertained. I imagine it would be easier to get planning permission for more buildings if needed.

The airfield alternative I'm not so keen on they tended to be isolated, because of the noise, which raises the question of schools etc.. On purely personal grounds I would not want to live somewhere flat and featureless. If you are going to talk about Nisson huts no mother will want to put her family in one. I can not believe I have been much help to you Jim, I will talk at length to Harry, we are both impressed with all you are trying to do. I will ask him to ring you tomorrow, if he has anything to add or not. Jim how is Sarah?, how are you two getting on? How are we getting on, as far as I know very well! We tend to lead our own lives, but get on very well when together. Jim they say that love is blind, but you're not just blind but you are not listening to your guide dog.

I have no idea what you are talking about, LOVE!! we are just very good friends. Sarah is way out my league, she has real class, and a proper education. She would never be interested in a loser like me. You are quite right Jim why would any girl ever be interested in a man like you who wants to build a better life for people he has never met, who are in need of a fresh start. Certainly not a warm hearted girl, I should say mature woman like Sarah. For heavens sake talk to the Lady. I'm going now Jim love, I have probably said too much, certainly enough to get me in trouble with Harry, goodnight Jim God bless you.

It was a sleepless night for Jim, Carol's remarks about Sarah and love had set his mind in a whirl, he had never dared to think of them being more than friends. Surely she won't want anything else, she has her life pretty well sewn up. A job she loves and is very good at, why would anyone give all that up to be with me. What did Carol say talk to Sarah!!, what on Earth am I supposed to say? Now what's all this Sarah about you loving me?, I don't think so, she would knock me out before walking out. Sarah's friendship is too important to take chances with. Sorry Carol but your idea is a none starter.

The melancholy thoughts continued through the morning Jim was relieved when Harry rang, as promised. Although hoping Harry wouldn't take up where Carol left off. Luckily Harry led of with agreement with Carol that Airfields are a none starter, for all the reasons she gave. The derelict farm seems a much better bet, I dare not guess at how much it will cost. Do not worry Jim replied its only money.

I'm sorry Carol meddled in your private life, but I know the two ladies had a long talk, and perhaps it all came from that. Do what Carol says "talk to the Lady", what can you lose. With that he hung up, leaving Jim no closer to knowing what to do.

Needing to clear his mind Jim set off for Country and City Estate Agents, to see if they had made any progress. Having apologized for not allowing them the week they had asked for, but had there been any developments. Our agencies in Devon and Dorset tell us they have a couple of possibilities, and are preparing photographs and details of buildings, domestic properties, land acreage and location. We should receive all this in the next two or three days. It will be sent to us electronically and we can forward it to your phone or home P.C. if you wish. One of the Airfields has been taken off the market but we can arrange a visit to the other at your convenience. My advisors feel Airfields tend to be very isolated, with Nisson huts a non starter for the kind of development we envisage. Of course we may not find our first choice and have to return to them. I don't suppose at this moment you have any general idea of what a farm might cost? We would need to know which farm to even try to guess.

Jim sat at home that evening, his mind in a whirl, for the first time wondering if he was a complete fool to even think about achieving his dream. A secondary education, never higher than the middle of the class. A hard working but uninspired engineer, recently left behind by all the electronic innovations making the simplest job a computerised nightmare. Give up moaning Jim, you know what is bothering you is not the commune its Sarah. You're not the first man to be bewildered by a women, you have to ring her sometime or lose her completely. At that Jim stopped arguing with himself and took himself off to the pub.

The next day, an ideal day for his ill will, strong winds and heavy rain. Jim did what he always did when he was in a quandary, he made a list.

SEEK HELP WITH PROJECT "MASTER" AND "TEAM"?
ASK FOR HELP WITH REAL ESTATE
CONTACT SARAH ARRANGE TO MEET A.S.A.P.
TELL HER EVERYTHING THAT CAROL SAID AND WHAT "MASTER AND "TEAM" SAID.
SORT OUT YOUR OWN MIND AND TELL SARAH YOUR THOUGHTS.
STOP BEING SUCH A NINNY!!!

Starting with the easy bit Jim made himself comfortable and called up "Disneyland Space". To his pleased surprise he got straight through to the "Master". Hello Jim, said the familiar voice in his head, I have been wondering where you had got to. Please tell me all (no need to speak Jim just let your thoughts flow). How much easier that was for Jim he just let his brain ramble disjointedly through the happening of the past weeks, leaving the "Master" to make of it what he could. Jim I think your idea of a self help "commune" is brilliant, and think a farm sounds ideal. As you say near to village or town, I note you have listed a local Pub as a priority!! I have contacted our Earth bound Estate Expert and he will do some research and contact you directly. I certainly feel he should be with you whenever you view a property. I picked up on your slight worry, if the money will last out, Jim, Jim, Jim don't be daft we have Billions up here we haven't even counted yet.

Now; am I to comment about you and Sarah?, you know I have always said you two are in love, and I am never wrong! Lets hear no more of your lack of education and working class rubbish, we sent you home with an excellent brain, believe me you will cope. Overcoming any obstacle if you will only believe. Sarah is not your problem, she loves you! I have spoken.

Jim I believe in you, do not let me down. Call the "team" any time. At which point Jims brain went silent and the "Master was gone. Guess what! Thought Jim the ball is back in your court, you have got to face it everyone wants to help, but not until you have made all the decisions. No change there then.

Jim rang Sarah, feeling more nervous than he had ever been. Hello Sarah its Jim; Oh! Jim this is a lovely surprise I was hoping to hear from you, Is everything O.K.? Yes! I'm fine its just I really want to see you, when can we get together? Your timing is great Jim, I have a whole weekend off, Friday to Monday next week. I have nothing planned and would love to spend it with you. Sarah that is great news, I could come down to you Thursday evening so we don't lose any of the available time.

James Fields a good idea, but I have been thinking it would be better if I came to you, apart from the saving on hotel bills, we would be able to please ourselves, and just "chill". I'd love a couple of days with nowhere to go, and no-one to answer to. I love my job but some of these University types can be a pain. It gets better, let me know all the details and I can meet you our come and fetch you. No need I now have a reliable car, and Sat/Nav. Just keep the home fires burning and the kettle boiling. I am longing to hear all about your wonderful scheme, face to face and not a disembodied voice on the phone.

A week feels a long time, but I will work very hard and perhaps have plenty to tell you. Goodnights were exchanged and the long week began.

The next morning Jim received the long awaited details of the south coast farms on "City and Country Estate Agents" books. The photographs showed everything to be truly beautiful, both the farmhouses and the landscape. Well they would wouldn't they thought Jim, the photographer is going to show the best bits, if he knows his job. The acreage or hectares meant nothing to him, he tried judging by looks but soon gave up realising he would have to wait for the Earth bound estate expert to contact him. True one of the farms appealed to him more than the other, he decided not to think about that, in case the Estate expert didn't agree and he felt disappointed.

The agent called him later in the day, making an appointment for the following morning. Like all the "Team" members had always done, he arrived dead on time, with a hand shake, big smile, and call me Simon. His relaxed manner soon put Jim at ease, his enthusiasm for the project lifted his spirit. He agreed with Jim it was difficult to judge the suitability of the farmland from photographs. I know of a couple of farms not far from those we have looked at, which may come up for sale in the near future. If you are free I suggest we scoot off down there and get a closer look. Are you available for two or three days? Yes said Jim but I must be back by midday Thursday, without fail! Good said Simon, I'll dash off now and pick you at ten in the morning. Jim offered him a bed for the night, but he claimed a previous engagement and hurried away.

Jim spent some time preparing a substantial meal "you never know when I'll get the next one. Packed a small suitcase, laid out his new lightweight suit, and silk shirt, told himself it is not all bad being a millionaire. Went to bed and had his first good night for too long.

Prompt as always Simon arrived at ten the next morning and they were soon on their way to Devon. A long but comfortable journey, by Jims standards a quick one. The first farm they were to see was one of the ones identified by Simon as likely to soon come on the market. Simon had insisted on stopping in a nearby town for light refreshments. To give him time to inform Jim of aspects of the art of farm buying he might not be familiar with. The owner has until recently farmed with his father and prior to that his grandfather. His parents died recently and as he has no family, he is thinking of selling lock and stock and barrel, to start a new life.

From you Jim I would like a lot of head shaking, and a lot of muttering about how much work you would have to do, though not always in just those words. Good for us it is a dairy and beef farm, all fields set with grass and hay etc. so no expensive harvesting machinery to complicate matters. There are a number of barns etc. all in good condition, but possibly not easy to convert to your requirements If we are offered refreshments and you can refuse without causing offence do so. We don't want to risk becoming too friendly, its harder to haggle with a friend.

Jim was beginning to see why the master had suggested he took

Simon with him. He at first thought Simon was being a bit parsimonious, until he realised any bartering would be for thousands of pounds not peanuts. Right I get the message mums the word. There followed an hour of learning for Jim not all of it making sense to him, Simon and the farmer talked at length about hectares, drainage and access. With Jim doing his best to look pensive as if not convinced. The tour of the house and buildings was more to his liking, As Simon had suggested the house was very old and beautiful, with an annex with all mod con's, which he thought would do for him in the beginning. The other farm buildings all seemed to Jim in good repair and would probably convert to workshops, but not housing.

The amount of land staggered him, seeming to stretch to the horizon, he felt it had too many hills and valleys to be suitable for the kind of development he dreamed of. He kept these thoughts to himself, hoping to get Simon's opinion when they were alone.

Having said their goodbyes to the farmer Simon seemed anxious to hurry to the next appointment. Jim had to agree and curb his impatience to talk, as they had a prearranged time to meet. The next farmer an elderly man was reluctantly selling up as the work was too much for him and he was unable to find the help he needed. Again the farm was beef cattle and a small flock of sheep. It was obviously on a smaller scale but although not flat the land was far less hilly. To Jims delight it included a small acreage of woodland, something he had hoped for, but wasn't sure why. The farmhouse was also smaller (4 bedrooms) but with generous sized rooms. Along side was a pretty two bedroom thatched cottage, on a short term lease to two school teachers. The farm buildings though not as big were brick and stone structure and may convert to housing. Simon and the farmer briefly touched on the asking price. The farmer firmly stating his rock bottom price, Simon shaking his head and looking pensive.

Shortly after they said their goodbyes, and drove away. I cant speak for you Jim, but after that long drive down here I've had enough for one day. I suggest we find our hotel, freshen up, and have a talk over dinner. Now that, I understood and agree with said Jim and I can't say that about everything I've heard today.

Back at the hotel, Simon asked Jim for his thoughts. Accepting that part of what you were discussing

with the farmers went over my head, I thought the land on the first farm was too hilly for the development I hope for. The farm buildings would require extensive alterations to be serviceable as either workshops or dwellings. Purely instinctive but I thought the young man was convinced the property was more valuable than it really is.

The second I thought the lie of the land was far better for my purpose. The farm buildings being brick, stone and slate were more suited to development. The farmer named his price more in hope than expectation, or so I thought. To summarize No. One no, No. two Perhaps. Thank you Jim, that is clear enough, you may not have any experience at this game but your instincts are working well. I agree with your assessment of the land on both farms, No.1 certainly not suitable. No need to worry about the owners attitude as we wont be going back there.

The stone and brick structure of the farm buildings lends itself to development, but it would be costly to match it. I have three sites lined up for tomorrow, and would like to make an early start, please, bring that sharp intuition with you please.

After an early start, their day started with disappointment, their first farm had a large "sold" notice and the gate locked and bolted. It seems we are too late, said Simon, I suppose we can't win them all. I'm not too sorry said Jim, the lane we just came down was very narrow, and looking at your map the nearest village is about 10 miles as the crow flies, probably more by road. Our next call is rather different, much less land and it has converted to the holiday trade. All buildings and all suitable land has been turned into holiday lets of one type or another. How do you convert land into holiday lets? Asked Jim. Ever heard of Yurts, or Glamping? Replied Simon. No! should I have done? Jim said Looking bemused. I wont waste time trying to explain, all will become obvious when we get there.

Simon swung the car into what had once been the farmyard and Jim got his first clue. The farmhouse had become an office and reception area. With B&B lets on the upper floors. The centre a large parking area surrounded by old and new buildings all converted to various forms of dwelling. Having reported to the office they were taken round one of the

"Houses" to Jim's eye pokey ill lit rooms without any redeeming features. I suppose they are O.K. for a week or so thought Jim, but not for me.

Happily for Jim they soon moved on to the land area which to his mind was a nature nightmare. The field was criss-crossed with innumerable paths to a selection of large ornate "tents" many with side extensions. "Yurts" for Glamping Simon explained to Jim, while asking their guide if they could look inside one. Certainly agreed the guide and led them to a nearby example. Jim could see that the interior had once been opulent, although now faded and worn. He thought with proper maintenance it could provide a comfortable dwelling. The side extension confirmed his thoughts supplying ample cooking and bathing facilities. Again all in poorly maintained condition, offending his engineering instincts. "Seen enough"? asked Simon, more than, said Jim. Lets go, said Simon, right behind you, said Jim.

With that they said goodbye to their guide, and left. If I thought that was all I could have, I would forget the whole idea and take up fishing. Where is next? To be honest Jim this next place is a gamble, the few remaining buildings are derelict, fit only for demolition. The land should be O.K. as a local farmer has been using it on a rental basis, but he has no wish to buy. Right said Jim lead on and I will try not to wear my rose coloured spectacles.

Sure enough the problems with the buildings were all Simon had said they would be, no admittance could be allowed. Leaving Jim no alternative but to walk round the outside in the hope of assessing the foundations. The land offered no problems, except a small stream leading to a medium sized pond. Jim would have loved to have a large water feature, but knew that children and water features do not mix. Meantime Simon had been in discussion with the agent about the cost. On Jims return from his inspection of the land, Simon met him with a shake of the head, and a dubious expression. I'm afraid Mr. Fields, the agent and I have not been able to agree on the value of this property, and I must advise you to continue to look elsewhere. Thank you, Simon, as you know I have complete faith in you and trust your decision. The gulf between us is not that wide surely we can work something out, said the agent. Not much of a gulf to you, sir, often means a lot of money to me! Keep a note of my colleagues number and let him know when you reach our offer. At that , with a crisp good afternoon Jim walked away, leaving Simon to catch up.

Once in the car Simon turned to Jim with a look of admiration, saying well done, you said and did exactly what was needed that agent now knows you are no pushover. Up to that point he seemed to think he and I could swing any deal that suited us. Jim laughed and told Simon I took my lead from you as soon as you called me Mr. Fields I thought I had better play up. Brilliant Jim just Brilliant exclaimed a still smiling Simon. Just tell him no thanks if he contacts you again, the land includes a large water feature which is a no go where children are. Much as I would love one.

The remaining two sites both had problems, deciding Jim and Simon to discount them. I must be home by Thursday lunch Jim reminded Simon, if I plan to leave here early Thursday morning can we plan to spend most of Wednesday at the second farm, of all we have seen it remains my favourite. Too late probably to be asking this, do the "Team" have a tame architect we could take along with us? I understood your point about the existing stonework being more expensive to redesign, but I am hoping to tempt families to live on the site and have to make everything as pleasant as possible. Yes, Jim there is an architect we can call on, when we get back to the hotel I'll give him a ring to check if he is available.

Simon you are a a font of all knowledge, by way of thanks I will buy dinner and expect you to pick all your favourite dishes. There is no need but I accept, I'm not allowed to charge the best food on my expenses. Good man enthused Jim I'll see you in the dining room in an hour. The meal turned into a real feast, Simon confessing a love of red wine, he and Jim had a long discussion with the wine waiter before buying two bottles of his finest. Fine food and fine wine! They parted the best of friends.

After not quite as early start as they had planned, they arrived at farm 2 and were soon joined by the architect, who in the manner of all the "Team" warmly shook hands and announced himself as Walter. Walter but never Walt! May I suggest Jim you and Simon go and have a good look at the land to decide where you want my input if at all. I will get my overalls on and give these buildings the once over, I must warn you I do love them.

Jim agreed and he and Simon set off. At the first field which had only a slight gradient, Jim reminded Simon of the "Glamping Yurts" they had seen previously. I see them as good quality accommodation for any single people wanting our help. If there are fewer people than "Yurts" some of the wives could let them out as holiday lets and create themselves some income. Or offer them to friends and family who wish to visit. Great idea! It's a wonder to me your head does not explode with all that is going on in it. Lead on Jim and I will try to keep up. Learn to go easy on the red wine and you should be able to follow, said a smiling Jim. Since you ask, the next field is almost flat and may be viable as a games area and Crochet ground. I am keen to explore the wooded area, I love the idea of it but don't know how to use its potential.

The two men spent some time exploring the wood, with Jim becoming more convinced that it would prove a great asset, even if only for him to escape to if ever he needed some peace.

Time to get back and see how Walter is getting on with examining the buildings, insisted Simon, and they hurried back to find him. Walter had clearly been very busy with his outer clothing getting the brunt of it. Missing stucco and patches of exterior plaster gave evidence of his thoroughness. You have been busy Walter, said Simon, what have you to tell us? First things first, the lady of the house has offered us tea and bacon sandwiches. Home made fresh bread and home cured bacon. You gentlemen can please yourselves, I'm off to eat. Lead us to it, said Jim, giving Simon no chance to worry about time.

A smiling farmer and wife welcomed them in, the farmer leading them into a small cosy "snug" room containing a small table and three chairs. The table laid with tea cups and side plates, The farmers wife, soon known as Ethel, had headed to the kitchen, but reappeared with a large tea pot and milk and sugar. Followed by a large plate of bacon sandwiches. As they began to eat, the farmer popped his head round the door, just to say you wont be overheard if you have anything to discuss among yourselves. If you need us for anything, just stick your head out and shout Bert and we will join you.

The food, the best of its kind ever tasted, was soon eaten, and

Walter encouraged to tell all. I think you have found a winner enthused Walter. In a nutshell, all the buildings are first rate, whoever laid the foundations was a master craftsman There is no rising damp and those foundations left in peace will ensure there never will be. Only one building shows any sign of damp and that is due to a faulty water pipe, no problem to any plumber worth his salt.

Simon tells me stone buildings can be more expensive to develop, what is you're feeling about that?, asked Jim. They certainly can be, agreed Walter, a lot depends on the ability of your builder, a man experienced in stonework can lay a course of stone almost as quickly as a bricky laying bricks. Bearing in mind a course of stone is often equal to two courses of brick. I was more concerned about the cost of stone compared with the cost of brick. A good point, speaking new stone compared with new brick. An additional idea of mine while the large high roofed barn just past the other buildings is sound, its size alone makes it more difficult to develop. Correctly demolished, leaving the foundations intact, would provide almost all the stone you would need. With careful planning the site could be redesigned to provide workshops etc., utilising the old foundations where possible. Of course it would require a talented architect to make the most of the potential!! Luckily for you I know of just the man and as he has already been asked to provide plans for the other buildings, you may be able to persuade him to take on the job.

Gentlemen, I have seen and heard enough to convince me this site will suit my dreams very well. My suggestion is we call in Ethel and Bert offer the full asking price, Subject to the usual provisions I'm sure you have as standard. Tell them we will need the farmhouse quite soon, but would be happy for them to live in the cottage, until they are able to find other accommodation. Making sure they understand the farmyard will be a building site, with all the noise dust and disturbance that entails. During that time we will be altering some of the farmland and would be happy to have Bert's advice on how best to proceed. Paid of course.

Simon I have said before I don't know how you manage with your brain racing along at the speed it does. It goes against my nature to offer my highest price from the start of negotiations, however you are the boss. There will be no negotiations my offer is final, said Jim. May I give Bert a shout? Both men nodded, Simon adding you tell them your terms, and good luck. Jim stuck his head out and shouted Bert, getting the swift reply "coming".

Once the nervous couple were settled Jim began, and listed all the items he had outlined to his friends. I have to tell you the money I have offered is my money and is my limit. There can be no negotiations, unless you agree with my advisors who think it is too high. I am sure you would like time to talk it over but I'm sorry I must return north I have other problems waiting. If Ethel would be kind enough to make us another pot of tea we could be drinking it while you talk. Ethel stood to go and make the tea, saying you can talk to my Bert he has made all the farm decisions and never let me down yet.

Bert sat for a few moments gathering his thoughts, before saying, thank you Gentlemen our answer is yes. I have one or two minor questions, that is minor to you, more sentimentally important to Ethel and me. Behind the farmhouse we have a sty with four pigs, and a small cowshed with a couple of cows. The pigs provide the bacon you enjoyed earlier, and the cows milk and butter. The surplus goes to a local home for old and disabled people, and we would like to keep them if possible. Ethel returned in time to hear Bert's last remark, don't forget the "War Graves" in the wood, Bert I wouldn't like them forgotten.

I hadn't forgotten, love, I was about to explain. You see Gentlemen in the wood down at South Acres there are the remains of a "Lancaster Bomber", shot down at the end of the Second World war.

All the crew were killed. They had been hit while still over France, before struggling to get this far finally running out of fuel. Its believed they had flown too low to show on Radar, and no-one knew where they were and it was assumed they had crashed into the sea. The poor men were not found until after the war, explained a tearful Ethel, the R.A.F. took the remains away to try to identify them. So awful for their poor families. There are no graves in the wood said Bert, two memorial plaques listing their names. I have tried to keep them clean, but you can't hold back time and the weather. Its been a year or two since any of the families visited, the Airmen are all in proper graves now, I expect the families go there.

Thank you, said Jim, we expect that a large percentage of our guests will be from the Armed Services and I am sure they will be happy to undertake the care and maintenance of the memorials.

You were asking about the pigs and cows Bert, I'm very keen for you to keep them, in fact I am disappointed you haven't mentioned hens. A fox got in the hen house a few weeks ago, as we expected to be leaving soon we didn't bother replacing them, explained Bert. Sorry to hear all that and would like to discuss that sort of thing at length when I come back, it fits in with one of my ideas!

Thank you both for your kind hospitality, even if your farm hadn't been suitable it would have been a real pleasure to meet you. I look forward to a long association and friendship, good for all of us. Hear, hear, said Simon and Walter. They took their leave with a smiling Bert and Ethel waving their goodbyes.

Well Jim, said Simon as soon as they were in the car, if you are not tired after all that you ought to be. You have had a busy day, made some important decisions, and done very well. You have certainly made my job easier, I have worked with many an experienced business man, with nothing like the grasp of things that you have shown today. I put it down to two things, thought Jim. One! I really do dream about all this, Two!, the "Master" keeps telling me he sent me back to Earth with a very good brain, and I keep surprising myself, so who knows.

Back in the hotel Jim did not linger over dinner, explaining he had his packing to do and wanted an early start in the morning. I still have much to do once I am home, and my guest is never late. Lucky you, said Simon, there is nothing worse the waiting for late visitors. Promising to be in touch, Jim said his goodbyes and retired to bed.

Early Thursday morning saw Jim, groomed, packed and ready to go, feeling more excited than he ever expected to feel. He believed the day would present him with problems to solve, and decisions to make, but none of that mattered, when compared with the pleasure of seeing Sarah again. The journey went quickly and smoothly, with Jim having to check himself a couple of times for dozing "Now Jim better to be late than "dead" on time. He called in the Supermarket and stocked up with everything he could think of, plus one or two last minute ideas.

By early evening Jim had his home spick and span, a meal prepared, himself showered and groomed, all I need now is the Lady. No sooner the thought than the deed, car headlights shone in through the window, a sure sign that a car had pulled onto his drive. As he reached his door the car door slammed and as he opened the door Sarah ran in pausing only to plant a warm kiss on his lips. Hello!! he said, if you want to go out and do that entrance again I'm game!! No need said Sarah come here and I'll take my time this time.

Jim went and Sarah took her time, kissing Jim in a way he hadn't been kissed for a long time, with Jim returning her kisses, their hello left no doubt they were glad to see each other. They finally broke apart, both starting to say how they had been looking forward to the weekend. If it is all as good as the first ten minutes it will do for me said Jim. Oh!! Jim I have been longing to see you and at last I am here, you must tell me all you have been doing and what progress you have made.

First my love you must be hungry, I have food prepared and can have it ready in ten minutes, if you wish. Give me fifteen minutes to wash and brush up, and you're on. Well done said Jim, bathroom first right, dump your case etc. any room you like. Sarah was true to her word and returned looking refreshed and to Jim's eyes truly lovely. Jim this is delicious, any chance of a second helping? With pleasure same again coming up. The dessert was equally, well received, much to Jim's relieve. If you would like to go and make yourself comfortable, I'll bring some coffee through.

Sarah seated herself on the sofa and pulled a small table nearby, just to be sure Jim sat next to her. Once the coffee had been drunk she drew closer to him and snuggled next to him. Good show thought Jim I was hoping to do that but didn't know how. Sarah turned towards him, kissed him, and started to speak. Jim please believe I do want to hear all your news, but first can we talk about us? Ever since I first met you on "Disneyland Space" I have been very fond of you and my feelings have been growing stronger with time. It is such a thrill to be here with you now, but I can't go on pining for you while pretending my exciting job is all I need. In my heart I know you have feelings for me but I don't know how deep they are. Since you called me to tell me you wanted to see me,

I have had alternating dreams and nightmares over why you called me at this time. Please tell me the truth about your feelings, I have simply got to know.

Like you from day one in space I have strong feelings for you, I have never dared admit even to myself how these feelings have grown. When one is young it is wonderful to have, great feelings of total love for someone. At the age I am now it feels too late, and unfair to you, to cherish dreams of a long life together. I cannot expect you to give up your exciting new life, nor can I drop all my plans, disappointing so many people, seemingly depending on me. You ask me to tell you my true feelings, Sarah I simply love you, want you, and yes, desire you. The problem is I am in my 73rd. Year far too old for a young vibrant lady like you. I know the "Team" have given me a younger body, but for how long.

Sarah pulled Jim to her and covered his face with kisses, thank you my darling for telling you love me!! Please! Never another word about age and time. So you're 73 let me tell you I am 62, like you the "Team" have given me an unreal youth. Why don't we embrace all the good parts. Have the wisdom of our age, and the energy and joy of our youth. We can live more in the time we have, than many will live in a lifetime. Tonight lets only talk of love, and only think of each other. Tomorrow we can plan our life together.

In this frame of mind and with joy in their hearts they cuddled together with no further need for words. With the evening fading into night, Jim lifted Sarah to her feet, come on sweetheart time for bed, which room did you put your bag in? Sarah kissed him smiling, yours of course, silly question. Good said Jim that saves us both trying to get into the spare bed. They passed the night as lovers should, later they both swore they heard a familiar voice say, "I told you I was never wrong", but neither could be sure.

After a leisurely breakfast a stroll round the town centre and a pub lunch, the happy couple were back home cuddled on the sofa, Sarah asking Jim to tell all that had happened about his dream. If I'm to tell all I shall need a pot of tea. If you will get that while I sort my memory into some kind of order. Slave driver! said Sarah hurrying into the kitchen, quickly returning with a large pot if tea, cups and saucers. Your refreshments are served my Lord, your humble slave awaits your every wish. Glad you have learned you place so quickly, now please sit in silence while your master speaks. Sarah sat obeisant but spoilt the effect by putting her tongue out at Jim.

It took Jim over an hour to tell Sarah all that had happened, and how helpful Simon and Walter had been. He tried to explain how he felt he was a lot more aware of all that was happening than he had expected to at the start of the week. To give an example he told Sarah the story of the Estate Agent handling the sale of one of the farms. Simon and the Agent had been in lengthy negotiation, while he had looked over the land. When Jim joined them he was surprised when Simon addressed him as Mr. Fields, for the first time ever, before explaining he had been unable to reach agreement with the Agent and felt they should continue their search elsewhere. When I agreed with Simon the agent said he felt the gulf between us was not too wide and we may still find common ground. I told him I tended to find his "Gulfs" ended up costing me a lot of money. Make sure you have got my colleagues contact details and give him a ring when you can meet our offer. With that I wished him a good afternoon. Leaving poor old Simon to catch me up. Simon later told me I had played my part to perfection, and had taken an unpleasant man down a peg or two.

Once she managed to stop laughing, she said, Oh!! Jim I can see I'm going to watch myself with you or I will soon be the poor little down trodden woman. No worries there said Jim, for a start I'll never be able to catch you! Please Jim tell me all you can about the farm you have bought. First the location, only a mile or so from a very nice village complete with a school, church, and a couple of nice shops. A butcher, general store come grocer, greengrocer, and bakery. Add to that a pub, sadly on its last legs, I think with a small investment and an influx of new customers, it could be a winner.

You will love the farm, the farmhouse and barns etc. are all built of a local stone, beautiful to look at and as sound as the proverbial bell. The land is all in excellent condition, ideal for the developments I have in mind. There is also a thatched cottage, which I have offered to the farmer and his wife (Bert and Ethel) as temporary accommodation until they find somewhere suitable. I hope to keep them until the "Commune" is well on its way, They have some pigs and a couple of cows, together with a hen "Coop". Kept for their own consumption, with the surplus going to a local Old Folks Home. Trust me until you have tasted one of Ethel's bacon butties you haven't lived.

Jim my darling I want to come to all these wonderful places, not just to be with you, but to be part of all you are trying to do and to help you in any way I can. Perhaps I could be your P.A. at least until you need a new secretary. Is there any way I could help you now? Yes said Jim I need to find out all about "Glamping Yurts" and hopefully trace a British manufacturer able to modify to our spec if necessary. If you fancy giving it a try you will save me trying to fit it in. I'm afraid "Glamping Yurts" is all I can tell you, so good luck.

Jim Fields, I accept your challenge, be ready to become one of the country's leading experts on the subject. Now can we please have a cup of tea and a cuddle, while we talk about our future. Just one last thing on the farm there is a beautiful wood which contains memorial plaques to the crew of a bomber that crashed in the wood killing all the crew. Any R.A.F. personnel we may have might wish to maintain it.

Tea made, biscuits dunked, cuddles in place, Sarah returned to the subject of their future together. I really do want to be with you in all you are trying to do, but I still have six months to run on my contract with the university. There are two more tournaments this season, and I owe it to my athletes to be with them. I am proud of the reputation I have gained and would like to finish at the top. Of course you must stay with your runners, my love, knowing how hard you had to work while on "Disneyland Space" you must stay and gain all the credit you deserve. It will be at least six months before any building work takes place, and I shouldn't need a P.A. or secretary before them. My dreams about "Yurts" etc. are one of my wilder schemes, if you sort that for me I can hit my advisors with a properly researched plan. For myself I see at least six months of, meetings, planning conferences, and staffing crises. If I survive it at all I will be back to being an old man. Do not dare to say that Jim Fields, I haven't finished with the young you yet, said a smiling Sarah.

I believe you are right in all you say Jim, and see we cannot be together for six months, but can we please at least ring each other once a week and meet up every month. Yes!, Yes! Yes!, agreed Jim, roll on six months. Will you ring Carol and Harry asked Jim I don't want another lecture from Carol, but I would like them to visit the farm to give their opinions. To be honest I am keen to hear "Mark" and "Wayne's ideas as well. We will ring them tomorrow my love, you can talk to Harry and I will talk to Carol, that should save you from another lecture. The rest of the day is ours with no more talk of projects, and problems.

Sarah rang Carol and Harry after breakfast the next day and was surprised to find them both at home Carol had a day off and Harry resting before a top of the league basketball match that evening. Sarah brought Carol up to date with the developments on the romance front, Carol whooping with delight, and insisting Sarah give Jim a kiss from her immediately. Sarah called Jim to the phone and gave him a kiss, before handing the phone over allowing him to talk to Harry. Congrats old man, Harry's first words, although everyone who knows you both will be wondering what took you so long. Had to be sure she wasn't just after my money said Jim, ducking quickly to dodge a cushion that came flying at his head. When he explained to Harry he was told he was lucky, had it been Carol it would have been his head flying at the wall. "Ouch" said Jim.

Harry I was hoping to tell you and Carol the developments so far, do you have an extension she can listen on, I'd like her to hear it all. We are ahead of you Jim Carol is already listening. After some days searching with the help of an experienced land Agent, I have bought a beautiful farm with most of the benefits I hoped to find. The large farmhouse and all the farm buildings are built of a beautiful stone and all bone dry. The architect assures me that although stone is more expensive to buy than brick less of it is needed to build comparable walls. He has promised me he will keep alteration to existing outer walls to a minimum. The previous owners Bert and Ethel are staying on for a bit until they find a new house. Together they have lived and farmed here all their lives, and I hope to pick their brains.

The land which has been kept to pasture is in marvellous condition, and flat enough to suit my needs without being boring. I am hoping you will all come and visit a soon as possible. With your permission I would like the boys to tour the land to give me their point of view. With luck Bert (who is proud of his land) and his Dogs will show them the best features. You are invited as our guests and advisors, and all expenses charged to our parent company. Carol and Harry both began to protest as they would prefer to pay at least some of the cost. Not possible I'm afraid said Jim, we cannot cover your visit on our insurance if you are not on expenses. Jim Fields said Sarah, also on an extension, I swear you get more like a boss by the minute, Carol we are going to have to watch him before he gets above himself! Sarah I do not make these fool rules I just try to live by them. Yes but what happens when you realise Bosses make the rules for others to live by. Good point "wench" I'll keep it in mind for when I get a P.A. With these exchanges Carol and Harry roared with laughter, soon joined by Sarah and Jim. Carol was the first to speak, I guess you were to have been the Boss man's P.A. He will be lucky if I speak to him!! Down girls said Harry remember the poor souls new to the job.

So boys and girls what is the unions decision, do I get a visit from my advisors or not? I don't mind begging if you wish. Jim we would love to come, we both have a weeks holiday due, it was to have been at home but we are sure the boys will love a few days in the country. Thank you said Jim, did I mention we are only a dozen or so miles from the sea. Perhaps we can all have a day out suggested Sarah, Jim is a swimmer of some note, and worth a quick look when stripped to the waist. Not if it is cold, Jim's final word. Dear friends can we please leave it with you to let us know when you are free, and we will make all the arrangements, Even the BOSS may take some time off. We will be in touch, said Harry, bye for now.

Jim had just put the phone down when it rang again, the caller introduced himself as Clive and explained he had been given Jim's number by the senior "Pro" at the Grange Golf club. I am hoping to play a round this afternoon, but my usual partner has cried off. The Pro said you haven't played for a couple of weeks and may be glad of a game. Before you decide I must tell you my niece will be caddying for me, she is well behaved but some people find her a distraction. Oh! Jim came Sarah's voice from the extension, if that means I can come as well please say yes I would love to see you play. I'm sorry if I startled you Clive, I am Sarah a friend visiting Jim at the moment. What can I say Clive except what time are we teeing off. Thank you Sarah and thank you Jim, Tee off at 14-50hrs, hope that is O.K. Just fine said Jim, see you there.

Well my love you have done it now said Jim you have agreed to pull a heavy trolly through long grass for at least 4hrs. With two increasingly depressed old men and a young girl for company. However thank you I'm sure I shall enjoy myself. Sarah put her tongue out at him, saying when you have finished gloating please tell me what I should wear for the sporting event of the century. Trousers but not jeans, some kind of long sleeved blouse, and if you have one with you a light weight shower proof short length coat. The coat can go in the Golf bag in case you need it.

They arrived at the club in good time and Jim made his way to the "Pro" shop to sign in and collect his handicap certificate. He had been rated by the committee as a 16 handicap, slightly higher than he had expected, all the better for that he thought. The senior "Pro" came in to the shop while Jim was signing in, Jim exchanged greetings and introduced Sarah. Clive got in touch then, I hope you didn't mind my giving him your number, you should get on well, he is very funny once he gets to know you, He tells us his niece can be a distraction, said Jim, I think that's why Sarah was keen to come, to make sure I kept my eye on the ball. Well I would always recommend you do that anyway. At that point Clive arrived and further introductions made. Clive's niece turned out to be a 5ft. nothing bombshell, causing Sarah to turn Jim round and push him out the shop, muttering down boy.

Once on the tee, Posy the niece, passed Clive his driver, ball, and tee, then stood well back keeping out of the players eyeline. Clive a 20 handicap player hit a straight, if not overlong, drive to the middle of the fairway. Jim took his time to get the address right and also hit a straight drive many yards beyond Clive's. This set the pattern for the round, Clive's tee and ground shots much shorter than Jims, but always on line putting him on all the par 4 holes in 3 strokes, where his putter saved him all too many lost shots. Jim's best holes were the par fives, Jim's longer shots putting him on the greens in two shots. Gifting him a Birdie and an Eagle. Jim ended four shots in the lead, cancelling Clive's four stroke handicap advantage. The game a very satisfactory draw.

The query about Posy causing a distraction was solved when she began a series of balletic exercises as she followed Jim and Clive down the fairway. Sarah telling Jim he could turn round and look once, any more than once and she would kill him, unless he went blind first.

In the clubhouse after the game, everyone expressed their pleasure with thanks for a successful afternoon. Jim explained to Clive that his business was taking him away for sometime, may he contact him on his return. As they set off for home Sarah asked Jim to stop at the Pro Shop as she wanted to talk to the Pro. Whatever for, asked Jim, come and see she said, it will save me the trouble of explaining later.

Luckily the Pro was in the shop, and happy to give Sarah all the time she needed. I wondered if you had a couple of ladies clubs I could buy just to try my hand at this golf lark. I'm working at Cambridge University and can probably get free tuition if I get enthused, Yes I can sell you as many clubs as you

wish. Buying clubs separately is an expensive way of doing it, the clubs I would show you are anything between £55 and £110 each. I have a very good second hand ladies set including bag, tees, and half a dozen or so quality balls. I don't usually deal in second hand equipment, but this person was the Ladies Captain and bought all her equipment from me deserving any help I could give her. You could have the lot for £400 pounds, a real bargain. I hadn't expected to pay that much as I don't know if I will enjoy playing the game, as much as I have enjoyed watching it today.

You know I will be happy to buy you anything you may want, buy the set and a trolly if you don't take to the game Egg developments will buy them from you to try to get the resident ladies interested.

Knowing how independent you are, Jim added, If you prefer to pay what you expected to pay I could pay the balance, and you could repay me if and when you get a handicap. On that basis I agree said Sarah and solemnly shook hands with both men.

Glad to have got that settled said Jim I was going to suggest a pub or restaurant meal but I am wondering if we could get a meal in the Clubhouse. The Clubhouse meals are quite wonderful, but I doubt your dress would meet the exacting requirements. The same food is available in the bar where dress is optional, although the bar can be rather noisy. What do you think asked Jim, I would prefer somewhere not too crowded, saying the bar can be noisy suggests it may also be very busy suggested Sarah. Fair comment said Jim somewhere quiet it shall be.

Once in the car Sarah said I know of a very nice little house on a quiet street where we could be alone. There are sausages in the fridge and potatoes and onions in the cupboard, sausage and mash fit for royalty. You have convinced me said Jim, and headed home smiling.

The sausage and mash proved a great success, and was soon eaten. So what's next asked Jim I suggest a cuddle on your lovely sofa while we cross the "Ts" and dot the "Is" on our future plans. I still feel we must allow the six months we spoke of, to each put our life in order before getting together for ever and ever. Not a day more than six months please. Oh! Jim not a moment more than the six months, I am sure I couldn't bear it. I know we said we would ring each other once a week I feel if we each rang the other each week it would be twice as good. Agreed, said Jim and I promise that whenever possible I will fly up to Cambridge for extra weekends. Actually flying might be the answer I will check for local airfields, to see if it is possible to fly to Cambridge and back, giving us more time together.

That would be lovely Jim, you really are thinking like a multi millionaire these days. Being rich is a lot easier to get used to than being poor, Jim's reply. Seriously my love, if we can increase the number of phone calls and pull in extra weekends time should pass more quickly. I'm sure you are right Jim, agreed Sarah. In that case can I change the subject and spend a few minutes telling you I love you. Well Mr. Fields this is all a bit sudden, but yes so long as you are gentle with me. Mind you not too gentle!

The couple spent what was left of their weekend together, very relaxed and generally taking life easy. The only surprise contact from one of the "Masters" Team, (I am one of the "Masters" accountants) and I am happy to inform you a further £25, 000.000 has been paid into your bank. A small gesture from the "Master" and his Team, to show our appreciation of all you are doing. At that the voice went silent, as did Jim and Sarah. Just when I think nothing will ever surprise me again, Mr, Egg pulls one of his stunts.

All too soon it was Monday morning, time for the lovers to split up and get back to the real world. Jim faced the longer journey and was to contact Sarah as soon as he arrived, in order to make sure they both had safe trips. Jim's mobile phone had rung twice while he was driving, he expected there would be messages. Someone was anxious to get him back into work mode. His first call was to Sarah, who had beaten him back by half an hour. They managed to keep the call fairly brief as apart from the messages Jim had received, Sarah had been contacted by one of her runners needing help and advice. I really do not mind Jim the busier we are the quicker the time will go.

Jim was not too surprised to find his calls were from Simon and Walter, both of whom sort audience with their lord and master. Or as they put it, Jim please ring as soon as possible I have news, it seems he had been the only one not working over the weekend.

Simon First thought Jim, surely Walter cannot have hit problems so soon. Hello Simon don't tell me there has been a major Earthquake and Bert's farm uprooted. That's right Jim, the worst part is we had just exchanged contracts and the farm was your property at the time. You win Simon you're much better at fake news than I am, may I take it the contracts are ready for signature?, I do not know if your position as land agent qualifies you to sign or if I have the sole privilege. Its all yours Jim, I can be at the farm this afternoon if you wish to get it sealed. Although why anyone would be keen to sign a document that is going to cost him millions of pounds, I cannot imagine. If you ever figure it out let me know please, begged Jim. Thanks I will see you this afternoon.

Hello Walter, what can I do for you, Good news, I hope, depending on your cash flow. I have been contacted by a local demolition company who have a quantity of stone the same as the farm buildings. He is anxious for a quick sale and offering a good deal, if we can accept delivery this week, with full payment this month. Walter I am completely in your

222

hands, I have no knowledge of stone, may I take it the stone is clean ready for use, or will we incur some extra expense cleaning it ourselves. I'M sure you must think it worth buying. Just for my experience go back and tell him your Client is concerned about the cost of cleaning the stone, and try to get the price down a bit. Sorry if I sound like I'm trying to teach my Granny to suck eggs, but I have to learn. Do not lose the stone if you can help it. While I think about it size of ground to dump it all on until we need it? Simon and I will be at the farm this afternoon, if you or one of your staff has the time to help us find the most suitable dumping ground. I can't spare the time myself, although the thought of Ethel's bacon sandwiches is very tempting, I will brief my son Peter and send him along, one day soon he is going to be better than his Dad. Please don't tell him I said that. One other thing a very good local construction company has just been thrown off site, the company they were working for has gone bankrupt owing them thousands. Keep in close touch with them Walter and get them to work A.S.A.P. It happened to me once and it was the shop floor workers who were hardest hit. Bye for now I look forward to meeting your son later today.

Jim made his way to the farm to find Simon and Peter had both arrived, Jim joined them saying hello Simon, hello peter, when is God due? Very droll, said Simon, I gather you had a good weekend, or are you always this happy on a Monday morning? Only when I am to meet someone of your wisdom and Peter's charm, replied Jim, and Simon held up his arms in a gesture of surrender.

To business then gentlemen in his best authoritative voice, have you had chance to look for a suitable dumping ground. Or can we leave that to Peter while we go to talk to Bert. I have all the documents for Bert to sign, said Simon, so if Peter is happy for us to leave the dumping site to him, we could go and get the contract signed and sealed. Having sampled your collective humour, I need some time to recover, with your permission I'll toddle off on my own, Said a smiling Peter.

Jim and Simon headed off to find Bert and Ethel. As usual the couple met them at the door and waved them both inside. After the exchange of pleasantries, Simon produced the sale documents, saying, just a couple of signatures, and all will be signed and sealed. Not quite said Bert there is still the small matter of the money. Very true said Jim if when you have signed I may have your bank details, I can have the money transferred today. Failing that I can give you a cheque which will no doubt take a week to clear. Cheque please said Bert, Ethel and I fancy strolling into the bank and paying a few millions in. Make a nice change from asking for loans they would rather not give us. Anyway we have never seen the manager smile! Ever practical Ethel asked if she could sign first and go and get the kettle on, Not really said Simon you will be signing as a witness and should see us all sign. It is not a problem go and make the tea and poor Jim can hang on to his money a moment or two longer.

The tea was soon made, and the signing completed. Hand shakes all round, Jim writing the biggest cheque he hoped he would ever have to write, with apparent nonchalance. Simon is there anything else you need to talk to Bert and Ethel about, if not I would like to pick their brains. Always assuming they can spare the time. I have finished said Simon except to thank you all very much, I have completed quite a few farm sales over the years, but never before as pleasant as this one. I will go and see how Peter is getting on. Bring him in for a cup of tea if he wants one, insisted Ethel, will do Simon called over his shoulder.

Now friends I was hoping to pick your brains. You have probably guessed this is my first time on a farm and I have lots of ideas but I'm not sure if they are workable. You mentioned a couple of days ago you have cows and pigs and the potential to keep hens. This made me think maybe we could run a course for people who might be interested in Market Gardening, or Smallholding. Is there any spare land behind the house, which perhaps I haven't seen? Some, but not enough for the kind of development you are suggesting. What about the corner of Joe Kerry's field, it joins our land and he never uses it, suggested Ethel. I doubt Joe will give it away and it will take a pretty penny to put right.

Could we go and look Bert asked Jim, good idea are you coming Ethel you know more about Smallholdings than I do. Yes I will get my coat, Ethel's family are all smallholders, so was she before I wooed her away from it. While we are out we will look at her garden behind the cottage. The pig sty and cow shed were in first class condition, although the Hen Coop would require some repair. Bert's land was larger than he expected, but not large enough, although like all Bert's land in good condition.

However, the adjoining piece of land was sadly neglected and given over to weeds and wild flowers. What's the soil going to be like if we decide to clear it, Jim asked Bert. Clear the big stuff plough the rest under over winter it, harrow it and away you go. Will I need all the scrub land or will that be too much?

Well Jim, if I may call you that, land is wealth if properly kept. If you are going to be teaching visitors, you will need to be fully equipped which means storage units, potting sheds, rest rooms and probably a shop area to sell the surplus. That will take a year or two but you will have to plan now, at least that's my opinion said Ethel. My brother Sam is about to retire, and will be glad of something to keep him interested. No doubt his children will be pleased for him to have something to keep him out of their hair.

In that case, if you have Joe Kerry's number I will give him a ring and see if I can start a ball rolling. Best let me ring him first, he is a "cranky" old bugger but I reckon I can handle him. Ethel has called your friends in and is busy boiling kettles and making bacon sandwiches. So you won't be bored for a minute or two. Good I'm getting peckish, lead me to it.

Jim sat near the door of the snug hoping to hear some of Bert's conversation, thinking I didn't ought to snoop but there is a lot at stake. Joe must be hard of hearing as Bert was having to shout, together with Jims much improved hearing, meant he caught most of it. Bert was saying Joe you know I sold my farm, yes best thing I ever did. The gentleman I sold it to is interested in that bit of old scrub land, you do know, the bit that runs up past the back of my house. Louder mumblings from Joe sounding like protests! Joe yes it is a bit of old scrub land, you know it as well as I do, I doubt if you have set foot on it this ten years. Yes he will know it's no good, he might not be a farmer but he is not blind nor daft. Look I think if you play your cards right he will probably clear it all himself, and put a fence between his bit and yours. No, I don't think you can charge him for the land he will be saving you a lot of trouble and expense as it is. I'll bet you already have the ministry on your back for not doing anything with it. If I bring Mr. Fields round to see you are you going to be civil to him or not? More mumblings from Joe. Yes I know you're always civil as long as you're getting your own way, well I'll tell you now Mr. Fields is very fair but when he says no he means it, now I'm missing my supper can I bring him or not? Right I'll tell him Tuesday afternoon, if he can't make it I'll give you another ring. More irritated mumbling. I told you not to talk rubbish, if he can make it he will. If not I have a bit down my bottom field might do him.

With that last salvo, Bert hung up and came to speak to Jim. I'm sorry Bert I've been eavesdropping and heard all your side of the conversation, perhaps you can give me the gist of his reply. He says it is a valuable piece of land he has big plans for! That is flannel he has been nowhere near it for years and it takes him all his time to work the rest of his land. He is talking about asking top price for it and says he won't budge. You heard me tell him if you clear the land and fence it, he cannot expect to be paid as well. I think you should talk to your friend Simon to estimate the lands value. I will cost out the clearing and fence building, take one from the other and you should have a better idea of its value to you. A point to remember there is no water supply, which you will need for market gardening. Thank you Bert I will do all you say. Today is Wednesday I have six days before Tuesday and promise to do my homework, and turn up with my business head on.

Now friends I have to go, I have no hotel booked and have an important phone call to make tonight. Mr. Fields my son's room is vacant now, it has it own bathroom and a small sitting room, we would be delighted to have you stay here if convenient for you. Ethel that sounds wonderful Jim enthused, throw in a couple of meals, and permission for my better half to visit and I'm in. You must, of course, let me pay you the going rate, and call me Jim. Ethel and Bert both shook their heads, we will call you Jim with pleasure, we will not charge you a penny, until we are living in the cottage and you charge us the going rate, said Bert, with Ethel nodding her agreement. May I remind you I promised you the cottage free of charge argued Jim. We haven't forgotten and that is why we say we will only charge you when you charge us, Ethel the spokesman this time. Ethel give me a hug, Bert let me shake your hand we have a deal.

Bert and Ethel complied with his wish and then took him to view the room. Jim would have struggled to find a more comfortable set of rooms anywhere. A spacious bedroom with a "king size" bed and large windows overlooking the best views the farm had to offer. Bathroom with bath, shower, washbasin with mirror and toilet. The small sitting room again had wonderful views, two large armchairs and even a desk for Jim or his P.A. to use. Jim tried to say he couldn't expect such luxury for nothing. Rubbish said a surprisingly forceful Ethel if you ever go in the cottage you will find real luxury. Now supper in half an hour, while you eat I will put clean sheets on your bed and air it.

Jim's phone call to Sarah was full of news of all his doings, but mainly about his new digs, and Ethels superb cooking. He was at pains to outline his plans for his P.A. to work at the desk while he reclined on the bed. Oh! No big man let me tell you if I am anywhere near and you lie on the bed so do I, said Sarah laughingly. If you are thinking that puts me off the idea, you are quite wrong, Jim's reply. Sexy beast, any more off that kind of talk and I will hang up. So be quiet while I tell you my news I have had a couple of Golf lessons, apart from not hitting the ball very far or very straight I've just about mastered it. Lots of the lady Golfers have admired my clubs, a couple offering twice I paid for them. The Pro says no golfer is ever better than their clubs, so hang on to them they are good. I have been checking up on private airfields, and there is one, better still one of my fellow instructors flies from here and is licenced to carry paying passengers. He only has a four seater aeroplane, which restricts his ability to carry the kind of family groups most planes like to carry. Of course this means he would be ideal for us. He didn't know if there is a suitable airfield near you, but promised to find out and let me know at the next team talk. It really would be lovely to just jump on a plane and be together in no time. On the other job you gave me, no news yet, but at least I now know what I am talking about. The talk moved on to more personal things, until it was time to say goodnight.

Jim settled in very quickly in his new "digs", enjoying the convenience of being on site without having to commute. Most days walking with Bert and his dogs, all the time learning more about the land.

The second hand stone he had bought was now stored in three tidy mounds behind the barns, handy but not intrusive. Walter and various members of his team had visited the site on several occasions, checking details, and revising ideas that hadn't proved workable. Walter had explained many of his plans to Jim who was in the main very impressed. Walter was also impressed, when Jim queried one idea which was the one Walter had come to check its feasibility. Jim was fretting about losing the local construction company, begging Walter to find them something to do, before they found work elsewhere. Can they start on roads and pathways? Not yet Jim perhaps next week.

Simon arrived to check and measure the scrubland, his first comment "only you could see value in this mess". I look with my eyes not with pound signs, Jim's reply, and with Bert's help we are going to get it cheap. Then you will spend a fortune getting it usable, said Simon. Then we will train a disabled person a happy contented way to keep their family. O.K. you win I give in said a smiling Simon, applauded by Ethel and Bert.

Tuesday arrived and Jim and Bert set off to do battle with Joe Kerry, Bert promised to show approval of what Jim said, I know you will be fair. Be warned though Joe will try every trick in the book, fair or not. Sarah, my girlfriend, says I think and talk like a "Bossman", let's hope it works today.

Joe met them at the door and after brief introductions said you had best come in I suppose! Thank you said Jim although I will not keep you long, like yourself my time is very precious. I am sure you understand I have a slight interest in the plot of scrubland, and my advisors tell me the cost of clearing and fencing will negate its value. So all there is to decide if you will let it go on my promise, in writing if you wish, to clear and fence the plot at my expense.

Now look here said Joe, sounding flustered, you can't march in hear laying down the law, telling me what my land is worth. Mr. Kerry I am sorry if I have upset you in some way, I have merely laid out my offer as one businessman to another. I'm sure you know the law as well as I. Having come this far I will be delighted to hear what you have to say. That is a prime piece of land, and I have plans of my own for it, I don't know that I want to sell it at all. I reckon there must be the best part of four acres, and I couldn't think of any less than £2,000, I'm robbing myself at that. Two things then Mr. Kerry, being a city man we tend to measure ground space in "Square Yards", so I had your scrubland measured properly by my Land Agent" and he assures me there are just under two acres, needing a hundred and thirty five yards. of fencing, your estimate of £500 an acre is totally unacceptable. Will you please give my offer some proper consideration as it really is realistic.

I may have over estimated the size of the plot, but I'm not that far out with cost per acre, I will come down to £400, what do say? said Joe offering his hand for Jim to shake. Sir, said Jim, you have my offer, and if £400 per acre is yours I'm afraid we are wasting our time. I will tell you what, you probably need something from me to tell your friends how you took me for a ride. So here is my final offer which I need you to accept without further discussion, as time is pressing, I will pay all expenses as agreed plus £75 per acre for two acres. With that Jim stood up took the agreement and a pen from his pocket and looked at Joe expectantly. Oh! Give it here said Joe, I wonder you don't ask for a couple of pints of blood while you're at it. Both copies signed and witnessed by Bert, Jim shook Joes hand and made a quick exit.

Thank you Bert, if you hadn't warned me about that old reprobate, I would never have been able to cope with him. Well I thought you handled him like an angler with a fish, that bit about giving him something to brag about was brilliant.

Ethel greeted Jim excitedly saying you have had a phone call from "Sarah" she wants to speak to you urgently. You go and make your call and I will bring you a pot of tea and a piece of cake. If you have been arguing with that Joe you must be parched. Thanks said Jim, running up the stairs before dialling Sarah's number, she answered on the first ring, can I come and see you this weekend. I can fly down Friday evening arriving seven thirtyish. Returning early evening Sunday. The airfield is a private one about ten miles northeast called Oldsmith Airfield, on the fringe of Oldsmith village. My friend is bringing his wife with him and staying the weekend. Which is why we can have a lovely long visit, of course you will have to pay him, I am Not a multi millionaire. Delighted to, must check with Ethel If only out of politeness, she has just come in with my tea. I wondered who you were shouting "come in" to. Loudly Hello Ethel, thanks for passing the message on. Ethel says a pleasure, and she does not mind you sharing my room, but don't tell Bert we are not married. He will not mind but he might chat you up, said Ethel, and left laughing. The two lovers chatted on a little longer, before hanging up, Jim promising to ring Sarah on Thursday, to make sure her flight was still on. Jim felt that was enough excitement for one day, dozing in his armchair until Ethel called him to supper. Its!, not a bad life sometimes he thought.

The next morning Walter and Peter appeared on the doorstep almost before Jim had finished his breakfast. May we come in we have plans to show you and ideas to put to you. You had better come up to my office said Jim, hiding a smile. The two men followed Jim upstairs, exchanging puzzled glances, impressed by the sitting room come office they congratulated Jim on his ability to get his feet under the table wherever he went. Walter began by saying he knew Jim was concerned not to lose the services of the local construction company, with this in mind we are thinking of starting work on the roads, paths, and parking areas sooner than would be normal. If you would look at Peters plans, he will show you the areas we hope to start with. A few minutes looking at the plans bought over to him how much he had to learn about construction. Peter began to enthusiastically explain the drawings to Jim. Whoa there mate I'm sure you know what you are talking about but you will have to slow down for me to keep up. Sorry Jim dad is always telling me not to let my enthusiasm run away with me. Now you know why Said Walter, nodding his acceptance. The plans showed outlines of where the houses would be and pathways and roads in greater detail, Including the main route from farmhouse to the public highway.

Jim could find no fault with the lay out, asking why were the roads normally left until building work was finished. The roads are liable to suffer damage due to the heavy delivery vehicles and accidents during unloading. I need to explain if you allow us to build the roads in advance, we will have to build them to a higher standard than may have been necessary. I understand said Jim but in my view the extra strength may be a boon. One of my dreams is to have a course for would be motor mechanics, and repair and maintenance of heavy farm machinery. With a possibility of such vehicles used to train would be farm hands correct handling of same. I notice there is no details of walls around the dwellings, I would have thought some kind of barrier to keep children safe essential. Walter smiled, saying I told my team that would be the first thing you would say, we are engaged at this time looking at a variety of walling and fencing to find the most appropriate material. Surely, Jim replied, nothing beats a good brick wall.

In many ways you are right, but build a brick wall next to a busy road, Not if it gets hit by a car, it may stop the car but a section of the wall will collapse, at least blocking the pathway, or injuring a passerby. If we can find something the car will bounce off, so much the better. Of course if it also lets

light through even better, explained Walter. My instinct is to say yes go ahead, however if you could leave the plans with me for a day or so I can take my time with them and be sure I am not being too hasty, due to my desire to get started. Not a problem said Walter, if you only take a couple of days, you will confirm Simon's claim, you are a man of very quick decision.

Refusing Jims offer of tea, Walter promised to contact him in a couple of days, to get the ball rolling.

Jim spent some time standing in the middle of the square formed by the existing building, studying the map trying to get the proposed road lay out firmly in his mind. He continued with this study every spare moment for the next two days until he felt he was ready to face Walter and Peter. To his surprise Walter rang to suggest he and Peter come to the site, rather than phone, to be more able to answer any problem Jim may wish to raise. Jim agreed, saying I do have one or two minor queries, as you say lets get the ball rolling.

The two men arrived promptly as arranged, and were soon closeted it Jims office. Right Jim you said you had some minor queries, poor Peter here couldn't sleep last night wondering what they might be. Simple enough Jim assured him, I expect it is my lack of experience reading plans that is causing my concern. You have most of the pathways along the side of the barns etc., which suggest the footprint of the new dwellings will remain as is. Does this mean that there is to be no drainage from bathrooms kitchens etc. into the area where the paths will be. Your plan does not show the two Sycamore trees which I am anxious to keep if possible. You have shown a plot of land to the right of the main gate, with the outline of a derelict building of some sort. I confess I had never noticed this and it intrigues me. May I suggest, I try to persuade Ethel to make us some tea, while you two think about what I have said. We are certainly ready for tea, and need a couple of minutes to wipe our furrowed brows.

Ethel was as always happy to make tea and with Bert's help soon appeared with trays of tea and cakes. Little was said while the tea and cake were consumed with relish, and cries of "I needed that"!! Now Jim to answer your questions, we have to confess you have caught us out slightly we didn't expect you to pick up on the missing drainage. We have had problems with the exact sighting of the drains and the final drawings are still to be printed. The builders will not be here for at least a week, you have our firm promise the sumps main drains, and domestic drains will all be in position before the builders are ready. We perhaps should have explained all that to you yesterday, we will know better in future. Good said Jim smiling. We have been in touch with a local tree surgeon, and he will examine the trees to decide how best for us to proceed with the road passing so close to them. Thankyou said Jim, please make sure the tree surgeon knows his priority is to save the trees if he can. The plot of land by the gate is a bit of a puzzle, we have carried out extensive checks on your behalf and have definite conformation that it is your land. Short of going to the county archives to do a search, there are several conflicting theories about the ancient building remains. Perhaps Bert may have some clue that has passed word of mouth down the years. Again thanks for your efforts, perhaps when you are less busy you can have it all surveyed, it may prove suitable for a site office or even a short stay car park. With that the two men made their departure. Having promised the builders will be on sight in two days to work on the drains. The civil engineers on site as soon as the materials needed were available. What Jim didn't hear was Walter telling his son, "Simon warned me he has a brain like a steel trap", we will have to be on top line when we deal with him in future, Peter nodding in agreement.

Jim asked Bert about the ancient building near the gate. The local legend that Bert had learned at his grandfather's knee, was the entire area had once belonged to a Feudal Lord, and the building had been a gatehouse guarding the road. It was thought to have been fortified to explain the large and strong foundations. Of course over the centuries much of the upper stonework had been taken for building materials. It was rumoured the South Porch of the village Church had been built in this way, and that had to be hundreds of years old.

The drainage team arrived as promised, and were soon fans of Ethel's bacon sandwiches, even though Bert and Jim had persuaded her to charge, If you don't you will be swamped when there are up to a hundred hungry men on site. It does seem mean Bert when we are millionaires, but I'll give the money to charity!

Friday arrived at last, and Jim set off to find Oldsmith Village and Airfield, arriving in good time in spite of taking a wrong turning on the way. The office and control tower were one and the same building, controller "call me Frank", telling Jim your pilot has been in touch and says E.T.A. in Twenty minutes. Fifteen minutes later the radio bleeped into life and Sarahs pilot came through loud and clear. Calling Oldsmith this is SAC 497 have you on visible request permission to land. Thank you SAC 497 we have you in our orbit all is clear you are free to land. Thank you control over and out.

The shining silver and blue aircraft came calmly into view, making a perfect three point landing before taxiing to the "Hard shoulder" and cutting the engine. A door opened and Sarah came flying out to throw herself into Jim's arms. Oh Jim that was such fun! It is the only way to travel, don't forget to pay Alec. I'm not sure I will pay him argued Jim, if I don't, he won't fly you back and you can stay here with me. You can't buy me that cheap said Sarah calling Alec and his wife "Margaret" over. Introducing them both, before saying pay the man, or else. Yes dear of course dear said Jim producing a large sum of money from his pocket. I assumed it would have to be cash Alec, lets you and I go somewhere away from Sarah's gaze. Do not let him short change you Alec, he gets more a miser every day!

Jim and Sarah were to run Alec and Margaret into the seaside town just beyond the farm, Jim managing the journey without getting lost. Dropping them outside a small hotel near the sea front. You will have to let me know what it is like, we may need a decent hotel some time in the future, said Jim.

Sarah was excited and delighted at her first view of the farm, loving the stone work of the buildings, and enchanted by the vista provided by the beautiful farmland. Jim no less excited by Sarah's pleasure. As expected Ethel and Bert were at the door, having seen Jim's car arrive. Ethel and Sarah were instant friends, sharing a cuddle of welcome. Not to be out done Bert embraced Sarah while kissing her on the cheek. Everyone laughing when Ethel said, I told you to watch him, no woman is safe. Especially not you said Bert chasing her into the house.

I have your supper on and you can have it here with us or we can bring it up to your room. Oh! Please have I time for a quick shower and then eat in our room, we have so much to talk about, with both my news and Jim's. Promise we will share meals with you while I am here, and Bert I want to go on one of your walks with the dogs. A pleasure my lovely said Bert but don't go near them until I have introduced you, they have to be taught who their friends are. Sarah fell instantly in love with Jim's rooms, saying honestly Jim I don't know how you do it. I swear if you fell off "Big Ben" you would land in "Harrod's bedding department!! Now, Now, dear let's have no jealousy, you know you can share my bed anytime you wish. Go and get your shower and be ready for as nice a supper as you have ever tasted. You see nothing but the best for you ever, said Sarah, rushing into the shower. Just emerging as Ethel and Bert arrived with the food.

After a lovely meal they settled in the armchairs to exchange news. Jim started, briefly explaining about the construction company, and all the business about paths and roads. You will be able to see where work has begun, I dream we are at last under way.

Sarah spoke of how lovely and quick the flight had been, I don't care what it cost you it was worth every penny. My Golf is starting to improve and I have applied to join a local club. I explained I am only in the area for six months, and they are allowing me a six month membership. On the track my runners have continued their winning ways, other teams are beginning to ask about my training methods. I have told them nothing doing until after I leave Cambridge.

Now my big news! I think I have found a manufacturer of "Glamping Yurts", a company in Somerset well known for the manufacture of tents, canopies and windbreaks, are hoping to begin manufacturing "Yurts" if their sales team can drum up sufficient interest. I thought you and I could arrange to go and see them with the intention of placing a large order if their prototype met our requirements. I have brought their brochure and will show it to you when I unpack. The brochure does not show the "Yurt" but gives a good idea of their manufacturing capability. The sales manager is going to send you a photograph, and details of the size etc. Sarah that is such good news, thank you very much, you are very clever, as well as lovely. Well James Fields if I am so lovely why is there so much space between us. Follow me, she instructed heading for the bedroom.

After breakfast the next morning Jim led Sarah on a tour of the former barns, for her to see their potential as future homes. Jim had always thought the "front" of the houses would face towards the central parking area. Sarah was insistent that it would be better if they faced the other way, asking who wants to overlook a car park when they could be overlooking those beautiful fields. Jim had no answer but to promise he would contact Walter and see which way his plans faced. I hope he agrees with you as the plans are drawn up and it would take weeks and cost a lot of money to change them now. Jim rang Walter, explaining Sarah's thoughts, fear not Jim, we have ladies in our office, who thought of that on day one.

Lunch, and Ethels bacon sandwiches, Sarah asking Bert if he had walked the dogs yet. I want to see the farmland close to, Jim is such a city boy, he wouldn't have a clue. In about an hour my Lovely, Ethel and me have a bit of a rest now, we used to plan the farms day, but now we talk about our future. I don't know which is the bigger worry.

The details of the "Yurts" had arrived that morning and Jim excused himself from "Walkies" to study them. Tired of me already are you? Sarah wanted to know. You may live to regret that remark it does not do to upset the BOSS too often. Come on Bert lets you and me escape before the nasty man attacks me said Sarah with a broad grin.

The walk was all Sarah had hoped for, Bert so completely knowledgeable, and the dogs, now her best friends, chasing everything that moved. They miss having sheep and cows to herd explained Bert. Sarah told him about the "Yurts" and Jim's idea that they may make ideal temporary homes for single guests. I think upper left field would be best for that idea, it doesn't slope much, and is always well drained. We have passed it once, so I will show it to you on the way back. Do you mind if we start back now, I have promised to give Ethel a hand in the kitchen before supper. I think just she doesn't trust me on my own with you. I heard her telling the dogs to keep an eye on me. Do not worry Bert I'm a very fast runner and I'll put her mind at rest. I'm not worried about you running away its your feller running towards me, I don't fancy. If he does Bert I'll stand in his way! After this exchange they arrived back at the farmhouse still laughing. Hearing their laughter, a smiling Ethel met them at the door, saying, it sounds as if he hasn't behaved too badly! No problem Ethel, I have told Bert I am a very fast runner and he would never catch me. I can vouch for that, said Jim as he came down the stairs, we once trained together and she was always too fast for me.

The next day was Sunday and Jim and Sarah were saddened to know they must soon part. With this in mind, apart from meals and a quick walk to look at the medieval ruins near the gate they remained in their room. Spending their time in ever more wonderful dreams of what their life would soon be. It was a subdued couple who set off to pick up Margaret and Alec, and onward to the Airfield. Bert and Ethel seemed genuinely sad at Sarah's departure asking her to come back as soon as possible. Ethel holding her tight. While Bert called her friends the dogs to say goodbye, before kissing her on both cheeks, saying don't worry about your feller we will look after him.

To their relief, Sarah rang later to say she was safely home after a pleasant hassle-free flight. Alec and Margaret had a great time, hoping we can all do it again soon.

Monday saw the arrival of the road laying machinery, and the end of peace and calm at Sycamore Farm. As Sarah had renamed it with Bert and Ethels permission. The good news, the schoolteachers occupying the cottage left as arranged, Ethel pleased to find they left the cottage in good clean order and no breakages. For the first time Jim was able to have a careful look round, being delighted by the cottages great charm and the beauty of the rear garden. All of it down to Ethel's hard work, Bert was quick to tell Jim, she has always worked longer and harder than me.

Jim's day was made when he received a long-awaited phone call from Harry, the Edwards family were having a week's break in two weeks' time and hope they can pay the long proposed visit. Carol has spoken to Sarah who says she has not booked any time off but as most of the staff and students are away she can see no problem. If the powers that be turn awkward they can have my instant resignation and I will run away to the great love of my life, Bert and his dogs! Jim and Harry joined in the general laughter. Please come as soon as you can, Sarah has been working so hard a holiday would do her a world of good.

Jim was pleased and surprised when a second team of builders arrived, and began digging the trenches etc. for the drains. The foreman sort Jim out with a message from Walter, saying he would be coming to see Jim that afternoon with the final plans for his approval. Jim very excited by this news, promptly rang Sarah's number hoping to speak to her. Having no luck he decided to wait until that evening when he would have the plans, and could explain them to her.

True to his word Walter arrived, for once without his son Peter. He and Jim retired to Jim's office, and began a close and detailed examination of the plans. I will have to keep the plans overnight Jim explained, I want to talk through them with Sarah tonight. Since she noticed the way the new dwellings were to face, I feel her input can be useful. If it will help I can get the girls in the office to E-Mail them to her, If you have her number. I have, and that sounds a great idea, thank you said Jim. Of course Sarah's copy won't be full size but must be better than nothing. I agree said Jim. The two men continued their examination of the plans, Jim finding no serious problems. Good said Walter if Sarah has nothing to add, I can get the foreman started on the secondary drains straight away.

How long before its all finished, your best guess, asked Jim. Even for you Jim I am not going to try to answer that on day one of the build.

If ever an architect does that for you will know he is a charlatan. I had an idea I was pushing my luck said Jim.

At that Bert knocked and came in, Ethels doing bacon cobs for the builders, would either of you gentlemen like one? Yes please said the men in unison, put kettle on Bert and I'll come down and make some tea, save you another trip, offered Jim. Oh! No, you don't, said Bert, at the moment I'm in her ladyship's good books and want to stay that way. Anyway now I'm not working I need the exercise. Bert was soon back with tea and cobs, and Jim and Walter settled down to discuss the possible future of Egg Investments.

To be honest Walter it is rather like rolling a snowball down a snow laden slope. The further it rolls the bigger and faster it gets. I have this fear that one day it is going to roll right over me. Do not worry Jim, both Simon and I feel you are doing brilliantly, we have both worked for large investment companies where the C.E.O. and his minions have a far weaker grasp of everything, than you have always shown. No doubt because to them it is just a job, to you it is something you care and dream about. May I assure you Simon, Peter and of course me, firmly believe in what you are trying to do and are with you all the way.

Thank you for that said Jim you can have no idea what it means to me. I hope you all do not live to regret it. While you are here can I show you this plan of a "Glamping Yurt" if it proves at all practicable, I hope to purchase a number of these as housing for any single quests we may have. If we cannot fill them perhaps the wives of patients may be able to run them as holiday lets. Walter was very interested in the drawing but thought drainage and mains water supply may prove too expensive. Perhaps we could talk to your drainage consultant, to get his thoughts. I think it might be a good idea to ask Bert as well he has been working this land all his life and may have a trick or two up his sleeve. Agreed said Walter, if at all possible I would like to accompany you to the works to see the actual product. I have another project in the pipeline, and these tents could possibly solve one of my clients' problems.

This has been Sarah's project up to now, and I will tell all you have said. One last thought if Egg Investments and your client both order "Yurts" I shall expect priority of delivery. Simon said you don't miss a trick, I agree, said Walter, ruefully. As I said this has been Sarah's project, I am disinclined to go any further until she can be with me, subject to her consent I will keep you informed. Thank you said Walter.

If there is nothing else you wish to discuss, I will get off, and look forward to hearing from you in the morning. As soon as he had gone Jim ran down the stairs hoping to speak to Bert. Sorry said Ethel he is out walking the dogs, it's their second walk today so he won't have gone far. You can wait here for him and I can put the kettle on, or you can go down passed the top fields and you're sure to meet. Thanks Ethel I'll do that; the walk will do me good and it's the top fields I want to talk to him about.

Jim soon found Bert on his way back with the dogs. Glad I caught you Bert, Sarah told me you thought the top left field would probably be the best if we decide on the "Yurts" option. That's right Bert agreed, this is the one, as you can see it doesn't slope as much as the others, and has always drained well. I'm not a builder but I think it is nearest to the electricity mains, which might be useful. You are right about the electricity Bert, the drainage has been much on my mind, why do you think this field drains so well? That's a question that has puzzled my family for tens of years. My father thought and so do I, it is because the field is higher in the middle than at the two sides. The water drains not just from top to bottom, but also from the middle to the sides. Kind of a double action if you like, you can often find the ground under the side hedges fairly wet where it catches the extra water. If you do set a number of these tent things on there, your Architect will need take that into consideration, or the tents could get flooded. Bert you are a bloody marvel, I've now seen the slope and I'll bet you and you're Dad are right. Now Bert do you think Ethel will have the kettle on? She has never failed yet said Bert, can't think why she should start now.

Ethel had the kettle on the boil, and soon provided tea and delicious cakes. Bert, she said, you had a phone call while you were out, Sam Button rang to say his ploughman "Colin" will be here tomorrow to turn over that bit of land that you got off Joe Kerry. He said to tell you it will cost you a couple of pints, and whatever Colin wants. If you still frequent your "Local" now you have come into money! You will have to remember to open the fence, or he won't get the plough in. Thanks love I hadn't thought of that. I'll give Sam a ring and arrange to meet him and Colin in his "Local" sometime next week.

Would that be your local or his, Jim wanted to know, I only ask as I have not yet been to the Pub in the village and wondered what it is like. It used to be a lovely place, and could be again if someone could spend a few thousand on it. Mind, it would have to be done properly or you could ruin the beauty of the place. Claude the owner is to retire shortly, he reckons he can't afford to do the repairs. I think he has made his pile out of it and wants to take it with him. Sarahs coming to stay for a couple of weeks isn't she? take her up there she will soon put you on the right track, she is a very bright lady I say. My word Bert you have got it bad said a smiling Ethel, and they all laughed.

I'll ask Simon and Walter to have a secret look at it and give me their "guesstimate" of what it may be worth and how much to redevelop it. It might be useful to have somewhere to train people interested in running a Pub. Mr. Fields, how many more irons are you going to have in the fire? before you are satisfied, asked Bert. Tell me how many I need to be able to meet my guests needs, and I will try to answer that question. Well Jim, if I can be so bold, Ethel and I have been wondering what happens if a guest wants to learn something and you spend a lot of money providing facilities for their training, only for it never to be used again. Then I will have trained that person which is what I said I would, Jim answered. Yes Sir, said Bert but you will have spent a whole lot of money for very little return, money that may have help train half a dozen others. Thank you both for your concern, I agree that the point you make is a valid one and may have to be taken into consideration at some time in the future, happily not yet.

It may be in a few years time we will run out of space for more facilities, and outsources for all the demand. In that event I suppose we will have to produce a list of trades and occupations we have available, and only take guests requiring the help available. Unless of course we start other communes!!! If you do break it to Sarah very gently, she might be hoping for a retirement, opined Ethel. Good point said Jim, I'll have to stick to financing someone else to organise everything, I pity them if they have to keep pace with you, said Bert shaking his head.

The next few days proved to be a quiet time for Jim, with no one asking for decisions etc. Berts friend "Colin" came to plough the land behind the farmhouse, promising to come back in two or three months to harrow it. Then you can dig away to your hearts content he added, me I'll stick to ploughing, it's easier on the back! Ethels market gardening brother Sam came and took at lot of measurements, and soil samples. I will draw up some plans for the layout, then Ethel can tell me which bit I got right. If any voice said from the kitchen, remember to think about water supply while you are at it. Thank you, sister dear said Sam, I would never have thought about water. Calling, Bert give me a call when she is out sometime and I will come back.

Jim's thoughts turned to Harry and Carols coming visit, the next week promised to be fine with plenty of sun and very hot. A couple of days on the beach a must. Throw in a day exploring the farm, and a good time will be had by all. Jim contacted a local taxi firm and arranged for them to collect the Edwards family and bring them to the farm. Being from a coastal resort they were used to transporting families from many parts of Britain. After lengthy discussion with Bert and Ethel it was decided to give them the cottage for the length of their stay, with all meals except breakfast in the farmhouse. Ethel looking forward to cooking for a family again. You had better keep them away from Bert, he gets excited enough when there is only Sarah, goodness knows what he will be like with two young ladies to ogle, said Ethel. Before having to hide in the kitchen, as Bert was shouting," I heard that woman, now you are for it. All said while laughing aloud, and Ethel shouting "Promises. promises" from the safety of the kitchen.

Sarah had decided to drive down, thinking they may need two cars, if they all went out together. However, she was coming down on the Friday night, to be on hand for their guest's arrival. Also to book a walk with her friends Bert and the dogs.

It looks like being a busy week, I had better get some work done. I have still to have words with the drainage man, about top field and "Yurts". I must see when Bert can be available, I don't want to decide anything without his input. Bert promised to be free the next afternoon, so Jim set off to try to find the drainage expert. To Jims disappointment, he had left dead on time as he had to take his men's "Time Sheets" to the office. His men promised to tell him the Boss had been looking for him as soon as he arrives in the morning. Thank you, please just tell him I need his advice if he could spare me an hour or so tomorrow afternoon. If he can't no doubt one of you could let me know when you come for a bacon cob. Sure enough one of the gang gave Jim a shout the next morning to confirm the "Gaffa" would see him at 2pm.

By ten past the hour, the three men were gathered at the field. Jim explained to the engineer about the "Yurts" and showed him the plans. For his part Bert explained about the fields drainage, and pointed out the slope from the middle to both sides. The engineer (call me Ted) asked if it were to be just water or sewage as well? To be honest I hadn't considered mains drainage, thinking more of "Elson" type toilets, but now you have mentioned it perhaps I'll look into it. Well Jim you are already looking at huge expense Just for mains water supply and water drainage. It is all uphill from here to the main drains and water mains and drains. You are going to need a serious pump just to take the used water away, and its not a hundred percent certain that standard water pressure would be enough to get it to the top of the field. Unless Bert here knows of a way we can run it downhill. There is a minor road about a mile and a half down that way, it should have road drains but I don't know of any other. Some of the route would be across Joe's land and he would no doubt charge more than three pumps. If it were possible to run the water in from the top of the field, it could be simpler said Bert. Now who has missed the obvious, replied Ted, Bert you are probably right, be assured I will check.

Jim was disappointed by the difficulties raised by the drains expert, consoling himself with the notion that these experts only saw problems and it was his job to verify the probable benefits. Luckily, While the Edwards family were only coming for one week, Sarah was staying a fortnight. Giving them time to visit the tent maker, without cutting into the time for their visitors. If the drains expert and Walter had reached any conclusion about the "Yurts" field in that time, everything may fall into place.

Sarah arrived early on Friday evening, to be warmly greeted by everyone, including the two dogs. Jim was prepared to swear the smiles on Bert and Ethel's faces were enough to light up a fog. Sarah cuddled and kissed Jim, whispering how much she had missed him. Then turned to greet Bert and Ethel, and of course her friends the dogs. Asking Bert when can we walk please. Supper first, then time to let that settle, and we can all wonder down to Topfield to see the sun set. Sunset has been glorious all week, and you don't want to miss it. All agreed that was the best plan.

Sarah used the time before supper to shower and change into what she called her country clothes, an old track suit, woolly socks and walking boots. Jim commenting, it covered too much of her, Sarah told him not to worry as she would not wear them in bed. Cheeky said Jim. All went as Bert had planned, the sunset seen from the highest point on the farm was truly spectacular.

Breakfast had hardly been cleared away, when a motor horn announced the arrival of the taxi, bringing the visitors. Jim and Sarah hurried out greeting Harry and Carol hugs and handshakes. Jim and Sarah both delighted when the two boys asked, do you mind if we call you Uncle Jim and Auntie Sarah? Mum and Dad say its O.K. if you don't mind. O.K. by us, there only one snag you have to give Auntie's a hug. Both boys obliged, grinning broadly. This formality over Jim helped Harry with the luggage, and showed them into the cottage. We decided to put you in here there is more room than you would have had in the Farmhouse. Ethel hopes you will take all your meals, except breakfast, in the Farmhouse, so that we can all dine together. Trust us Ethel's meals consist of the finest ingredients cooked to perfection, and plenty of it. One small warning Bert has two beautiful dogs, but you must not go near them until Bert has introduced you, they are trained to guard against strangers.

All the family expressed delight with the cottage, and thankful for the kitchen well stocked with all they could possibly need for breakfasts. That must be Ethels doing, Jim confessed, he had not given it a thought. Anyway lets go and meet them, I'll lay odds the kettle will be boiling. The two couples met, with the usual joyful greetings that were B& Es speciality. Ethel hugging all four of the visitors, Bert shaking hands with all the males and giving Carol a kiss on the cheek. Ethel giving Carol her usual warning don't let Bert get you on your own, he tends to get over excited!! Luckily Bert did not hear, as he had gone to get the dogs, in order for them to get to know everyone as friends. Bert spent a lot of time with Mark and Wayne getting most of the training. They fed the dogs "titbits", (thoughtfully) provided by Bert, taught to shake doggy paws, and generally make friends.

As expected the kettle was on and Ethel quickly produced hot tea, bacon cobs and cake for the greedy. With Bert and their fathers permission, the boys soon went off with the dogs and a couple of balls for a quick run around. Jim asked Harry and Carol to come and look at some plans, Sarah showed Carol to Jim's rooms, Harry staying to check on the boys. Reassured when Bert explained he was on watch, if only to make sure his dogs came to no harm. When Jim and Harry arrived the Ladies had already toured Jim's rooms, Carol telling him he was a lucky blighter! Harry slapping him on the back saying well done mate.

Both visitors thought the plans for houses were very good, thinking the "front" of the houses facing the fields an excellent idea. They had admired the stone farm buildings as they drove in and thought the house conversions in the same stone could only be beautiful. The "Yurts they saw as suitable for a single person or perhaps a couple, but a nonstarter for Families. A lot would depend on how long the stay. Harry was curious to know where Jim hoped to put them. Let's go and see the buildings at close range, suggested Jim, and then I can show you the "Yurts" field on the way back. Saturday is a good day to look round free of noise and dust.

Harry told his boys not to tire the dogs too much, go into the cottage when Uncle Bert tells you, rest a bit, mum and I will give you a shout on our way to see the field.

Using the plans as a guide and the new secondary drain covers as markers they were soon able to understand the layout of all the rooms. A first even for Jim and Sarah. Carol was keen to learn what freedom guests would have regarding internal décor and gardening ETC. Oh! Said Jim a totally free hand, apart from any form of structural alteration, all the houses need to be identical, to save any talk of favouritism. Fair enough Carol agreed, in that case any time Harry wants to come here I'll happily bring my Family. O.K. said Jim I will reserve you a couple of "Yurts".

James Fields shame on you cried Sarah before punching him on the arm. Ouch! Said Jim turning to Harry and Carol, the trouble is she is too fast I can't even run away.

Come on let's go and collect the boys and go and look at the fields. The boys met them at the cottage gate and they were all soon on their way. Jim did his best to explain the problems with mains water and water drainage, but without Ted and Bert to help thought he had left a lot out. What if you go to all this trouble and expense, and don't get the response you are expecting. Well I find an ambitious Family to run it as permanent and holiday lets. They could live in the cottage, have posh guests upstairs in the Farmhouse, reception, and a shop/ café downstairs, and go on a months cruise every winter.

Meanwhile Sarah and I could travel the world, sparing no expense, aging gently. Boring said Sarah, I like you better when your head is busy with all new ideas and planning the old Ideas. With me "bossman" as your P.A. Friends you see my problem, I must work long into my old age, or lose the woman I love, I will probably retire to my bed to nurse my aching heart. At this all his friends burst into false tears, crying Oh! You poor thing. Sarah through her mock tears, saying, poor little millionaire all this money and all alone. Wayne and Mark who had watched the adults behaviour in startled disbelieve, began to laugh, with everyone else soon joining in.

They returned to the Farmhouse, chattering and laughing, to be greeted by Ethels inevitable pot of tea and slice of cake. Carol asked to excused once the tea break was over as she still had to unpack, explaining she needed Harry to carry the cases upstairs, and the boys to come and unpack their luggage,

From the speed at which the three males stood up, it was clear when Carol spoke they all listened. Just before you go, said Bert there will be another glorious sunset to night, Ethel and I are strolling down to High Field after supper for the best view and would welcome the company of anyone interested. Sounds lovely said Carol, we don't get a good view of many sunsets where we live, thank you. As they left the boys could be heard asking if they could go as well, packing first, Carol's voice all they heard.

Your friends are a wonderful family, Harry and Carol have taught the boys obedience and good manners, but always with love, opined Ethel. With Bert nodding agreement. You will get no argument from us said Jim we have never known the boys to do anything without permission, nor have it refused without explanation.

The Edwards family did not reappear until supper time, but could be seen enjoying the cottage's beautiful garden. Asking, later, who looked after the garden, and could they come round the garden as Carol had so many questions. There is nothing I would like better said Ethel, perhaps after breakfast tomorrow if the men all go with Bert to walk the dogs, we ladies can have some peace and a good natter. Sounds lovely said Carol and Sarah in unison, Ethel smiling happily. The viewing of the sunset from Bert's top field was again wonderful, even the boys sitting awed and asking their usual questions. Mainly answered by Bert, to Harry's relieve.

The women got their peace the next morning, the men dog walking as predicted. Bert had some initial doubt over Harry and his missing foot being able to cope. Harry explaining he needed practice over rough ground, and would turn back if it became a problem.

The boys didn't care how far they went while they had the dogs for company. In fact they spent so much time and energy, running the dogs up and down the fields, the adults were able to shorten their walk as the dogs had enough exercise. For the afternoon, the adults all felt a rest was called for, even the boys not looking to run with the dogs. After an hours rest Bert suggested the boys might like to see the pigs and the two cows, yes please said the youngsters accompanied by the adults all wanting to come. Sarah and I have never seen them, said Jim and I do want them to be part of my grand scheme. In the event Harry and Carol joined them, with Ethel to follow after a few minutes. Mark and Wayne looked for the dogs, but Bert explained the pigs didn't like the dogs, and got too aggressive.

The "townies" were all astonished by the size of the pigs in particular the eldest sow the head of her reaching over the side of the sty. We will be moving her on before long, said Bert, before she puts on too much fat. Where will she have to go? Uncle Bert asked Wayne, Bert looking flustered, got a nod from both parents, before answering. Do you know where pork joints and bacon come from? From the Butchers said Mark nudging his brother and laughing. Oh! You mean she is going to be made into pork, sausage and bacon, said a crestfallen Wayne. Now! Don't you go feeling sorry for her, she has had a wonderful life, explained Bert, she has always had the best of food, a warm dry bed to sleep in, and no predators to worry her when she was little.

As a wild pig she would have known cold, starvation and fear from all the many beasts after her. What beasts were they asked Mark with Wayne nodding. Well, her own kind for a start, any large pig from a rival passel would find her a welcome meal. In times when food was short her mother would have to hide her away from the larger Boars in her family. Then there would be Foxes, Badgers if threatened, larger birds such a Eagles and Falcons. It was even known for a couple of Stoats working together, to take a very small pig. Wow! Said the boys beginning to look a bit more cheerful. Thank you, Uncle Bert, we have seen diagrams at school of pigs showing where all the different types of meat are taken from, but it isn't the same when you see the real pig. I don't mind telling you Aunt Ethel and I have shed many a tear over an animal going to market. That's why we have always tried to care for them as well as possible. I couldn't begin to tell you how many lambs Ethel has hand reared over the years, even some I didn't think worth the effort. Now go and have a look at the cows next door, but don't go in the shed they might get fidgety and stamp on your foot. Trust me you wouldn't want that twice. Tomorrow if your Mum and Dad will let you out before breakfast, I will show you how to milk them and perhaps give you a try. Please don't ask Mum and Dad now, wait and see what time you all wake in the morning. Do not worry about missing it, milking happens every day.

Ethel had now arrived and took the adults to see the soon to be market garden area. Explaining her and her brothers planned lay out. Of course it will all depend on Jim providing the money, and my brother deciding where to get the water from. A single or at most double domestic pipe could be run from the Farmhouse, any more than that and a commercial supply would be called for, probably meaning running new pipes from the nearest main. That would drill a big hole in Jim's money pit, and keep draining it while the Market garden lasted. Point taken, said

Jim, looking pensive.

While training on Dartmoor during a hot dry summer, we kept open topped bath shaped containers along the top off hedgerows and such, with filtered drains into steam cleaned barrels, it was surprising how much we collected when it rained, of course it was not used as drinking water, but was acceptable for washing clothes and equipment. Said Harry, hoping to make a contribution. Of course, yours could be a more permanent structure, possibly Aluminium, with an annual clean they should last for years. Thank you, Harry, said Jim, now smiling again. Being rain water it would be better for the plants than tap water, if you build a staff hut you can run single feed water pipe for tea ETC. I'm not expected to provide tea as well am I? asked Jim with a mock frown; no but you will expect one every time you visit said a smiling Sarah.

Harry, asked Ethel, would you mind if in the beginning I tell my brother this was my idea. I want to see his face when I ask him why I have to do all the thinking for him. He and I were born only fifteen months apart and have always been friendly rivals over everything. Fine by me said Harry. Explaining to his sons Ethel will be teasing not lying.

The holiday began in earnest that night when the four adults finally made their way to the village pub. Ethel and the dogs being on child watching duty. From the moment they entered they fell in love with its charm and ancient features. The beer was from a local brewery and to Jim's mind not the finest, but well cared for. It became apparent, the longer they remained in the pub that beneath the charm there was a lot of decay and neglect. This place is truly lovely, said Harry, but it is going to need a few thousands to put right. Well that alright then, said Jim with a rueful smile, I have spent so many millions this past month, a few thousand does not sound too bad!! Sorry to rub salt in your wounds dear, said Sarah, but it's your round, and mines a large G&T.

The fine warm weather continued, the boys got their two days at the seaside and Jim got a chance to show off his swimming prowess. Carol and Sarah, "cooing and whistling" when he first stripped off his shirt. Starting a round of ironic applause from Harry and the boys. Trouble came on the Friday, the last full day of the Edward's family holiday. The boys had been allowed to take the dogs for a walk unaccompanied. A first time Bert had felt justified in staying home. The boys had been gone for some little time, when one of the dogs was seen to be racing home on its own. On arrival it was found to have a note tucked under its collar. "Wayne has had a fall and hurt his ankle can't walk Please help". Carol was all for rushing off to find her son, please wait said Jim. Sarah get your first aid bag and get the dog to guide you to the boys. Carol trust me Sarah will get there far quicker than you and is very experienced with ankle injuries. Sarah soon returned with her bag and having made a big fuss of the dog, they set off on their mercy mission. Watching Sarah running with the dog, Carol asked if Sarah would be able to maintain her speed. Speaking as one who trained with her I'd say she has got some in reserve, Jim replied.

Now Bert I know you have a small trailer! What have you got to tow it with? I'll see if my old Land Rover will start and then you won't need the trailer. It will take three adults and two children with ease. As he spoke he was hurrying behind the Farmhouse, to return moments later behind the wheel of the Land Rover, giving a thumbs up. I'd better drive said Bert this old girl can be a bit temperamental, but I'm used to her. Harry and Carol if you want to come with me, Sarah can make her own way back with the dogs. All were in agreement, Jim saying I will run behind and come back with Sarah. Don't worry I'm not as fast as Sarah, but I will get there. They had not gone too far before they saw Mark in the distance, waiting to show them the way.

I shall have some words to say to these boys, said an upset Carol, no you will not said a surprisingly forceful Harry. Accidents will always happen and as far as I can tell they have behaved very sensibly, Sending the dog with the note was good thinking, if the rest of their behaviour has been to that standard, I for one will be proud of both of them. Carol took his hand and gave him a kiss. By the time the Land Rover arrived Sarah had diagnosed a slight sprain, and was applying a support bandage. Mark had arranged their jumpers under the ankle to give it a cushion and lift it off the hard floor.

Mark explained to his father, Wayne had tripped over a log hidden in the long grass and fallen heavily. Although it hurt him a lot he did not complain, and it was his idea to send the dog for help. You have both done very well, Mummy and I are proud of you. By the time they had reloaded the Land Rover Jim had arrived, thanking Sarah for all she had done. Carol and Harry joined in with the thanks, saying they could not believe how fast she had set off. Once I knew there was nothing serious to worry about, I realised how much I had enjoyed the run, its been a long time since I did some serious running, I will have to chase Jim about more often. The last word came from Bert asking Sarah and Jim not to rush the dogs coming back, they have had enough excitement for one day.

The next morning found Wayne feeling better Sarah assuring him by the time he had sat in the taxi going home he should be able to put his foot to the floor, provided he was careful. The Taxi arrived all too soon, and the holiday was over. Everyone turned out to say farewell, and keep in touch, the adults with cuddles all-round, the boys cuddling their hero's the dogs.

Sunday was taken as a day of rest, Jim helping Ethel with food preparation while Bert and Sarah walked the dogs. Monday found Jim and Sarah out and about, checking with the various building groups how things were going. Everyone seemed fairly relaxed and sure of their part in the grand scheme of things. Walter was due on site that afternoon, Jim sort out "Ted" the drainage specialist and arranged for him to join him and Walter on the top field, for further discussion about how best to deploy the "Yurts". Jim had almost decided that ten "Yurts" should be sufficient, subject to the expert's opinions. Sarah was anxious to finally visit the manufacturing company, as some weeks had passed since her initial contact.

Walter had preliminary drawings of the field showing different layouts of the "yurts". At first agreeing with Jim that ten was the probable right number. After several trial layouts had decided that eight would be preferable. I believe he explained that more room between each dwelling was needed to allow for pathways and social areas around each tent. When asked what he meant by, "social areas" he said he thought room for lying sunbathing, deckchairs and visitors, would prove popular.

At this Jim brought Ted into the discussion, Ted of the opinion that eight or ten was all the same to him. The more room I'm allowed for water supply and drains, the bigger the "diggers" I can employ. I suppose you mean bigger machines, said Sarah, I was hoping you meant big muscular Navvies. Giving Jim one of her cheeky grins, To be told by an equally smiling Bossman to "report to me in my office this evening". If I may be allowed to continue, interrupted Ted, smiling at them both. Mr Field I did some rough costing based on ten "Yurts", For anything more accurate I shall need Walters final drawings, for length of trenches pipes ETC. I guess that throws the ball back in your court Walter. Sarah and I will try to visit the manufacturers, tomorrow and confirm delivery of eight units, subject to price. Walter reminded them he hoped to visit at the same time, to ensure the design was not flawed. Not to mention the "Yurts" may suit a problem another of his clients was having. Please let me know what time you are leaving and I will try to meet you there.

The "Yurts" maker, Canvas Construction Ltd. were delighted to see Sarah and Jim the next day. A time of two P.M. being agreed. Jim let Walter know as promised, he decided to make his own way there, promising to be on time. Both parties were delighted with the design and quality of the "Yurts". The actual tents were lavish in design, but extremely comfortable for two. The extensions for kitchen and bathroom/ toilet were compact but practical. Jims commenting "I've stayed in worse digs than this in my time, some of them for weeks at a time. Walter with his architects' hat on found no problems with the manufacture, so everyone was happy.

With prompting from Jim, Sarah was to do the important negotiations for price and delivery. A decision he was pleased to have made as she proved to be a fierce buyer, working hard for the best price. When Jim later praised her efforts, Sarah said well they are on thin ice with a product as yet unproven. I have agreed to give them access to bring clients to see ours in situ. Best publicity is a satisfied client. Fair enough said Jim, you once said you would have to watch me or you would become the down trodden little woman. After that exhibition, I am quaking in my boots.

Delivery for all eight was to be four months, Walter saying I suppose you will want the hard standings and water and drainage in situ by then, shaking his head. Certainly Jim replied, what's a bit of drainage, a cold water supply and a concrete base between friends. You won't want to be keeping Sarah waiting will you?!

As they were parting, Jim said, not to rub it in Walter, I'm thinking of buying the village pub and renovating it. If you and Simon could call in one day, on expenses of course, you could give your opinions. Of course if it is viable I shall need an Estate Agent, Architect and Expert renovators, perhaps it's a project Peter could help with. It will be done "Oh Master" said Walter, smiling but still shaking his head.

As they arrived back at the farm, Bert was at the gate waiting for their return, after the usual greetings, Bert explained he had had an offer of some very good hens from a friend who was selling up. I was pretty sure that you would want the hens and I had a word with one of the carpenters, (he came for bacon rolls) and he has had a look at the hen coop. He says he and his mate could fix it this weekend, as good as new. His boss allows the men to buy small amounts of materials, so the timber and felt are on hand. If you want them to do the job they are coming to see you when they finish for the day and they will do a proper measure

Bert I don't think I am ever going to be able to let you and Ethel go, you are much too helpful. I have been wondering how to sort the hen problem out and here it is solved. I'll bet your good ladies got the kettle on, I will beg a cup of tea and sit out here and wait for them, its nearly knocking off time anyway. Many thanks again Bert, I owe you a couple of pints. Maybe said Bert, but don't forget who gets the eggs until your market gardens running! O.K. Bert make that one pint I owe you.

Jim had just time to drink his tea and eat his piece of cake, before the two carpenters arrived. One of the two men had yet to see the job and they asked if they could have a look and do some measuring together. Just a moment while I check where the dogs are, they need to be introduced to strangers. Jim called through the door to see if Bert was available to keep the dogs calm while the workmen had a look at the hen house. He is ahead of you, said, Ethel he is out the back with them in case you wandered round there without thinking. Sure enough as they rounded the farm house the dogs let out a mixture of snarls and barking, bringing Bert out of the cowshed to call them to heel.

Wow!!, said the carpenters, that is some reception, are they really the two dogs which were playing with the young boys last week. We thought they were armchair pets. Not to worry said Bert we will make sure you are properly introduced before you start work. While on the subject, if Mr. Fields employs you I can bring the Land Rover down to your store and help you to bring the materials here. Thanks Bert that will be a big help, said both men while sidling warily past the dogs. Bert shut the dogs in their kennel and joined the others at the coop. Explaining to the men "Len" and "Ryan" It is no use building a little palace if that old Fox can still get in. Of course we want it weather proof, and all the creature comforts, but leave a week spot and that old Fox he will find it. He killed all the hens a couple of months back, and you can bet he has been round a time or two since to see if we have replaced them. Rest easy Bert now we know the score you will be lucky to get the hens in and eggs out, by the time we have finished.

We can let you have a price tomorrow Mr. Fields and do the work over the weekend if that suits you. That's fine lads thank you, just remember we are more interested in quality than price. Adding with a smile, if that Fox gets in we will seek you out and set the dogs on you.

Jim joined Sarah telling her I have had enough of work for one day, what do you say to a couple of pints in the village. Ethel missed it last time, we could always invite them both and try to get them talking about local history. Those foundations near the entrance still intrigue me, they might know more than we have already heard. Good idea said Sarah, after this I will want you and me to be alone for the rest of my holiday. I'm reminding you that I have to go back to work on Sunday.

The evening in the pub was a great success, Ethel and Bert proving to have a great line of banter. Any and all other visitors to the pub that night were friends of the farming couple, and joined in the fun. A couple of local farmers assuring Jim he would have been better off buying their farm. Than that stretch of waste land he calls a farm. Oh! Dear said Jim, if your place is that much better than Bert's, I'd never be able to afford it would I. Shame that, I was thinking of looking for a couple of other places, but you just priced yourselves out of the market. The two farmers laughed the loudest, as several locals shouted, "EE's got EE There" right enough. Jim and Sarah got no new information about the ancient site near the farm entrance, although several locals said there is some kind of inscription on the church porch. They do say as that porch was built of stone from your site.

For the remainder of Sarah's week Jim kept away from all those likely to take up too much of his time and concentrated on Sarah. They swam in the sea, ran in the fields, sunbathed on top field, and rejoiced in a wet day that gave them a reason for doing nothing. All too soon the week was over with tearful goodbyes from everyone. Sarah promising to ring as soon as she was safely back in Cambridge.

Monday found Jim looking round the building site catching up with how the work was progressing, telling any of the workmen, "Don't mind me I'm just checking how many of you aren't sweating yet". All said with a large grin!! Jim could only be pleased with the speed of progress all round the site. He was again very pleased when he saw Peter and an assistant checking the various levels of "Top Field" in preparation for designing the hard standings for the "Yurt's". I seem to be falling behind thought Jim, I had better go and find "Ted" the drainage and water supply man to see how he is getting on.

Ted assured him he had got as far as he could go, having priced the drainage pump and piping as far as the main drain, he was now waiting for the architects to give him the details of where and how the "Yurts" were going and he could get started. Simon was able to assure Jim he had no outstanding problems, and all invoices had been forwarded to the accountants, who would deal directly with Jim's bank. Have you been to the village pub yet? I still need to know if it is a viable project, or not. Yes, Walter and I have had a look, we think the building is worth restoring, but the owner has not decided on the asking price yet.

We thought the beer was drinkable, but a bit bland! Did you know there is half an acre of old building land at the back. Complete with a drinking water well. With planning permission someone with money could perhaps site a "Micro Brewery there. There is a big opening in these parts for a pint of really good beer. By the way ever heard of Nine Pin Skittles?

Jim was back in his office, sat at his desk, trying to bring some order to all the projects he had begun. Mr. common sense, Bert, had asked him how he was getting on with trades etc. ready to train his first visitors, this building work will seem as if it is going to take for ever, then suddenly be over before you are ready. Jim thought Bert was giving him a nudge to get cracking, before he had extensive accommodation, but no reason for visitors to come. Oh!, help now what do I do?

I have the Market garden on the way and possibly bar staff training if I manage to buy the pub, but that could be a year away. It is not much though, time I got a grip. First things first, get a valuation done on the pub, contact a solicitor to take us through the jungle of rules about licenses, opening hours, and insurance etc. "Hello, Jim to master"!! "Master here Jim I have just been asking the "Team" if they had heard from you. How can I help? Just let your thoughts flow, and I'll sort them out as we go along. Right thought Jim here we go: I am anxious to make some headway with buying the village Pub. I'm ahead of you now! Have we got a suitable solicitor, yes he will be in touch, a suitable estate agent to value the pub, again, yes and he will be in touch. Thank you, "Master", I was beginning to get bogged down and you have got me going again.

Jim all decisions are yours, but the team and I think you will soon have a lot more irons in the fire and perhaps you should get some help. Perhaps not Sarah, you will need her charm when you have bickering families to deal with. Jim all the team have been listening, and are unanimous in their praise for all you are doing, and wish you well with all you are still to do.

That has got the pub underway. Now what else, I think I will give Harry a ring to see if he has any thoughts on the sort of job injured soldiers might fancy. To his surprise Harry was at home, sounding more subdued than his normal cheerful self. After the usual pleasantries, he explained he had been made redundant from his temporary job, leaving he and his family struggling to make ends meet. My army pension is just not enough. Harry I'm sorry to hear that, and angry that a man who had paid the price you have finds himself in this position.

I rang originally to see if you had any ideas about the sort of jobs your contemporaries might favour. Now I would ask you that question, what line of work truly appeals? Firstly Jim I would have a go at anything that helped feed the family. The most fulfilling job was when I was in "Logistics and Procurement" in the Army. A pressure job, finding where to get supplies from and then getting them to where they were needed, usually to a deadline. Harry I need someone with very similar experience to come and work for me. Can you get Carol on the extension, and I will try to explain to you both. Carol is ahead of you Jim and has been on the extension since you rang. Hello Carol, said Jim. I need an assistant who will be able to interview injured or sick servicemen to get an accurate idea of what to supply as training facilities. In addition, the successful applicant would have to track down tutors and companies willing to take in handicapped people to train to a high standard.

From what you have told me today, and from my previous knowledge of your personality I believe you would be ideal. Of course Carol it would mean you and the boys would have to relocate to this area, although I have no idea what area Harry would have to cover. Salary? Again I have no idea, but you can rest assured it will be over the national scale for this type of work. You will realise I cannot expect prospective employers to pay top rates, if I underpay my own staff. If you are interested I think Bert and Ethel will be happy to stay in the farmhouse, leaving the cottage for you until alternatives are available.

Of course you must take your time and be sure you want to give it a try. If you want to come down to check on schools etc.. I have no idea Harry what sort of aftercare you receive, but we can always fit it in. The cottage is available to you, please come down, expenses paid to all applicants of course. I will ring you tomorrow to confirm the cottage will be available long term.

Ethel and Bert were delighted to hear the Edwards family were probably coming to stay long term, and happy to stay in the farmhouse for the foreseeable future. To be honest Jim we are so enjoying being part of all that is going on, we are in no hurry to move. Jim rang Harry with the good news, delighted to learn all the family were pleased and excited at the thought they may be coming to stay long term. Harry hire a van or something similar and bring lots of clothing with you, you can always hand the van in to a local branch.

Jim's call to Sarah that evening was a very long one as he explained all the news about Harry and Carol's problems. Sarah applauded loudly when she heard of Jim's offer of a worthwhile job, for Harry and accommodation for the family. It got better when Jim learned Sarah intended to play golf that Saturday. If I fly up there Friday night is there any chance I could join you? Oh! Jim of course you can, there are only two of us and you can make a third. What time can you be here and how long can you stay? Down girl I have only just had the idea, I need to contact your flying friend, to arrange flights. Sorry dear said Sarah I got over excited, I can't think why. Have you got Alec's phone number? I hope he is not already booked. I will try him now, and ring you again when I have spoken to him, their luck was in, not only was Alec at home but free for the weekend. I can be at Oldsmith Airfield just after 17.00hrs. Refuelling etc. half an hour or so E.T. D. 18.00hrs. I will have my car at the airport and can drop you off in Cambridge. Thank you said Jim, I will ask Sarah to ring you and tell you where we are to meet.

Many things may have happened that week, but by Friday Jim and Sarah could not remember any of them, thinking only of their weekend together. Alec dropped Jim off at the main Cambridge hotel, where Sarah had booked them a room. Porters took control of Jim's luggage and Golf clubs, leaving Jim free to give Sarah a huge hug, warmly returned, and the weekend was under way.

Early the next afternoon and they were ready to meet their playing partner and keen to get under way. When he met her Jim began to wonder if he had been suckered. Nancy! A strongly built redhead some six feet tall, all of it muscle, admitting to being a shot put champion. With a fourteen handicap, smiling but only on a good day. Jim tore his eyes away from her to look at Sarah's face covered with the biggest grin he had ever seen. I'll get you for this he thought.

As the lowest handicap Nancy was first to tee off, sending her drive well beyond the holes 150 yard marker (indicating the distance to the green). Oh! Help said Jim, I don't go that far on my holidays. Taking great care over his address position, he hit one of his better drives, ending on the 150 mark, not too far behind. Now both have a rest while I play my three shots to catch up, said Sarah. For such a beginner Jim thought Sarah's swing was very good, like her running very smooth and balanced. Nancy and Jim pared the hole, Sarah having taken four to reach the green putted in from 10 feet for a creditable five. Nancy remarking, if you were playing off a high handicap you would have won that hole, I shall be watching you.

The round proceeded in much the same way, Nancy winning four holes to Jims two. The big excitement being Sarah winning one of the par threes, with a splendid birdie. Jim thought he had done well to come through unscathed, until Nancy gave him a big hug, leaving him gasping for breath. Sorry to dash off, I've still to do a couple of hours in the gym, and some course work after that. Sarah when you get your handicap give me a ring I have a feeling anything around 30 and you will probably win. That doesn't seem fair said Sarah, she is so much better than me. Not really said Jim your handicap is the club's assessment of your ability, and while you play to it you can give any other player a good game.

The main thing is we all enjoyed it. I am so pleased you did Jim I was afraid you would get fed up waiting for me to catch up. No way, he replied, Nancy and I were constantly worried you were going to pinch the hole.

I am hungry, can we go back to the hotel, clean up, and eat? Of course my love never let it be said I allowed you to suffer any kind of hunger, Sarah replied with the usual grin on her face. Showered and fed the lucky pair returned to their room, tired but happy. Sunday saw them out and about, Jim learning the charm of the city and its collages. Awed as millions before him had been by the grandeur and beauty of Kings Collage Chapel. We think of ourselves as being skilled, the chaps who built this had no computers or machinery.

Sightseeing over they became sad at having to part, consoling themselves with the thought they only have three months to wait, until they never need be apart again!

Alec was punctual, as he always had to be in order to keep his take off slot. The flight was pleasant experience for Jim, though he felt sorry for Alec who had the return journey to face alone. Jim was soon on his way back to the farm, looking forward to a cup of tea. As usual Bert and Ethel were on the doorstep to welcome him back. Go and tell Sarah you are home safe and sound and I will bring you a cup of tea up, commanded Ethel, the poor lass will be worried.

Monday morning saw a refreshed Jim, compiling a list of things requiring his attention, time he started to put pressure where needed he decided. Top of the list chase Walter for the layout plans for the "Yurts" in top field. Walter answered the phone with the words " I wondered how long before you started chasing me", If convenient Peter can be with you this afternoon. He has done all the work, under my supervision of course, and will be able to give you chapter and verse. To, I hope, your complete satisfaction. Jim hung up the phone and dashed off to see the drainage expert, hoping to have him on hand as soon as Peter arrived. Next to buttonhole Bert to ask him to come along, as Jim wanted his local knowledge.

To Jim's consternation, he received a call from the Solicitor and the Estate Agent, sent by the "Master", to assist with possible purchase of the village pub. They were meeting at the pub that afternoon and hoped Jim could join them. Jim explained he was about to meet with the Architect and Drainage Expert, but would be happy to join them late afternoon (5 o'clockish), if they could wait that long. Both men were happy with this, explaining they had plenty to occupy their time until he arrived. His time with Peter, Ted and Bert, proved very successful, all praising Peter for an attractive lay out. Ted believing the spacing between the "Yurts" would be Ideal to allow easy fitting of drains and mains. Bert impressed with the provision for draining the field, without drying it out.

Peter gave copies of his plan to Jim and Ted, while assuring Jim a copy had been E-Mailed to Sarah, as a matter of standard procedure. In that case nobody start digging until I have Sarah's approval. Up to you then boss, not a sod will be turned, until you give the word. I need time to recruit some well-muscled Irishmen, as Sarah requested, Teds last words.

Happy so far, Jim rushed off to join the experts at the Pub anxious to hear their thoughts on the viability of his plans. He found the Solicitor and Estate Agent sat at a corner table nursing pints of beer. Jim was about to make some comment until he realised the table was covered with sheets of paper. The papers covered in sketches of various buildings, and the interior of the Pub. Well gentlemen said Jim, having first armed himself with a pint, what is your verdict, and your guess as to what it will cost me. We think the Pub would prove a sound investment for anyone prepared to spend the money to get the most from its undoubted charm. Getting the balance sheet into the black would take some time and depend largely on the Landlord and his ability to bring people in.

The micro brewery is a great idea, and should go ahead if the Well can provide sufficient water, of a suitable quality. You will need a qualified Brewer and the local water authority to give the go ahead. Once the go ahead is given, the actual build would be relatively straight forward as it is a brown field site needing very little preparation. As for cost you will have to get your Architect and Builder to tender. I would say get quotes for the copper vats, and be sat down when you read them!!

The licences and other rules are mainly concerned with opening hours and cellar and pump hygiene. They are of course Law!, and cannot by treated lightly. We feel you must be ready to spend a lot of money, but you will find our bills very moderate. This last bit said with large smiles, let me have that in writing Gents, said Jim also smiling.

Jim was about to leave when the Landlord asked to speak to him. I just wanted to tell you I AM selling the pub and the land. To be honest I had not given much thought to the development of the land, hearing of your plans has made me wonder if I have undervalued it. I'm a fan of what you are trying to do, and will stick to my original valuation in my dealings with you and give you first refusal. I expect to be able to go public in a couple of weeks and hope we can do business together. Thank you said Jim, shaking his hand, and turning to leave, Oh!, one last thought do you have any very old records I wonder if the Well has been used for Brewing in the past. A Public House this old must have brewed its own beer at some time. There are old records, in poor condition, I will get them out for you but you will have to sort through them yourself, drop in one night next week and I will have them ready.

Jim set off back to the farm, wondering, not for the first time what he had let himself in for. A refurbished Pub, a micro brewery, drainage and water supply for eight "Yurts", with all that going on you had to ask about dusty old deeds, who do you imagine is going to plough through them.

A telephone message left for him added to his workload, Harry and family were arriving the next day, excited at the prospect of a new job and almost a new start in life. Jim was pleased that the Edwards family were all coming, it showed a willingness to commit, to Jim's dream. He could only guess at Sarah's reaction when she learned they would all be here, while she would be stuck in Cambridge. I guess I had better ring her without delay.

Ethel had made some tea and promised to send Bert up with it, allowing Jim to ring Sarah straight away. Sarah answered on the first ring saying she was about to ring Jim, Sarah had spent a long time studying Peter's layout for the "Yurts" on top field. As the person responsible for this project she had hoped to find something to query, but had to admit she could find nothing she wasn't happy with. Good said Jim, can I leave you to give Peter the go ahead, I will tell Ted and the Forman builder to get cracking as soon as possible. O.K. said Sarah I will tell Peter to get them started tomorrow, the sooner these posh tents are in situ the sooner I can retire. Dream on sweetheart Dream on, the work is piling up here and I need my P.A., before I expire.

Now news, Harry, Carol and the boys are arriving tomorrow, excitedly hoping to start a new chapter in their lives. Oh!, Jim and I cannot be there!!, do not make any plans for Friday night I am going to ring Alec to see if he can fly me to you on Friday night and back again on Sunday, If not I will get there somehow. Ring off now and I will ring you as soon as I find a way to get to you, sometime this weekend. Bless you my love, spare no expense I still have a million I haven't spent yet!

True to her word Sarah rang within minutes, having found Alec home and free for Friday and Sunday. If you don't mind taking them into town and back he and Margaret would like to come down for the weekend themselves. If it means you can get here I would buy the bloody aeroplane. I will be delighted to collect you from Oldsmith, perhaps I will be able to smuggle you into my rooms before Bert and dogs etc. pinch you off me. James Fields I hope you are not hinting at what I think you are hinting at. All in your mind, said Jim, all in your mind.

The next day, Wednesday, saw Jim up and about with the Lark, anxious to try to catch up with some of the jobs needing his attention. First check with Peter to see if he had survived Sarah's phone call. No problem Peter assured him, I only have to achieve the impossible by yesterday, at half the price, and I get to keep my scalp. That's alright then said Jim, so long as all the other jobs stay on schedule, or you could lose more than your hair. I am going to tell my Dad about you, so there, said Peter. Seriously Jim, Sarah made her wishes very clear, and promised to talk to Ted, to make sure he is aware of the "Yurts" delivery date. Thanks Peter said, said Jim, I'll be on hand if you need me, but this is Sarah's ball game.

He found Ted on top field, he and his surveyor hard at work marking out the routes for the pipelines, and wanting final decisions on the Pump housing. Sarah wanting as much stonework as possible, both on the "Yurt" sites and the Pump housing. She is adamant that the whole site is to be beautiful, Bert's field deserves no less. Please give the lady all she wants, subject to there being sufficient stone to complete the houses as well. Believe me when I tell you Sarah will go through your invoices with the proverbial fine-tooth comb. What she wants includes the best price, but not necessarily the cheapest!!

Returning to the farmhouse, an excited Ethel told him young Mark had been on the mobile from the van and they hoped to arrive in half an hour. I told them I would have tea and bacon butties ready and waiting. I don't know what their parents thought I only heard the boys cheering, and the line went dead. It is so lovely to see them again, I hope everything turns out right for you all. We all do Ethel, we all do, was all Jim could say.

True to their word they arrived on time, to be greeted with warm hugs all round. The boys first question after eating, "where is Uncle Bert and the dogs". He has taken them down to high meadow, he is checking on the grass. If you stand by the door you should see him coming back. Dad may we go and meet him please, asked the boys, yes the reply but trot don't run flat out we don't want any accidents. Thank you, said the boys trotting off at a speed that seemed to get faster the further they went. Just as I thought said Harry smiling broadly.

Harry, we have a lot to discuss but can we leave it until tomorrow, take today to get settled in, and catch your breath, you have had a long drive. After lunch perhaps Carol can join us to have look at the houses and a chat about how things are going. Oh, and Carol, Bert is going to want a hug, and I have promised Sarah I will ring her, on my bill not hers as it will be a long call. You have been warned.

The afternoon inspection of the houses and other buildings was very successful with Carol saying she would be happy to have her family live in either one of the houses, or the cottage, for as long as needed. Both Carol and Harry, saying, they both liked the village and would be happy to live there, if it became expedient sometime in the future. Mark and Wayne, wanting to stay at the farm, because of Bert and the dogs, and the freedom of the fields. Do not get too fond of that idea, warned their parents, wherever we live you will have school, homework, and jobs around the home to consider. If Dads gets his new job, he may not be around as much as he used to be.

Sarah rang soon after they had finished the tour. Having caught up with developments with Jim, she spoke to Harry and the boys. Finally settling for along chat with Carol, the men as usual wondering what they found to talk about. Jim remembered he had the Pub records to collect and managed to persuade Harry and Bert to come with him to the Pub with him. Promising not to make a night of it, Carol reminding Harry he and the boys still had their unpacking to do. Not to worry, said Harry, Mark and Wayne will do theirs now, and I will do mine as soon as I get back. I'm much better at unpacking after a couple of beers!

The trio found the Pub to be very quiet, with just one or two farmhands calling in for a quick pint on the way home. The Landlord of the opinion things would pick up a little later. If he is hoping to sell you this place, he would say that wouldn't he, Berts opinion. The landlord handed Jim the records thankfully in a clean bag. The three men, then settled down to a discussion about what car would be best for Harry. Who soon pointed out it would have to be an automatic as his artificial foot wasn't up to operating a clutch, I am lucky it is the left foot.

Bert said his son had a B.M.W. which was a delight to drive, but cost an arm and a leg for servicing and spare parts. Jim, with Harry's agreement, thought one of the Toyota Hybrid family saloons would probably be best. A good sound reliable car, but not so flashy to make possible tutors think the commune threw its money about. Of course, said Jim smiling, he still has to pass the interview tomorrow, and accept the pittance I am offering along with the seventy hour minimum week. Harry, also smiling, said I'm off then, at least I don't have to bother unpacking. Bert's comment, I reckon you two will get along just fine. As they got up to leave the Landlord passed Jim an envelope, saying that is my price for the Pub and land, I hope you will find it acceptable. Thank you, said Jim, I hope I do, although I am sure my advisors will want to negotiate.

The next morning after breakfast, Jim took the time to ring all the people involved in the purchase of the Pub, including Simon and Walter, to pass on the asking price for the Pub. He had hoped to settle a time for a meeting of all concerned to form a plan of campaign, but had to leave it to the four very busy men to arrange a mutually acceptable time, and hope he could make it.

Now it was time to speak to Harry, all the time hoping there would be no problems. The two men settled in Jim's office. Jim opened by saying he had told Harry probably all he could about the job but would happily take any questions. Harry thought he understood the basics of the position offered, the interviewing of prospective service men presented no difficulties. The Armed forces is like a great big club and with my injury I will be welcomed anywhere. The finding people to take on trainees will be more difficult, but I am hoping we can produce a leaflet which I can leave with my card, and follow up later.

Harry that is great said Jim, I can see you have been giving things some thought. I am suitably impressed and can say the job is yours if you want it. I hope you realise it may not always be possible for you to get home every night, and understand the impact that could have on your family. Jim it is good of you to mention it, but my family have been used to my being away for months at a time, often somewhere not safe to be. If we can settle the boys happily this could be the best posting we ever had. Only thing I now need to say is what are you paying? I knew there would be a snag said Jim smiling, you surely don't expect all this luxury and pay as well! O.K. said Harry I will work for nothing if you tell Carol. On second thoughts how does £40,000 a year plus expenses and a company car sound.

At the moment Ethel and Bert are allowing me free use of the cottage and want you to live there free, in exchange for any help you are able to give. Mainly Carol and the boys helping with the bacon butties and general help around the farmhouse, of course the boys school work will take priority over all other work. This will run until a better alternative becomes available or they need the cottage for themselves. On the Job front I would like you to sign a six month contract, to cover your training period. Assuming you are happy the contract can be extended, if you wish, or be replaced by a months notice on either side. Shall we call Carol to tell her what we have decided, I'm sure she will have thought of something we have overlooked.

Carol joined them and expressed delight at all that had been decided, you have not mentioned holiday entitlements, may I assume standard allocation? Although why I bother about holidays I do not know, living in this delightful place is going to seem like one long holiday. In that case Harry can have standard holidays, while you can carry on working. No change there then said Carol, with happy smiles all round.

Friday saw Jim again making an early start wanting to be sure the afternoon was free to fetch Sarah from the airfield. He Harry and the boys, set off to a nearby town which boasted a Toyota sales room. Having already decided to buy a Toyota, the choice of model was soon settled. The showroom had an "ex" showroom "Corolla" with less than 1,000 miles on the clock, classed as second hand. Harry who claimed never to have bought anything that wasn't a bargain, declared himself satisfied. Jim who had saved a few thousand, was delighted. The boys liked the colour, it was, they said, the colour Mummy said she liked. So everyone was happy.

Back at the farm Jim had time to check the progress with the "yurts" sites on top field. The drainage and water ditches as far as the site for the new pump, were all in place, and the piping was to be delivered Monday morning. Ted assuring Jim drainage experts and plumbers would be available as soon as the piping arrived. If you can keep Sarah away until after lunch, she will get a better idea of our progress.

To Jim's relief and great pleasure it was soon time for him to set off to Oldsmith to collect Sarah. The time they were apart was growing harder to bear every time they were parted, a good thing thought Jim there were only six weeks left on her contract. He would have to speak to Alec about increasing the number of trips to and from Cambridge.

His journey to Oldsmith was uneventful, and the silver and blue aircraft arrived ahead of schedule, all to do with following winds according to Alec. Jim didn't care why just happy they were. Sarah was keen to see Carol and Harry, together with the boys. Do not try to kid me, said Jim, I know it is Bert and the dogs you really want to see. You know me too well, said Sarah pushing him towards the car. Do you mind if I drop Sarah off at the farm before I take you into town. It will give Sarah time to say her hellos.

No problem said Alec and Margaret, in fact we would like to have a look round, we are both excited about your project and would love to see the progress you are making. Fair enough said Jim I always enjoy showing off the work everyone else has done. Makes me feel important, so it should my darling, said Sarah, none of it would exist without you. Now I really am worried, if you are going to say nice things about me, where will it all end?

Harry and the boys offered to show Alec and Margaret, Ethel insisting they first have a cup of tea, don't forget they have been all that time flying down here.

If you want the full tour you had better ring your hotel or they will think you are not coming. Quite apart from the houses nearing completion, there is the Yurts foundations on top field, the Market garden area, new hen house, for starters. For the full tour you will have to visit the village Pub, Which the boss is going to buy, refurbish completely, and train would be Landlords. I shall say nothing about having a microbrewery built next door to train brewers. Oh! Said a smiling Ethel let me guess who is planning to be the guide for that part. Wrong you and I will be entertaining the boys. While the young people have a pint and a gossip!

Bert and the boys were soon on the way with Alec and Margaret, to begin their tour, the houses were indeed nearing completion, wow said the boys, lovely rooms said Margaret, just look at the view said Alec. The top field, and its "Yurts" met with more amazement than understanding none of the visitors had ever seen a "Yurt" and couldn't imagine a field full of them. Strangely it was the Market Garden area that excited Margaret the most, Bert explaining that it looked at its best, as Colin the local friendly Ploughman, had run the heavy Harrow over it a couple of days ago. Are you doing the design for the lay out Bert, I can see someone has been marking out pathways. Not guilty said Bert, Ethel and her brother are the Market Garden experts, Ethel's brother Sam has just retired from the family firm and he is coming to help get our Garden started. Mark and Wayne had not seen the restored Henhouse and were thrilled to find it already had a dozen or so healthy looking Hens, I wonder where you find the eggs!! You will have to ask Aunt Ethel, she does not allow me anywhere near them. Margaret explained her interest was due to her family always having a large allotment. Her father, an enthusiastic gardener, keeping the family supplied with fruit and veg.

Harry and Carol elected to run Alec and Margaret into town, provided they did not stay too long in the Pub, as Harry was on taxi duty for the Boss and his P.A. Apart from allowing Jim time for an extra pint, he also had chance for a chat with the Landlord. I passed your valuation over to my Land Agent and Architect, one of them should contact you in the next couple of days, no doubt they will want to start negotiations, I hope they won't be too far from your price. The speed at which you can vacate the property will be a big factor.

The next day being a Saturday Jim declared a holiday, asking for suggestions where they could all go for a day out, the day to include Bert and Ethel. If we could include a slap up meal, so much the better. I would love to repay Ethel for the wonderful meals She has given me, if only for one day. Then let's ask them where they would like to go, and see what they say!!

Bert and Ethel were thrilled with Idea of a day out altogether, Bert insisting Ethel chose the venue, unless you want to spend the day looking at "livestock" and Farm machinery. Can I really choose asked a smiling Ethel, I would love to go to the Jurassic coast area. We could all take hammers and break open some of the stone that has fallen off the cliffs. No doubt it has all been picked clean, but you never know your luck. Afterwards I would love a posh Chinese meal to get away from my boring menu.

Wonderful said Jim, Sarah and Carol will you get on the internet and sort out a suitable piece of coast, and Harry maps out to get us there and back. Would you all listen to him, said Sarah, this being the boss lark has gone to his head. Sir may a humble servant know what our lord and master will be doing. Naturally I shall be accompanying Bert and the boys taking the dogs for a walk. We cannot ignore our friends in pursuit of our own pleasure.

At this the two male adults blocked the doors, while the three ladies attacked Jim with cushions accompanied by enthusiastic cheers from the boys. You are wasting holiday time Jim begged until they finally let him go. Not really said Sarah if the rest of the day is this much fun, then roll on. Not too long on the walk Bert, warned Ethel, You will need to change before we go. YES dear, said Bert, Quickly closing the door behind him and calling for the dogs.

With the boys keeping the dogs running Bert soon thought they had enough exercise and hurried everyone back to join the others. Bert rushing to change, while Ethel loaded the cars with flasks of tea and sandwiches. Ethel we are only going for the day, said Jim. Might be a long day, said Harry, to emphatic nods from the boys. Harry took the lead, in his new car, together with his family. Jim right behind, with the rest of the party. Sarah and Carol kept their phones handy, for inter car communication.

They were soon on the coast road, with many views of the sea and fishing boats.

Are we really going to live here all the time, asked the boys. Yes for at least six months, said Carol. We may stay for much longer if your father likes his new job, and Uncle Jim is happy with his results. Do not run away with the idea it will be one long holiday, your father will have to work long hours, even being away some nights. You two will have to settle into new schools, there will be homework, and jobs to do about the cottage, and the commune. You and I will have to pull our weight to make sure you dad can concentrate on his work. Often when he gets home he will have records to update and reports to write for Mr. Fields, and you may end up doing your own homework. They won't mind that said Harry I got the last three lots wrong. Now you can please yourselves I am now on holiday.

Harry, who had studied the maps, led the way and they soon arrived at a suitable beach complete with nearby car park. Bert explained that easy though it may look, it was not safe to climb the cliff. There were plenty of fallen rock pieces to keep them all busy. The hammers etc. were soon handed out, happily carried by the boys, who were keen to start exploring as soon as possible. They were lucky to find a recent rock slide which offered the possibility of new stones, unlikely to have been tampered with.

Bert again issuing a warning, if this area has slipped recently it could easily do it again, so no climbing. Harry designated an area for himself and the boys, explaining he would allow them to move if they found nothing of interest. Everyone chipped away happily for half an hour or so, all finding clear traces of where crustations had been set in the stone but had rotted away some time in the last 180 million years or so. A break for a drink and paddle, Harry taking the boys to the side of the rock fall where they were able to reach rocks from higher up without climbing. Bert and the ladies thought this a good Idea and went to the other side. Jim stayed at the bottom of the rock slide, Having found many traces of fossils, he hoped he would find the real thing.

Ethel and Wayne both let out cries of success as they both found small crustations hidden in the rocks. Both specimens were very small, but had not rotted at all. Wayne was disappointed his find was so small, until his mother reminded him it was many millions of years old and he could hold it in his hand to examine its beauty. They had no further success, and it was soon time to go. Mark had split a piece of stone, although there was no crustations there were twenty or more scars showing where they had been. Mark was pleased with this find and decided to keep it as his memento of their fun day.

They found the Chinese restaurant with not too much trouble, but had to park two streets away as there was no parking available at the restaurant. At Harry's suggestion he and Jim went to find parking leaving the others to get settled at a table ready for their return. The meal was excellent, Ethel was thrilled and thanked them all for their enjoyable company, and Jim for his kind generosity. Jim answering, he would take Ethel out any time she liked, but could they please leave the rest of the rabble behind. Sounds good to me Bert, said Sarah, smiling at Jim.

Their way to the parked cars took them along a busy road, as they were passing a side alley a young boy came flying out of the alley on a skate board, clearly out of control. He was heading straight for the road, when quick thinking Harry grabbed him off the skate board, saving him from racing on to the road. The speed and weight of the boy spun Harry round almost pulling him over. The skate board carried on and hit the side of a passing car.

The driver stopped the car with a shudder of brakes, loudly shouting abuse aimed at the child. Seeing Harry was still holding the boy, he demanded to know if the child was Harry's. Being told no, he tried to grab him from Harry, shouting he would soon sort the little brat out. He found himself being spun round and confronted by a very angry Ethel. You drunken lout, one step nearer to that boy and you will wish you had never been born. The best thing you can do is get in your scrap heap car and slink away, my friends will be phoning the police in the next few seconds, and I am sure you don't want to see them. You don't know what you're talking about spluttered the man look at the damage his damn skateboard has done to my car. That's fifty quid's worth if it's a penny. We wouldn't give you an old penny for the lot, said Ethel jabbing him in the chest with her finger. Mr. Field would you come round this oafs car with me and make notes of all the problems. First a blowing exhaust next two bald tyres on the rear, the number plate is suspiciously dirty I think the driver don't want the police reading it. Calling to Carol Ethel asked to see if she could read the number plate, make a note and phone the police. Now Mr. Field shall we look inside, as I thought the seat belt is frayed and he hasn't applied the hand brake and I assume it doesn't work. Now if everyone would note our friend here's staggering gate and catch a whiff of his breath I think we can wait for the police content we have done our duty. Now!! Where do you think you are going, not adding leaving the seen of an accident to the list, I hope.

Too late the driver had fallen into his car and driven away as fast as he could. The friends gathered round Ethel full of praise for her command of the situation. Now you know why I try not to cross her said a smiling Bert. Sarah rescued the boys skateboard and handed it back to him, while advising him, practice on the flat before trying any more slopes.

Sorry to put a damper on the party said Harry but I'm afraid I have twisted my foot must have been when I caught the lad. Shall I have a look asked Sarah, not unless you're an engineer as well as medic, it's the other foot said Harry. Jim then, said Sarah, he's the engineer. Jim helped Harry to lean on a nearby wall and bent to examine the foot. You have twisted it all right said Jim, the foot has spun round on the leg, if we can get you sat down somewhere we might be able to force it back again.

Bring him in here said a man who had been stood in his shop doorway interested in all that had happened. The man, a Barber, soon had Harry seated in his chair and Jim was able to get a good look. It looks as if the locknut holding the foot was forced loose by the foots movement, probably a safety feature in the design. If Bert and our friend here can hold against me I should be able to twist it back in line. The foot turned with a bit of a struggle, but the locknut stayed loose. Have you put your spanners in the car yet asked Carol, thankfully our sons reminded me just before we left, so the answer is yes. I just knew you wouldn't remember, said Carol, turning to thank the boys. Harry give Jim your car keys he knows where you are parked and can fetch them. Jim left at a fast speed, while Harry and Carol apologised to the Barber for the inconvenience. Nonsense he replied if you lost that foot how I think you did it is an honour to help.

Jim returned with the spanners, in a very short time, and Harry's foot was soon fit to walk on. Jim had been tempted to fix it facing backwards, Carol saying don't bother he hardly knows whether he is coming or going when it's on correctly. With renewed thanks to the friendly Barber, and many puns about close shaves and enough to make your hair curl, they finally set off on the homeward journey. Completed with no further problems, Ethel as usual heading to the kitchen, only to be stopped by Sarah and Carol insisting on playing housemaids.

Sunday, Sarah, Bert and the boys set off to give the dogs a long run, Ethel and Carol, in the kitchen cooking lunch. Leaving Jim and Harry free to spend time trying to plot the best way for Harry to spend his time, in his first week on his new job. Jim felt something of a fraud since he really hadn't a clue where Harry should start. Fortunately, Harry had given it a lot of thought and decided to start in the area where had had been hospitalised, believing he would get a better reception where he was known. Good Idea said Jim, just don't get thinking it will all be that simple. When you start to meet would be employers, I will always be glad to accompany you, if only to discuss money problems. Harry was happy to know he had the boss's full support.

Monday bought a strange change about the commune, only one team of builders, following their top man and Peter the architect around retouching any area not thought complete. It spoke well for the construction company that found very little needing their attention. As each building passed its inspection, teams of decorators moved in and began the final preparations before the houses could be handed over to Jim. The busiest person seemed to be the interior design expert, hurrying from house to house to see her design plans were being followed.

Jim interrupted Peter long enough to ask him to come to the office when he was free. No problem, Peter ensured him, Dad will be here in an hour or so and I know he will want to see you then. Walter arrived as expected and armed with a pot of Ethels tea and plate of cake, he Peter and Jim were settled comfortably in Jim's office. By the end of the week the houses should all be ready to hand over subject of course to your complete satisfaction, Walter assured Jim. If I can possibly postpone my final inspection until Saturday, I would like to have Sarah and two prospective guests with m0e, all of whom will have a better idea of design and decor than I'll ever have. I only ever bought the one house, and my late wife chose that. Fair enough agreed the architects, what if we leave the keys with you for the weekend. You will be able to look round with whoever you wish, make all the notes you need and we will spend Monday with you to finalise the deal. Suits me said Jim.

You're planning to be here Monday brings me to the next problem. Things seem to be at a standstill with the conversion of the large barn. I have Harry out interviewing potential guests and suspects there will be a large demand for mechanical and engineering training. Is there a problem I should know about? Hopefully not now, said Walter, there has been a delay with the supply of steelwork to support the new floors. As you will remember you are to have two floors and an attic. The Steel is promised for Wednesday and Thursday of this week. I am told by the steel erectors, although large, the work is very simple and should be completed no later than Saturday. The room divisions are all stud work, many of the partitions are already made, and the flooring and joists cut to size. Your building and construction company have always been thankful for your financial support at the start, and are now pulling out all the stops for you.

Further news the owner of the village Pub has accepted Simon and my offer for the Pub and extra ground. He agreed to a reduction of £5,000 on the asking price, on the understanding that he be invited to try the first drinkable pint from the proposed Brewery. Simon and I feel you should accept his offer without delay. Great news said Jim, let me know when the landlords last night is, and we will have a bit of a party. Sounds good to us agreed the architects with smiles all round.

Peter, said Jim, before you attempt to dash off, how are we progressing with the top field. The "Yurts" are expected in four weeks, and I would like bases and drains etc. in place by then As you know this is Sarah's project and we don't want her upset. There is a delay on power supply to the pump, it seems the new workshop building requires a three phase electric supply and that is to be run first and then the drainage pump can be wired in. Once this is completed, a bit of a tidy up and it will be finished.

Jim was eager to ring Sarah that evening, and a little surprised when she insisted in telling her news first. The thing is Jim I'm coming home to you for good, I shall be driving down on Wednesday with all my worldly goods. I arrived here on Sunday night and was immediately accosted by one of the non athletic boffin types wanting to know where I had been. It appears his secretary had hurt her ankle and he expected me to be there to attend to it. I explained that my responsibility began and ended with the long distance runners. He shouted me down, saying he would see to it that the terms of employment would be changed to include all university personnel. Furthermore he would expect to be told when I was to be off campus for more than 12 hours at a time.

Having told him what I thought of him and his ideas. I made it clear that he had altered the terms of my contract without prior discussion and I considered the contract broken and would terminate my employment with immediate effect. I shall of course expect to be paid all moneys due to me, and will be seeking legal advice in the event of any delay. He began to shout and bluster again, so I told him one more word and I would charge him with assault. Other people were now approaching wondering what all the shouting was about and he left in a hurry.

Are you really coming home for good? I miss you so much while you are away and need you so much said Jim. You can come home just to be with me, but in truth there is so much happening I need my P.A. more than ever. It is true I have finished with the university, but I have to go back for two days in two weeks time to see my team through the years final competition. No one from the athletics club have ever given me a minutes hassle and all my runners have worked so hard, it is the least I can do. You are right my love and deserve to go through the year without losing a race. No guarantee of that my love but I still have a couple of Disneyland Space tricks up my sleeve.

When I get home on Wednesday Jim Fields I shall expect you to have details of all that has been happening, so that we can spend long periods in "the office" without fear of interruption. Sarah Barnes I am fitting new bolts on the door even as we speak. I shall be asking Bert to keep the dogs out of your sight for at least a week, so there will be no sneaking off for private walks. They talked on for a long time, dreaming of and planning for their future, believing they were lucky to have found love this late in life. Thanking the "Master" and his team for the health and strength to enjoy it.

Once the Phone call was over, Jim rushed down the stairs to tell everyone the good news, his timing was a long way out! Bert and the boys were out walking the dogs and Carol had not returned from walking to the village school, hoping it would be suitable for Mark and Wayne. Harry was still out on his travels, although he expected not to be late home. Jim called to Ethel, and wearing his most unhappy face, asked if you would ask everyone to meet in the lounge as soon as they had all eaten. I've had some news that is going to affect all our lives. Oh!, Jim whatever is wrong?, can I help? Just ask everyone to come, including the boys, I'd sooner tell you all together. Thankyou. To himself he could only say, Jim Fields I didn't know you could be this rotten.

Sooner than he expected, Ethel knocked his door to say everyone was ready, thank you Ethel I will be right down, said a solemn sounding Jim. Dear friends, said Jim, I received some news today, I can't pretend anymore it is the greatest news ever!! Sarah has finished with the university and will be home for good on Wednesday. One of the idiot "boffins" thought he could bully her and change the terms of her contract, and she declared the terms of the contract broken and resigned with immediate effect. When he continued shouting she threatened to charge him with assault and he ran away. There was instant applause and some cheering, even the two boys doing a war dance.

The two ladies kissed him while threatening to kill him if he ever put them through anything like that again. You are a wicked man. Bert went to the sideboard and produced a bottle of whisky and glasses, saying this calls for a celebration. Ethel taking the boys into the kitchen giving them lemonade, to drink the toast proposed by their dad. Sorry to warn you Bossman, but I have a lot to report to you and so has Carol, so don't get too far into that bottle. Not a problem Harry, I'm already higher than any bottle could send me, and hope I never have to come down.

Carol was elected to report first as it was approaching the boy's bedtime. Two things Jim, the old deeds etc have been gone through by me and a historian based at the local library. A very old parchment, almost to bad to read speaks of a Brewery on the site and of the well supplying the water for all the Brewery and Pubs needs. There are other records of stone from the ancient ruin near your entrance being used in the building. The stone from the Brewery being taken by persons unknown, to be used elsewhere. Computer copies have been made, and all originals have been forwarded to Exeter University history department for urgent restoration. The library historian will contact you shortly, to give you more details. Just quickly, as it is not your problem, but we know you will be interested. The village school is no use to Mark he is well past their curriculum. I want both my sons to go to the same school and will be looking further afield in the hope of finding a school taking a longer age group to include them both. Wayne will of course go to the village school if necessary. Carol I can't tell you how grateful I am for the time and effort you have put in on the old records. I dream of a time when the Commune runs itself and we can give more time to the local history. Keep me posted regarding schools, charge the commune for all expenses, we may have many children here in the future and a knowledge of nearby schools could prove useful.

Right Harry how did your first day go? I hope you had no difficulties. None at all Jim thanks, my day went very well, said Harry. I met with about thirty invalids who are coming to the end of their treatment. Many already have some kind of job to go to, none of them very well paid. All were excited by the idea of affordable training for proper employment. Pub landlord rated high with many, often because their wives / girlfriends had experience. Others to avoid an immediate ever present boss. I.T. was another popular choice, especially among the more disabled. Could be very expensive, and involve a university. A few with injuries like mine, able to kneel, and full use of their hands, hope to become some kind of driver or motor mechanic. Market Gardening, farm work, and builder were also mentioned. I think I or someone must start some serious work on getting the training started. The demand is there, and the housing in place, I feel we must set up some training facilities without delay. I have a list of several other employments we might be able to help with, but when?

Wow! Harry, thank you have clearly got to the heart of the matter, and thank you for telling me so clearly that I have neglected to press hard enough with training facilities. Rest assured it will be my priority from now on. In fact, if you could carry on as you are for just this week, I and my P.A. will attempt to draw up a plan of campaign and we can set up a three pronged attack. O.K. by me boss agreed Harry, first job chase up that Pub.

Jim felt that Harry had lit a large fire under him and it was time he stopped being complacent. He had been feeling so proud, with all that had been achieved, the fine houses and the well laid out site for the "Yurts", all worthless until he had facilities for training. What sort of a fool am I.

Tuesday morning found him on the phone trying to organise a meeting of all his advisors, and builders. To include Ethel's brother Sam, for up to date details of how the market garden was progressing. Simon and Walter were first to promise a full day of their time as soon as needed. The C.E.O. of the construction company. Brewery experts, and all the legal aids. After consultation with Ethel and Bert it was felt the farmhouse could provide enough space for separate small meetings if needed. Ethel and Bert agreeing to spend their time in either their bedroom or the kitchen.

All was arranged for the following Monday, Harry and Sarah both attending. Jim felt all this activity might have an unhappy effect on Sarah's homecoming, and offered, his apologise. Oh! Jim she replied it is all so exciting, I am so pleased to be a part of it. Perhaps you ought to have a word with the "Master" and "Team", after all he is providing the money. Good idea my love I will do that today and tell you all about it tomorrow.

To Jims delight he got straight through to the "Master", who sounded pleased to hear from him. Jim go and make yourself comfortable, I will gather up some team members and recontact you shortly. There will be no need for you to speak, we will all get your thoughts and offer our conclusions. We are all very happy Sarah is coming home for good, you two should be together.

Jim settled into one of his armchairs and was soon asleep, later realising it was the "Master's" doing.

When he reawakened, he found his mind was full of new information and helpful Ideas. He recontacted the "Team" to say thank you, for all you did while I was asleep, our pleasure. We are glad you have called again, we forgot to tell you we will be telling Sarah in her sleep all that was discussed today, so she will be a fully informed P.A. We are still here for you at any time. At that Jims head became quiet, except for his own racing thoughts.

To everyone's joy Sarah arrived early the next morning, having finished her packing the night before and left after breakfast. The boys were the first to see her, and their yells brought everyone to meet her. With hugs all round, a few tears and many happy faces, Sarah could be in no doubt she was welcome. Her car was soon unloaded Bert Jim and the boys making short work of carrying her worldly goods upstairs. Tactfully leaving Jim and Sarah alone, Ethel leaving them the inevitable pot of tea and plate of cake. After a long hello, Sarah asked what is this head of information I woke up with this morning. I assume you have been in touch with "Disneyland Space".

Harry came home with news of a lot of people who would like to join our scheme. He also explained his embarrassment at there being no courses as yet available. All after one day. He has agreed to complete this week as he has started, and from then on go looking for people happy to give tuition at minimal cost to themselves. You as my P.A. to help me formulate a plan of campaign, how best to go about it, without covering the same ground twice. I have arranged to meet with all concerned on Monday, it would be great if we could have some sort of agenda for that, and the campaign plan for all it may concern.

It occurs to me a first priority must be some sort of brochure to give prospective employers some Idea of what we are about. Do we know anyone clever enough with a computer, to be able to whip up something in a couple of days. Carol and the boys are pretty good, Sarah told him, why don't we go and see them, at least they can give us some idea of what's possible. This is what I have been needing a good P.A. said Jim. Not to mention all the fringe benefits said a broadly smiling Sarah.

Minutes later they were stood at the cottage door, speaking to Carol, Mark and Wayne. Once they had explained about the brochure, an urgent discussion broke out, with the boys wanting to give it a try. Do not go jumping in you two Carol cautioned, we will need photographs and somebody who can write decent grammar. Wayne get a few sheets of paper out of the computer box, Mark get your and your brothers phone, I've got mine here. Check them for suitable photographs of the farm buildings etc. If you haven't got one of things like the "Yurts" lay out and the market garden, whoever is the best at taking pictures take my phone and give it your best shot. Wayne is better than me Mum, said Mark, that's true Mum, Wayne confirmed he is always too impatient. There are photos on your phone Mum, but both sites have moved on since they were taken and there is more to see now. Good lad said Mum off you go then.

Bring the paper over to the table please, and gather round while we try for a lay out. Holding the sheet portrait, Carol roughly wrote a headline, then set out blank areas for photographs. Leaving room alongside for script. Taking the second piece of paper she sectioned it the same, but with the pictures and script alternating on different sides of the paper. I like the second lay out better, but will accept either with many thanks, said Jim. Save the thanks until we have printed it, if we manage it at all, said a doubtful looking Carol. Wayne returned with what everyone thought were excellent pictures, and the process of downloading on to the computer began. Jim and Sarah do you mind, leaving us to it, you have us worrying about keeping you waiting, while you sit there. The boys and I know our individual strengths, and work well as a team.

Sorry said Jim and Sarah we should have thought of that, please don't neglect anything else, we would never forgive ourselves. Once outside Sarah asked Jim if they could please go and look at top field, I want to see the "Yurts" lay out, pictures are only two dimensional. O.K. said Jim but after that it is on with the agenda or I will be stopping your salary. Thank you for reminding me, about salary, I shall be opening negotiations first thing in the morning, be warned. I'm trembling, said Jim, but I don't know whether its fear, or anticipation!

The trip to top field took rather longer than expected as Sarah took long close looks at several of the sights, before expressing her satisfaction. Delivery of the "Yurts" is due in two weeks' time, I must remember to ring and check they are still on schedule. Yes dear, tomorrow, today we have an agenda to plan.

Back in the "office" complete with tea and cake, Sarah suggested that what was needed was an opening statement from Jim. Clearly stating his reason for calling them together and listing all the things he needed finishing in quick time. Top priority the Pub and Brewery. Spend too much time renovating the Pup and some of the regulars may go elsewhere. That's not to say we need anything less than the highest quality finish. The main barn conversion to a garage, capable of handling farm machinery. First floor Possibly a print shop, second floor, probably I.T., plenty of power points and phone lines. All floors capable of holding machinery and sound proofed. A last thought said Jim the I.T. centre would have the most disabled students and some kind of lift essential.

Well done Jim, you rattled that of in quick time and it was exactly the type of thing I had in mind. If you think of all the other problems before the meeting and have notes ready for your opening address. For now it is perhaps time we saw how the Edwards family are getting on with the brochure. I think we should wait for them to contact us, I'm sure they will call for us as soon as they have anything to say.

Quite right Jim, I hope your not going to be the kind of boss who is right all the time! I don't expect I'll be the boss all the time, Jim's reply. Almost as if they had heard Jim, Mark appeared within minutes, to say he and his mother and brother had got as far as they could and would you please come and have a look. I think it is very good, Mark explained, but mummy is not so sure.

Carol allowed the boys to show Jim and Sarah their work, both were delighted, and unable to believe it was all their own work. Across the top in a stylish font:

SYCAMORE FARM COMMUNE
SPONSORED BY EGG INVESTMENTS.

The remainder of the A4 sheet showed pictures of the best of the accommodation and the "Yurts" layout in top field. Together with a brief explanation of the building or view shown. The second A4 sheet listed the aims of the commune, followed by a list of the trades and occupations to be offered. A final paragraph stating that in the event of a not listed occupation being requested every effort would be made to supply tuition. Carol and the boys assured Jim and Sarah they had sufficient Ink and Paper left for about twenty more copies, if they thought the sample was good enough.

"Good enough"!! said Jim you have exceeded my wildest hopes. With your kind permission we will use your work as the basis of all future publicity. Sarah declared "wonderful" don't forget to submit your bill, for copyright and time and expenses. The boss here has got to learn to pay his way, or lose his best staff. Mark and Wayne both stood shaking their heads, asking their mother please tell Uncle Jim, and Auntie Sarah we don't want anything, we had lots of fun and learned many things. Carol said Jim and Sarah you heard my sons they are right and we will not be submitting any invoice. If you would like to replenish the Paper and Ink we have used fine, otherwise the boys are right to refuse.

Thank you Carol said Jim, if you could run off the extra copies, I would be very grateful, No problem said Carol, in fact it sounds as if my sons are running them off as we speak. Once they get started they like to finish. They get it from Harry he hates having to leave a job half done. Good for all of them said Sarah, I won't ask how many things you have unfinished but I'll bet it isn't many. If you would keep ten copies for Harry, and send the lads to my office with the remainder, it will save my P,A. from turning out again. To Carol Sarah said I swear one day I will kill him! To Jim, my salary demand just went up by another £1,000, I'm getting a clearer picture of the kind of Boss you would like to be. Now get out before I have the boys throw you out.

Back in the office, both still smiling Jim settled down to complete his opening statement ready for Monday's meeting. Sarah ringing the "Yurt" manufacturer, to check he was on schedule for delivery. To her delight he was able to promise delivery in two weeks as originally agreed. If it would be helpful he could deliver four units complete with staff to erect them next week. Although Sarah would be responsible for water and drainage connection. A thrilled Sarah asked for delivery of the four, any day from Tuesday onward, adding thank you very much you have made my year.

While you are on a roll please ring Simon and ask when the Pub will be closing. I thought I might buy any beer he has left over, and throw a free beer while it lasts night for the regulars. Good idea don't forget the ladies make sure there is more than beer to drink. O.K. said Jim find out if Simon knows if Walter has drawn up the restoration plans yet; if he doesn't know please ring Walter's office, they should know. As she began dialling, he called Oh!1 do love having a P.A., and ducked, in fear of flying cushions. No cushions were thrown just the two words spoken, "Salary negotiations".

The rest of the week passed very quickly, Jim and Sarah enjoying being together, knowing it was permanent. The day for the meeting of all involved in Egg Investments activities arrived and a proud though nervous Jim called the meeting to order.

Thank you all for coming. I know how busy you all are; and I hope that by the end of today you will all be much busier. In a very short time we have achieved a great deal, providing potential living accommodation for our first batch of students. Harry has been out canvassing for applicants for only one week and has a substantial list of interested people keen to be involved. Thank you, Harry! I must now eat humble pie and confess I have been so self satisfied with the progress, I have failed to drive forward with the need for training facilities. The large barn, destined to be an important part of our plans, is only now being fitted out. I feel I should have given it a much higher priority than I did. I have talked glibly about a garage with facilities for car, lorry, and farm machinery repairs, but so far not ordered a spanner. The Pub and Brewery site have now been purchased, and only now am I beginning to think about copper vats etc. The pub is to be renovated and fitted out suitably for use by disabled people, on both the bar and public areas. Gentlemen I can carry on in this vein for some time. Bert and Sam have done Trojan work preparing the ground laying out paths and planning future planting. For my part I have failed to match their progress, with plans for a water supply, shop and staff facilities. The purpose of this meeting is to rescue me from my folly and supply tuition facilities for all, in record time. There is no agenda I hope you will all recognise where you skills apply and get together with other skills to plan and produce!!

I am delighted to say Sarah has agreed to be my P.A. and will be adding her drive to my dreaming, to keep me up to the mark, please contact either of us at any time. Sarah leaned over to Jim and whispered in his ear. My brand new P.A. has just pointed out to me that I have not asked you all if you are happy to stay involved. I again apologize, I think, I didn't want to give any of you the chance to drop out. At this several of them got up and made as if to leave, before sitting down again laughing or smiling, One thing, that worries me said the C.E.O. of the construction company, I am well aware of the amount of money you have already spent, and hope you realise you are about to spend a lot more. I understand it is all your money I hope it is a bottomless pit.

I know of your recent problem with a company unable to pay their debts, I am happy to assure you ample sums are available, now and in the foreseeable future. It was true that the money was all mine originally and to a degree still is. However, I have spoken to an organisation and they have offered to meet all our costs for the life of the commune.

I notice Sarah and Bert have slipped out, this must mean tea is on the way, if you would like to form your groups you can exchange ideas while enjoying a break. Bacon sandwiches were mentioned, and Harry went to check on availability. One further thing I should have mentioned the Pub, Brewery and the Motor Garage, are the most in demand. I hope all concerned will be able to give your maximum effort to these projects. As always I would like the highest quality, and again assure you, until further notice don't worry about cost. Egg Investments will be happy to pay overtime rates when required. To the C.E.O. of the construction he apologised sincerely for not introducing himself earlier, I'm Jim and hope we can be friends as well as colleagues I already think of you as a friend, and my name is Jules. Please don't spread it round too many of my workers. Walter started laughing, while assuring him they already know.

The discussion groups quickly formed and were soon engaged in animated discussion. Jim and Sarah visited each group in turn, hoping to assure all parties of their fast response, in any future emergency. After a couple of hours of intense sharing of views, with the groups reforming many times, to ensure everyone knew who was responsible for each task.

"Jules" of the construction company soon proved a tower of strength, promising to put full teams of men into the Large barn, promising maximum effort throughout. While asking Jim to apply himself to procuring the necessary machinery, tools etc. as quickly as possible. Two other teams of specialists would tackle the Pub and Brewery as soon as plans were ready. Jules had taken the liberty of employing the teams, believing they would be urgently needed. Walter was quick to respond that the plans were drawn up and now going through final checks, and should be available by the end of the week. If needed plans for the brewery groundwork, including a small car park, were available should Jules wish to start immediately. After consultation with Sam and Bert, the water and drainage experts were ready to lay suitable piping as soon as required. Sewage drains had not been mentioned earlier, Ted promised to check the nearest drain to assess its suitability. He had also given Sam the name of a company to supply the water traps.

Harry had a short list of potential Tutors and employers, and had been given some good leads for printers and I.T. and computers. These he would follow up in the next few days and was optimistic of a positive response. Sarah suggested it may be worthwhile to prepare some form of sports facilities, to encourage general fitness and good health. Or even Para Olympians.

The meeting finally broke up with everyone feeling it had been a worthwhile exercise, and excited to be involved in all that must be done. Jim in a final address thanked them all but warned them he had some new ideas, and they ain't seen anything yet.

Jim had a final word with Harry as he was leaving, I would like to offer Carol a job she can do from home, or at least locally, hours to suit her. I know how important Mark and Wayne are to you both, and hope you know how fond Sarah and I are of them. I can promise Carol will never be under any pressure from anyone, the boys will always come first, You too!!

I will pass the message on and ask her to contact you tomorrow, as always Carol will make her own mind up. I will say this you will be lucky to get her, she was in great demand by prospective employers, when she worked. A couple of would be employers told me off for daring to take her away from them! think I have always known Carol was a special person, in fact I am lucky to have found both of you, said Jim. Please tell Carol to seek me out when she gets a few minutes. Right now I have to tell Sarah I am hoping to employ this very attractive young women, to strengthen the clerical staff and leave her more time to do my work. Luckily we have completed her salary negotiations, and she can't ask for more money. You want to bet said Harry and walked away laughing.

Jim asked Ethel for a pot of tea to be brought up to his office. Certainly said Ethel your P.A. has asked me to do that as soon as you made your way to the office, you have a good girl there. Do not let her hear you say that or she will want to restart salary negotiations. Oh! There you are, your "Bossiness", I am just writing a summary of todays events, and need your input on a couple of things. Sorry my dear, it will have to wait I have something else to tell you, while we have our tea. I'm hoping to persuade Carol to join our staff, with hours to suit her family commitments. I am hoping you and she will become the "buying team", I was going to suggest how best it may work but then thought it is no use employing the best, and then trying to teach them how to think. Buying must be the most important task, as thanks to my letting it slide we are now behind schedule.

Carol is going to contact me tomorrow, and I would like you to sit in on our discussion. Provided of course you are happy to have Carol on board. Happy! Said Sarah how can I not be happy, she is clever, quick thinking and will stand no nonsense from suppliers. I feel she may ask for my assurance that she will not be treading on my toes. No that's my job said Jim. Now lover you have been very good up till now don't go and spoil it! I have finished my tea, back to the summary. Jules has already allocated his biggest team to the garage barn and has a second team ready for the all clear to start the Pub and Brewery. I mentioned your idea of a free beer night, he is going to say nothing there are a hundred and seventeen drinkers on his payroll. He will need Garage equipment and Brewery vats etc. urgently.

Carol contacted Jim early the next morning, but could not see him for an hour or so as she had to get the boys up to two bus stops to get them to their schools. No problem said Jim, I'll not need my car this morning, why don't you take It and save yourself some hassle. If that's o.k. send one of the boys across for the key. Take your time, if you have any shopping to do don't hesitate.

Carol duly arrived for her meeting, and she and Sarah settle into the two armchairs, leaving Jim the office chair. I know Harry will have told you all that I said to him, and hope it wasn't too much of a shock. The meeting proved we have got to do a lot of buying in as short a time as possible, I had thought of it as something Sarah and I could pull in it our spare moments, I'm sure you know it's more important than that. I am hoping your will join us to work with Sarah, until the buying is up to date. After that, hopefully, at that point you can assume overall responsibility. I have only now thought we will always need a buyer to replace expendables and breakages. Perhaps even a stores supervisor. Watch him Carol he is starting to think again, you could find yourself running the whole show, said Sarah smiling broadly. If that puts me in charge of the money, I might take it Carol replied also smiling. Which brings us to what you intend paying, said Sarah, I'm going to leave the two of you together for that, I really don't want to know how much more you are paying her than me, you certainly can't pay her less. With that final salvo Sarah left still smiling.

Carol my dear, said Jim, I have no idea of the going rate for this type of work; may I say £25 per hour as a starter for ten, and sort out any problems later. I promise if it proves I am paying too much I won't ask for a refund of the over payment. Carol was happy with that arrangement, but wondered how her hours were to be recorded, since they were unlikely to be the same every day. Good point said Jim I will ask my on site printing team to produce time sheets for you. If they/ you take on the job you can charge it at your hourly rate. Oh! And don't forget a column for expenses. Well that is settled, when do I start said Carol, I will contact Sarah tomorrow. Please do said Jim, I think in essence you need to create a buying dept. In time there will be a need for a system of buying consumables, and replacement items. I expect the Pub and Brewery to do their own buying, but "Head Office" may need to keep an eye on their spending. Carol I have enjoyed our friendship since day one, and I hope, and believe, working together can be as much fun, Any problems or worries knock my door, and if I don't know the answer I will probably know someone who does.

Carol went off to be a housewife again, and Jim sought out his P.A.. I have noticed Sam is here with Bert on the Market Garden and I need to talk to them. If you can bring your note pad, you can record my words of wisdom. One page will do for that but I will bring the pad in case Sam and Bert have anything to say. Sam and Bert were clearing up after a good days work. Look out Bert, said Sam, its knocking off time and here comes the Gaffer. Sorry chaps, said a chastened Jim, I don't want to keep you, but Sarah and Carol are taking over buying and I wondered if they could help you with anything. Well said Bert as you know we were given the name of a company to supply the water catches. We need them to be contacted, to discuss what they can offer. Perhaps I should make the call said Bert, otherwise I might not be around when you ring them. We are almost ready for the staff shed, and water and drainage, a toilet will be required. While on the subject a fresh water supply for tea and personal hygene, again with drainage, added Sam. Better not mention all the garden tools we are going to need,said Bert. I expect we will have to make do with a rake and a spade between us. Jim sat on a nearby log hanging his face in his hands, begging Sarah please deal with them. I now know why people don't like employing pensioners. A laughing Sarah was too busy congratulating Sam and Bert and shaking their hands. Between us we should be able to teach him who is Boss. Now sir, was there anything else you wish to discuss, or shall we try again another day. You can, said Jim I dare not. He too shook hands, and they parted laughing.

Back in the office, Sarah asked if Jim would help her to compile a list of all the things he expected to buy in the near future. Of course, said Jim, but don't be surprised if I pass out half way through, I prefer not to think of all of it at the same time.

SARAH'S LIST.

No. One Garage equipment. Hoists. Pressure tanks. Heavy duty Jacks. Tyre changers.
Engineers tools. Larger tools for farm equipment. First Aid Kit.
Fire extinguishers. Office and Staffroom Fittings, i.e. Kitchen sink.
Minimal stock of tyres. Bulbs ETC.
If buying new Dealer to supply comprehensive list.
Hope to have our own expert to advise.

Pub and brewery. Copper Vats. Barrels, Bottles etc. Brewers Tools.
New furniture. Lighting and soft furnishings.
Check with Walter he may have a colour scheme in mind.

"Yurts" and other housing floor coverings. Bath and Shower mats

Market Garden Please ask Sam and Bert for a list of all their requirements. Rotavator? Greenhouse?
IT School Computers Printers etc desks, cupboards, and stationery

I am sure there are many more things I have not thought of, but I expect that will be enough to get you started. I would like to buy another car for general use. Mainly for Carol if needed. While on the subject how happy are you with your car, it might be better to get you a new one at the same time.

Thank you my love, said Sarah my car is better than it looks but I can see if I am likely to be out seeing suppliers, a new one would be better for our image. However Bossman have you any idea how much you are thinking of spending, even the "Master" must have his limits. I checked with him before Monday's meeting, and he assured me the pot was unlimited. He told me if anything had happened to him there would be repercussions throughout many Galaxies, and possibly the destruction of the human race. Compared to that the money you are spending is as a grain of sand in all of space. By the way he said don't forget to spend some on yourself, and was gone.

Thus began a period of great change in the calm of Sycamore Farm. Gangs of construction workers descended on them and the garage building soon began to take shape. The "Yurts were all delivered and connected to necessary services. Sarah not allowing Jim to look closely until she had completed her inspection and was satisfied. Jim and all other interested parties thought they were excellent, Mark and Wayne asking to be allowed to sleep in one. Concrete bases laid for the shed in the Garden, engineers trying various designs of water traps. Before promising quick delivery and fitting of the chosen model.

Carol proved to be a tower of strength setting up the buying dept. as Harry had said she was a very experienced office manager, Sarah confirmed her strength as a no nonsense buyer. Harry was beginning to find companies and individuals willing to give a trial of tuition for disabled interested persons. Jim thought he was the only one with time on his hands, but soon found keeping up to date with all that was happening and sorting queries from all sides kept him busy. Latterly he was to spend time showing would be families the available accommodation, and the training facilities to prospective trainers and employers.

In this way some Five years were to pass almost in a blur. Five years when Jim and his team could see the dream come to fruition. Years when they saw the housing all filled, mainly with happy families enjoying the very popular houses and the freedom of the beautiful fields.

Of course, thought Jim it had not all been sweetness and light, and happy smiling faces. He remembered only too well, the Walsh Family. One of the first families to arrive. They brought nothing but trouble and chaos at every turn. Four noisy undisciplined children, a bossy argumentative wife, and Corporal Walsh. A typical wide boy who thought anything not being held down, easily portable, sellable, was his to take away. He and his wife liked to borrow from all and sundry, but always forgot to return or pay back. Often denying having borrowed the item at all. Corporal Walsh was anxious to be trained as a bar and cellar man, and seemed to have many of the traits needed for the job. Until it was noticed the Pub takings were always down on the days when he was working. A trap was set, and a specially marked Five Pound Note was found in his pocket as he left the Pub, together with other money he couldn't account for. With a sad heart Jim, backed by Sarah, had to order them to leave, by the end of the week. Mrs. Walsh became very abusive, while blaming everyone else for their problems. She finally turned her rage on Sarah threatening her with all manner of violence, becoming quiet only when Sarah pulled her into the kitchen, and begged her to try something to give me an excuse to teach you a lesson you will never forget. Sarah was later to say she didn't know what she was going to do, but knew it is always better to tackle a bully head on.

Jim often wondered if the Walsh family didn't have the last laugh, as they hired a large van and left in the very early hours when no one saw them go. Several items belonging with the house and work sheds were never found. Causing Jim to tighten up on security, routine inspections, against his personal wishes.

An unusual problem occurred when Mark and Wayne had gone down to the wood to look for Conkers, to their dismay they were chased away by two unpleasant men who were trying to remove parts of the crashed Lancaster Bomber. The boys hurried back to tell Jim all that had happened, he was all for going down to the wood and telling the men to "get off my land". No you don't said Sarah, come with me, I think I know where we might get some help. To his surprise Sarah led him to the Market Garden where they found ex Military Police Sergeant Gregory. Sarah explained the problem and asked him he had any advice on the best course of action. Yes!, he said get me to a phone and then leave it to me.

After a few minutes on the phone, he declared it was all fixed. What we call the "Heavy Mob" are only about 5 miles away and will now be on their way. All I need say, they are very angry at someone messing with a memorial site and I for one do not envy their Quarry.

Sure enough it seemed only minutes before Police sirens could be heard approaching and a large Land Rover bearing regimental markings roared down the road. Shortly followed by a police car. Six of the largest men Jim and Sarah had ever seen jumped out of the Land Rover, greeting Sergeant Gregory, as an old friend. Which way Sarge? Sarah said come on fellows I'll show you the way. With respect young Lady, we will be going flat out I doubt you will keep up. Worry not said Jim I'll give £50 to any of you that can get passed her. Sarah then set of leaving the men to follow, Jim was not surprised when no one claimed the £50. The MPs returned with the three men in hand cuffs and looking very sorry for themselves. The police who had chosen not to accompany the MPs, later explaining they did not want to cramp their style, took statements, and formally charged the men with desecrating a war memorial and trespass, plus damage to a private woodland, and warned not to give any trouble as we are trying to think of more charges. In that case said the leading MP. the big chap with the black eye can be charged with resisting arrest and attempting to assault a MP.

The police having taken the men away, the MPs joined in on a feast of tea and bacon rolls, while keeping all amused with stories of their many adventures.

A constant in the commune were practical jokes, probably the most ambitious when a trainee motor mechanic was locked in a customer's car boot, just as the customer called to collect the car. The customer returning in a few minutes complaining of a knocking at the back.

Do you James Alan Fields take this woman Sarah May Barnes to be your lawful wedded wife, the I do, as clear and happy as ever heard. To Jims mind as joyful and happy a day as any day could be. The marriage took place in a packed Village Church, with a congregation of friends, trainees and their families. Simon, Walter, Jules and their families, villages and even the local press. With Harry as the best man, Bert to give the bride away, (after he had been persuaded he couldn't keep her). Carol as Maid of Honour, Mark and Wayne as Page Boys. Ethel as Major Domo, and Master of Ceremonies, a position earned by all her help and advice with the Wedding Planning. Jim and Sarah set off for a long cruise, happily leaving Harry and Carol in charge, feeling. as many times before, how lucky they were to have them

As result of a short article in the local press making the Tabloids, a reporter and camara man from a national paper appeared wishing to do a feature on Jim and the commune. Commune yes , me, definitely not said Jim, I have always been a private man and wish to stay that way. We need to say something about you argued the reporter or it will seem the commune just suddenly happened, and I promise you that will really get the press excited. Jim promised to give his decision the next day and hoped by then to have contacted the "Master" to get his assurance that EGG Investments Co. would stand up to close scrutiny, and he could not be accused of money laundering. The "Masters" accountants were happy to put his mind at rest, in fact seeming surprised he should ever doubt it.

Jim was content to allow the newspaper to contact Egg Investments, sure that they would learn nothing likely to cause any embarrassment, to him or anyone else. Jim refused to give any details of his life prior to starting the commune and as the reporters were unable to trace his past, the papers could only write about his present situation.

Jim was to later learn the press had attempted to check his tax returns only to find his file could not be found. A fire in one office was blamed for missing documents although no one was sure if Jim's old file had ever been in that office. Luck, or the "Masters" work Jim was never sure and preferred not to speculate.

The Pub and Brewery, had been completed and working three years earlier, although it took the Master Brewer a further year before he produced a range of beers, to the standard he demanded. The Pub, now doing light snacks, had been very popular from the first day, with all praising the beautiful new décor. Once the range of new beers was available the former owner and Landlord came for the first tasting, as he had promised. He pronounced the new beers as good, if not better than any he had ever tasted, had I have had these beers to sell, I would never have needed to retire. When word of these beers gets out into the drinking public, you will need extra bar staff, and the Landlord will be able to sit back and count his takings. I don't know how much you are able to brew but there will be lots of Free Houses wanting to sell it. One last thing, pull me another pint lad, Cheers!

Most of what the ex Landlord said came true, except the local water company insisted on a year of weekly quality checks to test the purity of the well water. Earlier checks having shown that while the level in the well dropped during a busy days brewing it normally restored the level overnight.

The one great sorrow of the past five years was when Ethel and Bert retired to the village, where they had bought a beautiful old cottage. The much loved dogs their main concern; they had aged quicker than the adults. Becoming more and more nervous as the Commune filled up with ever more people. Bert believing the dogs could no longer differentiate between who were friends and who were strangers to guard against.

The boys were the most upset by the dogs departure having been used to walking them every day. Unknown to them Bert had long discussions with Carol and Harry, who agreed to the boys having dogs of their own. Provided Bert would help Mark and Wayne to train the new dogs to a high level of obedience. Although as pets and not guard dogs. Of course Bert knew where there was a new litter and took the boys to choose their own dogs. Bert never told anyone how much they cost him.

Through all of this time, Sarah, Harry and Carol had been towers of strength to Jim, seeing him through many a crisis, always assuring him his dream was working and was truly worthwhile. Only now when every thing was running well, had Carol and Harry decided to leave the cottage, moving in to a house of their own in the village. Jim was tempted to try and change their minds, but Sarah talked him out of it. Explaining that he couldn't expect a couple like them to be content to live in his shadow for ever. Not to mention that living free in the cottage all this time, must have seemed like charity to them and we all know Carols view on charity. They have no desire or intention to leave your employment, and even less lose your friendship.

Jim and Sarah had a long look at the cottage and instantly agreed they should move in. The charm of the cottage would have been sufficient. The Farmhouse could now be used for some of Jim's earlier ideas. The upper floor becoming the main office, and the lower floor to be refitted and offered to some of the wives as a cafeteria. Jim would cover the first three months expenses, after which the wives would pay a nominal rent, and keep all profits. A large sign to be erected at the farm entrance announcing the Café open for business.

The business of the ladies owning and running the Café proved to be a pain as the ladies all seemed to have different ideas how it should be run. In the end Jim employed two experienced caterers to come in and teach the Wives the correct and best way to carry on. It proved a time taking and expensive project for Jim, but was vindicated later when a couple of trainees choose catering as their career. A bonus for the ladies as the trainees worked full time for minimal pay.

Jim received a great shock a few days later when he received an official document offering him an O.B.E. (Order of the British Empire) in recognition of his work in creating and maintaining the "Sycamore Farm Commune". An organization dedicated to the retraining of injured forces and civilian personnel, unable to follow their previous employment due to injury or occupational illness. Jim's first inclination was to decline the honour as he felt it was unfair to his "team", all of whom had worked as hard as him. Often with more knowledge and experience than he possessed. None of the team agreed with him, pointing out it had all been his dream from the beginning. His ideas, drive and enthusiasm, at times all that kept things moving. Sarah knew how many times he had started his day in despair, faced with problems beyond his experience. Harry and Carol reminding him of the early days when having become newly rich, he risked it all on his dream project. Bert and Ethel saying how his great kindness had made, for them giving up their beloved farm, a pleasure rather than the sacrifice they had feared. Bert also spoke of his clever handling of Joe Kerry when purchasing the land for the Smallholding.

Simon and Walter also sang his praises, saying he had always shown a firmer grasp of negotiations than many an experienced businessman they had worked with. Jules, the construction company owner, spoke warmly of the man who had rescued his firm from closure, with his thoughtful generous early payments keeping my company afloat.

Mind you I am not saying he is a pushover when it comes to getting what he wants, when he wants it.

Jim remained unconvinced until Harry told him privately that in the forces O.B.E. was said to mean "Other Buggers Efforts". That's how I shall always think of it , thank you, said Jim.

So it was that Jim and Sarah went off to Buckingham Palace, where Prince William invested Jim with his medal. To every ones annoyance Jim was so nervous he never could remember a word the prince said. On their return home they enjoyed a super meal prepared by Ethel and Carol, with Bert, Harry and the boys also in attendance. The boys now being old enough to be left, all the adults, joined the rest of the team and some of the trainee's and their families at the pub for a lively celebration. To Jim's surprised delight even the "Master" came into his brain to offer his own congratulations.

The buying team, Sarah and Carol, contacted the printer who had been given the task of printing the quality version of the brochure originally printed on Carols computer, hoping to be in time to add O.B.E. to Jim's name. They received bad and good news, bad, they were too late to add Jim's Honour, but the printer was able to accept two trainees, with the proviso they would need two working hands. Harry delighted to have two more positions to talk about. Jim relieved, he wasn't keen on it being advertised anyway.

Jim was later contacted by a group of officials from the M.O.D. To ask if they and two high ranking Medical officers could visit Sycamore Farm, with a view to examining all it had to offer. Jim and Sarah felt this could only provide further publicity, and promptly set a date.

The group duly arrived, and set off with Jim and Sarah, on the grand tour. From the start they were anxious to assure their hosts they were on a fact-finding visit, not a fault finding one. Sarah quick to assure them she and Jim were always pleased to receive constructive criticism. We are probably the only people attempting to do this, and have had to make it up as we go along. Mainly thanks to my husband who had the original dream and has made it work. Jim giving Sarah a warm hug, saying thank you and adding my main boast is gathering a wonderful team of friends about me.

All of the group were full of praise for the housing, the Army Doctors declaring it far better than most married quarters. With great pride Sarah took them to see her "Yurts", explaining they had originally been intended for single personnel but have proved popular with several couples. Many of whom had over wintered in them declaring the "Yurts" warm and cosy. Opposite the Top Field, field Three was undergoing extensive alteration, Jim's latest idea, the field was soon to be a crochet lawn, and two tennis courts. The tennis courts to be hard, for wheelchair use if required.

The hosts, then gave the guests lunch in the Farmhouse Café' where they were able to see the current trainees in action. After a very well received meal, the group moved round the back of the Farmhouse to see the Smallholding in all its glory. Here again they met trainees all of whom were happy and enthusiastic. The remainder of trainee workshops were all viewed with enthusiasm, the Tailors room and the I.T. and computer room surprised the visitors who confessed they would never have thought of them. One of the visitors saying how he wished the M.O.D. would supply computers of that quality. When we can we buy the best Said Jim. One of the joys is the number of companies offering discounts when they learn who the equipment is for. Feeling it was growing late the visitors began to talk of leaving. As you wish gentlemen, but we have two more highly successful projects to show you which we are sure you will enjoy. The site is in the Village a two minute drive from here, if you would like to take your cars, you will be able to start your return journey without coming back here.

All were happy with this arrangement and followed Jim and Sarah to the Pub. What a beautiful building, surely this is not one of the projects you spoke of. Yes, said Jim, but first we must go round the back. The Brewery soon came into view, to Oos and Ahs from the visitors. Passing the Well Jim explained it supplied the water for the brewery and the Pubs domestic needs with no discernible lowering of the level of water. The gleaming interior of the Brewery with its shining copper vats delighted the visitors and here again they were able to meet two trainees. Both working supervised by the Brew Master, trying new formulas for a stout they hoped to add to the existing range of beers. Apologising for disturbing their concentration, the visitors left the Brewers to it and headed to the Pub.

Jim deliberately ushered his guests into the bar before him, happy to hear their cries of delight at the old world charm of the décor. Heaping praise on Sarah and Jim for the surprising beauty, all around them. All his ideas none of his work, said a smiling Sarah. The best is yet to come, said Jim, ordering pints of the best bitter all round, explaining the beer was their own brew. All who have tried it so far have sung its praise, many thinking it is the best beer in Devon. All the visitors agreed saying they envied the trainee bar staff, and wished they didn't have a long drive facing them and could make a night of it.

Thanking Sarah and Jim for a pleasant and informative day, the group left with promises of a very favourable report. Most of them very sorry to be leaving the Pub. I reckon if they could have stayed an hour or so at the Pub, we would be getting Knighthoods in the next honours list. Said James Fields O.B.E., only to be mocked by Sarah, as the man who said he wasn't interested in honours. To Sarah and Jims surprise and delight, Harry was able to tell them a letter singing the praises of Sycamore Farm has been sent to all M.O.D. rehabilitation centres, suggesting anyone interested in retraining should apply and good luck.

All of which brought a large increase in applicants wanting training in various skills, not all of them currently in the syllabus. Jim calling a meeting of all his staff, to try to find the best way round the problem. Harry felt that this fell mainly on his shoulders, as vetting new applicants and finding new training facilities were his responsibilities. Maybe said Jim but the job has grown beyond what one man can do. You will have to employ someone to assist Harry. Since Ethels departure Carol and I have little enough spare time to consider taking on any more hours insisted Sarah, with Carol nodding agreement. Before you think of suggesting you take it on Jim, it is essential you are on site most of the time. There are too many people on site now for Carol and I to cope with the day to day problems. They are not so bad Jim protested! Maybe not for you but for we females coping some of these "Macho" ex-service men is a different matter. We can cope but we would much rather not. You seem to all be agreeing we need someone new, and I agree. However, this is something

I have known must happen and I dread it, we have such a happy team working so well together I dread the thought we may get someone who does not fit in.

If Carol and I could slip out for a couple of minutes we may have the answer for you. Please do, said Jim, Sarah and I can't wait. Carol and Harry soon returned, but Jim could learn nothing from their faces. Speak he begged before Sarah and I have apoplexy. Well said Harry we have this friend Seb, our friendship going back many years, and we both count ourselves lucky to have him and his wife Terry as friends. I can only tell you, I have marched with him, fought alongside him, and been drunk with him and I have never found him wanting. I have to say, Seb was the one who carried me to safety after I was hit, but I must beg you to never mention that to him as I promised I would keep it his secret.

Harry he sounds a wonderful fellow and friend, but I have to ask is he suitable for the job. Carol spoke up saying if I may answer Jim and Sarah, Seb is a total people person who will plead your case with would be employers and trainers ardently but without offence. Jim tells me he is unhappy with his employers, who turn him down for any promotion, telling him it would be too hard with his disability. Even though he stands in on all the other jobs when anyone is absent. Like us he and Terry have two children and he will do whatever he must to support them.

Wow, said Jim, when can I meet him? He sounds perfect. If you can get him here for next weekend the Smith family leave on Wednesday and they can have No' 3 for the weekend. I will pay all expenses, or send a taxi if needed. Harry you and I will interview him, and if he proves suitable, I will pay him the salary you are getting and pay you £5,000 extra as his supervisor. With that the meeting broke up with smiles all round.

All went as planned, except that Seb and Terry elected to stay with Harry and Carol instead of at No 3. Sebastian Henry Windsor, attended his interview, Jim liking him on first sight. Harry had primed him regarding the nature of the job and together the two men suggested that one man could concentrate on recruiting visitors and one on visiting prospective trainers and employers. Jim was willing for them to give it a try, but not until Seb had completed his six months trial. Things had gone well so far, and Jim, was never happy with change for its own sake. Seb was delighted to accept the offered position, but explained he would need a month to put his present house on the market, and resign from his current employment.

I have had some thoughts about where you and your family might live and would like you to hang on for a few minutes, and I can share my thoughts with you. Perhaps Harry you could ask Terry to join Seb and I if convenient. Within a surprisingly short tine, Terry hurried in to join them, telling Jim Harry is making a pot of tea for us, I think he wants to keep you happy! Good, said Jim, its time he learned. Now, Terry, I have just been telling Seb I have some thoughts about where you may live. Let me first say it will always be your decision. I thought if you could find somewhere that suited you not too far away, I could buy it for you, Deeds in your names right from the start, once you have sold your present home, we can sort out a repayment scheme to suit your budget. I would, of course, want first refusal on the property should you decide to sell. Finally, Seb, Terry, you have got the job and I hope we can work happily together for many years. For my part if it ever stops being fun, I'll be the first to go!

I mentioned to Sarah and Carol that it would be nice to have a bit of a celebration tonight, early enough to allow the children to come as well. Find out what plans they may have made, and see if they suit you, my treat of course. The plan was to eat in the farmhouse canteen, two of the ladies in charge agreeing to help Sarah and Carol prepare the food and then act as waitresses, the two trainee men had offered to clean the kitchen afterwards. Their way of thanking Jim and the team for all their hard work. After the meal the children to return home, where Bert and Ethel would be on hand to keep order.

The adults then retiring to the Pub, to finish the evening in style. Seb having the last word, saying I think I could learn to live like this. Sign on and commit and you will said Harry,

So began a happy and less hectic time for Jim and Sarah. The Crochet Lawn and Tennis Courts were finished and proving very popular with Guests. Seb and Harry playing the odd game of wheelchair tennis, whenever they managed to book a weekend time. The spare land near the farm gate now had a reception office, for visitors, in particular unexpected ones. Local Archaeologists had spent a long time on the site, not discovering anything new, had proved many old believes to be true or folklore. At Jims expense there was now an unmanned museum, containing many ancient artifacts discovered on the site.

Seb and Terry had proved to be towers of strength in all aspects of life and work on Sycamore Farm. He and Harry proving very effective at persuading uncertain companies to take on trainees, always successfully. Terry always seeming able to provide an extra pair of hands whenever the other two ladies needed.

Sarah and Jim thought that perhaps it was time for them to consider retiring or looking for some new dream to capture their imagination. All very well thought Jim but we both still spend forty hours or so a week working and will need to appoint suitable people to replace us. An obvious choice Harry and Carol if they would like the Job. Mark has already gone to university and Wayne will be leaving home shortly, perhaps they may like a less hectic way of life. They live quite close and would not need to move house. Seb and Terry much the same if Harry and Carol needed to give them more responsibility. These thoughts occupied them for quite a long time, with ever sensible Sarah finally telling Jim to stop dreaming and concentrate on what are you and I going to do if we hand over control of the Commune.

Jim became very quiet for the next two days, and Sarah thought he had been in touch with the "Master" at least once in that time. I would love to know what is going on in that brain of his thought Sarah, but she was determined not to ask, sure that Jim would tell her as soon as he was ready. The next day Jim asked her to walk down the fields with him, as he had an idea to put to her and didn't want anyone near enough to hear if they started arguing. I'm always ready for you to walk me down the garden path my love she replied, hoping to lighten the mood.

Now my love give me a kiss said Sarah and tell all. Hear goes then, first I want us to settle the problem of who will take over from us and speak to Harry and Carol as soon as they are available. Any new staff that may be required to be the first problem for the new Boss. We then give them a month to settle in, after which you and I go on holiday, to test out my thoughts for our future. First I have been in touch with the "Master" and he has agreed to take us back to Disneyworld Space to check our general health and fitness, improving both if needed. That need only take a day of our holiday, with no one any wiser. After that we try to obtain a running track or stadium, together with a swimming pool, or a Golf Course. Then I can take up athletics training again and you swimming or golf prompted Sarah. Yes, said Jim, which is why I want the "Master" to have us looked over, to make sure we are still young enough.

Of course we would have to find what group of people would most benefit from our training, Para Olympians, Junior Olympians who lack sponsorship to train full time. Any other form of disabled person who would benefit from our help. The "Master" and his accountants are happy for us to build what we need from scratch if necessary, the "Team" wondered if it might be possible to find another Farm and have accommodation on site as before. Oh! Jim that sounds like a whole lot of work for you to take on,

I remember all your sleepless nights, and days of worry. Yes love so do I, but now I have you helping full time, and I will have done it all before, and I hope I will have enough sense to take on extra staff much earlier. It is Wednesday today let us ask Harry and Seb to stay here Friday as we have much to discuss. Both Carol and Terry will need to be available as well. I think whatever is decided will concern all four of them. Good said Sarah now you are starting to sound like the Jim of old, and not poor old Jim. Do you want me to draw up an agenda? No said Jim but if you could do a list of all the salient points, it would make sure I don't forget anything.

Friday came all to soon and the meeting began at 10am. At first all were nervous, worrying what it was all about. With Jim and Sarah concerned how their plans would be received. Jim opening with a summary of his plans, assuring the others nothing would happen without their approval. Harry was a little hesitant at first wondering if he would be able to cope. Happily, Carol would have none of that, telling him, a man who can lead a squad of recruits into a battle zone and get them safely out again, has nothing to fear in running an established Commune. As you know your leg has not been happy on long car journeys and a chance for more exercise will be good for you. On top of which I will be your P.A. and I have handled more paperwork than you can Imagine.

Seb and Terry were both enthusiastic, Seb feeling the commune now had a waiting list, and perhaps it was no longer a two man job to keep it full. Terry saying as she now had her new house spick and span, and the children settled in their new school. She would be able to give more time to helping the team than previously, and help Seb with his reports.

I am pleased you are all so relaxed about the changes, you are first my friends and workmates a long way second and I would have hated for you to be less happy. So to summarise Harry you will take over as C.E.O. Please don't tell anyone how little actual work I used to do, and spoil my image. Carol to be your P.A. I hope she is not as bossy as Sarah always has been. Seb you and Terry will carry on as before, until the new boss says different. Harry if you stay for a couple of minutes and everyone else stay nearby and I will call you in Individually.

Harry We are offering an additional £10,000 salary which we hope you will find satisfactory. Once the other members of your staff have accepted my terms, you will of course be given a full list of salaries and all other routine expenditure. If you are happy, please send Carol in next. Sarah told Carol her salary explaining it is the same as he paid me, and you won't be expected to iron his shirts. If that's O K. please send in Seb and Terry. Seb Jim explained you will have extra responsibility and we are offering an extra £5,000 which we hope you will find acceptable. Terry you are currently paid an hourly rate, and we are recommending to Harry he place you on salary, once your future hours have been defined. I can't believe Harry will be as tight as Jim, said a smiling Sarah, so you should be O.K. Sarah and I are planning a weekend off, can we meet again Monday A.M. To cross a few T's and dot a few I's. Thank You.

Monday saw Jim's team gathered and to Jim and Sarah's delight all looking excited by the new opportunities being offered them. Sarah and I will be here for the next month and happy to help in any way we can, but your first point of contact will be Harry. Harry was present when I first had my dream which became the reality we have today and he and Carol have given us their full support from the beginning, even when we had no idea what we were doing. We have no doubt in the following days Harry will call on you to explain any changes. Sarah and I hope you will always be happy and enjoying your lives.

You may know that at the beginning all the money was mine, happily the cost has now been taken over by Egg Investments, and they are happy with the changes and send their best wishes for your future success. Harry may I say they have never queried a penny I have spent and feel there will be no need to in the future. Far from counting costs they are hoping you will find ways of expanding in the future. Their words not mine! At the end of the month, providing, none of you have gone running screaming to the nearest high jump, Sarah and I will be starting a six month holiday, sun, sea, and I'm assured I am looking at being thrashed at golf in the very near future. A word of warning, said Sarah, watch this space the "brain" has started dreaming again. "I think he is after a knighthood" almost unheard in the laughter, Jim replying you just wait I'll get you at playtime.

Any questions? Just one for now, is cash available now? asked Harry I fancy a farewell party is called for and we will all need a "sub" to pay for it, and anyway my chief buyer assures me routine supplies are needed, and petty cash is low. Sarah do an immediate forensic audit, I want to know where all this petty cash is going, said Jim, trying not to laugh. No can do Bossman said Sarah, first I am no longer employed here, second I happen to know a lot of it was spent getting you a new pair of work boots. Why you needed them a few days before retiring I don't know! Ouch! Said Jim that's my best .

friend speaking. The month to Jim and Sarah's retirement, past very quickly, and with two days left.

Jim sat on the top of high field waiting for Sarah to join him. Both hoping to enjoy a last glorious sunset. Jim found himself reminiscing about all that had happened these past few years. He had become a multi millionaire, built up a commune training injured people to live full lives. He had restored a Pub saving it from desolation. Created a Micro Brewery now supplying the best beer for miles around. Had gained many truly wonderful friends. In Sarah he felt he had the perfect wife, companion, business associate, lover, and beautiful in looks and nature. Now waiting to be at his side for the next impossible dream.

All of this began when he found a talking metal Egg, with its own light show, in his garden and started the weirdest, most exciting time of his life.

If you find one in your garden do whatever it tells you, and stand well back.

TRY IT YOU JUST NEVER KNOW.

To anyone who has struggled all the way through this narrative; please accept my sincere apologies.